MODERN Pen Pals

MODERN PEN PALS
Copyright © 2024 by Eva Chau

Cover and Interior Design © 2024 by Eva Chau
Editing by Sarah Ward

All rights reserved. No part of this publication may be reproduced, stored or transmitted in any form or by any means, electronic, mechanical, photocopying, recording, scanning, or otherwise without written permission from the publisher. It is illegal to copy this book, post it to a website, or distribute it by any other means without permission.

This novel is entirely a work of fiction. The names, characters and incidents portrayed in it are the work of the author's imagination. Any resemblance to actual persons, living or dead, events or localities is entirely coincidental.

Designations used by companies to distinguish their products are often claimed as trademarks. All brand names and product names used in this book and on its cover are trade names, service marks, trademarks and registered trademarks of their respective owners. The publishers and the book are not associated with any product or vendor mentioned in this book. None of the companies referenced within the book have endorsed the book.

ISBN: 978-989-35709-1-3

MODERN Pen Pals

EVACHAU

Trigger Warnings

This book contains scenes with anxiety, sex, alcohol, sexual assault and mentions of suicide. Readers discretion is advised.

Dicktionary

- **Chapter thirteen 'yeolset'** - Last half of the chapter.

- **Chapter eighteen 'yeolyeodolb'** - In the second quarter of the chapter and the last quarter.

- **Chapter twenty 'seumul'** - End of chapter, not as explicit as the rest, and contains some enlightenment for Delilah.

- **Chapter twenty-four 'seumulnet'** - In the middle of the chapter (small one).

- **Chapter thirty-one 'seoreunhana'** - Near the end.

- **Chapter thirty-four 'seoreunnet'** - In the second quarter of the chapter.

- **Epilogue** - In the middle of the chapter (small one).

To all the kind-hearted, independent people who have trouble asking for help or are too stuck in a place they wish they weren't.

A lot can change in a year, but only you can take the first step. Asking for help doesn't diminish your effort, it only shows how strong you are for allowing yourself to be vulnerable. Take the step. Sometimes you're already surrounded by those who'll help you live better, and if not, you'll find them.

Spread your wings, little bird.

The Playlist

1. Modern Loneliness - Lauv
2. Have We Met Before - Sarah Barrios ft. Eric Nam
3. 8 billion people - Kiran + Nivi
4. Blue & Grey - BTS
5. OK (Anxiety Anthem) - Mabel
6. Your eyes tell - BTS
7. Anxiety - LOVEONFRIDAY ft. Trevor Daniel
8. FAKE LOVE - BTS
9. stuck in my head - BLÜ EYES
10. BREATHE - LeeHi
11. Little Bit Better - Caleb Hearn ft. ROSIE
12. i can't breathe - Bea Miller
13. You're Sexy I'm Sexy - Eric Nam
14. OK Not To Be OK - Marshmello ft. Demi Lovato
15. She's In The Rain - The Rose
16. The Climb - Miley Cyrus
17. Friends Don't - Maddie & Tae
18. Never Not - Lauv
19. Lights - BTS
20. AH EE YAH - KARD
21. Hold Your Breath - Chase Atlantic
22. Tattoos Together - Lauv
23. Lonely Eyes - Lauv
24. Still Into You - Paramore
25. FRI(END)S - V
26. At My Worst - Pink Sweat$
27. Tattoo - Loreen
28. Anxiety - Blueyes
29. I Hope You Know - Sofia Carson
30. more than friends - Isabel LaRosa
31. Can I - Alina Baraz ft. Galimatias
32. Yes or No - Jungkook
33. wish that i could - UMI
34. Trivia 承 : Love - BTS
35. The Sun Will Come Up, The Seasons Will Change - Nina Nesbitt

하나
'hana'

ENTER USERNAME:

What username should I put?
This is so stupid.
My mind comes out blank when I try to remember the last time I joined a social platform. They used to be for connecting. Nowadays they seem more for show, but Ms Julie said it could help.

ENTER USERNAME: HeythereDelilah

**USERNAME ALREADY TAKEN
TRY AGAIN**

ENTER USERNAME: HeythereDelilah28

**USERNAME NOT TAKEN
VALID**

ENTER PASSWORD: ********
ENTER PASSWORD AGAIN: ********

CREATE ACCOUNT

HELLO, HeythereDelilah28
WELCOME TO MODERN PEN PALS

'Lilah? Where are you?' I hear Elisa's voice outside my bedroom.

Oh shit.

She can't know about this. At least not yet.

'In my room!' I shout.

My flatmate's face pops into my bedroom at the sound of the doorknob turning.

'I'm having some friends over for dinner. Is that okay?' Her deep-ocean eyes widen for an answer of only one option.

'Hmm...okay.' I don't know what else to say. It's not like she doesn't bring people here all the time.

'Thank you! You're the best,' she says.

The moment her back faces me, my head switches to its former position so I can continue providing personal information to a place that will most likely leak it or sell it without my permission.

'Do you want to join us?' The sound of Elisa's voice refocuses my attention on her. She bounces her smooth, chocolate-coloured curls as our eyes meet again.

A sudden heatwave consumes my body, and my heart palpitates faster as I take off my robe. There's this warmth inside of me every time she repeats those words, but contrary to the shaking beneath me, as my foot incessantly taps the ground, my mouth cannot move.

'Well, you know where to find us if you want to join.' Creases form under her eyes as the corners of her lips lift.

My ears don't catch her leaving as the image in front of me blurs together, her words taking me back to the moment we met.

I was reading a pamphlet near the university campus. Mixed housing, it said. I held the little paper with the phone number for way too long as those words repeated in my brain. *Mixed housing*, which meant I would live with all genders. I already had a hard time talking to my gender, but with the other, my throat dried every time. It's not that they couldn't be friendly, but the jitters made it very hard for any acknowledgeable sentence to be formed.

My shoulder felt an unknown pressure, and the little paper fell out between my fingers as I searched for the pressure's cause.

A young woman stared at me with breathtaking eyes. They just popped with her dark skin. My entire face relaxed at her sight. She had a magnetic energy around her—I've always imagined her as a descendant of sirens.

'Are you looking for a place to live?' I heard, still blinded by her pull.

'Huh?' I asked, the word leaving me close to a breath, so she repeated her question.

Just like that, the spell broke, and I came back to reality. 'Yes, I am.'

'Fantastic! I'm looking for a flatmate.' Her hands collided, and she smiled. 'It would be just the two of us. You'd have a room all to yourself, and it's just a quick drive or bus ride to campus.'

With no hesitation, I blurted, 'Yes.' I didn't know her then, but the words *mixed housing* still made my stomach churn.

At first, I kept mostly to myself. The snow on my balcony's flowers had time to melt before I opened up more to her, but there wasn't one day, even when her voice was the only one that filled the car, that we didn't go to school together. From the moment my feet crossed the gate, my existence would perish at the sight of Elisa Burk. Every single soul on the way to class would stop to either talk to her, talk about her, or simply stare.

So I know, even though she is my best friend, she wouldn't understand me trying to make friends through letters.

Anyway, Lilah, stop overthinking. Remember what Ms Julie said in our last session. *'Breathe. Not having friends isn't the end of the world, but if you don't have more right now, it is because the right people haven't shown up.'*

Let's see if this Modern Pen Pals thing will make me a friend. At least not being face to face, seeing the person's expression, might keep the flower's snow intact before I open up.

ENTER YOUR LOCATION: London, England
SEARCHING FOR PALS
63 PALS FOUND

AMAZING! YOUR LOCATION IS PERFECT TO MEET NEW PEOPLE.
SELECT A PEN PAL

Damn, a lot more people use this than I thought.

I can only see their usernames. There is no other information. *What if I choose a murderer?*

It's best if I open a PO box just for this. I don't want them to know where I live, but I wonder if people put their actual addresses on this thing.

Ugh, I hate meeting new people. I mean…I hate people in general.

This one has a funny nickname, Pamelicious. Let's see if they want to connect with me.

While I wait for the answer, I grab my recipe book and search through it to choose what I'm cooking for dinner.

The doorbell echoes through the house and a moment later the silent ambience ends. Laughs and voices fill up the air.

There is one voice in particular that makes butterflies slap their wings against my insides. Let's ignore the fact that if that expression was possible in real life, it would be creepy as hell.

I keep a low head around everyone, but with Elijah my whole world stops and I'm stripped down into the purest form one can exist, without a mask or anything to cover up how I feel. I can't even greet him sometimes. That's just how far out of my league he is.

On the lower left corner of my computer, the little bell blinks, letting me know I received a notification from Modern Pen Pals, so I click to read it.

**WE'RE VERY SORRY, IT SEEMS LIKE Pamelicious ISN'T AVAILABLE TO MAKE NEW PALS AT THE MOMENT. THE GOOD NEWS IS THAT YOU STILL HAVE 62 PALS TO CHOOSE FROM.
SELECT A NEW PEN PAL**

Perfect. Not even online am I lucky with people.
Ugh, let's try again. This is the weirdest homework my therapist has ever given me.
As I'm scrolling, the name Daldust stands out to me. I don't know what *dal* is, but dust is what I want to turn into sometimes.
To become bodiless, just a pack of tiny specks that float around. They travel more than any human can, and their size varies as they encounter more of their kind. Dust can exist from a multitude of things and is created from the essence of those. I wonder what kind of essence I'm born of.
Let's find out if they want to connect.
I stand up to place my recipe book back on the shelf, quitting on trying to make something from there.
Throughout the years this house's flaws became normal to me; how the third floorboard on the left side of the hallway squeaks letting me know someone is near the door, or how the lavatory door creaks allowing me to go on my turn, but there's one thing I'll never find normal. What was the architect thinking when he decided to create the only entrance to the kitchen from the living room? And how did no one else warn him about how bad of an idea that was?
I only wanted to go from the comfort of my room to my second safest place in this home, but for that to happen, I need to face my worst enemies.

Humans.

The soundtrack of a battlefield plays in my mind as I swallow every ounce of courage to enter the room. Hoping, praying to any form of higher power that I am as agile and noiseless as a cat.

'Lilah, you're here,' Elisa says.

Why aren't invisible cloaks real? I would sell my kidney to have one.

An invisible wall prevents me from walking further, and with a swift glance towards my flatmate, I say, 'Hi,' avoiding possible eye contact with any other person.

They greet me back. Elisa and Elijah get back to talking, and a guy I've never seen before looks down at his phone.

Withholding my breathing, I walk as fast as I can to the kitchen and pound my hand against my forehead as I breathe out in arrival.

Why can't you be normal, Delilah? Why can't you go back to that cheerful person, the one you were before him?

Nobody warns you that having your heart broken is not the worst part of a breakup with a crappy ex. The trauma they leave you as a parting gift is.

At least food doesn't mock me; it's made to please me. That's why I love my job. Cooking makes me happy, and it's my form of meditation, especially baking. And the people that come into my bakery are there for what I create. They don't judge me—quite the opposite—they celebrate me, putting a smile on my face with every order they take.

Moving my hair backwards with my headphones so my ears are free to listen to music, I touch the white metal handle to see what we have stored in the cold. The cherry on top is when my playlist plays something from my favourite seven boys on earth. There's nothing like the love of *Bangtan*.

The ingredients slide from the chopping board to the sizzling pan, causing tiny drops of olive oil to jump into the air at the same time as the beat I'm listening to drops. I take a step back to avoid the hot oil and move forward on the second beat, moving my feet as I hit all the notes.

Singing to myself with my eyes closed, I make a turn so I can check the time on the wall clock. As I open them, they widen more than needed to see the hours, and the wooden spoon I was pretending to use as a microphone hits the floor.

'Hi...' the stranger in my house says.

I suck the air out of the room and stare at the spoon lying on the kitchen tiles, where I wish I could descend to. A small ant approaches it, and I telepathically ask it to take me with it, back to my comfort zone. I inhale the food's aroma to make sure it isn't burning, as I'm trapped in this invisible box with no way out.

I remember Ms Julie's words: *'Whenever you face a situation where your first instinct is to flee, inhale and exhale five times. That will slow down your heartbeat and keep you in the moment. Remember that feeling of cooling down; make that your first instinct.'*

My eyes trace the way from the spoon to his eyes and as I open my mouth to greet him, Elisa enters the kitchen, saving me. The box vanishes in a flash, and I bend to pick up my wooden spoon.

'Lilah, that smells so good. Are you cooking for more than one?' my flatmate asks, looking over my shoulder at the stove.

'Yes, you can have some after,' I say, washing the spoon and drying it before mixing the pan.

Besides my therapist, the only other person I speak with is Elisa. We've been living together for almost ten years, and by now she knows how I function. She's seen me go through a lot and stayed every step of the way. I'm still not at that point where I feel a hundred percent at ease with her, but it's not her fault, it's mine. I have to work on my shit before I can open up to others.

'That's why you're my bestie.' The sweet smile she has on for me dims down as her head turns in the opposite direction. 'Moon Hee, do you need something?'

'*Gwaenchana*. I mean, it's fine, I'm okay,' he says, hurrying his pace back to the other room.

I recognise that first word. He spoke Korean. My eyes were mostly glued to the floor the entire time he was here, so his face's a blur to me, but his name is Korean, too.

I turn off the stove and peek at the living room. Elisa is gesturing with her hands as her mouth moves, and the guys' focus is on her. I take that as my chance to pass unknown on my way to the hall, and as I'm walking through the wall separating both areas, I face back.

'You can go taste it now.'

The moment I notice their heads turning towards the sound, my feet start and don't stop until I've crossed the line of my safe place.

'Thank you!' my flatmate says, and I can hear Elijah's radiant voice talking about the smell that comes from the kitchen.

'Elisa, your flatmate sure does know how to cook.' His words warm my heart.

The door's latch clicks and I place the plate on my dark wooden desk. As I sit down on the desk chair, my eyes capture the little bell blinking, impatient to share its news with me.

CONGRATULATIONS! Daldust IS EXCITED TO CONNECT WITH YOU!
CONFIRM TO BE PALS

My index finger hovers on top of the ENTER key, finding some resistance to move lower. I inhale as much as my lungs can take, and before letting that air out, I press it down, sensing the bottom of the key hit the board. Releasing my lung's capacity, the bright screen focuses as I attempt to picture what's coming, thrilled for the first step in getting out of my comfort zone.

둘
'dul'

Behind the counter of my bakery, I lean by the nearest window. The sunlight warms my hand through the glass.

Where there used to be empty seats outside, this time of the year people are talking, enjoying their cup of tea.

The gold bell on top of the door rings, diverting my attention inside. Two young girls enter the shop, allowing some red and orange leaves to fly inside and land on the soft-brown wooden floor. They're laughing, a rare sight in the usual grim weather of London.

The bakery has been busy for the last few days, so much so that I haven't yet set up my mailing box at the post office to receive the letters from my pen pal. Before I left the house this morning, I noticed a notification on my phone from Modern Pen Pals letting me know that Daldust had sent me a message, but I haven't got the chance to read it.

'Mrs Josephine, good morning,' I say to the old lady who entered my shop behind the girls.

She comes here every day to get her husband a slice of the cake of the house. My speciality is a light vanilla base with a creamy and sugary lemon frosting.

'My sweet Lilah, how are you this fine morning?' Mrs Josephine's wrinkles under her eyes deepen with her smile.

Many times when I stare into her eyes, the kindness that

sparkles in the hazel covering them reminds me of my grandmother.

I sigh and try to look cheered for this kind woman. 'I'm well, thank you very much. How was yours and Mr Blake's weekend?'

'It was good. At this age, all weekends seem the same. There isn't much to do, but we enjoy each other's company.'

'It doesn't matter what you do as long as you enjoy doing it together,' I say. 'If you're here for your usual, you're in luck. I'm about to take it out of the oven in a minute.'

'You're an angel. Blake can't go one day without eating that cake, and this time I'll take a slice for myself as well. We are having a little picnic by the river today. It's our anniversary.' Mrs Josephine looks at the bracelet on her arm and smiles. Her husband must have gifted it to her.

They make me want to believe in love, believe that everybody has a person, someone who is just waiting to find their other half and that those relationships can last. That love and care can outlive the traumas and regrets.

'Happy anniversary! I'll make sure to choose the big slices then.' I wink at her, and she goes to sit at the table near the window by the door.

I exhale at the sight of the clock hitting 1 p.m. Lunchtime.

When you're your own boss, you are supposed to make your own schedules, right? If I wanted to take a day off or get an extra lunch hour, I could. But if I do that, the regulars that come at those hours will leave, and that means less money to support the bakery.

I've had proposals to expand my business a few times, but the thing is, I do what I do because I love it, not to get more money out of it. Besides, it wouldn't be *Sweet Delilah* without Delilah.

Owning your own business is a lot of work—one of the most stressful things one can do—but it's also the most gratifying because you know everything you receive is based on your hard work.

I lock up the shop and walk towards the green-framed door next to mine.

Rebecca—or as her friends call her, Becca—is my waiter for the day. It rotates between her and her twin Jeremiah. They own this little place called *Greener's*. The food is organic and vegan, which I love since all my treats are vegan as well.

People in this neighbourhood call us 'the tasty animal lovers duo' because we show them that food can be delicious with no animal harm. We love to spread awareness through delicious food, and they say that the way to people's hearts is through their stomachs.

Becca walks to the kitchen in the back corridor to place my usual order. Their spaghetti carbonara is to die for. My eyes travel to Jeremiah, who's attending to a customer at the counter. As soon as the customer leaves, he walks over to where I'm sitting.

'H-Hello Lilah,' he says, avoiding eye contact.

'Hi Jer.' I smile at him.

'How's the bakery today?' He plays with his hands, glancing briefly at me before looking back at the ground.

'It's doing fine. How are you?'

I've known him since my bakery opened, and although at first my words were scarce towards him, they quickly grew as I began noticing that he's always more nervous than I am, allowing me to relax for a bit.

'I'm doing better now that you are here. Have a delightful meal,' he says, leaving as he watches his sister bring my plate to the table.

I try to thank him, but when I look back at him, he's already behind the counter, accepting a customer's payment.

'Here you go.' Becca places my order in front of me. 'Did my brother come to bother you?' she asks. 'That guy cannot keep his cool when you are here.'

'What do you mean?' I ask.

'Jer hasn't said it out loud, but I think he has a crush on you. He always gets jittery when you're around.'

Jittery? I've never seen him not nervous. I assumed it was his natural state.

'I don't believe you.'

'What's there to not believe?' Her eyebrows frown. 'He just never dared to ask you out. He can barely look you in the eyes.'

'Exactly. The fact that he can't look me in the eye makes it hard to believe he likes me. I would first assume he didn't like me very much.' I chuckle to hide the tightness around my chest.

'Anyway, enjoy. I'll go get a little dessert on my break.' Rebecca winks, moving to attend another order.

Some days I wish I could look at myself through someone else's eyes. Maybe I would find something I can't see with my own. But other days I don't want to fathom what they might see. It could be even worse than what I imagine.

I pause my thoughts and hold them for my therapy session on Friday. Ms Julie always says if I get a bad thought to not think about it at the moment, to let some time pass and see if I can handle it with a clearer head, or hold them until our session. By then it can either be gone or if it remains she'll help me face it.

After lunch, I make my way to the post office at the end of the street. At this hour you can catch the birds singing. I look around, inhaling the fresh air and letting the stillness of this calm hour relax me before I walk inside.

'Good afternoon, miss. How can I be of service on this fine day?' the man behind the counter asks as I arrive.

'I'm here to open a postbox...' I say, looking around for the correct area. I hope I'm doing this right.

The officer directs me to the side of the post office and hands me some papers to sign. I settle on postbox number nine since it was the day I signed up for Modern Pen Pals—it just seems to fit.

It's weird how eager I am about this. It can go very wrong and Daldust and I might have nothing in common, but because they aren't seeing me—even if they judge me, they don't know who I am.

I don't get nervous about talking to a stranger; I get nervous about the disappointment on their faces when I talk to them, and this time, I can't see it, so I picture a smile.

After setting up my mailbox, I go back to my bakery. The sun reflects through the window towards the painting I have on the wall.

I'm cleaning up the tables when Elisa comes into the shop. The corners of my mouth lift at her sight, but my whole body freezes as my eyes meet the people in the back. Elijah and the other guy that was in my house last night walk in behind her.

'Lilah,' my flatmate says, 'tell me you still have your delicious signature cake.'

I compose myself and walk fast behind the counter. *Be professional, be professional*, I repeat to myself.

'You're in luck. I still have a few slices from the morning.' I hope they can't hear the tremble in my voice.

'Amazing! I want three.' She looks back at the men that stand by the door and speaks to them this time, 'What are you doing standing there? Get here and grab your plates. I'm not your mum.'

I let out a light laugh. Elisa has an energy nobody can seem to ignore. She can be the life of the party but also scold you when you need it, and no one can ever be mad at her.

She winks at me before grabbing her plate and sitting at the table near the counter—the one I had just been cleaning.

The guys approach me and my words scramble in my mind, making it harder for me to speak. I hate that this happens.

'Good afternoon, Lilah,' Elijah says, and I smile at him, giving him a plate. 'Thanks.' He turns around to join Elisa.

The strange man—whose name I keep forgetting—approaches me later, looking at the table before looking at me.

'Hi.' The corners of his mouth lift.

There's a calm about him. He doesn't make me as nervous as Elijah, but that could be because of my feelings towards him.

'Here.' I reach my arm forward, giving him the slice of cake.

He grabs it and asks, 'Can you also make me a coffee?'
'Sure, what kind?'
'An iced Americano.'
I nod and turn my back to him to prepare his drink.

When I turn back again, preparing to call for him, I'm confronted with his body, still in the same place, the cake's plate on the counter. He never moved. He stood there waiting for me. That's rare. Most customers leave to sit at their tables and wait, but this man stood there.

With his stare on the painting on the wall in front of the door, a wave of serenity washes over me. It's the only painting I have hung because I want people to notice it. The rest of the walls are decorated with stencils of mauve-pink baked goods and acoustic-white flowers. Two soft-brown shelves filled with small cacti and some books for decoration stand on the wall opposite me.

'It was my grandmother's,' I say.

'It's beautiful,' he says, his eyes never moving from the cream wall.

'It's my favourite one.' I sigh, remembering how I begged to keep it when they were deciding what to take from her home.

She always said it reminded her of me; a beautiful garden filled with colourful flowers. Dull because of the grey clouds above it, as they seem to be about to cry, but behind it, you can see a light—the sun—trying to force its way out and illuminate the day. She said I was like that, a beautiful soul tormented by life's events, just waiting to shine again.

'I keep it to remind myself of her, of us,' I say, and his eyes move in my direction.

It's the first time I notice how dark they are, a deepness in them that matches the night sky. Where it's so dark you can't see beyond it, but just by looking, you know how vast it is, how many secrets it holds.

I glance at the coffee in my hand and reach out to him.

'Thank you, Lilah,' he says, quickly glancing at me once more before moving to join the others for their afternoon snack.

They stay for a while in the shop; eating, talking, laughing. Elisa tries to integrate me into the conversation sometimes, asking my thoughts about some topics and telling curiosities about the four of us.

Elijah and his friend work at the tattoo shop down the street, *InkPark*. From what I gather, Elijah is the owner, hence the name of the shop that comes from his last name, Elijah Park.

'If you ever want a tattoo done, we are the guys for the job,' Elijah says.

I noticed he has tattoos on his arms. What do they call them? Tattoo sleeves? One peeks from his shirt towards his neck, but I had no idea he was a tattoo artist.

I've always loved tattoos, the art of getting something you love, something meaningful, on your skin so you'll never forget it. It's the definition of wearing your heart on your sleeve. Each tattoo tells a story, one that you are displaying for everyone to see, even if they don't know the meaning behind it. To me, that's beautiful, but I've never done one. Not because I don't want to, but because I want to smile when I see myself in the mirror before getting them.

'I'll keep that in mind,' I say. Honestly, I believe that was the longest sentence I've ever said to him.

They get up and one by one come to pay for their snack.

'See you at home. I'm working there today,' Elisa says.

If I had a job like hers, where I could work from home, I would never leave my room. On one hand, that would be great for my introverted self, but on the other, I love seeing my customers' faces every time they enjoy one of my creations. Besides, my therapist encourages me to be around other people. Elisa might work from home, but in her free time she gets out. We are complete opposites.

Elijah speaks the best way he can—with body language—and winks at me, making my heart skip a beat when I hand him his receipt. But I know he does that every time and to everyone. He's a natural flirt.

He throws the receipt into a mauve-pink trash bin with cream crochet cupcakes near the door, and that reminds me to ask if they want it, or it's a waste of paper and judging by the portion occupied by receipts in the rubbish every time I take it out, I've been wasting a lot of paper.

I tell them both goodbye as they open the door to step outside. Today I had closed the door to keep the shop fresh in this warm weather.

Then the friend gets up. He has been counting the money in his wallet.

'Here.' He reaches his hand to mine, handing me the money. I count more than what it should be, but he's already approaching the door.

'Hey! Here's the change.'

'Keep it. It's a tip for your fabulous service.' His big, round eyes almost close when he smiles, turning back to the door once more.

'Wait! What's your name?' If I don't ask this now, I'll never ask again.

'Kim Moon Hee,' he says, looking down.

'In Korean, the last name comes first, so Moonie?' I say, unsure of my pronunciation.

He swiftly lifts his head and stares at me, making me hold my breath for the first time.

'I-I'm sorry, I'm terrible at pronouncing things.'

'No, it's not that.' He eases my nervousness with his gentle smile. 'I just...I'm surprised you knew that.'

'Oh.' I let out a chuckle. 'I listen to a lot of K-Pop, and K-Dramas are my favourite dramas.'

He nods, and before leaving, the man speaks once more. 'It's Moon Hee, but I like Moonie better.'

I smile and thank him for the tip, unsure if he hears me

before the white door closes behind him as he joins his friends.

I watch as they walk away, my focus on the last to join the trio. Even though we are complete strangers, something in the way his eyes landed on me felt so familiar.

셋
'set'

It's Friday. Therapy day.

A year ago I dreaded Fridays. Everybody was always happy for them, because it meant the weekend was near and they could finally relax and enjoy life, even if for a couple of days.

To me, Fridays meant having to open up to a stranger. Just the thought of it made me unable to leave my bedsheets for hours. I only opened the shop in the afternoon that day because of that exact reason.

I would get up when Elisa got home at lunch hour. Fridays for her meant having to go to the office and present her progress. Now she works as a freelancer, coding for games, apps, and even websites. She made mine and didn't ask for a cent. That's why for an entire year she would eat for free at *Sweet Delilah*.

Elisa would get me up by promising to go with me to Ms Julie's door. And so she did—every Friday—for six months.

Now, I'm eager for Fridays. Every session is a step forward. Each week Ms Julie helps me realise something about myself or something that surrounds me I have never considered. I am grateful for her and Elisa; she was the one to give me the courage to get up and work on myself, for myself.

'Good day, Delilah,' Ms Julie says as I walk inside her office.

'Good day, Ms Julie.' I sit on the sofa in front of hers.

Her office is beautiful. Very simple, but the view is

spectacular. The wall behind me has floor-to-ceiling windows from one end to the other, letting us see the entire city.

'How was your week?' she asks, beginning our session. Her long, slick brown hair is pulled back into a ponytail. I don't remember if I've ever seen her hair down.

'It was normal. The shop was busy, but other than that, normal.'

Her thick brows lift, urging me to keep going, so I do. By now, I already know what she wants to know. 'I didn't have any attacks, but I panicked a few times when I was with other people, especially every time Elijah stopped by to meet Elisa.'

'That's wonderful. You have been having fewer panic and anxiety attacks as the months go by. Last week you had one and before that, it had been a couple of weeks,' my therapist says, looking down at her notebook. 'Have you been exercising what I've taught you?'

'Yes, I've been breathing five times when being confronted by someone, or being put in an uncomfortable situation. I just don't understand why I get this nervous around people when I talk with others every day in my bakery.'

'You are in charge of your bakery. It's your place. There, people answer to you, so you feel in control, and when you do that, you don't panic.'

'So I don't panic when I feel in control?' I ask, and she nods. 'So, how can I feel in control outside my shop?'

'The only way for you to feel in control outside is knowing that you can't control everything and it's not your fault what happens beyond your abilities.'

If only it were that easy.

'How can I feel in control when I can't control everything?'

'True freedom is knowing you can't control everything.' She repeats herself; I've learned that's something she does when she wants me to interiorise those words. 'When you know that, you can control your reaction towards it. That's the only thing you can control: how you react to things, how you let others affect you. When you get in control of your feelings, of yourself, you get in control of your world...and ahead of people who can't control themselves.' She winks, leaning back into her seat.

Her relaxed posture allowed me to breathe during our first sessions, and her way of asking without prying, not minding if I answered but rounding back to the question in different words, was what made me talk in the first place.

'To feel in control, you must stop trying to control the world or other people. You can never control other people's thoughts. Start controlling yourself, your thoughts and reactions.'

I don't answer after that; I need to think better about it. It makes sense, like everything she says, but I can't shake the feeling that I can't do it.

'Did you do what I suggested you do?' my therapist asks.

'Yes, I've already got a pal. I'm waiting for his letter.' I smile.

'How do you feel about it?'

'At first, I was nervous, but because they don't know who I am, I'm now excited,' I say, letting out a trembled chuckle. It's still weird for me to think that I will talk with someone new without freezing at the beginning.

'There is a fine line between nervous and excited. They both trigger the same area of our brain, but it's us who decide how we look at it. You can always switch between them, learn to switch for the better one, the one that makes you smile, just like you are right now.' This woman always has a philosophical answer to my thoughts. I love that.

The hour-long session goes by fast. The sessions started to be over faster when I began to enjoy them. Before that, an hour seemed like three.

When I get home, Elisa isn't alone again. The guys are here. If they are moving in, they should at least warn me or divide the bills.

They don't see me as I walk through the corridor into my

room. I'm not in the mood to talk; I've been talking for an hour and it drained me.

I grab my computer and dive into the world of a new K-Drama. They always make me forget my problems when I'm involved in the character's issues. Some are more comical, others more dramatic and make you cry for days, but this one is more to the historical side. I like to change between genres.

In the middle of the episode, I find myself wondering when my first letter will come. The weekend is approaching, so it means I have to wait at least two days. Bummer.

I stop the drama and log on to Pinterest to look for pen pal ideas. People make their letters look so aesthetically pleasing, but I don't have that gift. It's hard enough for me to decorate my room, but an envelope? That's beyond my abilities. Elisa is the one with the design knowledge.

There hasn't been noise coming from outside my door for a while so I stand up to go prepare a meal. Before entering the living room, I peek inside and I'm faced with an empty sofa.

I text Elisa to know if she wants me to prepare dinner for her.

No need, I'm dining with friends. It's Elijah's birthday. Probably only coming home tomorrow.

I smile at the thought of having the house all for myself, but I can't help wanting to wish him well.

Tell him happy birthday for me, please.

I go back into my room, dress in my pyjamas, and grab my Bluetooth speaker. I place it on the kitchen table, the first purchase I made upon moving into this house. It's so worn off, and I deeply question its purity from all the people Elisa has brought home over the past years.

I turn on the speaker and blast on KARD. I've been obsessed with their songs lately. BTS, Stray Kids, ATEEZ, and more play a lot in the two hours I spend in the kitchen cooking dinner and baking biscuits. Tomorrow I'll be perfecting a new recipe I want to sell at my bakery.

I'm finishing the episode I paused earlier and munching down my buttery biscuits when a loud bell rings. At first, I thought it was in the show, but it rings again.

I look at the time: 2 a.m.

Who the hell is ringing my doorbell at this hour? Did Elisa forget her keys?

She said probably be back tomorrow. She wasn't certain, but usually is.

The bell rings again.

I grab my robe and step out of the room. Arriving at the front door, I get one eye close to the little hole that allows me to see a head outside. The person is looking down so I can't see their face.

'Who is it?' I ask.

'It's Jeremiah,' the voice outside says, dragging the name.

I turn the doorknob and pull it to me. In the space between the door and its frame, Jeremiah looks at me with bloodshot eyes. He's drunk.

'Jer, what are you doing here?'

'I was at a party and your flatmate was there. I asked for you, but she told me you were home.'

Elisa stopped asking me to accompany her to parties after three years of me telling her no. Now she only notifies me she's going out. From time to time, she asks again, hoping for a different answer, but I always tell her the same.

'And you came here because...' I tilt my head.

'Because...' he says, moving his hand to brush his ginger locks off of his face. 'I wanted...to...tell you...'

He stops, and I stare at him, waiting for him to continue. I step to the side of the door and motion my arm for him to enter the house, leading him to the living room. We sit down on the sofa and I ask, 'Tell me what?'

'Huh?' His eyebrows rise, but his eyes don't follow.

'You said you came here to tell me something.'

'Oh...fuck.' He closes his eyes and inhales deeply before

speaking again. 'I like you, Lilah. I've liked you for four years...since we met.'

Gravity takes a toll on my face as the shock makes my muscles weaken and my jaw drop. Becca told me her brother had feelings for me, but I never believed her.

'You can't like me,' I say, my voice low.

'I can and I do.' He stares into my eyes.

'How can you like me?' I stopped believing love was in the cards for me a long time ago.

'How can I not?' The dullness in his now widened eyes vanishes momentarily as his first normal-toned sentence leaves his mouth.

My eyes fix on a point on the grey rug, and he continues, 'You are the most amazing person I've ever met.' He grabs my hand but my mind can no longer control my body, every signal to move getting lost as it's sent. 'You are kind, smart, funny, and pretty as hell.'

That's not true. A song I listened to five years ago pops into my head: *8 billion people* by *Kiran + Nivi*.

Please don't say I'm pretty.

'I'm sorry, Jer. I-I only see you as a friend,' I say to him after a few moments.

I wait for his answer, but it never comes. His hold on my hand releases, so I glance to my side and find him leaning back on the sofa, passed out. Maybe that was all he had energy for.

I get up and grab the brown fuzzy blanket resting on the arm of the sofa to cover him.

Resting my head backwards on the mattress as my back touches the bed frame, my mind keeps replaying his words, still unable to believe his feelings.

My hands grip the soft fabric on my bottoms while thoughts float around.

I don't feel the same for him and I dread hurting him, but I also don't know what to think. He told me something I hadn't heard about myself in years, something I stopped believing. As the years went by, my self-esteem got lower. I used to like myself, but then *he* made me question everything. They all did.

Flashes from my past run through my mind, and I try to keep calm as my cheeks get wetter with tears.

Images flood my mind from every time my mother would dress me and how she would stare at me, trying to find flaws to fix. Images of how she would scold me whenever I was myself with others and the disappointment on her face. The same expression she gave me in everything I did.

Images from the only two boyfriends I had when I wouldn't give them what they wanted, when I wouldn't play the perfect girlfriend's role. How I just wanted to receive love when the only person whom I received it from left this world. The one person I could count on left me behind in a world where I had no rug under my feet to warm me, nothing to hold on to. Wherever I looked, disappointment filled people's faces whenever they stared at me.

It's okay, Delilah. You're okay.

Inhale, exhale.

Inhale, exhale.

Inhale, exhale.

I calm my breathing but break down on the floor, lying on my side, knees hugged against my chest. Crying for a future I thought I had and never happened, a past I wish I never had, and most importantly, crying for myself; for the one I hurt the most, the one that stopped shining...the one I want to retrieve.

넷
'net'

The cold floor jolts me awake as soon as my eyes open. I had dozed off before making it to my bed.

I fumble around, feeling for my phone with my hands. When I find it, I unlock it and glance at the screen, revealing the time to be seven in the morning. The soft glow outside makes its way in through the creaks on my blinds, but I'm tempted to go to my bed and stay a little longer.

Then it hits me. Jeremiah.

I walk to the living room and find him lying on the sofa, sleeping soundly; at least one of us got a good night's sleep. My bakery opens in three hours, so I try to sleep for at least one more. The sound of a door closing wakes me up. My hand reaches for my phone, tapping on the screen. 9:30 a.m.

Shit, I overslept.

I rush outside of my bedroom and encounter Elisa standing by the living room's entrance.

'Elisa?' I ask with my raspy voice.

'Lilah, don't freak out.' Her voice is for my ears only. 'But there's a man sleeping on our sofa.'

I laugh. 'It's Jeremiah, from *Greener's*. He stopped by last night drunk and fell asleep as we talked.'

At the exact moment words stop coming from my mouth, the man on the sofa wakes up.

'Lilah? Where am I?' Jeremiah asks, rubbing his eyes.

'Obviously at our flat,' Elisa says, rolling her eyes.

'Why?' He glances around the room.

Is it possible that he doesn't remember our conversation? That way, I wouldn't have to break his heart with his unrequited love.

'You came here last night—drunk, very drunk—to tell me something and then fell asleep on the sofa as we spoke.' I pray he doesn't remember what happened.

'Oh...' He scratches the nape of his neck. 'What did I say?'

'That you saw Elisa at the party and she told you I was alone and then...a little later you crashed.' I'm not lying, but I'm also not telling the whole truth.

'Nothing else?' He looks at me, eyes gleaming through the tiredness.

'Yep.' Okay, now I lied, but it's for his own good. I'm preventing a heartbreak.

'Oh, cool. I'm sorry for bothering you. I don't even remember why I came.'

Doesn't he remember, or is he lying like me? It's not always a bad thing though, as long as we lie to protect another. I'm lying to protect him, but I also feel bad about it.

Suck it up, Delilah.

Being a grown up sucks. It's filled with choices you need to make to avoid a disaster, even if most of the time those choices just create new choices and eventually everything explodes.

'No worries, I have to get ready for work. I'm supposed to open the shop at ten.' No way in hell that's gonna happen, but I shouldn't waste more time. 'Elisa can show you the way out.' I smile at them, and my flatmate looks sideways at me.

When I hear the front door closing from inside my room, I fall flat on the bed.

How am I going to look at him now? I can't avoid him, but I want to avoid this situation so much.

'Can I come in?' Elisa asks, knocking on the door.

'Sure,' I say, my voice a mix between a human and an animal.

'That guy is weird.' She sits on the corner of my bed. 'He was asking so much about you last night.'

My eyes pry at her. 'He was?'

'Yeah.' She chuckles. 'He really didn't say anything else before falling asleep?'

I look back at the ground and nod. 'He said he liked me.'

I wait for her to say something, but Elisa keeps quiet, waiting for me to go on.

'I don't know if he really doesn't remember, but I hope so. He's a good guy and I don't want to hurt him.'

'Remembering or not, if he had the guts to tell you once—even if he was drunk—he will tell you again. How are you going to react to that?'

She has a point. At least now it won't be a surprise and I'll be able to come up with an answer first, but I won't have a second chance often. I need to get better at controlling my emotions.

'I'll be prepared next time. Aren't you even a little surprised he likes me?'

Am I the only one who didn't see this coming? Even his sister has said he has a crush on me.

'Oh, no, you can see kilometres away that he likes you.'

'I guess I lost faith that anyone would ever like me. I just...I stopped feeling beautiful a long time ago.' My vision travels beyond the white framed window. The birds sing outside and in my mind *Blue & Grey* by BTS is playing in the background.

I just want to be happier...

My flatmate grabs my hand out of comfort and exhales. 'You are the only one who doesn't see your beauty. Fuck, Lilah, you are beautiful. You just lost your confidence. You still have the same face you had five years ago, the same one I saw people falling for at first sight. You just lost your shine and don't allow others to see you. Besides, outer beauty isn't everything.'

'That's easy for you to say. You are the most confident person I've ever met,' I say, glaring at her.

'That kind of hurt. I'm confident because I work my ass off every day to achieve and keep this confidence in myself. I have my bad days as well; everyone does. But I make sure they are just that: bad days. I don't allow the thoughts I have in those days to become my normal, to swallow me.'

'But how? How can I work on my confidence? How can I get that back?' I'm really desperate at this point. I'm a truck trapped in snow, giving its all to get out, but in the end runs out of gasoline before it can even move. 'I'm so tired of this. Sometimes I just want to scream until I have nothing else weighing on me.'

'Then scream.' The corners of her lips lift in mischief.

I'm bewildered, staring at her, so she grabs my hand and leads me outside our flat.

'What are you doing?' I ask as she pulls me all the way up our building's stairs. Thankfully we live on the last floor. We get to our rooftop, and she lets go of my hand.

'Go ahead, scream,' she says, pointing her head towards the sky.

'What? No...' I watch how every person looks tiny from here, nothing but ants running around.

'You said you wanted to scream, so do it.' I can tell she's dead serious.

'I mean, I can't do it here. People will hear it.'

'You have to stop caring about what others think. If you won't do it, I will.' With that, she releases a raging scream into the air until she can no longer breathe.

'Ah!' She exhales. 'This felt amazing. You should really try it.'

'Thank you. One day I'll try it. I need to open the shop now.'

We return to our flat, and I get ready to go to work. Elisa stays in her room the entire time. Most likely, she went to bed to recover from the night out.

I do want to stop caring about what others think. I don't

know how I'll do that, but I won't give up. That's my goal now, my priority, to get better.

The shop was slow today, so I closed earlier. As I arrive home, the place is silent. Either Elisa is still sleeping or she isn't home. So, I grab my speaker and some scented candles and walk to the lavatory. I turn on the water and let the bathtub fill halfway, pour a purple bath bomb, light the lavender-scented candles, and turn the speaker on low.

Confidence comes from self-love, and the first step to self-love is self-care.

I take my time, enjoying the water, the aroma in the air, the music, my body. There's a certain type of peace that comes from taking care of myself, and I'm saddened by the realisation that I can't remember the last time I did this.

I get out of the shower and moisturise my skin. After that, I do my skincare routine and take care of my hair. I leave the loo, a towel wrapped around me and the Bluetooth speaker on my arm, still listening to music.

As I pass through the hallway towards my room, the sound of people laughing fills the air, drowning out the music from my speaker. Despite the relaxed state of my mind, my feet refuse to quicken their pace. I walk, slow and steady, to my room. The moment I'm about to turn my doorknob, Moon Hee comes out of the living room.

He halts when his eyes meet mine and smiles, opening his mouth to say something. Something I don't let him say as I get inside and close the door.

I'm still in my self-care zone, and I don't want to think about what he thought when he saw me like that. I get dressed and concentrate on myself, ignoring every thought that pops up about the situation.

You can't control other people's thoughts, Delilah. Focus on your own.

Before heading to the kitchen, I stop by the mirror I have near my door, a mirror I rarely use, a mirror I avoid looking at. For the first time in years, I look at myself. Not only at my appearance, but truly at myself. I see a woman in her late twenties, with brown wavy hair down to her shoulders and dark brown eyes, smiling at me. A cute dimple forms as she stares deeper into my soul. A broken spirit, trying to regain its strength, to rise above all the past traumas. A resilient soul, a kind one, too. That's me, the Delilah Scott I've been trying to hide for so long.

A tear rolls down her cheek, but unlike all the others that she's felt before, this one doesn't carry sadness within it. It carries hope, hope for her future self.

'Come join us!' Elisa says from the living room as I finish cooking dinner and snacks for them. They are preparing to play some board games. 'Four is better than three.'

My instinct is to say no, hide in my room and stay there until they leave, but I also know this can be another test to get out of my comfort zone as Ms Julie has been saying I need to do. It's not like they are complete strangers; they come here almost every day.

I grab the pan of mac and cheese I made and take it to the living room, placing it in the middle of the table in front of the sofa without exchanging a single word or a glance. And as I leave to go grab plates and snacks, they all get up to help me.

'You could have asked us to help,' Elijah says, grabbing the cups from the kitchen counter.

'You know Lilah, she likes to do it all by herself,' Elisa teases, and I fake laugh at her.

'Oh, she speaks!' Elijah plays, and I smile at him.

Every time they direct their words at me, I feel like a fish out of water, reaching for a breath to utter back. Especially with him—my heart threatens to leave my chest with every interaction.

I grab the plates from the cabinet, and as I'm about to leave for the living room, Moon Hee stops in front of me. 'I'll take these; bring the snacks.'

'I can take them.'

'I know, but they seem heavy and I don't want you to break any plates.' He smiles, biting the left side of his bottom lip.

Did he just call me weak? Oh no, no, no. Now I'll have to beat him at the games.

I can see why Elisa spends so much time with them; they are really chill and funny. My presence is still more of an observer than a speaker, but the more I enjoy being with them, the more I open up.

'Are you sure you've never played this?' Moon Hee asks as I beat him for the third time at whist.

'Call it first timer's luck. But it's for calling me weak earlier.'

'Weak? When did I—Oh...' His eyes widen and he chuckles. 'I wasn't calling you weak. I just really wanted to help because you had already done so much for us.'

'Oh...*Bianhae* (sorry),' I say, eyes down to the floor.

'Wait, you speak Korean?' Elijah asks, surprised.

'No, I just know a few things I've picked up watching K-Dramas.' I rarely say anything in Korean, but for a strange reason with Moonie, I want to show what I know.

'So, are you a Koreanboo or something?' Both my and Moon Hee's head spurt to him.

'*Hyung*!' Moon Hee says.

'What? I'm just asking. I hear her listening to K-Pop and she knows a few words, so she could be.'

'I am so lost in this conversation,' Elisa says, and we realise she has no clue what we are talking about.

'I love K-Pop and K-Dramas, but I'm not learning Korean to get a Korean guy. I'm learning it because I truly enjoy the country and the culture, and I do want to understand what the songs mean without looking up the translation or what my idols say without waiting for subtitles.' I sigh. This is the reason I don't speak Korean on the street; people just assume things.

'That's great. I was just checking that you wouldn't start calling me *Oppa* or something.' I take offence at Elijah's comment and as my eyes glance past Moon Hee, I notice the discontent in his face as he glares at his friend.

'If we were close and speaking in Korean, I might because you are older than me, but don't worry, I won't. Now if you excuse me, I'm going to bed. It's late and I'm tired.' I stand up to leave.

'No, wait, Lilah!' Elisa says. 'You're right. It's late; they should be going home.'

'Yeah, I agree. I'm also tired,' Moon Hee says, getting up. 'Thank you for this lovely evening and for dinner.'

'Yeah, thank you,' Elijah says, and they both walk towards the door.

After they leave, I go to my room, and my flatmate follows me.

'I don't know exactly what happened, but I've never seen Elijah being rude like that. I'm sorry,' she says, sitting next to me on my bed.

'You are not the one that needs to apologise. It's fine. It's not the first time someone has called me that.'

'Can you explain what a Koreanboo is?' she asks.

'Well, simply put...Koreanboos are people obsessed with Korea and the Korean culture, so much that they renounce their own ethnicity and say they are Korean. They can also be very cringy when talking about their idols and do everything to get a Korean man.'

'Got it, yeah, definitely rude, and what are the other words you were saying? Moon Hee calls Elijah *Hyung* a lot, but I have no idea what it means.'

It's weird but refreshing having someone asking me about the Korean language and culture with a genuine interest and not to make fun.

'Basically, Koreans, when they are close with someone, rarely use their names, unless they are calling or referring to them. Even then it comes attached to another word. They call them *Hyung or Noona* when guys speak and *Oppa or Unnie* when girls speak, when the other is older than them. It means older brother or older sister. It demonstrates your affection and respect towards the other person. In this case, Moon Hee calls Elijah *Hyung* because he's older. In Korea, age plays a big part in everyday things, including speech.'

'So, why did the way Elijah said you would call him *Oppa* sounded like such a bad thing?'

'Because Koreanboos basically sexualised the word *Oppa*, as calling them Daddy, and use it even if they don't say another Korean word, which is just cringe. The word is supposed to be cute, friendship or relationship wise. It's also weird for Koreans when foreigners call them that, but only if they aren't speaking Korean, because it's their culture,' I say. 'But now let's end this Korean class and sleep. I'm really tired.'

She chuckles. 'Yes, let's go. Thank you for the lesson; at least with you I won't feel as lost when they start speaking Korean out of nowhere.'

'I'm not fluent. Trust me, we will both get lost.'

'Well, at least we will get lost together.' She winks, and this time we both laugh.

I fall asleep thinking that Elijah might not be how I fantasised in my head. People rarely are what they seem, but I believe he's still a nice person if Elisa hangs out with him. She's the type of person who has a sharp sixth sense for people and is not afraid to cut someone off if she thinks they aren't on the same level as her vibe.

Moonie seems like a decent man, but only time will tell how both really are.

다섯
'dasot'

It's finally Monday. I can't wait to go to the post office today and see if I've received my first pen pal letter. I haven't been this eager in such a long time. The adrenaline of knowing something I've been waiting for is arriving makes me feel younger and I love that.

Oh, to be a teenager again…Being an adult sucks most of the time. I know being a teenager isn't always easy, and I certainly do not want to return to all the high school drama, but times were simpler. I miss simplicity.

'Hello,' Elisa says, walking inside the bakery.

'Just you this time?' I grin.

'I came from the gym, but yes, today it's just me. Elijah is grounded.' Her firm tone tells me she hasn't forgotten yesterday, and even though it didn't happen with her, I appreciate how supportive she is of me. How supportive she's always been.

I watch her walk away from the door. The blue matching sports bra and leggings she wears pinching in all the right places. Elisa's shape is amazing, but I know she worked hard for it, as she goes four times a week to the gym to lift weights on top of doing yoga every day. Her golden skin glows from the sun outside, and a few of her curly strands frame her face while the rest is in a bun.

Instead of going down the rabbit hole of comparison, I

remember her words of bad days, bad thoughts. They don't reflect our life but are a trigger to recognise what's wrong in our mind and life so we can improve it.

Returning to reality, my eyes catch Elisa sitting at her usual table, looking out the window.

'I'm sorry, I got distracted...The usual?' I ask her and she nods.

A few more people walk into the shop, and my thoughts focus on work. Work is always the best way to not stress about the little voices in my head.

Right before I close for lunch, two very familiar faces come by the bakery for a few cupcakes and a latte.

'You are seriously the best baker I know, Delilah!' Becca says with a mouth full of chocolate and flour.

'That's impossible; I'm no Master Chef.' I look down and take a small breath in.

'No, you are a five-star Michelin,' she responds, making my head lift and the breath I'd just inhaled to be expelled as a chuckle.

This small, red-headed girl always makes me laugh. Her Scottish accent helps with the enthusiasm.

Jeremiah has been silent since he came into the shop. He's looking at his latte, swirling it with the straw as he stands behind his sister, closer to the cream wall.

Does he remember our conversation? There was something about the way he walked towards me that felt different, although I can't quite put my finger on it. Maybe it's just my imagination, now that I'm more focused on him. Maybe he's feeling a bit blue today.

'We have to make a collaboration again soon,' Rebecca says, shifting my gaze from her twin brother. 'Everyone loved your desserts in *Greener's* and it was a full week we had.'

'Indeed, I got more clients that week.' Many of my now-regulars came from the week I collaborated with the twins a few months ago.

Their restaurant has a lot more movement than my shop, since many people try to stay away from sugar but never skip meals. I'm trying to incorporate healthier goods in my bakery for those who avoid sugar and flour, but it's already all vegan, so that checks the lactose-free box already.

I need to think of more marketing strategies to bring people here.

'Then it's settled. Let's talk about a menu this week and prepare things to make it happen. Maybe a two week collab instead of one?' The small woman getting up from her table bats her eyelashes.

She comes to the balcony with their plates and cups, and I say, 'Sounds good. And you didn't need to do that.'

'I know, but I also know what it's like to work in places like this, and you already have many to pick up.'

While she pays, her brother steps outside without a word.

'Is something wrong with Jeremiah?' I nod towards him, and she turns her head nonchalantly around to his location.

'Honestly, I don't know.' She sighs. 'He has been quiet for the last few days. I even joked that he looked like he had been through a breakup, and he didn't even flinch. It's so weird.'

Bloody hell, he remembers.

I'll have to do what I dreaded: face him.

I stay silent and watch as they pass outside the white-framed window. Jeremiah's eyes glance to the side and meet mine before he disappears through the frame.

Maybe if I give him a few more days, he'll get better and things will get back to normal.

All my regulars came in today, and Ms Josephine even came with her husband.

I love this little piece of the world I created in the bakery. My own little world. Most customers are quite nice, and the neighbours as well.

London is huge, and this street is not very well-known—most

visits are from locals; we don't get many tourists—and that's why advertising gets a little rougher.

I have a letter!

I can't believe it, I actually have a letter.

I'm at the post office, smiling from ear to ear. My excitement bursts enough power to light up a Christmas tree.

Despite the temptation, I refrained from coming here during lunch hour. I wanted to do it, but I also wanted to enjoy reading in the tranquillity of my room.

The post office is closing soon, so I'll send my first pen pal letter during lunch hour tomorrow. I wonder how long it takes for them to receive it and respond. Since we are in the same city, it will most likely be a shipping day, but the sensation I get from holding this grey envelope in my hands transports me to a film where I have to wait weeks or even months to receive a letter from my beloved one.

When I get home, I don't even check if Elisa is home. I run straight into my room, close the door, throw my purse towards the bed, and sit at my desk.

The letter is quite simple on the outside, the only pop of colour coming from the London stamp on the right hand corner. On the front, written with a bold black handwriting, my username covers the paper in a pretty script.

I try to not ruin the envelope by opening it. I want to preserve this letter.

After unfolding the white A5 paper inside, I read it.

"**Hey there Delilah,**
The first time is always the hardest. Therefore, let's play a game to break the ice.
I was going to ask you your name, but let's not know each other's name for now. First, I want to know what

you like. Let's find something in common.
　Here are some things I enjoy:
　Art
　Music
　England
　Rain when I'm inside reading
　Irish bomb (no clue what else start with I...and yes, the drink)
　Cooking
　trAveling
　daNce
　fOod
　This was harder than I thought...Good luck!
　From your new pen pal,
　Daldust"

I had nothing in my mind about what to expect, but this was better than anything I could have imagined.

They sound funny. I look forward to getting to know more about Daldust.

'Lilah?' A voice calls from the hall. 'You home?'

More voices mumble around the house, but I can't figure out what they're saying.

A few seconds later, a knock sounds on my door, and I hide the letter under a book about *The Secret to Make your Bakery Rise*, a joke for bakers because we always have trouble making cakes rise well in the beginning.

'Yeah?' I say, and the door opens as my voice still sounds through the air.

'Great, you're here,' my flatmate says. 'There's someone who wants to talk to you.'

I tilt my head, wrinkling the skin between my eyebrows. She moves away from the door, and Elijah shows up in her place.

My heart skips a beat when I see him. He's wearing tight

denim jeans and a white T-shirt, black ink covering the rest of his arms. I can see his dark hair growing in the back as he pushes back the front. He stays at my door, looking down at the floor.

Never in my life have I seen Elijah shy, or whatever he is right now.

I stare at him—it's easier when he's not looking at me—but decide to speak soon after. 'Come in.'

He finally looks up, and my eyes move elsewhere. I hate this annoying inability to look someone in the eyes.

'I'm sorry.' He exhales, walking into my room. I still can't wrap my head around the fact that he just stepped foot inside my room. 'I'm sorry for the other night.'

I keep quiet, my eyes still avoiding him.

'I was an arsehole, and I ruined the night despite how much I was enjoying it. You are a lot different from what I anticipated, and I just went all evil on you.'

I clear my throat, trying to push the nervousness away. 'I was enjoying the night as well, and I'm sorry if I offended you in any way.'

'No, I'm sorry. I'm sorry for offending you when you did nothing to me. I just…Honestly, I don't know why I acted that way, but I promise I'll behave from now on.'

'I-I accept your apology. And don't worry, I won't speak Korean again unless I already know it fluently.' I bite my lower lip and glance up at him, flinching when my eyes meet the ones still looking at me.

For years I wished he looked at me, and now he's staring, bluntly, in my room. It feels surreal.

'Please, don't. Speak all you want. You can ask me if you need any help or just someone to practise with.' The corner of his lip lifts, and I nod.

'We are actually ordering Korean food tonight. Do you want to join us?'

'Only if you have *japchae* and *gimbap*,' I say as a joke.

There's a sense of fingers wrapping around my lungs after I speak.

I'm not funny. I've never been the funny type. Sometimes I question why my humour is so weird and now I just showed my weirdness to the last guy I should be weird in front of.

But when his expression lifts, wrinkles showing at the sides of his eyes, and he chuckles, the hand holding me hostage softens. 'We'll have that and a lot more.'

'I accept. I just need to finish up some things and I'll meet you outside,' I say. He leaves, closing the door behind him.

The moment I'm left alone my hand reaches for my chest and I exhale as if I've just got out of a corset—not that I've ever worn one, but from what I see in shows, that's the closest comparison I can think of.

I move to my bed and lay down, stomach up, looking at the ceiling.

Did I just have a full conversation with Elijah Park? I even made him chuckle.

I must be dreaming.

Please don't let this be a dream.

It's just Monday and I already have so much to talk to Ms Julie about.

But first, let's respond to the letter.

I'm even happier now.

It's hard to leave my comfort zone, but the rewards do make it worth it. I wish this feeling never ends.

I grab my pen and paper and start writing.

"Hi!

That's not fair! My name is in my username, so you already know it. What am I supposed to call you? Daldust?

Okay, Daldust, let's play games. I see what you did there, but I don't like coffee.

  Honesty
 bOoks
  Tea
  Cooking
 eart**H**
 k-p**O**p
  Cake (especially when I bake it)
my bedr**O**om
  Lilacs
  Animals
  ki**T**chen
 danc**E** (but can't do it well)
 1st thought before filling the letters: I'm fucked…why so many repeated letters??
 Final thought: H's are hard, oh look, an H word…
 What game is next on your agenda?
 Delilah"

I tap my phone's screen to check the time and realise it's been half an hour since Elijah left the room. Time flew as I wrote the letter.

I leave my room and walk towards the living room.

'Didn't you apologise?' I hear before stepping inside the room.

'Yes, I did. She said she would come,' another voice sounds.

I don't let them continue the conversation and step inside.

'Sorry, I took so long,' I say.

My eyes glance at the table and see that the food has already arrived. I was so focused that I didn't even hear the bell.

'No worries. Join us,' Elisa says and hands me a plate to serve myself.

'Do you drink? We brought *soju*,' Moon Hee asks, and I acknowledge him for the first time today. He's always so quiet, I sometimes forget he's in the room.

Is that how people feel about me?

'Yeah sure.' I'm not much of a drinker, since I don't have many friends and I don't like to drink alone, but I enjoy a drink once in a while.

'Well, let's get this party started!' Elijah says, raising his glass of *soju*.

여섯
'yeosot'

'Not me,' they say in sync.

'That's not fair!' I object.

'You were the last one,' Elisa says.

'I didn't even know it had started. Shouldn't you count to three or something?'

'Were you confused, guys?' she asks, and they both shake their heads.

'Fine.' I pout and stand up.

Damn the time I suggested for one of us to ask the neighbours for lemons. It's two in the morning. I don't think anyone will answer the door.

I observe all the doors on my floor, trying to hear any sound from the inside—any slight chance someone is awake. As I approach one door to listen closer, it opens.

I jump backwards and look down, catching my breath.

'Oh, fuck!' I feel my heartbeat through my chest with my hand. 'You scared me.'

'Sorry, I'm taking the rubbish outside,' the woman says.

I remember that I'm standing in front of her door, preventing her passage, and move to the side. 'Right, I'm sorry.'

She's near the end of the corridor when I'm reminded of the sole reason I was spying on her door.

'Excuse me,' I say, trying to keep my voice low for the

neighbours but loud enough for her to listen.

She turns around, and I take that as my cue to keep going. 'Do you, for any chance, have any lemons?'

She chuckles and nods. 'Help me take out the rubbish and I'll give you lemons.'

I smile and run up to her. We stand in front of the elevator for a few seconds, waiting for it to arrive at our floor, and I watch my reflection through drunken eyes.

Did I just run up to a stranger as if I'd known her all my life? And am I really going into a dark alley with her?

Inside the elevator, I have the urge to ask, 'Why are you taking the rubbish at this hour?'

'Why do you need lemons at this hour?' she asks.

'Because I want to drink tequila,' I respond, unlike her, and she laughs.

'I can see that you are a bit tipsy.' The corner of her mouth lifts. 'I like to take out the rubbish when it's calm outside.'

When we arrive at her flat, I stay by the door and she goes in.

'Here,' she says, holding two lemons. 'Is it enough?'

'It's more than enough, thank you.' I lift the edges of my lips, closing my tired eyes. I grab the lemons and before she closes the door, I ask, 'Do you want a shot?'

She smiles back. 'Next time.'

Inside my flat, music flows through the atmosphere and a few laughs come from the living room.

'Did you go buy them?' Elijah asks as I walk into the room.

'No, a neighbour gave me some,' I say, placing the lemons on the table next to the closed bottle of tequila.

'I went to check in on you and didn't see you,' he says.

'Aww, little Elijah was worried about me.' I am definitely drunk, sober me could never.

His cheeks turn red, and he looks down, so I put the focus back on me. 'I helped her take the rubbish out in exchange for the lemons.'

'You should have told us. Something could have happened to you. Do you even know who she is?' Moonie stands up, another person who talks a lot more when drunk.

I chuckle, lifting my eyebrows. 'What? Do you think she's a serial killer?'

'You never know.' He stares into my eyes and I know he's not joking. His dark moons stay on mine until my features relax.

I know she's not a serial killer. That would be crazy.

'Can you just shut up and drink? The game is called Truth or Shot, not Truth or Chit-Chat,' Elisa says. I look at the table and notice she has already prepared the glasses, cut the lemon, and opened the salt. She really wants a tequila shot.

'Moon Hee.' My flatmate points at him. 'Truth or shot?'

'Truth,' he says, and Elisa doesn't look amused.

'You are so not funny.' She scowls, preparing to ask her question, but he interrupts any line of thought.

'Not true.' Moon Hee smiles and drinks a shot without hesitation, making her laugh.

'Now, that's what I'm talking about!' My very drunk flatmate beams. 'Now Lilah-'

'Elijah, truth or shot?' I ask before she can get me into the spotlight.

'Truth,' he says, which is not what I was expecting.

'Is it true that you have a crush on Elisa?' I ask. I've seen how he looks at her. It's the way I look at him.

He chuckles. 'Who doesn't?' he asks and looks at her.

'Good point.' I nod. 'I guess it's my turn to drink.'

'I don't,' Moonie says, making me gaze at him.

His eyes—dark as the night—shine with millions of stars. They're the type of eyes that draw you towards them, the type that makes you question if the popular belief of light eyes being prettier is indeed true.

I take my shot with a small smile and watch the corner of his mouth lift. Elijah is the bad-boy type of hot, but Moon Hee is the mysterious type, and between the two, I've always had a hard time choosing a favourite.

'You don't count; you never have a crush,' Elijah says to Moon Hee. 'Are you sure you are not aromantic?'

'What if I am? My sexuality is not for you to have an opinion on. But no, I'm not. I have crushes,' he says calmly with a straight face.

Mysterious. He is bloody mysterious.

'You have a crush?' the guy sitting next to Elisa blurts.

'That's not what I said,' Moonie mutters.

'He said he has crushes, as in general, not a specific one right now,' my flatmate says, slapping Elijah's arm.

'Fine, fine.' He rubs his arm with his hand. It doesn't show much, but Elisa is strong. She has skinny arms that are all muscle underneath.

'Who's next?' Elisa asks, drinking a shot without even playing.

'My turn,' Elijah says. 'Lilah!'

My heart stops when he says my name and I glance at him, not sure how to react.

'Truth or shot?' he asks, tilting his head.

I want to swallow, but it's a desert inside my throat. I grab a shot and drink it, making him frown.

'Truth,' I answer.

'You know, the shot is supposed to be after...' he says.

'I was thirsty,' I explain, and he huffs out a chuckle.

'Okay. Do you have a crush on me?'

Huh?

I cough in surprise.

Of course, he knows I have a crush on him. But do I want to admit it?

I decide to take a page from his book and answer, 'Who doesn't?' and he smirks, nodding.

'I'm tired,' Moon Hee says, getting up.

'Me too.' I admit.

'No!' Elisa drags. It's definitely time for bed.

'Yes, you need to sleep. And so do I,' I tell her, and she pouts.

'We're leaving then,' Elijah says, moving next to his friend.

We walk them to the door and stay as they walk away. To my surprise, they don't take many steps. They get to the flat in front of ours and open its door.

'Wait! You live there?' I raise my eyebrows.

'How do you think I met them?' Elisa mutters to me.

'Well, goodnight ladies,' Elijah says, making a sign-off gesture with his hand. Moonie looks at us and does a little bow, ending with a gorgeous smile, and enters.

I'm still wrapping my head around them being our next-door neighbours inside our home.

'How long have they been living here?' I ask my flatmate. *How have I never seen them?*

'Elijah has been here for the past year, but Moon Hee only moved in a month ago. He was living with his mum before. She is also here in London from what I've heard, but he wanted a bit more freedom, and it's closer to their shop.'

How did I miss Elijah in the building for an entire year?

As if reading my thoughts, Elisa speaks. 'You probably never noticed because every time you saw them in the building you thought they were coming to meet me and you never saw them leave the flat before tonight.'

'Probably,' I say to myself, walking towards my room.

What a night.

I haven't had a social night like this in years. It felt good.

First the letters and now this. I already have so much to talk about in my Friday session.

But now, I need to sleep because I'm working in the morning and my body doesn't react to alcohol like it did ten years ago.

'Ah.' I groan, turning off my alarm for the third time.

I hate being responsible. I don't actually hate it—I think that is a wonderful quality, but I hate it right now. My head is pounding so much.

I make the effort and get up.

I grab the first thing I see in my wardrobe and put it on. It's in these moments I'm glad to have such a neutral wardrobe. It's all black for today. Black as my soul feels at this moment.

I get ready and grab my pen pal letter to send. I skip breakfast, since I can eat at the bakery. The moment I close my front door, I'm stopped by an early rising Moon Hee.

'Oh, hi,' I say as he stares at me.

He's wearing black trackies and an oversized black T-shirt. The hallway light shines on his hair, and I catch on to some sweat droplets on his forehead.

'Good morning. I was going to bring you this.' He lifts the corners of his mouth and raises the bottle he has in his hand.

I look at the bottle, intrigued.

'It's a hangover cure, my mum's recipe.' His chest rises and drops in strong movements.

'Really? Oh, thank you so much. I really need it.'

'Yeah, I figured. It does wonders. Elijah always asks for it.'

'Did you run here?' I ask.

'Hmm...not exactly.' He chuckles, rubbing the back of his neck. 'I went on my morning run before I came here. I saw the drink I made when I woke up as I got to the flat and thought you might need some. You were pretty buzzed last night.'

'Yes...I was.' I bite my lower lip and tilt my head down.

Moon Hee brings the cure into my line of vision and I grab it before looking up at him with a smile. It's funny how with him the conversations are so simple, yet enough. Words are unnecessary between us; we communicate through silent glances. That's something I've never had and I can't stop wondering why or how it happens.

I spent all morning thinking about how much my life seems to have changed from the moment I decided to take ahold of it.

From the outside, it might not seem like it has changed much. I'm still me, still baking and running a business, still shy, an introvert, but to me it has changed. It has been slowly changing since I entered therapy, figuring out my traumas and having someone I can talk to, with no judgement. Someone who I know is there to help me even when I break down while speaking. But the moment I got tired of my shit was the moment I let go, let go of my fear of change. I never knew how liberating change could feel.

I know I still have a long way to go—a lot of things are still triggering, and I still have panic attacks—but I can see a brighter future.

I just closed the bakery for lunch, and now I'm walking over to the post office to send my letter. From my first impression, Daldust seems like a cool person. I hope they like me too.

After sending the letter, I go over to *Greener's*. I haven't been there since what happened with Jeremiah, and I wonder how he's doing.

Becca is at the counter when I walk in. No sign of Jeremiah for now.

She greets me and points to the table near the window, my table—not that I bought it, but she knows it's the one I choose every time I can.

'So, when are you free to prepare the collaboration?' the redheaded woman asks.

'I'm free tomorrow after I close the shop. Can you meet then?'

'I can. I'll ask Jer if he's available.'

'Speaking of Jer...how is he? Does he look better?' I'm trying to be subtle. I'm not sure he has told her what happened.

'He seems better, yes. He's in the kitchen if you want to see him while you wait for your food.' She nods her head to the back of the restaurant.

'You know what? I'll take my order to him. That customer is calling for you,' I say, getting up and walking towards the kitchen.

I knock on the open door, and the chef looks behind in my direction.

'Lilah,' he says, eyes wide open.

'Hey Jer. How are you?'

'Good, working...' He glances at the food on the stove. I know he's busy, but I still have a gut feeling that he's rushing me out. He used to spend all the time I was here talking to me unless a customer called.

'Add my usual to your to-do's.'

'Of course,' the man with freckles says and turns again to mix the food.

I walk back to my seat, uneasy. It hasn't passed. I'm sure he remembers, and now I have to face him.

I don't want to, but I have to.

Ahh! I scream inside my head.

I spend my entire meal thinking about how to approach him, and after rounds and rounds of thought, I opt for the simplest, but hardest way: to be direct.

After paying, I go back to the kitchen.

I knock again on the door, and he looks at me. 'Are you leaving?'

'Yes...Can you meet me in my bakery when you have a break? I need to talk to you.'

Jeremiah doesn't ask why or about what; he simply nods and keeps slicing vegetables. He definitely knows what it's about.

일곱
'ilgob'

The bakery is calm when the little bell on top of the door rings. My eyesight moves to the entrance where Jeremiah is passing by, and my body tenses.

'Hi Jer. Hmm...take a seat and I'll be right there,' I say, receiving the payment from the only clients in the shop.

When they leave, I walk to the door and hang a sign saying, *I'll be back in a bit*, so we don't get interrupted.

I don't know if I can do this. The urge to run out the door is overwhelming.

'So...' I turn around to sit in front of him, exhaling the breath I hadn't noticed I've been holding.

I straighten my back and wobble a little in the chair, trying to find the position to make me look as natural as possible in this unnatural situation. I've never even had a serious conversation with Jeremiah before, other than when we talk about business.

Suck it up, Delilah.

'You remember what you told me the other night, don't you?' I ask, ripping the band-aid off.

He nods. 'Yeah...I didn't at first, but throughout the day my memory came back.'

'Oh, I see.' My gaze moves down at the table between us, and I fiddle with my fingers. 'I'm sorry. I had no idea you felt that way about me.'

'I thought I was being blatant, but you still never saw it. I've liked you since the day you entered our restaurant with a basket of cupcakes and cookies,' he says, looking out the window.

'The day I opened Sweet Delilah...' I match his glance.

'I have seen my fair share of beautiful women. I mean, they are all around us, but when I saw you—' He rubs the nape of his neck. 'When I saw you...I saw more than a beautiful woman. Your aura differed from anything I'd ever seen. You just lit up the whole place and your smile honed my day instantly. That's why I keep trying to make you smile, even if you don't do it often.'

'I-I'm really sorry. I just...I never saw you like that.' I search my mind for a better answer, but it never comes.

'I know, and I was okay, but then I got drunk and had to do something stupid and tell you.' He sighs. 'I wish I never told you.'

'Why?'

'Because that way I could keep making you smile, even if it was as a friend,' the man in front of me says. This mature side of Jeremiah is one that has always gone unnoticed by me, but I'm glad I'm finally seeing it.

The rays of sun make his red hair glow like copper and his freckles more visible.

'I would like that. To keep being your friend.' My eyes smile. In my mind, I've always seen him as an acquaintance, never a friend, but I might reconsider that now.

'Really?' There it is. The smile that was missing from his face in the last few days.

I stand up, and he follows, approaching me.

'Can I...Can I hug you?' Jer asks, and after looking at the hopeful sparkle in his green eyes, I nod.

After this brief moment, he goes back to work and I do the same.

I was so terrified of what our conversation would be like—solemnly the thought of it would make my hands tremble—but it went a lot better than I ever imagined. Maybe I should start being less scared of the unknown.

I'll add that to the list of things to learn how to do. I laugh at the thought.

'Why are you smiling so much?' Elisa asks. I didn't even notice her entering the shop.

'Nothing special. I was just thinking,' I say.

'Are you going home now?'

'Yes, I was about to close the bakery.' I take off my apron and fold it, leaving it on the counter.

'Great, let's go together,' she says.

'Were you at the gym?' I look at her clothes and she seems to have been working out, but I'm never sure since she wears sportswear ninety percent of the time.

'Yeah, I was working on my rear end.' She winks.

'I think I need to work on my rear end as well.' I laugh.

'Really? You should definitely come with me!' She beams. 'You know, working out does wonders for your self-esteem.'

'I've heard that. Maybe I should.' I bite my lower lip. I do want to, but I'm not sure I have the courage to work out in front of strangers.

'That would be so fun! I've always wanted a workout buddy. We could go after you close the shop. At this hour the gym is almost empty. I usually only see one or two people around,' she says, as if hearing my thoughts.

'Okay, I'll buy some workout clothes, and then we can start.'

I'll put my brave mode on and try to reach another goal; walk another step towards full recovery.

Fake it until you make it, right?

My body became an insecurity of mine as I grew up and developed all the normal shapes a woman is supposed to have, shapes my mum so frowned upon.

All those times she would give me an apple while my friends got ice cream or measure me to make sure I fit the standard for runway models even though I never became one, must have subconsciously tricked my mind to believe I'm never good enough.

I tried to quit her standards many times. In the last try I threw away the scale and ate the ice cream. When my loose pants became tighter, I cried the whole night because even though I broke the standard numbers, I no longer recognised myself.

I must be the most hypocritical baker there is: the one who doesn't eat pastries, only samples them, until I'm sure the recipe is perfect.

Will I become a fitness guru like Elisa? Doubtfully, I'm too lazy for that. But working out a few times a week? I think I can. Maybe that way I'll get to see my curves in the way they deserve.

When I get home, I take a long shower and order Korean food. I don't have the strength to cook today. After I eat and watch an episode of *The Bold Type* with Elisa—a series we absolutely love for their women's empowerment emphasis—I go straight to bed. Moonie's drink worked wonders. Unfortunately, it doesn't give you energy, and the lack of sleep drained mine.

In the morning, I count to five backwards when my alarm goes off, a technique I learned to stop procrastinating and to not hit the snooze button. I slept a lot, but I was so comfortable under the sheets that it was still hard to get up.

I do my normal morning routine and when I come back to my room, I notice my phone's screen light up, which can only mean I received a notification.

I check it and see a text message from my mum. They're coming here tomorrow.

No...I don't want to.

As I sit on my bed travelling through my childhood memories, a knock sounds on my door.

'Lilah? You up?' my flatmate asks.

'Yeah,' I say, and she opens the door.

'What's wrong?' she asks as soon as her eyes find me. *Do I look that bad?*

I get up and walk in front of her, showing her my phone with the text my mum sent open.

'Oh shit,' Elisa says. She knows how my parents are. 'Okay, so, I was going to ask if you wanna go shopping today, but we definitely need to go shopping today, for like, everything. Groceries, new outfits...Oh! We need a new hand wash. I remember your mum just going all out on how cheap soap was a big no for serving your guests.'

Despite my mind being hyperaware of my surroundings, trying to put on my mother's lens to find every flaw, Elisa manages to get a chuckle out of me. 'I'm sorry, my parents visiting makes you even more nervous than it makes me.'

'Are you kidding? Veronica Scott is no joke. I'm the one who's sorry for child you.'

The corners of my mouth lift slightly, in a way to not drag down the mood the way my honest thought would: *It's not like I spent much time with them growing up.*

'I'll close the bakery earlier today so we can clean the house, go shopping, everything,' I say.

She agrees, and I leave.

All the time at work, in between baking fresh goods, serving the clients, and a few chats here and there, my mind can only think of how this parent visit will affect my mental health. How it already is.

I stop by *Greener's* at lunch hour to get distracted and speak about our collaboration.

'Welcome.' Jeremiah smiles as I walk in. Relief washes over me, knowing we are back to normal.

'Hi Jer.' I greet him in the same way. 'I'll have the special today. It looked really good on your social media stories.'

'Coming right up,' he says, leaving for the kitchen.

While I wait, I go to Rebecca.

'Hello,' I say.

'Hi hi, how are you?' she asks.

'I'm good, thanks. I was wondering if we could speak about the collab at lunch hour, instead of after we close. Or another day, if that's not possible. My parents are visiting tomorrow and I have so much to do after work.'

'Oh, that's okay. Right now I can't, but we can talk about it after your parents leave. Let's just come up with menu ideas by ourselves in the meantime, so we can advance quickly after that.' Becca's eyes stay glued to the notebook in front of her the whole time she speaks.

I agree and move back to my seat, where Jeremiah is already serving my dish.

I close the bakery at 5 p.m. instead of the usual seven—hopefully I did not lose many clients. None of my regulars go after five, so I think it's okay.

When I get to our building's entrance, Elisa is there with her car, ready for us to go shopping. I enter the car in a rush, and as I turn around to place my purse in the back seat, my eyes widen. We are not alone.

'I brought extra hands,' she says as I look at her, perplexed. 'We'll need it, trust me.'

'So, we're meeting your parents,' Elijah says with a smirk.

'Oh no, you are not. Thank you for the help, but this is just between me and Elisa.' I do not want to bring more people into my parents' mess.

'Why? Parents love me,' he asks. 'Right, Moon Hee?'

'That's true; parents do love him,' Moonie acknowledges in a low tone.

'Well, my parents hate everybody, so, still a no.'

The car drive is short until the nearest supermarket, and inside it we decide to split into pairs so we can cover more ground.

'I don't know if joining Elisa and Elijah was the best idea. They both have their heads in the clouds,' I tell my designated partner. 'But Elisa knows what she needs to do, so hopefully it won't take them too long.'

'Don't worry. Elijah can be mature when it's needed,' he says.

We walk around searching for the items on the list we made, barely exchanging any words throughout the aisles.

He's not a man of many words; either that or he doesn't open up easily, which I can relate to.

'Why are you going to such lengths for your parents? You make them look like such monsters.' Moon Hee chuckles, searching for cloth napkins in the shade of Bavarian cream.

'They're not monsters, but they are beasts, as in the London Elite beasts,' I say as my eyes navigate the shelves for a matching tablecloth. Our last one got a wine stain we never removed, and it was the only one—in nine years of living in that house—my mum approved of.

'Wait, they're part of the London Elite?'

'You know it?' I'm surprised; nowadays people don't talk about the Elites as much, since all their members are getting old, like my parents.

The London Elite used to rule London at one point. They were celebrities around here, their influence was almost as big as the royal family, but millennials—like me—thought that it was too much of a boomer thing, so none of their children wanted to follow their parents' footsteps. Because of that, the London Elite is dying, and with them their influence.

Even though that hasn't made my parents less of beasts when it comes to appearances and social status.

'I used to know a few guys whose parents were in the Elite. My mum also works for one of the families.'

'Oh…Maybe we crossed paths before and I don't remember,' I say. I don't hang with those people anymore, but there was a time, before all hell broke loose in my life, that I did.

The Elite are bad, but their children are even worse. Elisa calls them entitled brats, because that's how they act.

He grabs the last item on the list, ignoring my remark. 'Let's find the others now. We have everything.'

I call my flatmate and we meet them in the aisle they are in. To my surprise, they're almost finished with their list as well, so we grab all that is needed and leave to checkout.

I can't wait to get out of here. Crowds make my head spin.

'Now you can go put the groceries in the car and I'm going to pick up some new outfits next door,' Elisa says.

'Sure, we'll wait in the car,' Elijah says.

The men walk away, and I take this chance to make sure Elisa is fine with our agreement.

'Are you sure you don't need help?' I ask.

'You sent me the pictures. I'm fine. I know how you feel about shopping centres.'

'Thank you.' I really mean it. She's an amazing friend for doing this.

I haven't stepped foot in a shopping centre in a few years. The crowds and fluorescent lights make up the perfect recipe to trigger my anxiety. I always shop online, but since we don't have time for that, I chose out the outfits I wanted and asked Elisa to pick them up at the shop.

We leave the supermarket, and she enters the door on the right that leads straight to the maze of clothing shops. I walk towards the car thinking of how funny it is when the four of us are together. You can completely make out the extroverts and the introverts from our interactions.

'I thought you were going with her,' Elijah says as I enter the car.

'She didn't need my help.'

I turn on the radio to fill the air around us. My social battery is running out and even though I know one of them is okay with the silence, I've noticed the guy that wears rolled-up sleeves showing his tattoos is not.

I close my eyes for a little, enjoying the sound of Lauv's song,

Lonely Eyes. The chorus plays and my eyelids open, glancing at the rearview mirror, where I find the two black moons staring back at me.

Moon Hee's lips lift slightly upwards as if saying, *I'm lonely just like you.*

The luggage door opens, jumping me back to reality, and when I look back at him, he's no longer staring back. Instead, Elijah is showing him something on his phone.

Elisa enters the car, and we go home. The guys also help clean our flat a little. They've been very helpful today, and I'm not used to getting so much help around me.

I go to bed dreading tomorrow. My only safe haven will be the bakery, but even there I know my parents will comment on something. Hopefully they won't be here for too long, since I have no idea when they'll get here.

My eyes close, hoping to wake up once tomorrow is over, but they somehow travel back to the dark night sky. I can't pinpoint the night, only a moon absolving my problems, giving me freedom, but somehow I know my heart was full in the moment, something that didn't happen very often.

8
여덟
'yeoldolb'

I still wish my parents coming today was nothing but a joke, but the dress I have hanging on my wardrobe's door says otherwise.

Dresses...I don't dislike them, but I rarely use them. When I was younger, I did all the time, but since I've become this spiral mess of a person, I stopped. It's funny to think that my body hasn't changed much since I last wore one, but I'm so much different. The body I once liked, and didn't have a problem showing, is now covered by layers of clothes.

I turn my back to the mattress and stare at the ceiling. I know becoming self-conscious about my body because of my childhood isn't the only reason for me to want to come by unnoticed. But I still don't remember the reason.

Why can't I remember that night?

I shake off my thoughts and get up. The day is stressful enough without me adding more to it. I walk to Elisa's room and knock to wake her up.

Today we're getting up earlier since we have no idea when they are coming. Last time they came even before I went to work, and we were still in pyjamas—let's not mention my mother's reaction—but the time before that they only showed up after I closed the shop. It's always a gamble with them.

'I'm up, I'm up,' Elisa says as I knock on her door for the third time.

She comes out to go take a shower, and I can see how tired she is.

'You went to bed late?' I ask.

'Yeah.' Her mouth opens, and she covers it with her hand, but not before it affects me. 'I was working on a website.'

I finish my yawn and nod.

Elisa does all types of work involving coding. I call her a coding genius because multiple big companies have tried to get her working exclusively for them, but she says she prefers to be a freelancer—this way she's not stuck to one place and can work for everybody. She also receives more by doing that since her time is constantly at auction for the highest bidder.

I've asked her multiple times why she still lives here with me if she has so much money, and her answer is always the same: This little house and you are my home; you keep me grounded.

As soon as we finish getting ready and I grab my purse to walk towards the exit, the doorbell rings. Elisa and I swiftly look at each other, eyes widened.

I peek through the little hole in the door and give a thumb up to my flatmate. It's my parents.

I'm not religious, but I pray for this day to go fast and well.

I open the door, and they get themselves inside without a single word.

'Good morning mum, dad,' I say.

'Honey, we missed you.' My mother smiles, her long, perfectly curled brown hair more still than a statue.

This is a surprise. I furrow my eyebrows at my flatmate.

'So, what are you doing here?' I ask, trying to understand what is going on. They are never this friendly, not my mum, at least.

'Well, we just wanted to come visit our precious child and her best friend,' she says. 'How are you, Elisa?'

I glance at my father, whose eyes are distant as always, but it's the smile on my mother's face that twirls my insides. Nothing good ever happens when she smiles.

'I'm good, thank you,' Elisa says.

'Were you leaving?' my dad asks, pointing at my purse already around my arm.

'Hmm...yes...I was on my way to the bakery.'

'Then we shall go. Goodbye, Elisa. We'll see you later tonight. Let's have dinner together.'

They walk fast to the lift, where I follow, but remain silent until we reach the shop. During the first hour of work, they leave me alone, conversing with one another.

What's going on? Elisa texts me. *They are acting so strange.*

When this happens, it can only mean one thing. They have news, and not the good kind. I write.

OMG, what if you are gonna have a sibling? I laugh at her text.

Hilarious. First, I think my mum is way past her fertile window and second, even if she's still there, I'm sure she had a tubal ligation after she had me. Hahaha

I'm sure we'll find out at dinner, but in the meantime they are freaking me out. I hit send before putting my phone away to keep working.

When the shop slows down a bit and my parents get bored with looking at the flies, my mum turns to me. 'You know, honey, I could tell some of my friends to come to this bakery so you have more clients. This could become the Elite's bakery, after some remodelling, of course, but for that I can give you the contact of an interior designer friend of—'

'No thank you, I have enough clients and I like the decorations.' Now that's the person I know, the one who can't keep herself out of other people's business. It took long enough.

'Veronica, leave it. We want a good day, right?' my father asks.

'As you wish.' My mum purses her red lips.

They want a good day? That can't be good.

'Well, honey, we are going to meet some friends for lunch.

We'll get to your house before dinner to discuss some things,' Mrs Scott says before the sound of her heels fades away.

I close up for lunch hour and go to the post office to see if I've received a letter. I don't know if Daldust is one of those people who writes right away when they receive a letter or waits a while, but it's better to go there than to be trying to figure out how dinner will go tonight.

When I open my postbox, I see a grey envelope like last time and smile. He sent me a letter.

I want to open it now, but something inside me tells me to leave it for later, and so I do. Back at the shop, I grab my phone to order food. I love *Greener's*, but today I want to vary and eat in the same beautiful place I'm able to call mine.

'Are you ready to leave?' Elisa asks, paying for the muffin she treated herself with for this stressful day.

'Yeah, I just need to close up,' I say.

'Do you already know what you are cooking?' she asks.

'Yes, my dad asked me to make my mum's favourite dish, which is still a surprise for me, since she is all fancy and mighty and the dish is so simple.' I look out the window, watching all the other shop owners eager to close their shops at seven on Fridays. Today I'm closing an hour earlier.

This street gets deserted after that until eleven, when the pubs open.

'So...what is it?' my best friend gesticulates impatiently.

'Right, sorry, it's carbonara.'

'Mmh, delicious,' she says, licking her lips, and I chuckle.

We get home and take turns getting ready and preparing dinner. First, I shower while Elisa chops the ingredients and sets the table ready. Then, while she's inside the loo, I cook.

The doorbell rings, and my heart skips a beat. I look at the clock: it's seven. My parents usually come only half an hour earlier, but they are so unpredictable that you never know.

I leave the pan on low heat and go open the door.

The two people who stare back at me on the other side of the door's frame get my thoughts to falter for a second.

'Elijah, Moon Hee…What are you doing here?' I ask.

They stay another moment mutedly staring. *Do I have something on my face?* My hands tremble a bit.

'Fuck, Lilah…' Elijah breaks the silence. 'You look…bloody amazing.'

My eyes glance down at my baby blue dress and I tug my hands on the hem, pulling it down. That's right, they've never seen me in a dress.

I bring my gaze back up, unable to speak, feeling the heat rise to my cheeks.

I remember I have the food on the stove and signal them to come in.

'We just came to see if you girls needed any help, but it seems like you have everything handled.' He looks around while I turn off the stove.

'Cut the rubbish, Elijah.' Elisa surprises us, coming into the kitchen. 'I know you came to see Lilah's parents.'

'Fine, I'm curious.' He raises both hands at her.

Moon Hee hasn't said a word, but I catch him looking at me a few times while everybody talks.

'Well, we don't need your help, and you won't meet my parents,' I say too late. Before I speak the last word, the doorbell rings, and this time, I'm sure it's them.

Bloody hell.

Elisa leaves to open the door. I hear my mother's voice echoing through the house the moment the door closes.

Thankfully the food is ready, so at least we won't have to wait any longer than needed to eat.

'Lilah, honey, who are these men? Is one of them your boyfriend?' my mum asks as soon as we walk to the hall to meet them.

This is why I didn't want them to come.

'I'm hoping not,' she adds, looking at Elijah's tattoo--covered arms.

'They are just friends, but what if I dated one of them? What's the problem with that?' I frown, trying to not raise my voice. Keyword: *trying*.

'Oh honey, you should know girls and boys can't be just friends. It never works out. And tattoos aren't elegant, you know that.' Her contemptuous look makes my blood boil.

'We are just friends, and tattoos are art, beautiful art. They are also great people and you shouldn't judge someone based on whether they have tattoos or not,' I say, trying to keep my voice calm in front of them, but I know I'm bound to explode at any moment.

'I'm not judging their character—'

'No, you are judging their looks, like you always do.' I'm not in the mood to hear any excuse she was going to give next, so I enter the kitchen and place the food on the table.

I decide to walk back to them to say the food is ready when I hear Elijah speaking, making me stop at the living room's entrance, his back turned to me.

'Actually, I am interested in your daughter,' he says, and they look at him surprised. I do too.

When I move closer to them—and he sees me—he adds, 'We were leaving when you arrived anyway, but feel free to stop by my parlour if you ever want to become less elegant,' giving my mother his card and winking before leaving.

I have to be honest; I enjoyed that way too much. He was so subtle with his disdain that he not only left me but my mum speechless. I'd never seen that side of Elijah.

'Let's go eat before the food gets cold,' I say.

The four of us sit at the table and begin eating in silence. My dad tries to break the ice a few times, but it stays intact.

My parents' visits are always energy draining. My mum usually finds something in me to criticise, and although I don't like it—when it's about me I can stand it—but when she attacks people I care about, it hits me harder.

One time she said something to Elisa about her hair, and even though she withstood it, I could see it affected her. I went off on my mother that day and she never said a word that wasn't kind to Elisa ever since. But now she did it again and it pisses me off how clueless she can be—or pretends to be.

Words hurt more than a punch. Just because you can't see the bruise doesn't mean it didn't open a wound. Emotional scars take longer to heal than physical ones, and I wish she would learn that.

My father is more careful with his words, but he allows my mum to act like that, and to me, a bystander can be as guilty as the direct offender.

'What was the big news you wanted to share?' I ask.

'Your dad and I are moving to Beverly Hills,' my mum says, her brown eyes glimmering.

'Beverly Hills, LA? As in the United States? The other side of the ocean?' My eyes widen, trying to wrap my mind around it.

'Yes, honey.' She gives me that unnerving smile. 'Since you are no longer little and there is really nothing for us here anymore, your father and I want a change of scenery.'

'Since I'm no longer little…there's nothing for you left here…' I repeat, my voice low, looking at my fresh plate of carbonara.

'Well, that's great, Mrs and Mr Scott. I'm happy for you,' Elisa says, trying to calm the very dense cloud of rage growing above me.

'Thank you dear,' my mum says. 'I thought you'd be happy for us, Lilah.'

'Happy that you are going away? For good?' My eyes fog as the water grows on them. 'I should be…but for some reason, I'm not.'

'We'll visit regularly. Our business is still here, and we have video calls now,' my dad says, caressing my mother's hand.

I've always questioned why he comforts her, when I'm the one who needs comfort.

'The same video calls you never make, even when we are in the same city? Visit?' I grimace. 'When? You barely visit now. When you go, you won't come back; I know that. You said it yourself: you have nothing here left for you.'

I get up and right before leaving the room I add, 'Have a safe trip.'

I leave the flat and walk upstairs to the roof, my feet fast but stumpy, my lips pursed and tears fleeing the safe space of my waterline.

The soft breeze brushes my face and I close my eyes, trying to understand why the thought of them leaving is crushing my heart. They've been a fleeting presence my whole life, but I knew they would always return, if not for me but for their home.

Elisa's words last time she took me to the roof echo in my head. So, I do it. I scream like it's the last time my mouth is going to make a sound.

As soon as I finish, my flatmate arrives next to me.

'I thought I'd find you here,' she says.

'You were right.' I glance at her. 'It does feel good.'

'I'm sorry, Lilah.' She rubs my shoulder.

'It's not the fact that I'll see them less; I barely saw them anyway. It's the fact that they are slipping further and further away.' I collapse on the floor, releasing all the emotion left from the scream.

'I know.' Elisa sits down next to me, trying to comfort the girl who questions why nobody can love her, not even her own parents.

9
아홉
'ahob'

With everything that happened last night, Daldust's letter completely slipped my mind. I stare at it on my desk as I shake the thought of the empty house I encountered when Elisa and I returned from the roof. They didn't even have the decency to say a proper goodbye.

I grab the envelope opener I bought just for this occasion—I called it a necessary unnecessary item to purchase—and put it to work.

"Yeah, I figured your name was Delilah haha. Daldust is fine by now.

What makes you think I have an agenda? I just want to get to know you.

Is this your first time pen palling or have you tried it before? If so, why did you decide to do it?

If you ask me, I think it's a great way to get to know people on a deeper level. No social media, no googling their name, judging them by their appearance. Call me an old soul, but I love the feeling of writing on paper.

Dear Delilah, tell me something about you that brings you joy.

Daldust"

I smile at the letter, and for a moment, all my worries vanish. Maybe Daldust can become my comfort person.

I'm glad I opened the letter today. Since it's Saturday, I closed the shop earlier and I am now at home with literally nothing to do, so I can actually take my time writing them back, still with the feeling he left me present.

"Yes, it's my first time and I'm doing it to meet new people—in this case you—and to open up more to someone since I have a hard time doing it face to face.

To be honest, not even this conversation I would have with a stranger, but I feel like since you don't know who I am, it's easier to be myself.

And your answer made me smile. Maybe you are a decent person haha.

Something I like about me? My passion.

I love profoundly, something I'm not sure I like since it doesn't always—rarely—benefit me. But the fact that I put my everything in the things I enjoy doing and I give my all to make them perfect is one of the few things I appreciate in myself.

What about you? What is something you like and dislike about yourself?

Delilah"

I meant what I said. They inspire trust in me, as if I can talk to them about anything. If they give decent advice, I think Ms Julie might be in danger of losing a client. I laugh at the thought.

Yesterday, because of my parents, I didn't go to therapy. They don't know about that side of my life. If they did, I'm sure they would criticise me. They are the type to bottle up everything and either explode at one point, or like my mum does, turn to everyone around you so you don't look at yourself.

To me, that's toxic, and I want to have a rapport with my

feelings and thoughts. They have dragged me to a dark place in life and I want to understand and face them so I can get out of it.

So, next week I'm having extra time on my session, but until I get there, Daldust will have to be my therapy. Hopefully I will receive a new letter before Friday, if I send mine on Monday.

Elisa is also introducing me to yoga tonight. She said it's perfect to let go of all your worries and focus on the present moment; that sold it to me. I'm just waiting for her to get home.

I want to check up on the guys, apologise for how my mum treated them, but then I remember what I overheard Elijah say, and I get jitters at the thought of seeing him. Maybe he just said that to get to my mother...

All this time I've had a crush on him, but the more I get to know him—even though I'm still very attracted physically—the more I see our differences and the more confused I get. I know people say opposites attract, but too much opposite isn't good.

Most of my feelings for him came from a fantasy in my head, so I'm still wrapping my thoughts around reality.

Elisa's voice sounds in my head, saying *woman up* as she once did before. When I asked if it wasn't *man up*, she answered: Women suffer a lot more than men, in all aspects of life, and have to put up with society on top of our own struggles, so we have a higher pain tolerance and have to be brave all the time. But once more they had to create a phrase to be more of a man—as if they are the better species—so no, it shouldn't be man up, it should be woman up, because we are bloody bosses who, if given the chance, would rule this universe.

That stuck with me, and I never said the words *man up* again.

So I do that. I endure my fears and put on my brave face, stepping out of my room and up to their front door.

I knock and listen to the sound of footsteps become louder on the other side.

'Good afternoon, Lilah.' The tall, Korean man with dark doe eyes greets me.

'Good afternoon, Moonie.' The corners of my lips lift as I peek inside to see if Elijah's home.

I can already pronounce his name correctly, but Moonie stayed with me and I believe he likes it.

'He's not home,' he says, and I pretend to be confused to whom he's speaking about. 'I saw you in the back of the room when Elijah said that to your mum. You heard it, right?'

'Is it true? Or was he just trying to mess with my mum?' I ask, avoiding his eyes.

'Honestly, I don't know. It was a surprise for both me and Elisa, but he has been talking more about you.'

'Oh...'

'I thought you'd be happier.' He chuckles.

'Why?' I try to hide the panic those words left me with.

'I've seen how you look at him, so I thought that knowing your feelings were mutual, you'd be happier.' Before I have a chance to speak, he adds, 'Do you want to come in? I have something in the oven.'

I nod and walk inside. Their flat is wider than ours and way less decorated. Neutral colours are the theme.

While ours opens to the hall—my room and the loo to the right, living room and kitchen to the left, Elisa's room at the end of the hall—theirs has an open space with a living room and dining area in the back.

I follow him to the left side of the open space where the entrance for the kitchen stands, and I stay by the wall as he takes the roasted vegetables out of the oven and puts them into a pan on the stove. I glance behind me to where another entrance like this stands, assuming the rooms and loo are through there.

He adds cooked rice and a bit of soy sauce. He's making fried rice, or how Koreans say it: *bokkeumbap*.

'You cook the vegetables in the oven first?' I ask. I've seen no one do that.

'Yeah, it's the way my mum does. It makes them extra crunchy.'

I'll have to try that.

'I'm still figuring out my feelings,' I say, going back to our conversation. 'Does he know how I feel?'

'I don't think so,' he says. 'Want to try?' Moon Hee holds a spoonful of fried rice in front of me.

I walk next to him and open my mouth for him to feed me.

'Careful, it's hot.' He blows on the spoon before giving it to me.

'Mmh, *mashisso* (delicious).' I beam with a full mouth, and his eyes smile. 'I always thought he liked Elisa…'

'I think he did at some point, but he likes their friendship more. He has grown to like yours too,' he says, and I nod in understanding.

Moon Hee grabs an extra plate and serves me a meal. We sit at their dining table and eat.

'Thank you for the meal.'

This was so random, but I'm glad I'm so at ease with Moonie.

I remember how he talked about his mum, and it brings back what I came here to do.

'I'm sorry for what my mum said,' I say.

'It's okay, you defended us pretty well.' He gives me a small smile, his eyes a world that pulls me in with every glance.

'Do you see your mum a lot?' I ask, trying to make small talk.

'Yes, I visit her at least three times a week.'

'Wow, you're a really good son.'

'We're the only ones of our family here, so I try to be.'

My whole family lives here, but I wish I had the connection with at least one family member like Moon Hee has with his mum. I had that once, but she's no longer here, and I miss her every day.

'How long have you lived here?' I'm trying to not be nosy, but he sparks curiosity in me.

'Five years,' the man sitting across the table from me answers. 'You don't get along with your parents?' he asks. I see…It's his turn now.

'It's complicated,' I say, getting up and taking our empty plates into the kitchen.

'You don't need to do that.' He watches me get the kitchen gloves on to wash the dishes.

'It's the least I can do, after you cooked so well.' I smile.

'That means something, coming from a professional chef.' He stands up and walks to me, coming closer to help me roll up my sleeves, which kept falling.

I look at him for a second while his eyes are on my arms and get a strange sensation, not an apprehensive one...a familiar one.

We hear the door close, and he steps back. I turn to continue washing the dishes.

'Lilah?' Elijah asks, entering the kitchen.

Yeah, this must look strange to him. It even looks strange to me.

'Hi,' I say, putting the dishes aside to dry and taking off the gloves.

'What am I missing here?' He looks confused, and Moon Hee and I laugh.

'I came to talk to you guys and Moonie was cooking, so I came in.'

'Oh...' he says. 'Moonie?'

'It's the nickname she created for me,' The guy standing by my side explains.

'Ah, I didn't know you two were so close,' Elijah says, his jaw tensing.

'Oh, no, we aren't! Not like that.' I shake my hand at him.

'Cool...' The man dressed in a tight black shirt and jeans leaves the room.

Moon Hee stays silent, staring at me. If I had a coin for every time he does that, I'll easily become rich.

'I wanted to apologise for what my mum said,' I say, walking after Elijah to the living room.

'It's fine.' He pats the top of my head.

They always say it's fine, even when it's not. It shouldn't be fine, but who am I to tell that to anyone, if I do the same?

'Either way, I'm sorry.' I glance up at him.

'We know.' The corner of his mouth lifts, and his tongue peeks out to wet his bottom lip.

I leave their flat and go to mine. Maybe Elisa is home already. I call for her, but receive no answer, so I move to my bedroom and grab a book to read.

A few minutes later, I hear the front door and Elisa calls for me. 'In my room!'

'Sorry, the lunch took a lot longer than it was supposed to.' She enters my bedroom. Elisa has lunch with some girls she grew up with every once in a while just so they can catch up. 'I'm just going to change and then we can leave for the gym. The yoga class starts in half an hour.'

We get ready and leave with fifteen minutes to spare. To our advantage, the gym is near our block of flats.

From the name alone—Hot Yoga—you could tell I was drenched in sweat by the end. It's more challenging than it appears and gets your present awareness heightened, otherwise you might just fall flat on your face.

I enjoyed it, and it actually didn't bother me that there were more people present. It felt more like a community doing something together, refreshing to my loner self.

When I get home, I walk straight to the shower—I won at rock-paper-scissors with Elisa—and it never felt better. My muscles will feel sore tomorrow, but I feel more relaxed. The movements also unlocked some knots I had in my back; a massage without the masseuse.

When I get to my room, I grab my phone to document my first time doing yoga on social media, and as I do, I receive a text from Elijah.

When did we exchange numbers? Flashbacks of drunk me

dialling his number on my phone come back to me.

I open the text and read: ***Can we talk?***

Talk? What can he possibly want to talk to me about?

A thousand thoughts run through my mind, endless possibilities, each more terrifying than the last. So, I tell myself: Woman up, Delilah.

Sure I send.

A few seconds later he responds. ***Meet me on the roof in thirty***.

10

열

'yeol'

I grab a big coat to cover up my pyjamas, which include an old shirt and tracksuit bottoms—I don't own any fancy matching pyjamas anymore—and my trainers.

The walk upstairs is slow as my feet drag, but eventually I reach the top. There are no visible stars in the sky, and the moon is shy behind grey clouds. Our primary source of light comes from an old, flickering lamp near the roof's door.

Elijah is sitting on some old boxes Elisa and I put up there a few years ago, when we attempted to make the roof some kind of hangout place for us. Nowadays we don't come here often.

As soon as he sees me, he smiles and stands up. He changed into a more comfortable outfit of an oversized black long-sleeved shirt and trackies—the pieces of clothes might change, but not the colour.

'You came,' he says, waving at me.

'Of course.' I give him a small smile.

I walk closer to him, sit next to his box, and he sits back again.

'So, what did you want to talk to me about?' I ask, looking down as I play with my fingers.

'I'm going straight to the point so I don't chicken out.' He titters. This is the second time I've seen him nervous, but it's still a shock to me. 'Will you go on a date with me?'

'W-What?' I ask, eyes wide, my lungs beginning to compress.

The sound of my heart muffles my ears to what he says next.

'I know I never showed how I felt, but you've always sparked my interest and I would like to get to know you better.' I hear him as if I'm underwater.

I can't utter anymore. My lungs are too desperate for air at this point. I fall to my knees on the ground in front of me, one of my hands holding tight to my chest while the other holds me in place.

My back senses a warm touch and I flinch, reaching lower.

'Are you okay?' he asks. I want to, but my body doesn't allow me to reach for him.

Please, calm down, Delilah. Please. Don't let him see you like this.

I get up and say, 'I'm sorry,' before racing to my bedroom—my safe place. I need it now. The four walls in which I can let everything out and eventually cool down.

The moment my back hits the cold, closed door, I gasp, searching for any air I can reach.

I try to count as high as I can, trying to divert my attention from the panic I encountered when Elijah asked me out and focus on something else.

I'm on number seventy-four when my breathing finally slows down.

I sit on my bed and see the letter from Daldust, so I open it and read it again, anything to make me calm. Their words have a calming effect on me.

I scan through the words repeatedly until the sentences make sense in my head. I finish the letter and grab a glass of water from the kitchen.

Returning to my room, my phone vibrates.

It's a message from Elijah.

Are you okay? I'm sorry if I scared you

My eyes water as I read the text. I lay down on my bed and stare at the screen.

I know I said I didn't know what I felt for him anymore, but for a split second, when he asked me to go on a date with him, I smiled. Before my mind betrayed me and the panic began.

Ever since that night, five years ago, every time someone asks me out, I have a panic attack. I don't know why; I never understood why that triggers me. There's so much I've forgotten from that night.

I close my eyes, letting the water run down my face. Crying not only for myself this time, but for Elijah as well. For the way he must be feeling now after I stormed out of there.

He didn't scare me. I'm just so broken that I shut down at a glimpse of an opportunity that someone might come to love me.

I haven't seen Elijah today and I'm grateful for it. I'm not ready to face him yet. In fact, he is here, with Elisa and Moon Hee in the living room, but I pretended to be asleep when my flatmate came to check on me.

Right now, I'm trying to focus on reading a book, but my mind keeps travelling to him.

Someone knocks on my door and it startles me, making me drop the book on my lap. I keep silent—maybe they'll go away—but a second knock sounds and this time a voice accompanies it.

'It's Moon Hee, nobody else,' he says, but I stay still. 'I know you are awake, I saw you go to the loo a while ago. Can we talk?'

Why did I have to pee?

I ponder if I should open the door or not. The thought of facing someone makes me want to hide under my blanket.

It's just Moonie, you can do it.

'Come in,' I say at last.

I wait a few seconds and wonder if he has already walked away when he opens the door.

Walking closer, he looks around the room, but doesn't speak a word.

I'm sitting on the bed, watching him as he approaches me and sits on the floor with his back leaning on the bed frame, facing the same wall as me.

'Do you want to talk about what happened?' Moonie asks. 'I know Elijah went to talk to you last night, and the fact that you aren't there with us lets me know that it didn't go as smoothly as he wished.'

The person I usually speak with about that kind of thing is Ms Julie, but I still have a week before I can speak with her again and I don't know if I can hold this in for that long.

'I panicked,' I confess, and he stays quiet. 'I didn't want to. For a second there I was happy, but then I couldn't control the anxiety taking over my body.'

'Do you have many panic attacks?' His voice remains steady and soothing, as if this was a question like any other.

'I've been having them for several years now. They're better though. I used to have them almost every day and now I go weeks without them. Last night just triggered me,' I say, thankful that he's not looking at me—it makes it easier to speak.

I watch his position again. *Maybe that was the whole point for him to sit like that.*

'Are you seeing someone about that?'

'Yes, that's how I've become better.' This is the first time I tell anyone else about being in therapy. Elisa was the only one who knew about it.

'That's good. I'm proud of you for taking that step. Not many people do it, and you should pride yourself for it.' He turns around to look at me and the corners of my lips lift.

'Thank you, really, thank you.' Water rises in my eyes.

It's paradoxical how overwhelming this situation feels, yet the act of discussing it brings a sense of release. But as much as I try to conceal it, it's bringing me to tears.

Even though Elisa knows, we don't talk about it. I never wanted to—I wanted to come home and distract myself from all the troubles of my mind, and she is outstanding at distracting me.

'In those situations, do you prefer to be held or be given space?' Moon Hee asks.

I sigh. 'Honestly, I don't know. I've never had anyone by my side in those times.'

Elijah tried to touch me yesterday, and I flinched. *Maybe I like to be given space...*

He holds my hand with a comforting smile. 'I know how hard it can be to speak about your issues, but speaking can be very freeing. He's not mad at you; quite the contrary, he's worried.'

'I'm not ready to speak to him about it,' I say, looking at his hand holding mine.

Or I might like to be held...

'You don't have to. Just come outside and be with us. He won't touch the subject if you don't. Just show him that you are alright. Come and have some fun. Dwelling on it will only make it worse.'

He gets up, but never releases my hand. I nod and lift myself up, only letting go of him when we walk out my bedroom door.

'Lilah, you're awake!' Elisa beams the moment we enter the living room.

'Yeah, I woke her when I went to the loo,' Moon Hee says, scratching the back of his head.

'I was wondering why you were taking so long.' She chuckles.

Elijah says nothing. He's looking at me with a small smile, but still the sadness in his eyes protrudes.

'Hey,' I say.

Moonie and I sit next to them on the sofa, where they are choosing a film to watch.

A film is good—we are together but don't need to speak to each other. This way I don't need to touch the subject.

A two-hour film goes by fast when you don't want it to end. I catch Elijah looking over Elisa at me a few times.

As they talk amongst themselves, I interject a few times, but my focus is mainly on observing their dynamic.

Elisa's blue eyes shine as she speaks, standing out from her dark skin. I've always found it curious how she has one of her eyes half-blue, half-brown, but it intensifies her charm.

Elijah, with his flirty nature, makes you stare all over his face. He has the habit of licking his lips and staring deep into your soul—which most people would assume is because he's interested in them, but it's the way he is with everyone. And when he pulls up his shirt's long sleeves, showing the tattoos on his arms, it sends me over the moon. To say I'm attracted to the ink is an understatement.

Moon Hee keeps pushing his dark hair back as he speaks. He has this way of being serious when talking, but also engaging. He just draws your attention to him, but then when he smiles or laughs he becomes the most adorable person you've ever seen. You can never understand what he's thinking, yet you don't want to do anything else but figure it out.

We agree on watching another movie and dining, no alcohol this time. It's Monday tomorrow and we need to be fresh for the start of the week. We all have to work early and a headache is a big no, even with the marvellous potion Moonie concocts to cure hangovers.

'Did something happen between you and Elijah?' my best friend asks as we stand in the kitchen, preparing more snacks for the evening.

'Why do you ask?' I avoid her stare.

'I just sense an odd vibe between you two. Besides, he's quieter than usual.'

'He asked me out, and I ran away,' I say, putting chips in a bowl.

'Oh...Don't you want to go out with him?' She frowns.

Elisa doesn't even ask why anymore; she already knows.

'I'm not sure.'

'Are you not attracted to him?' She bloody well knows I am.

'I am, but I don't think our personalities match.' I glance over to the living room, imagining what they're doing.

'Well, don't you want to find that out? I mean, you haven't had the chance to be with just him, to get to know him,' she says, grabbing some bowls of snacks and walking to the door. 'You're shutting off the idea without even giving it a try.'

I follow with plates of pizza in my hands and mumble, 'That's true.'

'Tell me something, would you regret not accepting his invite?'

I know future me would always wonder what if. What could have happened if I went on that date with Elijah?

'Probably...'

'Then what do you have to lose?' she asks, walking into the living room and joining the guys. The lack of chance she gives me to respond just shows how much she knows me. Giving me an opening to make an excuse would only get me to overshadow my true feelings.

I stand by the entryway, looking at them, looking at him, thinking, pondering multiple outcomes.

I walk in, and as Elisa smiles at the plates of pizza, both Elijah and Moon Hee smile at me.

열하나
'yeolhana'

What do I have to lose? Those words kept playing in my mind for the next couple of days.

As I stare at Mrs Josephine eating her daily slice of cake, I wonder what it's like to grow old with somebody. I still remember my Nana glancing at her nightstand every night and wishing my grandpa's photograph goodnight. And despite the lack of love my parents showed me, I could always tell how much they loved each other.

'Do you want anything else?' I ask her as I go by the tables to make sure everyone is enjoying their food.

'I'm good, sweetie, thank you,' she says, and I smile.

I stay still when, through the window, I catch Elijah walking outside. I stare at him and think about accepting his invitation.

'Are you okay, sweetie?' Mrs Josephine furrows her white eyebrows.

'Yes, I'm sorry.' I situate myself and notice I've been standing in front of her this whole time. 'Actually,' I say, before walking away. 'If I may ask...Do you have any regrets?'

She smiles. 'Many, my dear, but only for the things I didn't do out of fear. Everything I did, I don't regret because they all brought valuable lessons.'

I give her a small smile and nod in understanding. 'Thank you.'

She's right...What do I have to lose?

'Lilah, settle this for us: a cupcake and a muffin are different, right? Elijah is saying a muffin is just a cupcake without frosting,' Elisa asks as soon as I enter the living room.

I arrived home a few minutes ago and immediately heard their voices, but chose to go to my room first. I'm still preparing myself to talk with Elijah.

'Oh…Yeah, they are different. It's true that visually a muffin looks like a cupcake without frosting, but they have different recipes. Cupcakes are always sweet, while muffins can be savoury as well, since they're more of a soft crumbly bread. Cupcakes are tiny cakes that always have frosting.' My Nana taught me how to bake both, but it was only when I took a baking course—in order to receive a certificate to open my bakery—that I learned the difference between them.

'See? Told you they were different.' My flatmate pokes her tongue out at her opponent.

'They are still both made for one thing, to eat.' He rolls his eyes.

I look around and notice it's just the two of them. Moonie is not here.

'Where's Moon Hee?' I ask.

'He's still at the parlour. He had a special last client.' Elijah speaks to me with ease, but I notice the subtle glances. I'm sure he's waiting for my answer.

'Oh, interesting…' I wonder why the client was special.

'I've told you, you can always go there if you ever want a tattoo.'

'Are you offering me one?' I lift my eyebrows with a sly smile.

'No, but I'll give you a discount if you really show up there.'

'Will you be the one to tattoo me?'

'I can't wait to be the first one to have a taste of that blank canvas.' He smirks, his eyes glued to mine.

Now is the time. I should talk to him now.

'Aren't you thirsty, Elisa?' I turn my attention to her, giving her an eye sign to leave.

'Yeah, I'm going to get us something to drink,' she says, understanding my eye signal, and leaves for the kitchen.

Elijah is sitting across from me on the sofa, looking down at his phone.

I clear my throat. 'I wanted to apologise for running out on you the last time we talked.'

He looks up at me and gives me a little smile. 'It's cool, really. Are you okay now?'

'Yeah, I'm better. Thanks. I've been thinking and I want to take you up on that offer of us going out, if you still want, of course.'

'I still want to. Are you sure you're not going to run next time?' He smirks, and I chuckle.

'I'll try not to.'

'Great, I'll text you the details,' he says as Elisa comes back with three glasses and a few drinks for us to choose on a tray.

I'm sure she was listening and waiting to come back.

'We have water, orange juice, and wine. Pick your poison.' Her head turns to the side, facing me, and she winks before placing everything on the little table between the sofa and the TV.

I sit down next to Elijah, and Elisa sits next to me.

Not too long after we turn on the screen in front of us, the doorbell rings.

I open the door for Moon Hee and notice wrapping plastic around his arm. Something clicks on my mind: he was the special client.

'Did you just make that?' I say, pointing at his arm.

He looks at where I'm pointing and smiles. 'Yes, I've had this idea for quite some time, but hadn't had the opportunity.'

'So cool. Can't wait to see when it's healed.' I don't have time to catch everything under the wrapping, only an hourglass shape and some butterflies, but I'm sure it looks amazing.

'Can I come in?' he asks, staring at me. This whole time I've been blocking the door, amazed by the new ink on his arm.

I really want to have one of mine.

'Oh...Yes, of course...I'm sorry,' I say, embarrassed by my distraction.

'It's no problem.' The corner of his mouth lifts slightly, and the way he purses his lips after tells me he's containing himself from laughing.

He's one of the few people that sees right through me but doesn't make me feel vulnerable.

We join the others and relax watching a film. It's been refreshing to come home after a day of work and be with friends.

Life can pass by you at the speed of light when you are working and become monotonous. This has me feeling my age again, a young adult. I still have three years in my twenties to enjoy and I should make them count. People expect a lot of others when they turn thirty—as if we are supposed to have a family, a house, and a successful job by then. We still have over fifty years to live after that, so I think society is too determined to turn us into full-grown adults too soon. We should enjoy our youth as much as we can, and with them, I know I will.

Elijah and I have texted a few times over the last two days. Getting to talk one on one without having to face him to loosen myself up will hopefully ease me into being alone with him in a room. I've been having a wonderful time talking with him. He's funny.

On my way home from work, I pass by the post office and notice I have a new pen pal letter. I should be a better pen pal; Daldust always responds so fast while I take days. I know I'm not obligated to respond right away, but it makes me uneasy to make him wait too long.

I open the letter when I get to my room and smile at the first sentence.

"Dear Delilah,
I try my best to be a decent person, yes haha.

When I read your letters, I feel like we are on the same vibrational level. I don't know why, but it seems like your personality might match mine. I guess we'll have to keep talking to find out.

To answer your question, there isn't anything about me I dislike. I know people say it's normal to dislike things about yourself, but in my opinion, it shouldn't be. It's okay to want to improve. In fact, we should always improve but never dislike ourselves. That's society's bullshit to make money off our insecurities. We should embrace who we are. It's not until then that we truly start loving ourselves and, in consequence, live the life that is meant for us.

Something that I like about myself is how much I don't care about what others think of me. Others' opinion on another is nothing but a reflection of their thoughts about themselves; it has nothing to do with the other person.

You said you like to read. What are you reading?
Daldust"

Whenever I talk to Daldust, my confidence gets a boost for some reason. They bring out a side of me I haven't had in a while. That mixed with what's been happening with Elijah creates a wave of comfort inside me.

I write my answer right away so I don't forget to respond and put it in my purse to send it tomorrow at my lunch hour as usual.

"I like the way you think. Lately I've been trying to care less about what others think, and what you said about others' opinions reflecting their own insecurities and nothing to do with the other person really stuck with me. Thank you.

Regarding what I'm reading, I'm juggling between a few books. A romance, a guide to self-improvement, and a marketing one to help me stay up to date with my shop.

Do you like to read? If so, tell me what is on your To Be Read list.

You mention you liked travelling. I love that, but rarely do it…

I've only been to Scotland and Amsterdam. The one place I really want to visit recently is South Korea! I love the culture.

What countries have you visited?
Delilah"

The more I talk with them, the more curious I get. Getting to know Daldust has reignited my interest in learning different perspectives. The world itself intrigues me. That's why I love my bakery; I can see so many people and learn about different ways of thinking a bit more every day.

Elijah and I have a dinner date tomorrow. Elisa wants to help me choose my outfit tonight so tomorrow I only have hair and makeup to do, which she will help me with as well. I still don't understand how she manages the time. It amazes me how she seems to always be busy but free simultaneously.

After the last week and this one, I'm going to have so much to talk to Ms Julie about. I haven't skipped a session in a year, but leave it to my parents to ruin that for me.

I haven't spoken to them since that day, but I also think I won't for a while.

I sit on my bed and grab the guide Ms Julie suggested I read—it's a great guide, I'll give her that. It has a lot of quotes I think of daily and the overall aesthetic is quite pretty. Simple yet pretty; the dark blue title of *All the things I've never said before* bleeds to the white background, surrounded by various types of low-saturated, blue-hued flowers.

I wake up with a loud thump on my door—I must have fallen asleep reading.

'Lilah, are you there?' my flatmate asks.

I groan, letting her know I am, and she comes in.

'So...As you might know, my birthday is in a month and I hereby invite you to attend my party and free your weekend between the 26th and the 28th because we are going on a getaway trip.'

'A getaway trip? Where? With whom?' I get startled by the thought of too much social interaction.

'To Guildford and probably with the guys, and maybe one or two more people. It depends.'

Hmm...Guildford, Surrey. My parents used to spend a lot of weekends there, but I haven't been since I was six.

I grab my phone and search for images of the place.

'It's pretty,' I say, scrolling.

'It's beautiful, and I rented a little cottage there. It's going to be so much fun!' Elisa softly claps her hands in excitement.

A weekend with them sure sounds interesting.

'Okay.' I nod and watch her smile grow, showing just how happy I made her with my answer.

A year ago I wouldn't have accepted it, even her being my best friend. I knew it would be best if I stayed home rather than ruin her moment with my anxiety. Now, I've been doing better, and I have more faith in myself.

'Awesome,' she says, standing up. 'Now let's find you a dress for your date tomorrow.'

She rubs her hands together, making me laugh. 'I don't know who's more eager, you or me.'

'Well...this is a big thing, Lilah. It's your first date in five years, bloody five years,' my flatmate reminds me.

I sigh.
It is a big thing.

열둘
'yeoldul'

I woke up extra anxious today—not sure if it's the good or bad kind—but I was sweating, so my hopes aren't high.

The day at work has been calm, and I had time to send the letter to Daldust during lunch. Right now, I'm cleaning the tables and getting everything ready to close as fast as I can. With only an hour in between leaving work and my dinner with Elijah, I have to make the most of it.

The gold bell on top of the door rings, and I look in its direction.

'Hi,' Moon Hee says, pushing his black hair back. It looks longer every day.

'Hi.' I look at his arm. 'How is it healing?'

'Good,' he says, moving his eyes to the same place as mine. 'How are you feeling?'

'Good…' He stares at me, knowing bloody well I'm lying. 'Nervous,' I admit, and he gives me a small smile.

'Yeah…I wanted to check in on you before your date, since you know what happened.'

'Thank you, I think I can do this.' I move behind the counter.

'Well, if you need any help—at any time—just send an SOS text and I'll be there to help,' he says, walking in my direction.

My mouth's edges lift and I nod in agreement. 'Do you want anything to eat or drink?'

'Hmm...sure...I'll take one of those muffins to go,' he says, rubbing the back of his neck.

'You don't seem very comfortable with your haircut. You keep pushing it back.'

He chuckles. 'I'm still getting used to having any hair at all. I went to the military two years ago and after that I kept shaving it because it was easier to handle. But I want to grow it longer now, so it's been a journey.'

'The eighteen months of mandatory military service you have in South Korea?'

'Exactly. They called me and even though I had just started to work with Elijah, he said that once I came back I could have a spot next to him, so I went. It was better to go right away than to go now, for example.' His gaze lowers on my face.

'How is it better?' I ask, packing his muffin.

'Before I didn't have anything going on, and now I do...my job and you...you guys, I mean. I've been having a lot of fun with you...all.' He clears his throat and grabs a glass and the jar of water I placed on the counter for people to serve themselves.

He's always so sure of his words, so unfazed when speaking. This is like watching a piece of his mask slipping out of place; a breach in his composure.

'I've been having fun with you...all...too,' I say, handing him his pastry.

Moon Hee smiles and turns around to leave. As he approaches the door, I watch his head turn to me and he says, 'Remember, anytime,' before leaving.

'So? What do you think?' I ask my flatmate as I finish putting on my heels.

'Elijah is going to have such a hard time taking his eyes off of you,' she says, a naughty look beaming off her eyes.

'Oh, shut up...' I swat my hand at her arm, my cheeks warming up.

The doorbell rings, and before leaving my room, she gives me her reassuring smile. The one she used to plaster on when she dropped me off at Ms Julie's office door, right before I walked in.

I inhale and take a step to walk out of the room, but the moment I hear Elisa saying the name Elijah, I stop. A rush of reasons for not going burst through my head, so I grab Daldust's last letter and read the paragraph where he talks about how we should embrace ourselves. I read it twice and look at the mirror I uncovered to do my makeup.

Glimpses of the old Lilah Scott appear through my eyes—the outgoing and fun Delilah, the popular one. I grab onto those glimpses.

'I can be like that again,' I think and leave the room with my head held high.

'Hi.' I smile as I enter the living room, where Elijah and Elisa are sitting on the sofa, talking.

My date gazes in my direction, and his eyes travel up and down.

'Fuck, Lilah. Why have you been hiding all this time?' He gets up to greet me, taking my hand to kiss it.

I hope the warmth I'm feeling on my cheeks gets mistaken for makeup, because I'm burning hot.

'Have fun, but Elijah...not too much fun.' Elisa raises an eyebrow at him.

He chuckles and grabs my hand, leading us outside the flat.

His words keep echoing in my mind. *'Why have you been hiding all this time?'* I wish I knew.

'I made a reservation for us at *Gangnam*. I know they have vegan options and since it's fairly new, I was hoping you hadn't tried it yet,' my date says as we get into his car.

'Korean food with vegan options...you are really trying to

impress me.' I chuckle. 'The odds were slim, but you are in luck. I haven't tried it.'

His gaze stays on the road, but I see the corner of his lips lift.

Everything still seems like a mirage. Never in my life did I think this exact moment would happen. My life has been changing so much that the unexpected shouldn't surprise me anymore, yet it still does.

'You don't go out much, do you?' Elijah asks.

'Not anymore, no,' I say, looking out the window. Fluorescent lights fill the streets, with shops decorated for Halloween, waiting for its arrival in just a few days.

'Can I ask why?'

I spot the restaurant near us and a parking space on my side. 'You can park here. It's close enough to the restaurant and I don't see any open space nearer,' I say, changing the subject.

He nods and parks where I suggested. As we get out of the car, I notice what he's wearing—I was so nervous before I didn't get to check him out.

'You look really good too.' Elijah keeps with his signature colour; he's wearing a black shirt with rolled-up sleeves and a few open buttons, letting everyone get a peek at his tattoos. The black suit pants and shoes complete the look.

'Thank you,' he says, reaching his arm for me to hold as we walk towards the restaurant.

You don't even need to know him to know he's done this a lot of times.

'Reservation for Park,' he says to the hostess.

'Follow me, please.' She smiles.

We sit at our table, and I absorb our surroundings.

'Reminds me of some places I visited in Korea,' Elijah says.

'It's beautiful.'

The space is not big but the dark decor, with the black chairs and metal round tables, reminds me so much of the ones I see in K-Dramas.

'One day we'll all go there.' My date shows his perfectly lined pearly-white teeth, tucking a strand of my hair behind my ear.

'So Elijah, tell me, what made you open your tattoo parlour?' I ask, trying to get to know him better.

'Well, I love tattooing and wanted to have my space. Nothing too out of the ordinary,' he says, licking his bottom lip at the end, staring straight into my eyes.

The waiter brings our dishes, and we dive into the wonderful cuisine.

'And you? What made you have a bakery?'

'I've always liked to bake. Is makes me feel closer to my grandmother,' I say, stirring my *bibimbap*.

He says nothing. Maybe I made him uncomfortable. A dead grandma isn't probably something to discuss on the first date.

'It's funny how when we are all together, you barely speak to me. Hell, for the longest time you didn't say a word, but when we are alone, you can speak so freely.'

'It's not like you even knew of my existence until recently.' I chuckle, but his face turns serious.

'I knew. Trust me, I knew. I just didn't know how to approach you. I'm used to dealing with people like Elisa. I have no idea what to do with a Lilah,' he says, lighting up at the end with a smile.

'Well, I always assumed you knew with women. You are bloody Elijah Park.'

He laughs and tilts his head, smirking. He places his hand on top of mine. 'And who is bloody Elijah Park?'

'You know exactly who you are.' I avoid his gaze.

'Maybe, but you don't seem to know who Lilah Scott is anymore.'

My eyes travel to his instantly. 'And you do?'

'No, but I remember the one people talked about in the past. What happened to her?'

'You knew me?' The Parks are friends with a lot of The Elite's families, but I had never heard of Elijah during that time.

'Not personally, but you used to go to my parties with Vance,' he says.

My heart squeezes at the sound of that name, and my hands tremble. I look down at my spoon vibrating on the rice.

'Lilah?' I hear my date saying between the loud beating of my heart in my ears, holding my hands to prevent them from shaking. 'Are you okay?'

Words fail to leave my mouth, all the moisture having left my throat. I release one of my hands from Elijah's to reach for my glass of water, but my hand shakes so much that I end up spilling it, so he gives me his.

I take a gulp, my eyes scanning the spinning room.

'Air,' I manage to whisper. 'I need air.'

He gets up and places my arms around his neck for me to hold on to as he lifts me by the waist and leads me outside. When the breeze of the cold air meets my face, I inhale as if I had been underwater for too long and lean on the wall next to the restaurant.

'Maybe I should call an ambulance,' he says. I can tell how freaked he is by the way his wide eyes stare at me.

'No, it's okay. I'm okay,' I say in a low tone, glancing down and still focusing on my breathing.

'Lilah, you don't seem okay. I think it's best to at least go home.' Elijah places his hand on the side of my cheek, lifting it so my eyes meet his.

'I'm okay, really,' I assure him, placing my hand on top of his and giving him a little smile.

Why is this happening? Why is it always with him? Why can't I be normal?

I'm so fucking tired of this bloody bullshit.

I sit on the floor and he sits next to me. 'I know it's none of my business, but how long have you had these panic attacks?' my date asks.

'Five years.' I glare at the flickering light above the door of the store in front of us.

'And are you getting help for it?' His eyes dig into mine, and his thumb strokes my hand in a soothing gesture.

'Yes, trust me, I'm a lot better. Old Delilah would have never agreed to go out tonight.'

He smiles, relaxing his shoulders. 'I'm glad. So what do you want to do?'

'I want to go finish my meal before the waiter thinks we just left without paying.' I half-laugh.

He chuckles and agrees. 'Let's go.' Standing on his feet, he reaches his hand to help me get up.

The rest of the dinner goes by without a hiccup. We get to know more about each other and even though I notice the lack of similar interests, being in his presence is still enjoyable.

When we reach my flat's door, I turn my back to it and he places his hand next to my head, holding himself on the door, looking at my lips.

'This night was definitely interesting.' He spreads his famous smirk.

'Yeah, sorry about that...' I say, looking down.

He moves his other hand to my chin to lift it. 'Don't be. It's not what happens that matters, it's with whom it does. And I enjoyed every minute with you.'

'Me too.'

His eyes travel back to my lips, and he moves in closer to demolish our distance. A sudden tingle arises in my skin and I try to take a step back, hitting hard on the door, throwing my hand between us to stop him.

I know what he wants to do, and I can't say I don't want it, but a foreign sensation is preventing me. 'I'm not ready yet.'

He nods and backs away, clearing his throat. 'Have a wonderful night, Lilah.'

'You too.' I smile, and he smiles back.

I turn to open my door and wave at him before closing it.

The second I'm inside my house, I lean my back on the door and slide to the ground, looking up.

A swirl of emotions hits me, so many I cannot grasp how to react.

Why do I feel like crying when I just had a date with the one person I was crushing on for the past year? I had a decent time, so why do I feel like throwing up?

I get up and move to the lavatory. As I enter the shower, water runs down from my eyes, and I turn on the tap.

Time doesn't seem to pass as I sit in the tub, warm water flowing through my back, so I stay there until I've gathered enough energy to get up and move to my bed.

I lie awake, with no notion of time, numbness overflowing my body as I try to understand what the hell I'm feeling.

My goal is the only clarity in my mind: to get better. I want to come back from a date and smile, a date where I didn't have a panic attack.

열셋
'yeolset'

'So, how was your date yesterday?' Elisa asks Elijah in our living room.

I haven't been with any of them today. I got out of the house before Elisa woke up and came back while she was working. It's not that I'm avoiding her; I'm avoiding the exact question she just asked my date. Elijah texted me asking how I was today, but I haven't answered.

'What are you doing?' A whisper sounds in my ear, scaring the blood out of me. I jump with a gasp, trying my best to not make noise so the people in the other room don't notice my presence.

I look back and I'm greeted by big, round, dark eyes and a playful smile.

'Moonie, you scared the shit out of me,' I say, my words for his ears only.

He chuckles quietly and whispers back, 'Are you spying on them?' pointing at my flatmate and neighbour.

'No...' I say, deviating my eyes from his.

'Why are you hiding, then?'

'I was...just on my way to the lavatory and...stumbled upon...them talking about yesterday, so I just—'

'You just decided to stay and spy on them.' He bites his lower lip to prevent a laugh.

'Oh, shut up,' I say and walk back to my room.

Moon Hee follows me and closes my bedroom door behind him.

'So, how was it?' he asks.

'How was what?' I play dumb, organising some papers on my desk. I have a letter from Daldust that I haven't opened—I was waiting until everyone left so I could concentrate.

'Lilah.' He raises an eyebrow, knowing bloody well I know what he's talking about.

'It was good…if we ignore my panic attack.' I sit down on my bed, and he leans with his back on the door.

'If it makes you feel any better, he hasn't mentioned it.'

That's nice of Elijah. My fingers fiddle with each other as the silence fills the room.

My eyes are on the floor when a shadow appears in my peripheral vision. I look up and Moon Hee is standing in front of me—does he have cat paws for feet?

'Don't feel bad about it. It's not something you can control, and he knows it. It also doesn't change his feelings for you,' my friend says, reaching to hold my hands.

'How can you be so sure?' I say, my eyes pleading for hope.

'Because if it was me, it wouldn't. If anything it would only make me feel deeper, knowing how strong you are.' His eyes glued to mine.

I sigh and look back down. 'I hate it, you know?'

'Hate what?'

'Not being in control, feeling like at any moment my body can overrule me, betray me.' I bite the inside of my lip, trying to hold back the tears from leaving my waterline.

Moonie sits next to me and taps on his shoulder for me to place my head on it.

'Emotions can be a bitch.' He huffs out a chuckle, getting a sobbing laugh out of me. 'How dare they betray us like that? But you know what?' he continues. 'No one has them fully controlled. Some people might say they do, but it only takes something unexpected to lose control. Right now, you are just dealing a lot with the unexpected.'

'But that's the thing. I get like this over nothing. Out of nowhere!' I lift my head from his shoulder and look at him.

'Maybe to you they're nothing, but not to your body. Maybe you just need to start listening more to it.'

Ms Julie told me something similar today in our session: *your body tells you more than you think. Listen to it.*

As he finishes his sentence, a knock sounds on the door.

'Lilah? Are you there? It's Elijah.'

I look at the door and hesitate for a moment, so Moon Hee whispers in my ear, 'You got this.'

'Come in,' I say.

The moment Elijah opens the door, Moonie lets go of my hands, which were still holding on to his.

Elijah looks at his flatmate, frowning, but Moonie smiles and gets up, tapping him on the shoulder before closing the door as he leaves.

He stands near the exit, looking around my room. If I were him, I'd be stalling too.

'I'm sorry...' I break the silence, and he immediately turns his gaze to me. 'For not answering your text yet.'

The man in front of me stays still, so I continue, 'And for yesterday. I know it wasn't the date you had envisioned.'

'Don't be,' he says, taking a few steps closer to me. 'I just wanted to spend time with you, the real you, not the one that I've been watching for years, and I got to do just that.'

'But I couldn't even kiss you at the end...' I sigh.

He chuckles, biting his lip afterward, then closes even more of the space between us. With his tattooed hand, he caresses my face. 'Don't worry, I know I'm not. We will have plenty of time for that later, that and more.'

My heart beats faster, but this time I know why. I know why it's speeding up and why I'm having a shortage of breath.

Because Elijah Park just said he wants to do more with me.

The man probably catches on to my reaction, because he sits next to me and brings his face closer to mine, looking down at my lips. His tongue glides down to his bottom lip, wetting it along the way, and with his hand he strokes my hair behind my ear.

Coming even closer, he turns his head to whisper in the shell of my ear, 'You just need to tell me when you are ready.'

The warm breath on my ear sends a shiver through my body. This type of uncontrolled reaction is one I didn't remember what it felt like.

That's when it hits me. When I get a glimpse of what I was feeling yesterday: fear.

Why does someone getting this close to me make me tremble? Want to flee?

This is Elijah; I have nothing to fear. *No, I don't want to fear him.*

He pulls away and walks away to the other end of the room. In a fast movement, I stand up and grab his arm—something I didn't think I had in me.

Elijah turns around and after a quick inhale, I say, 'I'm ready.'

His lips form a smirk, and he grabs my wrists, pushing me to the nearest wall. With my hands above my head, wrists held by his hands, pinning me to the wall, his face returns to diminish the space between mine. 'Are you sure?'

I refuse to be afraid of him. Even if that means fighting my instincts.

The moment I nod, his lips close the space between us and a warm sensation fills me.

My hands move to his neck and one of his to my waist. The wet smooth feeling of his lips makes me crave him more. I've imagined how he would kiss so many times, but nothing compares to the real deal.

His tongue slides through my mouth, licking my lips and teasing my own. His warm breath embraces my being and draws me even closer to him.

One of his hands has already lowered to my face when his kisses trail down to my neck, kissing and licking me like that one ice cream flavour you never get tired of.

Elijah stops for a brief moment, guiding me to my bed, which gives me enough time to know I'm not ready to let go just yet.

I lay on my back and he hovers over me, his eyes penetrating mine before he's back on my lips. My hands pull him closer, so he steadies himself by holding his body with his elbow beside me, one leg parting mine and his other hand on my waist.

As his kisses move lower, the hand on my waist moves up to my breasts, caressing them. Suddenly, he gets on his knees on top of me, taking his shirt off and, as an instinct, my hand moves to his torso like two polar opposite magnets. I softly trace it with my fingers over every tattoo and defined muscle.

When I realise what I'm doing, I retract my hand and notice he's staring at me with a smirk. He grabs my hand and places it back on his chest, keeping it held by his own hand.

Lowering himself enough so his words touch my ear, he says, 'You can touch all you want,' and I swallow hard.

I lift my head so our lips touch and his hands grab mine to hold them above my head. Our waists touch and I can feel him growing harder inside his jeans. That thought sends another shiver through my body and a throbbing sensation between my legs.

I haven't had intercourse in five years, and I don't know if I'm ready for it. All I know is that this is the first moment through all these years where I'm actually enjoying the present; nothing else is on my mind and I don't want it to end. I want it to take me wherever it's meant to take me, to take us.

He releases my hands to grab the hem of my shirt and pull it above my head. I lift my torso enough to unhook my bra and throw it across the room.

'Fuck,' Elijah says under his breath.

Intrusive thoughts about my body try to creep into my mind, but I shut them off. *Not now, not at this moment.*

'Is Elisa home?' I ask.

'We're alone.' The man on top of me licks his lips.

Our eyes lock, transmitting the message that we both know what's about to happen.

'Do you have a condom?' Words that I never thought to ask him sound out of me and he grabs one from his back pocket.

I raise a brow at him and he remarks, 'Don't even try to judge me for thinking ahead, be glad I did,' and I chuckle, making him smile.

His lips touch my skin again, this time not holding back their trail, going all the way from my neck to my waist. He stops there to unbutton my pants and I undo his.

His bulge rubs between my legs, letting a moan out of me. It is at this point that I see how much I have been repressing my body, my heat, because an urge to get on top of him rushes over me and I switch our position.

His hands trace over my figure and he bites his lower lip as my hips move on top of him.

'Fuck, Lilah, you have no idea how crazy I am about you,' Elijah groans before grabbing my face with his tattooed hand to kiss me.

His other hand moves to my breast, and his fingers start playing with my aroused nipples. He releases his mouth from mine and moves it to the breast he was playing with before while his hand trails down my body to my undies.

With one finger, he traces my slit above the undies a few times before moving the fabric to the side and sliding a finger inside of me. A deep moan comes out of my mouth and he slides in another one.

While he's pleasing me, my lips kiss his neck as he did for me before, and my hand feels his hardness. After a while, he turns us around again and lowers himself all the way between my legs. He takes off my undies and his tongue touches my clit.

My legs tense from the encounter, so he grabs them tight until I relax. I can't control my breathing anymore and the moment he takes off his briefs and puts the condom on, I hold every breath I have inside.

Elijah places himself to enter me, rubbing his dick in my entrance to tease me first. When I feel like I'm about to beg for him, he comes back to hovering on top of me, and step by step gets inside me.

Our moans and groans get mixed up in the air and our breathing gets heavier each time he speeds up his pace.

'Fuck,' he says. 'Fuck, Lilah, you feel so good.'

I kiss him in return. Sex talk isn't my forte—never had the skill—so touching is my response in these situations. I pull him closer until there's not an ounce of air left between our bodies; until we feel like one.

Drops of sweat already cover our skin when my whole body begins to tense, getting ready to release. I fill the room with my moans and he smiles down at me, knowing I'm close.

I hug him tighter and lock my legs on top of his waist, preventing him from moving from the exact spot he's in. After I come, both my legs and arms relax, allowing him to move again. When he does, he speeds up and doesn't stop until he has come as well. The roughness at the end puts me back in a euphoric state, making me come a second time.

I don't know if it's his experience, if he's gifted, or if we just match, but I didn't remember sex being this good.

He drops by my side, both of us panting, covered in sweat, and smiling like cheerful kids.

'Wow...' I manage to say.

'Wow indeed.' He chuckles.

I turn to my side, and he does the same, our bodies facing each other. His hand holds my chin, and he kisses my lips, kisses that I am now addicted to.

His finger traces my curves until he reaches my ass, and he grabs it with a full hand. He pulls me close to him, where I feel him growing again.

'You are so hot.' His voice is husky.

'Save that second condom for later. I haven't done this in a while, so I'm going to need to rest for a little bit,' I say coyly.

'I never said I brought two.'

'Didn't you say you think ahead?' I wink.

He chuckles and lays his back down on the mattress, looking at me, arms folded by his side and hands under his head.

'This is going to be fun,' he teases back.

열넷
'yeolnet'

It was fun indeed. Last night Elisa came home around one in the morning and by then Elijah had already gone home. Before that, we went for a second round and even a third one in the shower.

I haven't felt like that in so long. It was as if every concern I had disappeared. For the first time in five years, I felt free.

'Good morning,' my flatmate says, staring at me as I walk into the kitchen.

'Good morning.'

I walk to the other corner of the room towards the fridge, but she never ceases to stare.

'What?' I ask.

'So? How was yesterday with Elijah? When I left, he was going to talk to you.' Her big eyes tell me she's expecting something good and wants all the juicy bits.

As I'm figuring out what to tell her, the doorbell rings. It's cliché, but I love that saying *saved by the bell*.

I open, and a smirking face greets me.

'Hey,' Elijah says, entering the house and closing the door before grabbing my waist and pulling me to him, connecting our lips.

The soft pillows of his mouth relax me, our surroundings vanishing. His back meets the door as I melt into him, one hand on my lower back and the other on the side of my face. Mine tug at the small amount of fabric they can pull off his skin-tight shirt.

'Lilah, who is it—' Elisa asks, coming into the hallway and catching us right in the moment.

I pull away the moment I hear her gasp, and Elijah looks at her.

'Oh, I didn't know you were here,' he says, moving both hands back to my waist.

'I guess it went well,' Elisa responds to her previous question.

I clear my throat and release myself from Elijah's arms, saying, 'I have to go get ready to open the shop,' and walk away to my room.

'Fuck,' I say under my breath, leaning on the closed door inside my bedroom.

I sense a wave of anxiety creeping out on me, so I focus on my breath, counting backward from ten.

Ten...nine...eight...Breathe, Lilah...six...five...It's okay...This is normal...You are okay...one...

Inhale...

Exhale...

When I calm down, I remember I still have a pen pal letter I didn't get to open yesterday. I grab it and sit on my bed. Daldust's words have constantly brought me happiness.

"Dear Delilah,

You are very welcome. I hope you start caring less then.

You have a shop? What kind of shop? What do you do for a living?

Me...I'm an artist. I do a bit of everything art-related. I'm an illustrator, photographer, tattoo artist, and all kinds of things.

My family wanted me to have a regular job, but as I stated previously, I don't care. They don't approve, not because they don't think I can succeed, but because they

don't know how to succeed in something that isn't conventional. That's what they learned.

I believe they'll understand better in a few years. The world is constantly evolving and people need to keep up or they get left behind, and my mum isn't one to quit. I'm like her that way. She's very caring and even not approving 100%, she has given in to me following my dreams and sometimes I even catch her smiling at my work.

Do you identify with your parents in any way? You don't need to answer if it's too personal.

Yours truly,
Daldust"

A knock sounds on my door, and I shove the letter under my pillow. 'Yes?'

'It's Elijah.'

'Come in!' I shout.

He walks in and I notice the outfit I only felt before; a tight black T-shirt grips his chest and grey tracksuit bottoms leave for imagination what I already saw yesterday.

The sight of him gets me tingling in places I hadn't in a long time until last night.

'I had a great time last night.' One of the most handsome men I've seen smiles.

'Me too, the greatest I've had in a while,' I say as he walks closer to me.

I can't understand why, but just him doing that gives me butterflies.

'I was wondering if tonight you'd like to have another great time at my place.' His index finger goes under my chin to lift it up, so my eyes meet his.

'I guess I can arrange that.' I push my bottom lip between my teeth, and his thumb traces my lip, plopping it out while his finger remains on my chin.

'Great.' His voice is husky when he takes a step backward, walking out the room. Leaving me stranded, longing for him.

I hear the front door of the flat and then mine opens abruptly.

'Girl, I need details now!' my best friend demands, and I laugh.

'Yes, things went very well yesterday. Three times very well, actually.'

'Ah!' she exclaims, her pitch higher than a squealing duck. 'That's my girl.' She comes to hug me. 'I'm so happy for you.'

I give her a blushing smile, reminiscing about yesterday's events. 'It's been a very long time since I've felt like this, and it's so weird to think that I did it with Elijah.'

'Last year Delilah could never.' She winks before the corners of her mouth drop. 'But seriously, I'm really glad therapy is working.'

'Thank you for encouraging me to do it,' I say. In all the times fear almost made me miss my appointments at the beginning, Elisa stood by my side and helped me go.

'But now I really need to go to work,' I say, and she nods.

On Saturdays, I enjoy to either close the bakery earlier or only do a half day. Today I'm doing the latter. I want to visit the boys at the tattoo parlour. I've been curious about it for a while and after my session with Ms Julie where she said how with each thing I'm doing out of my comfort zone I'm going back to living and enjoying life, I decided it was time. If only she knew I took a tremendous step with Elijah after our session. The last she heard of the story was the date.

I'm getting good at controlling my anxiety, but the panic screws with me. Both she and Moonie told me to listen more to my body and find the triggers. But I have to be honest, with the hot yoga I've been doing with Elisa and what's happening with Elijah, I feel a bit more confident, which helps with the rest.

As I walk into *InkPark,* I soak in the red and black decor. Elijah is behind the counter fiddling with some papers and Moon Hee is nowhere to be seen.

Elijah puts down the papers and looks towards the entrance when he hears the footsteps, only to be greeted by my smile.

'Lilah!' The corners of his lips lift. 'Couldn't wait until the night to see me?'

'Ha-ha, no, I just closed my shop and decided to visit yours. I was curious about how it looked.'

'Are you sure you didn't come to collect your first tattoo?' Elijah reminds me of his promise.

'Not today.' I get closer to the counter and look around once more before asking, 'Where's Moon Hee?'

'He's in the back with a client,' he says, grabbing the papers again.

'Hmm, okay...' I rock back and forth on my feet.

A door sounds open, and voices come out of there.

'You can go directly to my colleague at the counter to pay. Please tag us if you post it on social media. We would love to check out how it heals,' one voice says.

'Of course, thank you so much, I love it,' the other replies.

The client moves to meet Elijah, and Moon Hee goes back inside the room. I decide to go to him.

'Knock knock,' I say near the open door, making my friend turn around in my direction.

His raised sleeves show his latest tattoo. He's wearing black tracksuit bottoms and a matching shirt. Elijah was also all in black, which must be their work attire.

'Lilah.' His beautiful smile pops. 'Come in.'

'It's beautiful,' I say, pointing at his no longer covered arm.

'Thank you.' He glances at it.

'Does it have a special meaning?' I pry.

'It's a reminder of how beautiful but fragile life can be, so we should appreciate every moment before time runs out.'

That explains the broken hourglass with flowers growing inside and butterflies spreading to the background, while shards of glass and sand lie on the bottom.

'Are you here to do one?' Moonie asks, cleaning his instruments.

'I just wanted to check out the space.'

'That was my last client. I'm leaving in a few minutes to go pack for tonight,' he says.

'Pack?' I ask. *Is he going somewhere?*

'Yeah, I'm spending the night at my mum's. Elijah is having someone there to spend the night, so he asked me if I wouldn't mind giving them privacy.'

'Oh.' My voice is lower than a whisper. I wonder if I should tell him it's me; if Elijah didn't and knows him for longer, maybe it's best I don't.

He said to spend the night...I thought I was going there for a couple of hours and then leaving...I'm not ready to spend the night; I don't even know if I want it yet.

Fuck, breathe, Delilah. Breathe!

It's okay, it's okay.

Why is this triggering me? Am I just self-sabotaging?

Arms wrap around me, and I look up from the ground. I hadn't even noticed that I'd already dropped to an Asian squat, hugging myself.

'You're okay, Lilah. Everything is okay. I'm here. You are not alone,' Moon Hee says behind me, holding me in his embrace.

We count together until my breath steadies, and he releases me as soon as the door opens.

Elijah glances at us, frowning, and asks, 'Is everything alright?'

Moonie quickly jumps in and answers, 'Yes, Lilah just dropped an earring and I was helping her find it.'

I stay silent. My strength is still not enough to put together a sentence.

'I'm going now. I'll see you both tomorrow,' Moonie says.

'I'm just going to finish up some things here and then close up too,' Elijah says and turns to me after his flatmate leaves adding, 'I'll knock on your door when I'm ready,' giving me a peck on the forehead.

I nod and walk to my flat, still a bit in my head. I am trying to listen to my body, to figure this all out.

Why is dating so triggering for me? Sure, my last relationship wasn't the best, but that's not enough to be triggering. I wish I could remember what happened that night. They say ignorance is bliss and sometimes it's true, but in this case, it's driving me crazy.

I text Elijah, asking if I can be the one to knock when I'm ready, before I go to a hot yoga class to clear my mind.

My body is tired as I enter my building, but my mind is a lot calmer. I can focus on the positive now.

As I turn to open my flat's door, the one behind me opens.

'Hey,' Elijah says.

'Hey, sorry I took so long. I needed to clear my head.' I turn around to him.

'It's okay…' He looks up and down at me. 'I was about to take a shower. Do you want to join me?'

I stare at him as I consider my options.

'Actually…that sounds perfect.' I bite the inside of my lip, trying to keep my blush invisible.

I follow him inside his flat as he grabs my wrist to guide me to his lavatory.

The door closes, and Elijah pushes me against it.

'Wait, I'm all sweaty,' I say, avoiding his kiss.

He smirks and holds my face still with one hand, whispering in my ear, 'I don't care,' before locking my lips with his.

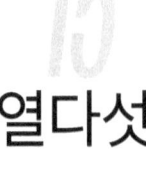

열다섯
'yeoldasot'

'You stayed.' Elijah smiles as I open my eyes.

I did…The realisation warms my heart and I give him a small smile.

He serenely brushes the hair on the side of my face with his backhand and tucks it behind my ear before his eyes travel down.

My eyes follow his, and I notice my bare chest. In a hurry, I grab the sheet and pull it up.

'Oh…I was enjoying the view.' His mouth forms a dramatic pout.

I divert the subject to hide my shyness. 'Do you have something to eat?'

'I don't remember, but there must be something in the fridge,' he says.

I get up and grab his shirt and my undies. I'm glad he was wearing an oversized shirt last night. It will cover enough for me to go to the kitchen.

As I'm rummaging through the fridge, footsteps sound behind me. I don't give them much importance because my mind goes to Elijah joining me, but when someone clears their throat, I know it's not him.

My body tenses and I stand up to turn around.

'Lilah?' Moon Hee frowns. His grip tightens around the sleeves of the grocery bags he brought home as he stares, mouth slightly opened, at me.

'Moonie,' I say, pushing my shirt's hem down as much as it can go.

Our eyes interlock, and the air around us thickens. I feel like I've been caught doing something I shouldn't by the one person who shouldn't know, and I don't know why.

Thankfully, Elijah interrupts us—nothing on his body but his briefs. Bloody hell, I keep forgetting how hot he is until he stands in front of me.

'Hey mate,' he says to Moon Hee—whose eyes are still on me—moving to my side and placing his arm around my shoulders.

'Did you find anything to eat?' Elijah asks, shifting his gaze to me.

I shake my head and look back at Moon Hee, who I'm guessing is still trying to wrap his head around the situation.

'Hmm...' Moonie's big doe eyes now hang low, looking around the room. He puts down the shopping bags he brought with him on the counter. 'I should go.'

'Moonie!' My mind didn't even think of what was coming out of my mouth. A sense of desperation fills my body, and it doesn't even make sense to be reacting like this. I don't like Moon Hee like that.

He comes to a sudden halt in the middle of the room, as if he's waiting for me to continue speaking. However, as I find myself devoid of any remaining words, he eventually departs.

'Is he okay?' Elijah asks.

'I don't know...' My voice is low as I stare at the door.

I lie in my bed, repeatedly playing Moon Hee's glance in my head. The look in his eyes, as if seeing me there with Elijah hurt him. I know it was unexpected to see me there, but why would that hurt him?

As I turn to my side, the sound of paper being crumpled reminds me I left Daldust's letter under my pillow yesterday. I get up to a seated position on my bed and grab the pillow to take the letter and re-read it.

Now, when I need a minute in my world, it's them who I want in it with me. There's a sense of security I get with every letter that warms my heart. It's a feeling that I didn't know I was missing, yet I'm becoming addicted.

I walk over to my desk to write back so I can send it tomorrow.

"I see you didn't answer my questions, but I'll answer yours.

I have a bakery here in London, so I'm a baker for a living and I love it. It's my dream job.

I don't have a close relationship with my parents. I talk to them probably once a month. It's not that we dislike each other, but I don't feel comfortable around them at this point in my life. They support my career. Actually, it thrills them. After my grandma died, they loved that I continued her legacy, but I'm a twenty-seven-year-old single woman who spends most of her time at home, and they keep questioning and pressuring me to find someone—which I'm not looking for. I'm not up to being let down at the moment, and honestly, I don't think I could handle it.

If I were a man, they wouldn't say anything. They would think, 'oh, he's just living his 20s, let's give him a break,' but because I'm a woman all they want to know is if I found a man. If they want a man so much, they should adopt one!

Sorry about the rant, but this rankles me.
Delilah"

Ms Julie was right when she suggested I get a pen pal. On paper, I let out my true feelings. I say things I couldn't even imagine saying in person, but I'm getting that tiny curiosity to know them.

'Hey,' Elisa says, knocking on my half-opened door.

'Hey.' I turn around from my desk.

'I passed by Moon Hee today and he seemed weird. Did Elijah comment anything about him?' she asks.

I sigh and tell her what happened.

'Oh, fuck.' She grimaces. 'Now I get it.'

'Get what?' I ask.

'Why he seemed so wrecked.'

'Wrecked?' I furrow my eyebrows.

'Lilah, you are not going to tell me you have never seen it...' she says, appalled.

'Seen what?'

'The way he looks at you. That man definitely has feelings for you.'

'What? Why do you say that?' I'm the appalled one now.

He's always been nice to me, and very understanding, but I don't think that means he likes me. It means he's a reliable friend.

'He just glows whenever you are around.'

'You are probably imagining it.' I chuckle.

'You've never considered him? To date, I mean?'

'Moonie? No, he's like a little brother to me!' I don't remember such a thought ever crossing my mind.

'Just because he's like two years younger?'

'I mean...yes. I do like him, and I might have a deeper connection with him, at least more than Elijah, but as friends.'

'Well, that's too bad. I think you'd make a very cute couple.' I'm still processing her comment when Elisa shifts the focus to our other male friend. 'And how are things with Elijah? You spent the first night out in five years, Lilah!' She claps her hands with a tiny movement of jumping up and down.

'It's been better than I could've ever imagined. He's so much fun and oh, so good in bed.' I bite my lip, thinking of all the times we've spent together.

'I'm happy for you. Do you think it's going to turn into something more than friends with benefits?'

'Honestly, no, and I'm truly okay with that. Like I said, our personalities don't match that much. We don't have much in common. Besides, it's Elijah…When does he ever catch feelings?' I chuckle.

'Maybe you're right,' my flatmate says, her tone lacking confidence. She turns around to leave my room, but not before adding, 'Talk to Moon Hee.'

I nod, but her back already faces me. My mind keeps replaying the word *glow*.

He *glows* when we're together?

No. It's Moonie. He's the one I've never felt self-conscious around, the one that holds me when I'm falling apart. If anything, he'd be a best friend, not a lover.

I leave my flat and knock on the door on the other side of the hall.

'Yes?' Moonie asks.

'It's me.'

It takes him a few seconds, but he finally opens the door.

'Elijah isn't here,' he says, looking at the floor.

'He's not the one I'm here for,' I say, and his eyes lift to mine. 'Can we talk?'

He stares at me in silence, only opening more of the door and moving to the side so I can walk in.

I sit on the sofa and he follows, waiting for me to say anything else.

'I'm sorry,' I say, fiddling with my fingers. 'For not telling you that it was me who was spending the night.'

He sighs and turns to face me as we sit. 'It's okay, I was

just caught off guard.'

'You wouldn't have been if I had told you yesterday when you commented about his date.'

'I just...didn't know it was going so well. It surprised me, that's all.' I can sense his discomfort. He doesn't look me in the eye like he usually does when he speaks.

'Trust me, I wasn't counting on it. It totally surprised me when you said that he'd planned for me to spend the night. I think that's why I panicked,' I admit.

'I guess you didn't have to worry about it. It went great by the looks of it.' Moon Hee smiles, moving his gaze to mine. A wave of relief washes over me.

I reach out for his hand and hold it between mine. 'I'm sorry if I made it awkward.'

He smiles again. 'Don't worry, you didn't. I did. I'm happy if you are. Are you?'

'I am strangely happy.'

Elisa was mistaken, after all. He doesn't glow. He might sparkle a bit, but it's all in the name of friendship.

'You are an amazing friend, you know? One of the best I have right now,' I say.

He stays silent with a smile.

The front door unlocks and Elijah walks in, not noticing us, so I signal Moon Hee to not tell him I'm here as I hide behind the sofa.

'Hey mate.' Elijah greets his flatmate and sits where I was before. 'Those five-hour tattoos can really get the best of me sometimes. I'm dead.' He leans backwards to relax.

I reach my hands to cover his eyes, startling him.

'Guess who,' I play.

'Bloody fuck, Lilah. You scared the fuck out of me,' he says, and both Moon Hee and I laugh.

'Hey,' I say, sitting next to him.

'Hey,' he whispers, pulling my face to his and kissing me.

'Well, this is my cue. I'm going to my room,' Moonie says, getting up from the sofa and leaving the area.

Elijah doesn't even acknowledge him. His lips don't want to depart mine and I don't mind. Once Moonie is gone, I get on top of Elijah and he places both hands on my waist.

'Do you want to stay over again?' he asks. 'Moon Hee bought breakfast this time.'

'I don't know...' My voice is low. I still feel strange about this morning.

'We can watch a film to relax,' he says, trying to convince me.

'Just a film?' Could we even just watch a film? Every time we are together, our bodies can't unglue.

Just the other day when Elisa caught us in front of the door, the day after our first time, I had to pull him away, and still, I felt the warmth on my waist. The touch of his fingers was one I easily got used to.

'Maybe...' He smirks, as his eyes face the bottom part of my face. I close my eyes at the soft trace on my left cheek in an attempt to soothe my mind, yet I can't help but feel uneasy.

Am I thinking too much into this? We're just having fun.

Fun I hadn't had in years.

But as much as I try not to, those thoughts linger in my mind, creeping at every calm moment.

'Enjoy it while you can. It won't last long,' one says.

'It's just a matter of time until I have you on the floor, reaching for air,' the other joins.

'Elijah will get bored soon. How will someone so pathetic entertain him enough?'

'You are not enough. You never were, you never will be.'

'Are you okay?' Elijah holds my face, the skin between his eyebrows wrinkled.

It's not until his thumb runs under my eye that I notice the wetness. Tears drip down my face, and my lower lip trembles uncontrollably.

I lift myself off his lap, and the back of both my hands spread the tears throughout my cheeks, attempting to wipe them off.

'I'm sorry, I don't know what went over me,' I say, my eyes drifting away from his to the left.

There's a slight click of the door's lock that makes me look in its direction. An empty hall stares back at me, so I return my attention to the man in front of me, the one whose eyes haven't moved an inch.

'You're such a mystery to me, Lilah Scott,' he says, getting up. My neck stretches up to keep his face in sight, and the sofa makes more noise than when I got up.

'I'm sorry.' My eyes meet his hands as they reach for mine.

'No, I'm sorry that I'm not much of a comforter. I never know the right words to say.'

'It's okay. I just think I killed the mood for a film. I'm going,' I say, briefly closing my eyes to prevent spilling once more.

His mouth parts, but no words come out. He knows I killed the mood. I'm a killjoy; I've always been.

My back turns to him and I don't stop until I reach the other side of my bedroom door. He doesn't try to stop me.

16
열여섯
'yeolyeoseot'

'When was the last time you two spoke?' my flatmate asks, holding her water bottle under the faucet as water pours into it.

'Sunday…I know, it's been almost a week, but I haven't been in the mood,' I say, closing my gym bag.

My only conversations this week have been with customers, Elisa, and through letters. Daldust and I have been getting to know each other a little better, where I also vented a bit to them about my situation with Elijah and he's been helping.

'Are you coming or not?' Elisa opens the front door.

'Yes, yes.' I rush. Maybe this spin class she's taking me to will help clear my head.

My pen pal's words are a comforting embrace, easing the burden on my heart when I receive them, but my dark thoughts linger in the background even when I'm not consciously aware of them.

I sigh, reminiscing about my days with Elijah. I'm surprised to admit that I've felt the void his hands left. There's nothing like the dopamine I get with him. Up until Sunday, my thoughts had subsided until they got louder.

I don't want them to get loud; I don't want to have them.

I promised Elisa that I would go with her, and that's the only reason I'm enduring the sweat dripping on my back.

'My legs are about to give up,' I whisper to her, receiving a pat on the back for a response.

I need my session with Ms Julie afterward. I'm hoping she'll have more answers than I have questions. The heaviness in my eyes is begging for help, begging to shut my mind, begging for one restful night.

Turning the corner of our building's stairs—yes, she made me take the stairs after a spinning class; this woman will be the death of me—almost out of breath, I spot someone leaning against our flat's door.

'Moon Hee?' Elisa asks, approaching him.

His head turns to the hallway and his back straightens, taking a step away from our door.

'Hey,' he says.

'Is everything okay?' She reaches with the key to the door's lock.

He stays silent, but our eyes lock. Elisa turns back to me and then to him again.

'Okay, I'm going in first,' she says, leaving the door open.

'Hi,' I say in a low tone, getting closer to him.

'Can we talk?' he asks, and I nod, leading him to my room.

I sit on my bed's edge, waiting for him to speak.

'Did you receive my text yesterday?' he starts.

My eyes meet the ground, and as it begins blurring, my mind travels to yesterday.

The room was dark until a bright white light illuminated the left side of my bed. I turned around, confused by why I was receiving a notification when I noticed the time. It had been four hours since I'd laid down, four hours and my head hadn't rested.

'Who's texting me at three in the morning?' I thought. *Moonie* appeared in bold, black letters.

It was a song, nothing else displayed on the screen except Miley Cyrus's face and the words 'The Climb' under it. I exhaled, and a strange contortion happened in my face—one I hadn't felt all week—my mouth's corners lifted.

I hadn't listened to that song in so many years, so I reached for the headphones on top of my desk and clicked play.

I sat down on the floor, my back feeling the comfort of the mattress behind me.

As I listened to the lyrics, my eyes began watering. I remembered listening to that song so much when it came out, but it felt like I was listening to the lyrics for the first time.

The only sound in the room was coming from me when the song ended. My face was covered with tears as I held my knees against my chest, my eyes closed for a moment.

It was the first time all week the aching in my head had stopped, but the heaviness became more prominent. The moment I laid my head on the pillow, an imaginary five-pound weight was placed on my forehead. Nevertheless, my eyes caught the morning light shining through the window.

The arms gripping around me take me back to the present. I lift my head from the hands that were holding it from hitting my knees and try to look at my back, where he's kneeled on my mattress, his chest sending warmth through my body.

'I'm sorry,' I mumble.

'There's nothing you have to be sorry about.' His words are a fuzzy blanket on a cold winter night.

'You keep seeing me cry.'

'Crying is the way our body cleanses the soul. So, that means I keep standing next to you as you clean your soul. To me, that's beautiful,' he says.

A strange sound leaves my mouth, making my eyes widen, and I smile.

This time it's not my soul that was cleansed, but rather my heart was embraced, so I continue the sound.

I make it more until I forget why I was crying in the first place. I laugh to my heart's content; I laugh until all the reasons why I haven't been sleeping all week vanish and the man next to me joins me.

We look like two lunatics, laughing just because.

He's the first one to stop, saying, 'It's so good to hear you laugh. I don't remember the last time I heard that sound and it feels so refreshing.'

My eyes water once more, but this time my mouth keeps curved up.

'Don't worry, these are tears of joy. It's been ages since the last time I laughed like this. Thank you.' I reach for his hands as he sits next to me. 'Somehow you keep comforting me, and I thank you for that. You have no idea how much I appreciate you, Moon Hee.'

'The pleasure is all mine.' He smiles.

I let go of his hands and stand up, walking towards the door, stopping before reaching the door knob to turn around. 'I made banana bread, want some?'

His eyes blink slower as his head nods, before walking behind me to the next room.

The long beige carpet in the corridor that leads to Ms Julie's office reminds me of the ones I had at home. I remember feeling so sorry for our house cleaner to need to vacuum it daily, that I learned to take off my shoes before stepping on it. Nobody else cared, and it's something that has always made me sad.

'Why does it make you sad?' my therapist asks after I told her the story as I sat on her cream sofa.

'At that time, I didn't know, but looking back...I think it was their lack of compassion towards everyone. I guess on a certain level I related more to the house cleaner than to them, and it made me sad because that was one of the first interactions I had with their sense of superiority.'

'Have you always felt inferior to them?' She writes something down on her notepad.

'Yes, if it wasn't because I was a child, it was because they were part of the Elite.' I clench my jaw at the mention of that name. All the Elite did was bring misery to those around, connected or not. 'I've always felt like a victim of the Elite, but I can't remember why. I just know that the thought of it sends chills down my spine and my brain simply shuts down.'

'Our minds like to protect us. That's why, after some traumas, we cannot remember the incident. There are ways to unlock those memories—it's not my speciality, but I do know someone who works with it if you'd like me to give you their contact,' Ms Julie says.

I take in the sun shining through her hair, creating gold highlights on her honey-brown hair, and nod. I'm afraid of what I might discover about my past, but I hate it even more than staying in denial. It's a part of my story that was completely erased from my mind. That's the biggest betrayal I've felt from my mind, even if it thinks it was for my protection.

'Here,' she says, handing me a business card. 'Call for an appointment whenever you are ready. It can even be while we are having a session if it makes you feel safer.'

She smiles and sits back down as I stare at the business card, the piece of paper that holds so much power over my future.

I speak with Ms Julie about how I'm feeling and all my doubts. She says that not knowing my triggers can complicate surpassing the traumas in my head, and that's why I want to remember what happened five years ago.

Before going home, I stop by the post office to see if I have a new letter—they have been coming almost daily. There's a grey envelope inside the dark box. I grab it and put it inside my purse so I can read it when I get home.

My mind keeps travelling to Elijah and how I should speak with him, but my courage keeps dissolving into thin air.

Closing the door of my room, I open the envelope and read what's inside.

"Sweet Delilah,

I see you copied my greeting, so I changed mine to keep it original.

I'm sorry I didn't answer before. I get so focused on a topic that I noticed I already didn't have space left to write. But I'll answer them now.

Yes, I like to read, but at the moment I'm reading more non-fiction books and poetry.

I've travelled around many countries, and I've been to every continent. Maybe one day I'll take you to South Korea. I have a house there.

I understand what you said about your parents. I see the same with my family. To me, they say nothing, but to my cousins, they wouldn't stop until all of them got a boyfriend and now all they'll ask about is when the first wedding will happen. I know after that, the talk will be about grandkids.

I'm lucky to have been born a man in that aspect (and others). But don't feel pressured. The moment you start not caring, all the pressure disappears. Their parents probably asked them that as well, so break the cycle and live life at your own pace.

I don't know much about relationships. I haven't been in a serious one, but I think no one is ever up to being let down, so don't let fear impede your happiness.

Yours truly,
Daldust"

That's right, in my last letter I wrote Dear Daldust. I laugh to myself. At least they're finally answering the questions I've asked so long ago. It must mean Elijah's topic is over. I hope it didn't bother *him*. He's a man...All this time I was unsure, but didn't want to ask—I was okay with the mystery—but now I know. Daldust is a man.

I'm preparing to write back when familiar voices sound on the other side of the door, a knock appearing a few seconds later.

I put down my pen and look back to answer. 'Yes?'

My flatmate's face shows in the opening. 'We're having some drinks. Care to join?'

I have work tomorrow, but between my letters with Daldust, my talk with Moon Hee, and my session with Ms Julie I'm feeling lighter, and a little alcohol in the system might be just what I need to gather the courage to speak to Elijah and finally get a good night's sleep.

Heck, I might even treat myself and not open the bakery tomorrow. After all, I'm the boss and my body is craving sleeping in.

'I'll be right there.' I nod and put away the letter to leave tomorrow's Delilah to deal with it.

Tonight's Delilah is tired of everything and wants to let go. Let go of all that keeps my mind hostage. And as Daldust said, I won't let fear impede my happiness.

The moment I walk into the living room, all eyes turn to me, something I'm not used to. If it weren't for whose eyes they are, I'd be a nervous wreck by now. But *these* people have been warming up my heart, helping me in ways they can't even fathom. *My* people.

My body sinks into our navy linen sofa next to Elijah, who, despite glancing at me, keeps quiet. There's sorrow in his expression—I know he wants to reach out but doesn't know how. He once told me he didn't know what to do with a Lilah, so I'll show him he doesn't need to overthink too much and tonight I'll do as I preach.

My throat burns as the liquid slides down, and when I hit the shot glass on the table, my upper body turns to the tall, tattooed, and handsome man next to me. Both my hands grab his face and as his eyes widen, I pull it closer, bringing my lips to his.

열일곱
'yeolilgob'

'So you two are okay?' my flatmate asks as I cut more lemon slices for the tequila shots.

My eyes look back at the living room, where the two guys are talking to each other, and I smile.

'We still have to speak, but I think so, yes.'

'I mean, that kiss was definitely something else.' She laughs, grabbing a plate to place the slices on.

There's something about the blurry buzz of being intoxicated. Everything around slows down and you transcend your body; your bones vibrate to the beat of the music and it all feels so much deeper.

As deep as the eyes looking back at me; they're big, round, and carry a raven's colour. But the most enticing thing is the soul they carry.

I tilt my head and give a small smile, and he swiftly glances back at his friend, the one I was kissing just moments ago.

'Do we have enough lemons?' I ask, and my flatmate looks back at the fresh bag of lemons we bought.

'I would say we have more than enough,' she says.

'Great!' I grab two of them and direct myself towards the exit door.

'Lilah?' she blurts, watching me walk away from everyone.

'Where are you going?' Elijah asks.

My free hand grabs our doorknob and turns it. My body knows precisely where to go. It travelled there the last time it was in the same state.

Checking the time on my phone, I knock on the door down the hall.

'Yes?' a feminine voice sounds on the other side.

'I'm here to give you your two lemons back.'

After a few seconds, she opens the door, frowning at me.

'A few weeks ago you gave me two lemons in exchange for me to help you take the rubbish out.'

'I remember. I just wasn't expecting you to return them,' she says.

The corners of my lips instantly turn up as it's the first time her smile appears.

'And I was also wondering if you'd like to join us tonight. We're having another hangout,' I confess.

'You sure like to have a good time.' The woman with long brown locks chuckles.

'It's easy to have a good time when people who make you happy surround you.' I glance over to my door where Elijah leans on the frame, watching us.

'Sure, I'll join you,' my ears catch the woman saying before I glance back at her.

I smile, and after grabbing the key by her door, she closes it to follow me.

Approaching Elijah, he frowns at me while wrapping his arm around my waist.

I signal with my head to get in the flat and we all appear in the living room, two people staring between me and the stranger I brought in.

'Guys, this is...' I look over at our neighbour, whose name I haven't asked.

'Sofía.' She completes my sentence.

'Sofía,' I repeat. 'The neighbour that kindly lent us lemons the other night when we wanted tequila.'

Her hand waves and Elisa, as the amazing host she is, sits up to greet her.

'I'm Elisa, or Lisa, as you prefer,' she says, reaching her hand out for Sofía to shake. 'This is Elijah and Moon Hee, and in case the person who invited you hasn't introduced herself, she's Lilah.'

'Hi,' Sofía says.

We all sit down and take a shot to loosen up the mood. Only drunk Delilah would invite a stranger to her house; sure, a stranger she had a good vibe with from the beginning, but nonetheless a stranger.

Sofía quickly matches our mood, and I can tell Elisa is interested by the way my best friend and neighbour talk to one another. Elisa's subtle touches on Sofía's arm and the way she leans in to speak, despite the music being low enough to hear each other well.

On the other side of the room Elijah and Moon Hee converse, so I join them.

'Hey guys.' I beam.

'You're so drunk right now,' the man with black hair and tattoo sleeves laughs.

The other keeps quiet, avoiding my eye contact. Sober Delilah would keep her thoughts to herself, overthink every movement the other made, and question whether it was her fault or not, but I'm not sober right now.

'Why are you so quiet?' I ask Moon Hee, whose head lifts right up.

'No reason,' he says.

My eyes fix on him for a few seconds, hoping for a change in answer, but I decide to leave it here. Who am I to force anyone to open up, when even I have trouble doing so?

My head turns to the first man and I say, 'I'm sorry.'

'No, I'm sorry, I didn't know how to approach you,' he says, looking down at his hands.

'And I'm sorry for being out of reach in the first place.' I grab his tattooed hand in comfort, making his eyes meet mine.

When we smile at each other, I sense a weight being lifted off my shoulders.

I wish I had the same courage when chemicals aren't being unbalanced in my brain.

The three of us walk back to the centre, to meet the ladies laughing. Laughter that lasts the entire night, laughter that rings in my head until the next day.

The warm arms wrapping around my torso pull me closer in my awakening.

'Don't you dare to get up,' Elijah says from beside me.

I chuckle. 'Fine, five more minutes. I need to pee after.'

The sensation of someone touching me would always send me spiralling, but his bare skin on mine makes me feel safe. I sigh and scoot closer to his chest.

The air hangs still, devoid of sound, leaving us in a state of uncertainty. Instead of trying to break the silence, we find solace in embracing one another, allowing a different kind of connection to flourish.

It's strange to think that a month ago I avoided his eyes and now they lay on my bare body; that in this short time, more people have entered my life than in the last five years.

It took a long time, but Ms Julie was right. When you step out of your comfort zone, each step is less daunting as they start to flow. It only took one drunk evening for me to gather the courage to engage with these men, a mere twenty-four hours to begin opening up to someone new, and a handful of weeks to venture into the realm of dating once more, surprising me on every level.

The last one is becoming more believable if I think the mutual desire had been simmering for longer.

My bubble expanded as what was once outside is now within and it will keep growing as I move forward, so the thought of going back to revisit the past threatens the slow and steady growth of the bubble. I'm afraid the memories will turn into a needle ready to pop all the progress I've made.

'It's been five minutes,' I plead, using the power of my dimples.

With a grunt, Elijah releases his tight grip on me and unfolds his arms. I rise from the bed and proceed to put on the clothes I wore yesterday.

'I wonder if it's safe to go to my flat by now. I need to change clothes,' I say, chuckling at my encounter yesterday when, after spending the night with Elijah, I opened my front door to two naked and playful women.

As I observed the happenings of our intimate Friday party, I couldn't help but notice the captivating interactions between Elisa and Sofía. How their eyes interlocked in a mesmerising way, their smiles lighting up the room, and their gentle touches that spoke volumes. But what I didn't see coming was Sofía spending the night, again and again.

'We can check it out after breakfast.' Elijah grins, knowing what I'm referring to.

I leave his bedroom and walk towards the loo next door, scanning my surroundings for his flatmate.

Moon Hee kept more to himself that night and barely spoke with us yesterday when the three of us interacted during meals or films. My mind can't shake the feeling that I'm making him uncomfortable.

When we step out into the living-slash-dining room for breakfast, Elijah moves to sit down on the table as I stop hearing someone opening the flat's door.

Moon Hee walks in and the world around me slows down as

I watch the sweat drip from his neck down. His right arm flexes while he pushes backwards the hair out of his eyes. Tattoos I'd never seen pop under his wet white tank top. He's always so covered up that I only see half of his arms, which now have one tattoo to show, but underneath all the fabric he's more inked than I'd ever imagined. All his baggy clothes don't do justice to the muscles he hides.

As his figure closes in on mine, it becomes harder to swallow, but I keep my eyes locked on him.

'Hey,' he says. The corners of his lips lift a little and the creaks under his eyes get deeper. Such simple features that I never cared for now seem so delicate.

'Hey,' I breathe, unsure if the sound left my vocal cords.

'You went running?' Another male voice sounds behind me, snapping me out of this trance.

I cough on air and turn to my side, avoiding both gazes. A gentle hand taps on my back, making me look its way, where Moon Hee's wide eyes glare at mine.

'I'm okay, I'm okay.' I step away from him and wave my hand back, in hope he takes the hint.

A sudden burst of courage compels me to seek out my flatmate and her date, even if it means subjecting myself to another uncomfortable encounter, just to escape from this situation.

'Yeah, I needed to clear my head,' Moon Hee says, confusing me until I realise he's perhaps answering Elijah's earlier question.

'Um...' I say. 'I'm going home. I need a shower and to change clothes.'

'What about breakfast?' Elijah lifts the plate of waffles he just unfroze.

'I'm not really hungry.' I grab my bag on the sofa on my way to the exit door.

As I prepare to leave, I steal a quick look at Moon Hee, who is standing directly in front of me, his gaze locked with mine. I don't know what in the bloody hell just happened, but I'm the one who needs to clear my head now.

So I barricade myself inside my shower.

I close my eyes and let the warm water flow over my face, savouring the soothing sensation that spreads through my body. When life gets too hectic, I often overlook how relaxing a shower can be, how something so mundane becomes special when you're enjoying the moment.

'It was just Moonie,' I think to myself as the water hits my shoulders.

It was just Moonie.

To entertain my mind away from strange thoughts, I sit down at my desk to write a letter to Daldust. Tomorrow is Monday, so I can finally respond to him.

"Fine, I won't greet you, but don't call me Sweet Delilah. The only person who has ever called me that was my grandma, so it's strange to hear it from someone else, not to mention that's my bakery's name. It almost sounds like you are directing your letter to it haha.

I prefer Dear Delilah, as if you are writing on a page of your diary. I would like to be that, your diary; a safe place you go to talk about anything that goes on in your mind.

You said you haven't had a serious relationship. Why is that? You seem like a pretty deep person. Or are you waiting for the one?

I do want to believe we have someone meant for us, but sometimes all love feels fake. Even my parents' love feels fake sometimes. The only true love I see around is this cute old couple that visits my shop; I want what they have.

And thanks, I'll try to make more of my happiness.

My therapist says that true happiness comes from within; if we keep searching for it in someone or something we will never get it, because we are the only ones who belong to us. Everything else can disappear and if we place our happiness on them when they go, so it goes.

I'm working on finding happiness within. I hope you are too.

Also, my best friend is having a getaway trip for her birthday soon, so I might be slower to respond next as well.

Delilah"

There's still a couple of weeks until Elisa's birthday weekend but I know the bakery will get my hands full. I'm working on new recipes I want to have for the winter. Soon I'll have Christmas-themed baked goods filling my shelves, and those need to be prepared to perfection.

The house was silent when I walked in, but I saw light coming under my flatmate's bedroom door. She's working or entertained, I'm sure; Elisa has never been one to stick to schedules.

I remember when in university, deadlines were her downfall. In group projects she always dictated the work each had to do, because she despised getting something she was unmotivated to perform. But when the time to focus arrives, she's a hurricane and won't stop spinning until the work is done.

By dinner time I'd heard the lavatory door once letting me know she'd walked out of her room, but remained inside as I got ready to walk out to meet our front-door neighbours.

The moment I ring the bell, I'm welcomed by those enchanting, dark, and round eyes that begin to leave me breathless.

Stop it, Lilah! He is your friend!

'Hi,' Moon Hee says, stepping to the side for me to walk inside his house.

Fortunately, he's returned to wearing his black oversized shirts, but the memory of him before still lingers in my mind.

'Hey.' I avert my eyes, scanning around for his friend, the one I should be having images in my head about.

'He's not here.'

I nod and walk to sit down on the sofa. The man beside me is the only one who has never left me speechless. My anxiety has never struck in his presence, but somehow today the words cannot form.

I can feel him looking at me, waiting to give him a clue. He adjusts himself next to me before speaking. 'What's on your mind?'

'Do you believe people can fall out of love?' I lift my gaze to his.

'Yes, of course. Why?' I watch as his eyebrows frown together.

'I was just thinking about something an ex said. He said that you either love forever or you've never loved at all.'

'If feelings were that black and white, the world would be a lot simpler, but people evolve. They are constantly changing and so are our emotions.' His face relaxes as he sighs. 'If feelings had a colour, it would be grey—messy and blurred. People's tastes change all the time, so why wouldn't feelings change? It won't be from day to night, but slowly they change if nothing stops them from moving. That's why we should never take anything or anyone for granted.' He holds my hands between his.

We're startled by the loud noise of a door closing. Moon Hee looks back as I watch Elijah approach us with pursed lips and a clenched jaw.

'Can we talk?' Elijah asks Moonie, who nods, following the first man towards his room. The man who did not even say a word to me. The man I don't remember ever seeing him this serious.

18
여열덟
'yeolyeoldolb'

Elijah's POV

We enter my bedroom and as he closes the door, my eyes meet the floor, trying to collect my thoughts. My hand pushes my hair back a few times as I turn circles in the room.

I'm trying to keep myself collected, not let the rage blind me.

He's your mate, Elijah. He's your fucking friend, and somehow that makes it worse.

'Is there something going on between you and Lilah?' I ask my flatmate.

My feet can't stay still, but if I keep this up, I'll wear out the floor, so I stand in front of him, waiting for an answer.

'What do you mean?' he frowns.

'Every time I walk into a room with just the two of you, I get the vibe that I'm interrupting something, not to mention that you are always awfully close to each other.'

My mind flashes back to after I asked Lilah out the first time, how when I entered her room to speak she and Moon Hee were holding hands, or how close they were at the tattoo parlour, or in the kitchen, or today. *I need to know if I'm imagining things.*

'Nothing is going on between us. We're just friends, that's all,' he says. But the way his lips purse at the end and the way he avoids my stare tell me there's something more.

One thing I've always praised myself for is understanding body language. I've been studying it for years.

So I shoot my shot. 'Do you like her?'

His eyes widen at me, telling me everything I need to know.

'What? No!' he bursts out, looking down to his left afterwards.

He's lying. *He's fucking lying*.

'Tell me the truth,' I say. I don't want to argue, or play as if she's someone's property. I just want to know.

'*Hyung*,' he says, his shoulders dropping in defeat.

'Before her, you were my friend. You know I consider you my *dongsaeng (little brother)*, and that's not going to change.'

'Do you like her?' Moon Hee asks. This time his eyes fix on mine.

'I'm not sure.' I've never been one to be in love, but to me, she is different.

There's no one thing that makes her special. It's the way the world feels warmer when I'm around her. The way her smile makes me want to protect her from the world.

I've never been one to be in love, but my heart grows bigger when I'm with her.

'I do,' he says in a lower tone, glancing back at the door.

I knew he was lying before, but hearing those words.... my heart sinks. Two simple words fazed more than a punch in the stomach.

'I have for a while, way before you two were together. I just kept my distance,' he continues, looking back at me.

I sit down on my bed, his words weighing on me. I never saw it coming.

'You might not be sure, but I think you do like her. I've seen you with a lot of girls, some lasted more than others, but I've never seen you how you are with Lilah,' my flatmate tells me.

I fucking know that.

And I fucking don't know what to do with it.

I stay silent, gathering my thoughts. I lay back on the bed. 'Tell her I'll be out in a minute, please.'

'*Ne (Yes)*,' he says, before leaving my space.

My eyes stay glued to the white ceiling, projecting as a film all my memories of us, trying to get me to decide, until a knock pounds on my door.

'Elijah?' a feminine voice sounds through the wood.

'Come in.' I move my eyes in the door's direction.

'Is everything okay? It's been fifteen minutes since Moon Hee left your room.' Her low tone and the way she's playing with her fingers give me the impression she's being cautious.

Why would she be cautious?

'I didn't even notice the time go by.' I sit up on the bed and pat the place next to mine. 'Come here.'

She walks slowly, still playing with her fingers. Is she nervous or being cautious? I can't tell. Either way, why?

'Why do I feel like you're walking around eggshells with me? Is something wrong?' I ask, grabbing her hand while staring at her chocolate-brown eyes.

'No, but you acted so…roughly when you entered the house and didn't even say a word to me. I'm afraid you are mad at me, and I don't know why.' She looks down at our interlocked fingers.

With my other hand, I hold two fingers under her chin and raise her head so her eyes meet mine. 'I could never be mad at you.'

The corners of her mouth lift and her lower lip gets pulled between her teeth. My thumb goes over it to push it down, so it can slowly enter her mouth. The wet warmth of her tongue makes me inhale, and it's enough to get me pulsating between my legs.

She sucks on it and my other hand moves to her belly, slowly sliding down inside her pants. I find her undies and pull the hem up, making her gasp. My finger leaves her mouth and I join my lips to hers.

My hand resumes its trace, now inside her undies.

'You're already wet?' I breathe inside her mouth.

She shyly mumbles, 'We haven't done it in a while.'

Smirking, my tongue's tip slides against her lip. Her eyes

close as soon as my finger finds her clit and I gently rub on it.

Lilah stays sitting on the edge of the bed and I move to the floor, placing myself between her legs. I pull her bottoms down, leaving her exposed to me, my mouth salivating for her taste.

My tongue traces her up and down, making her moan.

'Shit, Moon Hee is home,' she says, slapping her hand to her mouth.

'So, you know what that means…you can't make any noise, otherwise I'll have to stop…and you won't want me to stop.'

I spot her throat moving as if she's swallowed. With her nod, I place my tongue on her, licking first to wet her enough so my mouth can suck on it while my fingers slide inside of her. One, two, three fingers, and she rolls her head back, hands on her side gripping the sheets.

My other hand lifts her shirt, cupping her breasts; I love the way they fill my hand perfectly, not too large, not too small. I feel her nipple grow so I play with it, making it harder, the way I am for her.

I pump my fingers faster as my tongue flickers her at the exact pace I've learned she likes. I've been studying her face to know the exact pace and pressure; a bit too much, and she grimaces, too little, and she's too serious.

Her chest rises and lowers faster, and the sound of her breathing becomes more prominent. Her hands grip harder, rumpling the sheets.

There's something about watching how a woman reacts to a simple flicker of the tongue that drives me crazy, and watching Delilah on the brink of an orgasm requires all my self-control to not take her right here, right now, instead of letting her finish.

Her chest pauses, her grip tightening still, and she goes silent, mouth slightly open, her eyes closed. I slow down the moment she exhales, diminishing my pace not to stop too suddenly, letting her feel pleasure until her breath catches up.

'Fuck,' she curses under her breath.

'I told you, you wouldn't want me to stop.' The corner of my mouth lifts as I move up to meet her lips. 'You taste delicious.' I give her a taste of herself.

She grabs my pants and unbuttons them. I smile at the gesture.

That's my girl.

If there is one thing I haven't doubted for one second it's how compatible we are in bed. We never leave unsatisfied, we only stop until we are both exhausted, and we don't wear out easily.

Pants and briefs on the floor, her hand gripping me as her tongue now teases me. My hand fists her hair into a ponytail, so she can work better.

It's my turn to close my eyes as I feel the wet and soft trace on my cock, making it fluster with the sauna inside her mouth. The creases on her palate rub against me as she swallows me up to the back of her throat. I hear her gasping—fuck, I love that sound—allowing me to feel the brief pre-cum leave my body.

She uses her tongue while her lips close on me, faster as she knows I like. The hand that's gripping her hair pushes her closer to me, making her gasp once more; my butt cheeks contract as I pump her mouth full.

I take myself from her mouth and lead her to stand up and kiss me.

'You strangely taste good as well,' she says.

'Not strangely. I know what to eat to make it taste better.' I wink.

She chuckles and sits back down on the bed. 'I want to continue, truly, but I'm getting uncomfortable with the thought of Moon Hee knowing what we are doing here. We've been gone for a while.'

'He's probably in his room or distracted.' I clench my jaw at the thought of her thinking about him.

Please don't tell me I'm the jealous type. I fucking hate the jealous type. It's too stressful.

'Still...' she mutters, looking down.

Fuck. 'Do you want me to go check?' I ask.

Her head lifts, nodding, eyes wide open.

I put on my briefs—deep down wanting him to know that she just had me in her mouth—and peek into the living room on my way to the kitchen, pretending to go grab a glass of water.

'Hey,' I say, spotting Moon Hee reading a book on the sofa. He's in this wave of reading self-improvement books that I don't understand.

He looks up in my direction and says back, 'Hey,' looking down at my almost non-existent outfit. The grip on his book tightens, and I smile inwards.

Fuck, I'm terrible. It actually gave me joy to see my best friend in pain. *What's wrong with me?*

No, this can't be. I need to fix this. I walk towards him and sit on the sofa.

'I'm sorry,' I say. 'I shouldn't try to rub it in your face.'

He turns his face to me and sighs. '*Ottokeyo?*'

'How? How will we work it out? No idea,' I confess.

He laughs. This motherfucker actually laughs. 'Who would've guessed it?'

'That we like the same person?' I ask, and he nods.

'I don't think she *like* likes me though,' I say, looking down at my hands.

'She's had a crush on you since you met. Why do you say that?' Moon Hee questions.

'We might do intimate things, but we're not intimate. Anytime she's down, it's not in me she confides, it's you, and that's what's stinging me.'

He stays silent on the topic. I know he agrees. We might not know who she likes, but my relationship with her is purely physical.

'I never really imagined you in love with someone,' he says.

'Nobody ever said in love, mate, don't get ahead of yourself.'

I lift my hands in defence, and he chuckles once more.

This is better, this is the ease between us. That's how I want us, laughing at our downfalls.

'Fine, I never imagined you with genuine feelings towards someone. Is that better?' He stares with his lifted eyebrows.

I smile. 'I know you guys think I'm always cool, that I don't get hurt and I don't take anything seriously. But I do have feelings. I just know better than to show them.'

He nods his head, unsure of what to say. This is why I hide my feelings, I hate the uncomfortableness that not knowing how to comfort someone brings.

That's why I also don't know how to comfort someone because I don't remember ever being comforted.

My parents, even not being part of The London Elite, did everything by their rules to fit in as much as possible. They did everything with The Elite, went everywhere with them, and so did I when I was younger.

I remember overhearing my parents talking one day about how the only reason they couldn't make the name list was because they weren't born in London; so for Park Jae Seop and Park So Min, me being born here was their golden ticket to have a member of the family have their name engraved in the gold plate they keep at the entrance of their mansion hall. A plate that contains all the names of everyone that ever took part in The London Elite, all except my parents. My name is there, so is Delilah's, and like her, the moment I renounced the title was the moment my parents cut me off.

Now all I hear about them is through Moon Hee's mum. She and my mum are friends, within the possibilities between house mistress and house maid.

All my good memories with them are in Korea. Whenever we visited, I begged for us to stay because there they were my parents. Here they are two people too involved in the need to belong in a society that they forgot who already belonged to them.

That's another thing I like about Delilah. She might not know when I'm down, but she always knows the moments I need a lift of mood.

I get up and walk back to my room, knocking on the door before entering.

'Wait!' she screams as I enter the space, laughing.

The woman who has her hands and arms covering her parts blows out air at my sight and throws me a pillow.

'Bloody hell, Elijah. I thought you were Moon Hee. You scared the shit out of me!' she says. 'Why would you knock?'

'To have this exact reaction.' I needed a laugh. My last thought had been too depressing.

'You devil,' she says, lips tight.

'Oh, I might not be the devil, but I'll have you committing sins,' I tease, hovering on top of her on the mattress.

'I see someone's ready to continue.' Lilah licks her lower lip as her hand slides through my briefs.

'And I'm not the only one.' I bring my lips to hers, kissing her passionately, teasing with my tongue from time to time, making sure she's ready to move on. I lower my kisses and trail them around her neck, nibbling on her ear, receiving a giggle from her.

It's too sensitive of a spot for her, noted.

Bringing my mouth down to her breasts, I suck on one as my hand caresses the other.

It's for this exact reason I train single-arm push-ups, so I can hold myself up in these positions.

She lowers my briefs and grabs a handful; my cock always grows in her hand.

Her hand guides me to the middle of her legs, where she stops to tease herself with me. I like a woman who knows what she wants.

I take her lead and enter her pussy. The moan that leaves her is enough to know I need to cover her mouth with my hand.

As I move faster, I feel her warm breath against my palm, her moans trying to escape. I really hope Moon Hee either put on headphones or went on a walk because I've been containing myself too much and I'm about to lose all self-control.

The hand over her mouth moves to her neck as the other keeps me stable. I pound faster; her moans no longer contained, her back arching and legs wrapped around me. She wants me as close as possible and I'm already reaching deep inside her.

This bed, unfortunately, has had better days and I've treated it too roughly already, so there's only so much it can handle before it creaks.

My sweat drips down on her as I'm exerting all my strength. She signals me to switch positions, so I can rest for a while.

Going for one of my favourite positions, she rocks on top of me as I eye trace her curves. A woman's body, to me, is the purest and most enticing form of art.

I take her all in, every inch of her, and decal it into my memory, so if one day we're not together anymore, at least I'll have her embedded in my mind.

열아홉
'yeolahob'

Daldust hasn't written in a while, and sure, I said I was going to take longer to respond. Not hearing from him makes me realise how big of a part in my life he's become.

Someone I can go to forget about my day, because he doesn't know how it went.

'Hi Becca,' I say, walking into *Greener's*.

It's been a while since I visited. My life went from zero to hundred super fast over the past month and half, and unfortunately, the ones who have been there longer got left behind.

'Hi stranger,' she says. Her copper locks bounce in a ponytail as she moves around the counter to meet me.

'I'm sorry, I know I haven't been around much.'

'Is everything okay?' she asks.

I smile, avoiding actual words as a response before changing subjects. 'Are you still interested in a collaboration? It's been almost a month since we last spoke of it.'

'Girl, of course. I already have my menu done. You just need to hand me yours.'

'I'm close to finishing it. I just wanted to tell you an idea. Since December is coming up, I was thinking we could do a Christmas-themed collaboration. I've been working on new recipes for my bakery that I could use for this as well.'

'I love that!' Rebecca turns around and calls to the kitchen. 'Jeremiah, come here!'

Her twin comes out, wiping his hands on the black apron around his waist.

'What?' he asks right before looking up at us. 'Oh...Hi Lilah! It's been a while.'

'It has.' I chuckle. I'm glad to see him more at ease with me, stuttering less.

I understand him. I was his Elijah and although he didn't get a chance like I did, a crush is still a crush.

'Lilah had the brilliant idea for us to have a Christmas-themed collaboration. Do you think we can make our dishes more jolly?' his sister questions him.

'Yeah, we can make that happen. I have some ideas. I just need to make sure they work.'

'Awesome!' I say. 'I'll bring you my menu after I close the shop, and you can show me yours whenever you're ready.'

'Jer, do you think you can take this on? I have some other business I need to attend this week, so I won't have any time available.' Becca turns to her brother, placing her hands on his shoulders.

He looks at me for a quick second before inhaling. 'I can handle it.'

The corners of my lips lift after hearing those words, a weight that went by unnoticed lifting off my heart. It pained me to see him get hurt, so I'm selfishly happy he's healing.

My steps as I return to the bakery come lighter, one less burden trapped in me. Even the weather seems to have warmed up as people take off their winter scarves.

One thing that sets this street apart from every other road in London is how the sun illuminates it with a brighter glow. It could be the people who emit that certain aura, but the days appear crisper and the air carries a purer scent.

Today I change the ambient sound in the bakery from a

popular radio station to a jazz tune. I'm feeling inspired, and jazz has a way of making me believe I'm in a film—in this case, one where once colourful leaves drifted in the wind and now the trees lay bare. Where people have begun putting fairy lights on their windows and green pine trees stacked with dazzling ornaments welcome the holiday season approaching us.

The shop's movement is not substantial on a Tuesday, so it's a day I'm more productive in my baking, and as I prepare some treats for tomorrow, the music fills my soul. I take the chance to go to the small storage compartment I have in the kitchen for decorations and grab last year's Christmas box.

One particular thought pops into my mind as I hang the lights around the windows and decorate the small tree I place on the counter. Should I call the number on the card? What will I find if I do? Do I want to remember?

If I deleted the memory from my mind, it must have been for a reason. Should I betray my old self?

I am working on my issues without knowing the past. I know I can keep doing that.

Would it speed up the process? Yes. Is it worth it? I don't know.

'Lilah!' Elisa greets me as she enters the bakery. 'We're going shopping today.'

'Shopping?'

She nears the counter and the bell on top of the door rings, deviating my attention from my best friend.

Two young men wearing all black smile as they walk in.

'You're all hanging out today?' I ask.

'We were able to close the parlour earlier and met Elisa on the way here,' Elijah says.

'Yes, we're all going to shop for my birthday weekend!' Elisa claps.

'I don't need to buy anything...' I say.

'Yeah, you do. At least a dress for the party and a few bikinis.'

'Bikinis? But it's winter.' I don't understand how she thinks we'll be wearing something less than warm clothes.

'But it has an interior jacuzzi and a warmed pool. So, bikinis, yes.' She crosses her arms and tilts her head. My roommate wants to let me know it's not up for debate.

I gesture at her to come closer and whisper, 'But I don't feel comfortable. I'm fat.'

'You are not fat!' she says, missing the point of why I whispered only to her. 'You have skin, bones, and yes, fat, but that's being human. We need it to survive. No matter how little some may have, they still do. Everyone does. But you also have a kind heart. You are compassionate and gentle, funny and a wonderful friend. That's who you are. So if you ever want to objectify yourself, say you are beautiful, because you are. Inside and out.'

'But I used to be a lot skinnier.'

'Yeah, when you were unhealthy. Now you are healthy, so of course you have more meat on your bones. It's normal. And yes, you can get even healthier by working out and toning your muscles to add something more to the mix, but trust me, you are and look a lot better than you did before.'

Maybe, but it's hard to believe it when all your life your mother has made sure you never went up to a certain number on the scale.

I stare at her as she turns around. 'Elijah, help me out. You've seen her before and you know well how she looks now. Isn't she a lot better than before?'

'I don't remember very well how she was before, but I can say that now, Lilah, you are my kind of perfect.' He smirks and swiftly lifts his eyebrows at me.

'Of course, it's not just about how you look, but also how you feel. How do you feel?' Moon Hee, who has been nothing but a spectator, joins the conversation.

My eyes turn to him and I say, 'Better, I feel better than I did. Free as well.'

Moon Hee gives me a soft reassuring smile, reminding me to breathe.

'Then it's settled. We're shopping when you close,' Elisa says.

'Now, it's two coffees and an apple cinnamon tea, please.' Elijah orders.

'Add a few slices of cake, too.' Elisa smiles.

I get their order and as they eat I clean the shop, preparing to close and go on a shopping adventure when I haven't stepped a foot in the centre for a few years.

When we enter the shopping centre, I stop to take in the space. Elisa and Elijah keep walking, but I see a silhouette in my peripheral vision.

'Is everything okay?' Moonie asks.

I nod. 'I'm just remembering to breathe.'

He glances around. 'Are there too many people for you?'

'The last time I entered this facility, yes, there were too many. I couldn't walk past this exact spot before crashing onto the floor. But not today. Today I can do it. I have you to give me strength. As long as I remember to breathe.'

'I'm proud of you,' he says, looking into my eyes.

Elijah interrupts our locked eyes. 'Lilah! Moon Hee! Are you coming or what?'

'We're coming,' the man beside me says.

We join them again, and Elijah slows down to walk by my side.

'Can we talk later?' he asks me.

My head turns to him. 'Sure.'

Halfway through the shopping centre we split between ladies and gentlemen.

'Now let's go choose a jaw-dropping dress for you, my dear friend,' Elisa says.

'Your dress is the one that should be jaw dropping. Not mine.'

'We can both put those jaws on the floor.' She winks entering a store.

I walk into my bedroom and lay back on the bed, shopping bags still in hand.

Not for another three years. I don't need to go shopping for another three years.

We're going on a weekend getaway, yet Elisa bought clothes for a few months and got me way more than I needed.

I exhale and get myself back up again, ready to tackle the organising task before my whole body gives up.

Walking around shopping and tidying up the clothes after is sure to count as a workout. I think I even broke a sweat.

Sounds of people talking travel across the house and into my room, but I've drained my energy for the day. Even when a brief sound comes from my phone, I unsuccessfully try to lift my hand from the pillow my head rests on.

In between reality and dreamland, the sound of a knock on my door is too faint for my brain to process it well, not long after giving itself into the dream world.

Another morning, another day getting up, dressing in something comfortable but presentable for work. Walking to the loo and doing my routine. Getting breakfast and grabbing my keys and purse. Another day, putting on my shoes and walking out the door for work.

Six days a week—five sometimes—the same thing.

Most weeks, this doesn't bother me. I love what I do and I love waking up to do it. But others, the will to leave my bed is so weak it makes me forget the reason I love it so much.

It's only a day, Lilah. It's not every day, just one day.

It's interesting how time on the clock seems to go by slower when you're staring at it. Don't be shy, time, you love to sprint when I'm enjoying the day.

I've been doing this for so long my body runs on automatic when my ability to think and pay attention to reality is lacking. I fill in orders, take money, give money, give plates and cups, take plates and cups.

'Lilah?' the customer says as I hand him his cups of coffee to go.

I smile the smile I've ingrained into my face from the moment I walk into the bakery until the moment I step out. Although that last step has failed sometimes as I get home and smile at myself in the mirror; it's a hard switch to turn off.

'Lilah?' he repeats. My eyes focus on him, a face too familiar to ignore.

'Oh my god, I'm sorry,' I say. 'My mind is elsewhere today.'

'Yeah, I can tell. Is everything okay?' Moon Hee is someone I can always count on to ask me how I'm doing.

'Yes, and no.' And the one who has the ability to pluck the truth out of me every time.

He looks behind him at the two people in line. 'It's almost lunchtime for you, right?'

I nod.

'I'll be outside waiting.' He points to the table on the other side of the window near me and leaves.

When the smaller pointer on the clock stops at one and the bigger one hits twelve, I walk up to the entrance and hang the small rectangular wooden sign saying *I'll be right back,* on the door.

Lately I'm attempting to break bad eating habits, so I've been making my lunches. I grab my lunch container and join my friend outside.

'Hey,' he says.

'Hey.'

'It's nice today. Something I learned to do when I moved here was to enjoy every sunny day, because those don't come that often. In Busan it doesn't rain as much.'

'That's England. This week has been good. It doesn't seem like a November day at all.' I open my container and take out half of my sandwich inside. 'Have you eaten?'

'Yeah. Today I ate earlier. My schedule is light. Now I'm making time until my 2 p.m. appointment.' His eyes stare deep into mind. 'So...What's been bothering you?'

'How do you know something has been bothering me?' I ask, taking a bite of my tofu and mushroom sandwich.

'You're making your 'something is bothering me' face.'

I huff out a chuckle, attempting to smile but my face refuses to move. 'And what face might that be?'

Moon Hee makes a face, which I assume is supposed to resemble mine. 'You know, downcast eyes, drooping eyelids, lowered lip corners...the constant sighing and dropped shoulders. And most important, the fake smile.'

'It's that obvious, huh?'

'Just for me.' He winks, making my lowered lip corners rise for a few seconds.

'What's bothering me...' I sigh, 'is the question whether to meddle with the past or not.'

'The past is usually better left behind, but I know how hard some things can be to leave.' His head turns to the street, eyes lifted to the big white cloud—shaped like a jumping rabbit—in the sky.

There's so many more layers to him than he lets out. Even if I don't know what they are, I can see they exist.

I control the urge to ask what's hard for him to leave in the past and continue our talk. 'Yeah, but this one has the power to make or break my present and future.'

'It only has the power you allow it to have. The only way the past matters is if you give it importance in the present.' His black moon eyes turn back to me.

I decide to tell him what's going on. My bones feel he's trustworthy. 'Long story short, my therapist thinks my panic attacks and anxiety come from a traumatic event that happened five years ago, that I have no memory of. My brain locked it away to protect me, but my body remembers and it's sending signals every time it feels under attack.'

'Five years ago...' He mutters without saying another word.

'Yes, so now I have the choice to remember or not.'

His eyebrows furrow as he looks down.

'If I remember, I can work out the trauma easier, because I'll know the root of the problem. But remembering also means reliving it.' The light breeze blows on his hair as I speak.

Moon Hee glances up at me. 'I can see the dilemma. It's definitely a hard choice to make and whatever you choose, I'm here to support you.'

'Some say that ignorance is bliss, and that's true sometimes. But this ignorance is driving me insane. I have a memory I can't remember. Not just any memory, a crucial one. One that shaped me into who I am now.'

'It seems like you've made your choice.' The soft touch of Moonie's hand on mine sends me the reassurance I've been looking for.

20
스물
'seumul'

I've set up an appointment with Ms Julie's friend for her next free date, right after Christmas. I don't want to ruin Elisa's weekend, so I've decided to leave any issue at home during these few days.

No moping around unsolved problems. No moping around anything. This is a happy weekend.

'I'm so excited for today! And tomorrow! And the next day! Ah! This weekend is going to be *the* best!' My roommate beams, smiling from ear to ear.

For the last week, I've focused on work to avoid getting cold feet on my choice. And my collaboration with *Greener's* is on the move, ready for the holiday season.

'I couldn't tell.' I chuckle.

'Don't forget to take the dress and those swimsuits. They are a bit too covered up for me, but you do look amazing in them.' Elisa is busy sitting on her luggage as I attempt to close it for the fifth time.

'They're already packed. But Elisa, I think you're going to have to leave something behind.'

'Nonsense! Wait here.'

The woman storms out of the room, and the front door opens a second later. I sit on her bed waiting for whatever she went to do.

'Lisa, the fuck! Where's the fire?' the man she dragged all

the way to her room asks.

'Here.' She points at the luggage. 'Sit on top. You're heavier than me.'

His face turns to her in disbelief. 'What?'

'Sit!'

Elijah cautiously hops on the luggage, glancing at me in a cry for help, and I pat on his shoulder as a sign of understanding. My hand holds the zip once more and, at the sixth attempt, there's actual progress.

'Scoot,' Elisa tells Elijah and sits next to him on top of the luggage.

I glance at the big blue plastic luggage filled with clothes and shoes, mixed with makeup and other essentials, top to bottom.

While I push the overflow inside and pull on the black zip, I can only think, 'You've had better days, friend.'

'Finally!' I fall with my back to the bed. 'Seven is a lucky number indeed.'

'Seven? It took you seven tries to close this?' Elijah's eyes widen as he gets off the hard blue plastic. 'I'm taking a backpack.'

'That's Elisa for you.' I huff out a chuckle.

'I'm sorry if I need at least two outfits for each day and more choices, in case I'm not in the mood for the previously planned ones.' She struggles to carry the luggage down the bed and Elijah steps in to help her.

While my best friend rolls it into the hallway, Elijah sits next to me. 'Hey.'

His smile sends a few electric charges down my body. With everything in my head, I haven't been with him for a while.

'Hey,' I say, supporting myself with my elbows to lift my back a bit.

'We ended up not talking. I knocked on your door that day, but I guess you were already asleep.'

Shit.

'I'm so sorry! I totally forgot!' The palm of my hand flies to my forehead. 'I was so exhausted after shopping, it completely slipped my mind.'

'It's okay. But you know what?' he asks.

'What?'

He reaches down to my ear, his warm breath hardening my nipples. 'I've missed you.'

I bite my lower lip at the sight of his smirk. I've missed him too.

I don't think our relationship will ever evolve from more than friends with benefits, but I'm fine with it.

He fucks too good.

'I hear the mattresses are unbelievable where we're going.'

'Oh, we're going to have so much fun ruining them,' he teases.

The heat burns my face as I watch him lower himself on me.

'Hey!' Elisa says, closing in on us. 'Not in my room. Go to Lilah's.'

Elijah's face turns to her slowly, with his famous smirk. 'Gladly.'

'Elijah!' I swap my hand at his arm, sitting straight on the bed.

'What? You heard her. Let's go.' He grabs my hand and walks towards my room.

I'm not sure if the shock I'm feeling inside is truly displayed outside, because he pushes me against my door and lowers his head, his lips getting close to mine.

'I'm joking.' His breath hits the sensitive skin of my mouth.

I gasp, reminding my body how to breathe again.

'You should see your face. I can hear your heartbeat all the way from here,' the man with dark brown eyes staring at me plays.

My hand pushes on his left shoulder. 'What am I going to do with you?'

'Oh, a few ideas cross my mind.'

'Elijah Park!'

'I like it when you say my name,' he says, his tongue wetting his lips afterwards.

His mouth closes in on mine, this time leaving no space behind, allowing my lips to taste the softness of his. Elijah's hand travels down my back, grabbing my ass, while his other holds my neck.

I break our kiss and watch his eyes slowly opening. 'We need to leave soon.'

'I know.' He nods. 'I just missed your lips.'

'I think a few more minutes wouldn't hurt anyone,' I say, locking my mouth with his once more.

'Lovebirds, it's time to go.' Elisa knocks on the door, making Elijah grunt.

'We'll continue this later.' He smirks, grabbing the doorknob to leave.

I slide to the side so he can open it and then grab my luggage. Moon Hee is standing in the middle of the living room, watching my door.

I smile at his sight, and he walks near me. 'Are you better?'

'I am. Thank you.'

'I'm glad.' His words fade as his presence next to me moves further away.

I wonder if he's okay. Ever since that first day when he caught me in his flat after my night with Elijah, I've had this gnawing feeling in the pit of my stomach that something is off whenever he watches us together. I can't explain it. It's something I catch when I look into his eyes.

Maybe my mind is playing tricks on me. Maybe I'm the one who's being delusional, but I can't shake the discomfort I feel every time I'm with Elijah and Moon Hee is around.

'Earth to Lilah,' Elisa says, staring back at me from the other side of the exit door, no one else inside the flat.

'Sorry, yes, I'm going!'

'Elisa, this is such a cute house!' I say as we stand in front of the most adorable cottage with a view of the Guildford Castle.

'Only the best for the best.' My roommate smiles. 'There's

three rooms: mine and Sofía's, who's joining us later today, Lilah's, and the boys. Two are upstairs and one down. Now we just need to choose.'

'I'm okay with either, but maybe it's better for you and Sofía to stay downstairs. This way you have more privacy,' I suggest, peeking inside the house through the window.

'Who says they're the only ones who'll need privacy?' Elijah asks.

'You heard her, she said: a room for me and one for you and Moon Hee. There's no Lilah and Elijah room, so you're stuck with your roommate.'

'Oh, that's how we're playing?' He smirks, wrapping his arm around me.

'Let's get in and we'll decide inside. It's cold out here,' Elisa says.

From the outside, the house appears fairly small, but when you open the door, you see how vast it actually is. The stone walls give it a rustic side, while the brand new electronics show its modernity.

As we walk into an open space, organised to be the living room with a four seat sofa and two armchairs, one on each side. In the back you see the kitchen and a door to the extensive garden, where the pool's facility is. I've always wanted to have a warm pool.

On my left, there're the stairs to the second floor and a half-opened door leading to the small pink loo. We leave our luggage by the bottom of the stairs as we decide on the room assortment.

'How are we going to settle this, then?' Elisa asks.

'*Gawibawibo?*' Moon Hee suggests.

I chuckle. 'You want to play rock, paper, scissors?'

'That's indeed how we settle a lot of discussions,' Elijah says.

'Gaibabo...what?' My roommate looks at us, frowning.

'Gawi...bawi...bo, that's what Koreans call rock, paper, scissors,' I say.

'Sure, let's do it then.' Elisa chuckles.

'Wait, so who wins chooses the room first? Is that it?' I ask, and Moonie nods.

'Ready?' Moon Hee asks. '*Gawibawibo.*'

'We have all of them, so again,' Elijah says.

'It's a tie,' my flatmate says, looking at mine and her scissors and the guy's rocks.

'No, it's not. They're going to be in the same room and both chose rock, so they win.'

'Yes!' Elijah and Moon Hee high-five.

They look into the room downstairs first and then walk upstairs to check on the others. After a few minutes they come near us again.

'We're taking the left one upstairs. Has the biggest bed.' The man with tattoo sleeves picks up his backpack and hands his roommate his.

'It's up to us now,' Elisa says.

'Let's do like I suggested, you and Sofía stay with the one down here.'

My best friend accepts, and I pick up my luggage to walk upstairs.

At the top of the stairs I scream down, 'Be glad you stayed in that room, Elisa. I don't think you'd be able to bring that luggage up the stairs,' and she laughs.

I catch the guys' voices speaking, but can't figure out what they're saying. I walk to my bedroom's door and the moment I open it, their voices stop and the door on the left opens abruptly.

'Lilah, can we talk today?' Elijah asks.

'Sure, let me just organise the room and then we can do it.'

He gives me a small smile and enters the room once more. I wonder what he wants to talk about. He's been waiting a while for it now.

My room is mid-sized with a bed in the middle, facing the big window on the wall and turned to the left side when you enter the door. There's a big wooden wardrobe on the wall staring at me and a vanity table next to me.

The decor is simple: light grey stone walls, baby blue bedding and navy curtains that match the wardrobe.

I grab my phone and go to my chat with Moon Hee to play the last song he sent me.

The day we went shopping, when I was face down on my pillow exhausted, the message I heard and couldn't reach for was his. I only saw it the next night, after our talk in my bakery, and as if he knew I would need it, I played it on repeat with the one he'd sent me before until I went to sleep.

OK Not To Be OK by Demi Lovato and Marshmello sounds as I open my travel-sized luggage, unpack my essentials onto the vanity, and hang the dress on the wardrobe.

The upbeat track with heartfelt lyrics is enough to make my worries shrink and uplift my mood.

A knock sounds on my door. 'Come in!'

I turn to look at the entrance of the bedroom, where I see Moon He peeking with his head in the small opening he made between the door and its frame.

'I see you are enjoying the songs I sent you,' Moon Hee says.

'You seem to know which ones to send.' I place the last pair of shoes on the bottom of the wardrobe and sit on the bed, tapping for him to sit beside me.

'I just wanted to check in, nothing more.' His eyes are glued to the floor.

'Just because I'm listening to the songs doesn't mean I'm down, but they help me stay positive.'

His head lifts, and he stares at me. For a few seconds his gaze seems to stop at my mouth, so I swiftly shake off my lips with my fingers, afraid there's something there, making him look away to the wall.

'My mum sends me songs whenever she finds one she thinks

I'll like or whenever she doesn't see me smile around the house,' he says.

'She seems like a good mum. May I ask what happened to your father? You said it's just you and your mum here in London. Is he back in Korea?'

'He's everywhere and nowhere now.' He sighs, looking out the window.

My eyes widen at his words. 'I'm so sorry. I had no idea.'

'How could you?' His head turns back to face me and he smiles. 'It's been almost a decade since he died. Yes, it was hard at first—still is sometimes—but we've learned to live without him.'

My hand reaches for his. 'I rarely talk with my parents, and never had a relationship with them, so I don't know how I would feel if something happened to them. They're still my parents, but if you felt about your father the way you do for your mum...I can't imagine the pain.'

'Thank you,' he says, giving my hand a squeeze. 'Now onto happier subjects, what are we going to eat? I'm starving.'

'That's a question for the hostess, not me.'

'I'll go ask her then. Are you coming down too?' he asks, standing up and releasing my hand.

'Soon.'

The moment he closes the door, my back hits the mattress.

There are moments when I lock eyes with Moon Hee that I can't help but wonder about the depth of my affection for him. He's not just any friend; he's a truly remarkable one, someone I hold dear to my heart. But at times my breath comes out short when I see him, and a need to hold him close and hug him engulfs me, like I've been doing it all my life even though I never have.

He's a friend. Nothing else, just a friend.

Now I step away from my strange thoughts. *It's not like he even has another type of feelings for you, Delilah.*

Elijah. He wanted to talk to me.

I get up and knock on their door. Nothing sounds on the other side, so I knock again.

'Elijah, are you there?'

No answer. He's probably downstairs with the rest of them.

I walk downstairs where they already hold drinks in hand.

'No dinner first?' I ask.

'I ordered pizza for everyone. It's on its way,' my flatmate says.

'Is Sofía on her way too?'

'She'll be arriving in about two hours.'

Elijah is sitting on the sofa, looking at the liquid inside his glass. I sit next to him and peek at the drink. 'Is it not good?'

'Uh?' His face turns in my direction.

'Is the drink not good? You're staring at it so intensely.'

'Oh, I was thinking...' he says, looking back down.

'Didn't you want to talk to me?'

'Yeah, I just needed some liquid courage.' He chuckles, raising his glass at me. 'But, you know what...I think we should first continue what we started earlier today, then we can talk.'

His tongue wets his bottom lip so I take his drink from his hand and pour it down my throat. His eyebrows frown, so I say, 'Liquid courage, right?'

The left corner of his mouth rises and one of his hands moves to the back of my head, leading me closer to him. His lips touch mine and we get sucked into each other. In between kisses, I briefly open my eyes and see Moon Hee talking with Elisa in the back of the room. His head turns to us and our eyes lock for a split second before I close mine again.

Shit. No.

Be present, Lilah.

'Let's go upstairs,' I whisper in Elijah's ear and he nods, grabbing my hand and taking me to my room.

When the door behind me closes, I push him onto the bed.

'Lilah!' His eyes widen with a smile plastered across his face.

I climb on top of him and take his shirt off before our lips connect again. My hands trace his tattoos all over his arms and torso.

His hands lift my shirt and unclasp my bra. His right hand grabs my breast and he retracts his mouth from mine to suck my nipple.

'Wait,' I say, getting up from his lap.

I walk to the light switch to dim the lights and then take my phone out of my jeans back pocket to play my sexy-time playlist.

'It's just so they don't hear us.'

He gets up and walks up to me, his hands tracing my bare skin before removing the rest of my shirt off and unbuttoning my bottoms.

'You're so fucking hot,' he says with a low and husky voice.

My arms wrap around his neck and he turns our roles around, now pushing me onto the bed. I gasp from the surprise, and a devilish gaze takes over his eyes.

He takes off his pants and briefs and the rest of my clothes, hovering on top of me with one hand playing between my legs.

Today I'm not much in the mood for foreplay. I want to feel him inside of me.

I want him to help me forget all my doubts.

I slide my fingers through my wet tongue and wrap them around his cock, preparing it to enter me.

My eyes shut as he opens me up, sliding himself all the way inside me.

'You're not playing today, I see,' he says.

I smile, and as I open my eyes to respond to him, my vision tricks me, for the face I see is not his.

Fuck!

I shut my eyes closed, hoping when I open them again I see the man I'm actually with. I sigh, seeing Elijah's gaze on me.

'Yes, I missed you too much,' I say.

Why am I thinking so much about Moon Hee today?

My nails dig into Elijah's back as he rocks faster against me. My moans are buffered by the loud music.

After a few minutes, being immersed in the intense ecstasy the tattooed man is providing me, our naked bodies sweaty and sticking to each other, my mind calms down as I cannot think about anything else but the euphoria I'm reaching.

Calming our breathing, we lay side by side on the bed, mine gradually slowing until his words make my heartbeat rise again.

'I like you, Lilah,' Elijah says, watching the ceiling.

I sense all control leave my body as my jaw drops and I'm glad he's not looking at me.

Breathe, Lilah, breathe.

'What? Are you sure it's not just an attraction? I mean, we don't have that much in common...'

'It's more than that, and I can't remember the last time I felt this. It's true we might not have much in common, but oh, how I love to hear you talk about the things you care for.' He grabs my hand while staring into my soul. 'In that moment, there's no difference in what each of us like. Your interests become mine and I could hear you discuss them eternally.'

'Elijah...'

The man sits up on the bed and as he tries to hide it, I capture the sadness his eyes hold before they hit the sheets. 'It's okay, Lilah, really. I know you don't like me that way. I've seen how you look at someone you care about, and it's not the same as when our eyes meet.'

'I do care about you—'

'Not like that, not like you care for him. He's the one you confide in. I know our chemistry is through the roof and trust me, I don't want it to end. I've come to terms with only having you that way, but I wanted to tell you how I really feel and how much you mean to me.'

I'm speechless. I had a crush on him. *Me.* And now he likes me?

'Wait. Who's he? Who's the person you're talking about?'

'I thought it would be obvious.' He chuckles. 'Moon Hee.'

'Moon Hee?' My eyes widen and I sit up straight on the bed. 'No! We're just friends!'

'I still remember the first time we met,' he says, ignoring everything I just told him. 'You were nothing like you are now. You were extremely shy, you couldn't even finish a word to me. I found it adorable. You can even ask Elisa and she'll tell you how I would ask about you every time I went to your house, sad you never wanted to hang out with us. Look at you now.'

His gaze is back on mine, smiling even. Elijah has become so good at hiding his emotions; his face can make you believe he's feeling the opposite of his true feelings if you don't know him well.

But I do. My arms reach around him, holding him tight, letting him know I'm here for him. Even if it's not in the same way he wishes, even if it's nothing more than friends, I'll always be here to support him, to comfort him.

He releases our hug and joins his lips to mine. I close my eyes, allowing myself to be involved in the moment, a moment that doesn't last long after I taste something salty between our lips.

My eyes open and I watch Elijah's eyes closed as a single tear runs down his face. This is my first time seeing this man cry, and that thought alone is enough to fill my waterline.

스물하나

'seumulhana'

Elijah…Moon Hee…I really needed Daldust's amazing advice right now. But the downside to having a pen pal is they are not available at the moment you need. Unless you plan your breakdowns with two to three days in mind for the mail delivery.

Elisa. That's it!

I leave my room and walk to the edge of the stairs.

'Elisa! Can you come here?'

It's been a few minutes since a heartbroken Elijah left my room, and I'm freaking out.

'On my way,' my friend says, coming to the rescue. 'What's up?' she asks, standing next to me.

I grab her hand and pull her to my room, closing the door behind us so no one hears.

'I'm freaking out,' I say, walking in circles in my room.

'Lilah, breathe. Let's sit, count to ten backwards and then tell me what's going on.' She puts her hands on my shoulders and sits me down on the bed.

Ten, nine, eight, seven, six, five, four, three, two, one…

'Elijah told me he likes me,' I confess.

Her eyes widen, and she exhales. 'It's about time.'

'About time? It's not time. There was no right time to tell me that. What am I supposed to do with that information?'

'Do you like him?' Elisa asks.

I look down at my trembling leg. 'Not the way he likes me. But he just left with such a sad face. I hate this! I hated breaking Jeremiah's heart, and that was a dead-end crush. With Elijah...I don't want this to affect our friendship.'

'It might be weird at first, but he'll heal. It was wise to address it now instead of waiting for stronger feelings. But I do have to ask, is there a specific reason you don't even consider him boyfriend material?'

'We just don't have that much in common,' I say, looking at the ceiling.

'Lilah, you always say that, but I don't think that's it. You have more in common than you make it seem. When I look at you two, I see a great pair.' She waits until I look at her to add, 'Is it perhaps the mysteriously alluring flatmate of his that can't keep his eyes away from you?'

Words fail to leave my mouth. I have no answer.

'Is it Moon Hee?' my flatmate asks.

'What? That's insane,' I say, avoiding her gaze, but her stare is too intense for me to ignore. 'Fine, I don't know!' I sigh. 'All this time I've only seen him as a great friend, but lately my mind has been playing tricks on me, making me believe there's more there. I mean, he's two years younger than me. I shouldn't see him like that.'

'Just because he's younger?' Elisa laughs. 'Honey, he might be twenty-five, but we both know he's wise beyond his age. Forget numbers, also forget that Elijah's one year older. Age is just a number.'

Not for my mother...

'I don't know...my mind is a mess. I hadn't even thought of dating in five years, and now two amazing candidates appear.' My back drops on the bed.

Elisa joins me laying on the mattress. 'Dig deep into you. Tell me your reason for not dating Elijah.'

I stare at the ceiling for a few minutes, running my mind for the answer.

'I want a deeper connection. Besides sex, I don't feel it in my bones that Elijah and I connect. I can't explain it. And if I'm being one hundred percent honest, the closest connection I feel to the one I want is with Moon Hee.'

'So, why don't you go talk with him?' she asks.

'He doesn't like me like that.'

'I'm sorry, have you met Moon Hee? If there was a stranger in the house right now, I would ask them to tell you how he looks at you. Maybe then you'd believe it.' Elisa lifts herself up, glaring at me.

'Every one of you is delusional. Why would he like me? Even Elijah said we have something. No, there's nothing going on!'

'We're not delusional. You just refuse to see it.'

'Nevermind. I'm done thinking about this tonight. Tonight is to party,' I say, getting up. 'Sofía is almost here, right? Shouldn't we start getting ready?'

Elisa glances over at her watch and jumps off the bed. 'We definitely should!'

My friend rushes down to her room, and I move to my wardrobe. I take out a light blue textured swimsuit with an open back and side cut-outs; it was the closest to a bikini I allowed Elisa to get me.

On top, I dress in the black see-through dress she insisted I get. As I look into the mirror, I do like how the pair work; it's sexy but not too much. The see-through style gives a glance into the swimsuit, especially in the light, but it's opaque enough to not give it all away.

I put on some black short heels and move on to my hair and makeup. If we're going swimming, I'll leave my short hair out—it's not like I could do much with it either way—and only apply some waterproof mascara with a coloured lip balm.

When I'm ready to leave my bedroom, the doorbell rings and reminds me that with all of this, the pizza must have come and I didn't hear it under the sound of my playlist playing when I was with Elijah.

My belly growls at the thought of food.

Since the stairs are closest to the outside door, I open it when I reach their bottom.

'Sofía, welcome!' I say.

'Lilah! You look so pretty,' she says with her cute accent.

'Thank you.' I smile. 'Your room is through that door if you want to put down your baggage. Elisa should be there, getting ready.'

'Thank you!'

'Oh, and you look beautiful as well.' She's wearing a tight yellow dress with gold rhinestones across the sides.

I turn back into the living room and meet both men staring at me.

My body heats up and my hands tremble at the attention.

Fuck me. Fuck this life.

I run to the garden to catch my breath, hoping the cool breeze in the air will calm me down.

I hate attention. I used to feel invisible when I was younger, but five years ago I started dreading attention. Especially from the male gaze.

Footsteps sound running after me, but I need to be alone right now, so I run further away, getting inside the pool facility.

Inside, the air is warmer but comforting. The beautiful blue pool shines in the moonlight. The ceiling is transparent, allowing us to watch the stars while swimming or enjoying the hot tub. The walls might be opaque on the outside, but inside you can see the garden around.

From here I watch as the guy wearing black cargo pants and a bucket hat to match stands by the back door of the house, looking at the moon. His fair skin beams under the light and his shadows trace the muscles under his shirt.

I'd noticed Moon Hee's athletic build the other night when he returned home after going for a run, and now even with his oversized shirt my eyes can trace his contours.

A minute later, his roommate joins him outside and Moon Hee points to where I stand.

My body heats again, so I take off my dress and jump into the pool.

I'm curled up underwater when a wave swings my body and two arms wrap around my torso. Soon enough, more waves surround me, but I keep my eyes closed until I no longer sense the arms around me.

Coming up to take a breath, I glance around me and see Moon Hee leaving the pool behind me.

'Your Pisces self couldn't wait to get in the water?' Elisa jokes, diverting my attention to her.

'I guess not.' I give her a small smile, glancing back to watch him leave the facility.

'Hey,' Elijah says, closing in on me.

'Hey.' I avoid his gaze.

'Let's not let what happened before change us, please.' His words pull my eyes to his.

'I'm so sorry,' I say in a low tone.

His hands hold my waist underwater and slide me to him.

'Don't tell me you're sorry. Show me,' he whispers in my ear.

'Here?' I ask under my breath. I turn my head to the side and find Elisa and Sofía kissing.

'They're distracted.' Elijah say, seeing the same as me.

I glance once more outside, but there's no sign of Moon Hee anywhere.

'I'm not drunk enough for that,' I say, giving him a kiss on the cheek and leaving the pool.

I watch the time and it's twenty minutes until midnight. I'll be back before it to wish Elisa a happy birthday.

I open the house's back door to find Moon Hee pouring himself a glass of whiskey.

'Going for the potent stuff, I see,' I say, walking closer to him.

His head turns to me, but he stays silent. I hate it when he's distant.

The glass meets his lips, and he gulps down half of the liquid inside. Moon Hee licks the remnants of the whiskey from his mouth and my eyes cannot stop staring.

Somehow this man of lesser words—that keeps most to himself but is so gentle and seems to be at the right place at the right time when I need him to—has been slowly sweeping his way into my heart.

'Sometimes I wish I could read your mind,' I say, my voice light as a feather. My eyes turn down to the table as I speak.

He places the glass in front of me and as he walks away to the sofa, he responds in a tone that matches mine, 'Sometimes I wish I could tell you how every thought leads to you.'

I gasp. I must have not heard that right.

My gaze turns in his direction, eyes wide as the moon outside, but his back still faces me.

'Why did you hold me in the pool?'

I watch as his shoulders rise and lower in a profound breath and the need to hug him engulfs me once more. Before I know it, my arms surround him as my head lays against his back.

We stay in this position for a while, the only words in the air coming from the sound speaker.

I loosen my grip on him and take a step back. Moon Hee turns around and stares into my eyes. 'Why did you hold me just now?'

Then it hits me.

Does he understand my need to touch him? Does he have the same need for me?

The sound of the door opening interrupts our gaze and my body instinctively walks back to the table to grab a glass.

'Two minutes until midnight!' Sofía tells us. 'Elisa told me to get the bottle of champagne and you two.'

'On my way!' I say, not looking back.

This is Elisa's night, and it's on her I'm going to focus. In fact, that will be my focus for the rest of the trip.

Outside, they're all standing on the mowed lawn, my best friend's girlfriend serving everyone a cup.

'Elisa!' I say, wrapping my arm around her and kissing her cheek. She looks at me and I smile. 'Happy birthday!'

She looks at her watch that shows four zeros on the screen and smiles back. 'I'm born again!'

'Feliz cumpleaños, bebé.' Sofía kisses her.

'Here's to another year. Happy birthday.' Elijah toasts with his glass on hers.

'Happy birthday, Elisa,' I hear behind me, and a figure stops beside me.

My eyes trace his naked torso. His defined abs prominent in the moonlight. The shadows traced by the nine-tailed fox tattoo on his chest and the smaller ones on his arms. Everything is stripping the air out of me.

Before tonight, I thought Elijah was the hottest man I'd seen in real life, but it all changed three seconds ago when I laid eyes on Moon Hee.

He's been hiding. Oh, he definitely has been hiding his physique. I'd notice he had more than he showed, but not like this. And it's not even that he's very muscular—he isn't a bodybuilder—but if I ever needed an exact example of my perfect body type, he would be it.

'You're staring,' the man I'm utterly mesmerised by whispers in my ear.

My eyes widen and while still catching up my breath, I say, 'Well...Well...Your tattoos are really beautiful.'

'You know what?' I burst, desperate to change subjects. 'Elijah, I will take you up on that offer to get one. I think it's time.

I've always wanted one, or many, and I think I'm ready to take that leap.'

'Fantastic! Come by the shop this week and we'll talk details,' he says.

'You know what would be even better? If we all got a matching tattoo, something that even when all hell breaks loose and we talk no more, we can look at and smile at all these amazing moments we have,' I say.

'That's actually very sweet. I love the idea!' Elisa beams.

'Except Sofía, you all have met my parents, and you saw how little we get along. Besides them, my only other family was my Nana, but when she passed away, I was lost without anyone who I could count on until Elisa came.' I hold her hand and smile at her before gesturing to the guys. 'And then you two showed up, and well, I haven't felt this happy in a long time, maybe never.'

The stars become blurry and a fresh tear rolls down my cheek.

I chuckle, wanting to lighten up the mood. 'What I'm trying to say is that many are lucky to have a blood family they can rely on, but I'm even luckier because I got one, despite not being related to them, who feels more like home than the one I was born into.'

'Lilah! Why are you making me cry on my birthday?' My best friend hugs me and the guys join in.

I look to my side and watch Sofía standing by our side and gesture for her to take her place in the hug.

We release each other, and I turn to the new girl. 'From all the people that I've seen Elisa with, you are hands down my favourite.' I tilt my head in thought. 'There was Alexa. She was okay, but wasn't around much for me to get her to know her. Then there was John. I don't really remember him, just hearing his name being screamed throughout the entire house. Then there was Mark,' I say, now turning to the birthday woman. 'I'm so glad you broke up with him. He was the worst one of them all, like such an arsehole, I don't know how you put up with him...'

'Well, he was great in bed and he would also help me with my homework. He's the reason I passed geometry,' Elisa says.

'Yes, but his ego was the size of his head!'

'Oh, it wasn't that bad—his head I mean—the ego was for sure big.'

Everyone is staring at us, amusement plastered in their eyes.

'People went by him in the hallways saying, hey Arnold, it was that bad.' I look at her, dead serious. 'Anyway, Melissa was rude, and I think that's about it for the ones that I actually learned their names, because after a while I just stopped asking.'

'At least mine have names. For Elijah, I remember Jennifer, Vanessa, Serena...' Elisa directs the attention away from her.

'Serena? She dated you, not me,' Elijah says.

'Oh yeah, I remember Serena...I think.' My flatmate continues. 'Fine, not Serena. Oh, there was Megan, and after that just became the brunette, blonde, redhead. The one with the piercings, the one with the Dior purse or the Chanel purse. The one who left her earrings in my car, or was it her shoes? Probably both. I had to disinfect my back seats after that.'

'Wait, didn't you say you've only known each other for the space of a year?' Sofía asks.

'Yes,' I say.

'Oh, wow.'

'In all fairness, the ones I named for Elisa were throughout the nine years I've known her. For Elijah, I can't say much.'

'Lilah did not want to party with us, so I had to find fun in other places.' He winks at me.

'But is this party starting or what? I did not take my shirt off to stand outside,' Moon Hee says.

'No, you took your shirt off because you soaked yours before when you dove in fully dressed,' Elijah jokes, being the first to walk towards the pool facility.

스물둘
'seumuldul'

'What tattoo are you planning to get?' Moon Hee asks, lifting his head from the white soft water pillow he placed on the hard edge.

Yesterday, after partying until dawn, we slept way past lunchtime and then went on a walk to visit the surrounding areas. Today we're relaxing before going back to the busy life of London.

'I'm thinking of getting a fine line flower in watercolour style on the back of my arm.' I keep my eyes on his face as much as they want to travel down.

He scoots closer to me, waving the water in my direction. I look back to see if someone else is watching us.

'No one is here. They went to get food,' my friend—who's almost touching my body with his in the hot tub—says.

'I-I wasn't...'

'Why do you worry if someone sees us close? Aren't we friends?' He interrupts me as his arm touches mine and I flinch, making him frown.

'We are, I'm just...I don't want Elijah to get the idea that something is going on between us and get hurt.' I watch the water I sit under.

'Are you two together now?'

'No. We're just friends, and I don't aspire to be anything else.'

He turns to the side, facing his body to me, and I can feel his warm breath on my skin, sending goosebumps all over my body. 'So, is it just because you don't want to hurt him, or is there anything else?'

I hold my breath, unable to speak. He closes in on me, whispering in my ear, 'Breathe.'

Breathe? How do you expect me to breathe when you're this close to me?

He goes back to his first position, and I let out an unexpected breath, making him chuckle.

'Yes. That's the only reason,' I say, getting up to leave the warm and bubbly water.

'Lilah, wait.'

I stop, one foot out of the tub and one foot in, and glance over at him.

'Don't leave. We're friends, right?' Moon Hee's face stays stiller than the water, yet his eyes do nothing but plead.

'Yeah, we're just friends.'

Stepping back into the water, I am greeted by the comforting sensation of the underwater jets, their pulsating streams massaging our bodies. With each brush of our skin, an overwhelming heat radiates through me. We stay there, lost in the moment, until the rest of the gang rejoins us and we begin our preparations to leave.

'Hey Lilah,' Jeremiah says, greeting me as he enters the bakery.

'Hi Jer!' I glance up from the counter and smile at him.

'I came to tell you we have everything finalised for Thursday and will be announcing the collaboration today, both on socials and in the restaurant.'

'Sounds fabulous. Tomorrow I'll be starting on the samples for you to give your customers. Last time, a lot of them came here to take a dessert home after eating at your restaurant, and some have even become regulars.' I wipe my hands on my apron and walk around the counter to the front of the shop.

'Do you want anything before I close up?' I ask him.

'No, I'm good, thank you. I need to go to the post office, anyway.'

'I'm going there too!' I want to check if I have a new letter. With the weekend getaway and the collaboration, I haven't checked my postbox in a while.

'I'll wait for you to lock up, then.' He lays his hunter-green cardigan on the table closest to the door and sits.

As we walk along our street, most people have gone home and all the shops are closed, except for the restaurants serving dinner. The sky has grown dark, no star in sight. Our path is illuminated by big street lamps on the side of the road.

I watch my shadow on the ground as we pass under a lamp and say, 'We should do something together sometime. You, me, and Rebecca. I feel like we only see each other during work hours.'

'*You* want to do something with us?' His eyebrows raise as he stares at me, the shock noticeable in his tone.

'Yes, why?'

'Because we have invited you multiple times to have dinner, or go for a film or a carnival, but you always came up with an excuse. We just assumed you had a secret life after work where there was no time for daylight friends.' He grins, turning his attention back to the road.

I'm glad he didn't say he thought I didn't care about them. I hope they know I do.

'I'm sorry.' My tone is as low as my eyes on the floor. 'I'm working on it, I promise.'

'I know, we've seen you hang out with other people. That was a first all these years. Elisa we already knew, since she's been rounding you from the beginning, but not the other guys.'

'Yes. I'm pushing myself daily to do things I normally wouldn't,' I say.

'Is one of them...your boyfriend?' he asks. I glance up at him and meet the side of his face, his eyes not glitching from the path ahead.

'No, they're just friends.'

'Okay...because if they were, I would be happy to see you happy.' The light above the post office creates a sparkle in his green eyes, the ones that release from the building in front of us to glance at me. 'We're here.'

'Yes, we are.' I smile, and before walking in to find out if I have new mail, I watch him taking out an envelope from his back pocket.

'Those envelopes...they seem familiar,' I say, furrowing my eyebrows in an attempt to recall where I've seen the gritty light grey paper.

'Maybe you've seen them at the stationery shop in our street.'

'Oh, *Violet's Paperdise*? The one two shops away from *InkPark*?'

'Yes, exactly. I believe they're branded only to them. I've never seen any other shop with ones like these.'

'Maybe I've seen them in their window or something...' They seem too familiar to me, but I can't pinpoint why. 'Oh, and Jeremiah, thank you for before.'

He nods and smiles before delivering his letter to the mailbox.

I walk to my postbox and reach my hand into its darkness. The feeling of paper brings a smile to my face.

I have a letter!

I rush home to read it, noticing that Elisa might not be here since all the lights are out. Inside my room, I grab my letter opener. This one I bought at *Violet's Paperdise*—that I remember. It was too cute not to get when I saw it at her window. It's baby pink with a cupcake on top, so in tune with Sweet Delilah's brand.

When I grab the letter to open it, I stop at the sight of the envelope. Gritty and light grey. The same one Jeremiah was using.

I'm sure a lot more people use that paper, but I can't stop wondering if he could be Daldust.

I open the letter and read it.

"Dear Delilah,
I'm so glad you are finding happiness within yourself.
And you are becoming like a diary, yes. I've spoken more about myself with you than anyone else. Thank you for that.
I believe we have someone out there for us, someone who truly gets us. It doesn't need to be romantic, it can be a friendship, but I think we are not alone in the world; that there is someone with the same vibration as us.
I met my one a long time ago, but I lost her.
I promised myself that I would never let that happen again. If I found someone as special or more than her, I would hold tight to them, make them feel loved, and never ever miss my chance to share my happiness with that person.
How was your trip? Did you have fun?
Yours truly,
Daldust"

No, it can't be Jeremiah...but what he just said...he met someone a long time ago. He met me four years ago, and he lost me. I mean, he never had me in the first place, but now he knows for sure he doesn't have the chance.

No. It *can't* be him.

I read the letter over and over again, but I can't picture him saying these words.

Let's not jump to conclusions, Delilah.

Think.

Why would Jeremiah have a house in South Korea? And I don't think he's travelled a lot or reads a lot.

No. I'm eighty percent sure it isn't him.

I grab my pen and write back.

"I'm glad you feel like that about me. I feel the same. I confide in you as much as my therapist.

I hope to find someone on the same vibrational level as mine one day.

But I'm curious. How did you lose her?

About my trip, yes, it was refreshing to get out to the countryside and enjoy the view. I had fun with some friends that are becoming a big part of my life. Maybe one day we can all hang out.

Delilah"

Hopefully, with his response, I'll know for sure.

I pick my phone up to check the time, but the little green message icon pulls me in and before I can collect my thoughts, I've sent a text to Moon Hee.

Hi

That's all I said...Hi. *Stupid*.

I'm staring at the screen when the word *Delivered* changes to *Seen*.

'Ah!' I throw the phone to my bed, unable to see his answer.

Stupid. Stupid. Stupid, Delilah. Why would you text him?

My hand presses on my chest as I inhale deeply, trying to calm my heart.

Breathe. Friends text. It's okay. Everything is fine.

I rise from my desk's chair and approach my phone with a careful stride, treating it as if it were a fragile shard of glass.

Hey Moon Hee wrote back.

Fuck, now if I say nothing else, it will get weird.

But what? What will I say?

I can't say 'Nothing, I just felt like saying hi.' The palm of my hand hits my forehead a few times, trying to find an answer.

The moment he sends another text, I laugh, releasing some of the stress this was giving me.

I would have taken a day off if I knew you'd be texting this much xD

Sorry, I just...don't know what to say...

Are you home? he asks.

Yes, why?

The text gets seen, but he doesn't answer back. A minute later, I hear the house's bell ring.

I open the door and Moon Hee, wearing an all black outfit and slippers, stands in front of me.

'Have you had dinner, yet?' he asks.

I shake my head no and he gestures to me to wait, walking back to his flat which the door he left open. Moments later, he returns with two bowls. Moon Hee hands me one and goes back to close his door.

I look inside the bowl and my mouth waters.

'You made *bibimbap*?'

'I was making it for me and Elijah, but he isn't home yet and there's more than enough left for him to eat later.'

'I love *bibimbap*,' I say, and he chuckles.

'I'm glad.'

'Come in.' I lead him to the kitchen and place the food on the table. 'Elisa isn't home either. I think she's with Sofía.'

'So...' he starts, and I already know I don't want to hear the rest. 'Why did you text me?'

'I think we should start eating before it gets cold.'

'Lilah.' His tone is serious. This man is not letting it slide.

'I don't know. I did it blindly...'

'Was I on your mind?' Moon Hee tilts his head. A slight lift of the corner of his mouth threatens to unravel his composure, one he controls before it gets a hold on him.

I turn around to avoid him seeing my burning cheeks and grab spoons for us to eat. As I spin back, watching my reflection on the metal, I bump into the man that once was near the entrance.

His breath warms my ear, despite the shivers it sends down my body, as he whispers, 'Please, text me anytime I cross your mind.'

'You'd be constantly checking your messages if I did that.' The moment these words come out, my eyes widen and I press my palm against my mouth.

What. Did. I. Just. Say?

This time, both corners of his lips lift, and he lets them. I'm sure he can tell how embarrassed I am because he takes the spoons from my hand and walks backwards, his eyes never leaving mine until the moment he hits the table.

'You're right, let's eat before it gets cold.'

Now, Moonie? *Now* you want to eat?

Fuck me.

I sit down and enjoy the delicious rice mixed with vegetables, tofu, and a sauce I've never tasted before.

'What's the sauce made of? I usually eat it with soy sauce.'

'I've noticed restaurants here serve it with soy sauce, maybe because it's easier, but my family has a special *bibimbap* sauce.'

'You must share the recipe with me,' I say, mouth full of deliciousness.

'My mum made me promise to only share with family.' His big doe and dark eyes prevent me from focusing only on the food.

As much as I try to ignore it, I fall short of breath every time he looks at me. I've had crushes before. Hell, I couldn't speak with Elijah when I met him, but this is feeling bigger than a crush.

It seemed like yesterday the week was starting, but it's ending already.

I pass by the postbox to see if I have a letter before meeting

Ms Julie. Last week I missed our session because of the trip, so we have some catching up to do.

I've been skipping so much lately...I hope she doesn't think I'm bailing on her.

A little grey envelope greets me and I smile, placing it inside my purse before continuing my journey.

'How was the week before your trip?' Ms Julie asks as I sit in her office.

'Uneventful. I had a lot of work to do, so it kept my mind off everything that could bother me.'

'And the trip?'

'It went well. It was fun to get away for a while and just enjoy the present. I do see why you said it would become easier as time went by to get out of my comfort zone. The more I do it and get good results, the more I'm eager to do it again.'

'That's wonderful, Lilah. And how are things going with your friend Elijah?'

'We decided to stay as friends with benefits for now. I don't see more coming from there. We don't connect that much outside the bedroom, but he did say he liked me this weekend, so everything is a bit strange now.'

'Why do you feel that?' Her expression is welcoming to my thoughts.

'I'm not sure. It's just that we have fun in the group, but alone we don't seem to have much in common to talk about.'

'Having things in common does speed up the connection process, but there are other ways to connect besides that. If it's on an emotional level, you don't need to like the same things, but you need to feel the same way about the things you like. And as time passes, you actually create things to do in common, and each other's taste begins transmitting to the other person.'

'Maybe I just can't seem to open up to him,' I say, looking down at my hands.

'Then could the problem be not that you don't have things in common, but that you're afraid to connect?'

'But with Daldust, I can just be myself. I don't filter or sugar coat. I say whatever it's on my mind without the fear of being judged. I'm just me. With everyone else, I always feel like I have one foot in and another foot out, even with Moon Hee. He's the one I feel closest to now, but I can't make up my mind to give in to him. It's so much easier on paper.'

'On paper, you read emotions as you please. You can let out your deepest thoughts without having someone stare at you and react to your words. Perhaps it's the reactions you're most afraid of.'

Her words stick with me for the ride home. *Perhaps it's the reactions you're most afraid of.*

It always circles back to the lack of control. I'm amazed at how that twists my arm every time. I can't control their reactions, so they scare me. Every uncontrolled action frightens me.

With a sigh, I lie on my bed and open the letter to read, hoping Daldust's words soothe my mind.

"Dear Delilah,

I only realised my feelings for her when it was too late.

She doesn't remember me anymore. I only saw her a few times, and we barely spoke in those. She was kind, a bit shy, but so passionate about the world around her.

I got to have a conversation with her one night...Before I never saw her again.

We were at a party, and I went to the roof to get some air. She was there, alone, and drunk. I went to her and the way she turned to me is something I have never forgotten, how the moonlight reflected through her eyes, and the way she smiled like I had never seen.

She was so happy that night, and we sat down for what felt like hours and seconds at the same time—too

eternal of a memory for such a fleeting moment—while the party went on and talked. We talked about everything, but mostly about the universe, about people, humanity, and dreams, all that one talks about when one is drunk late at night.

We sat there until her boyfriend came searching for her. She loved him so much. I could tell by the way she looked at him because it was how I looked at her. He was an arsehole, and I heard through a friend that they broke up not long after. He did her wrong, but I was worse. I could have prevented that from happening if I told her how I felt that night on the roof. That was the biggest regret of my life.

I would love to hang out with you all, but first, we need to meet each other haha

Yours truly,
Daldust"

He's one hundred percent not Jeremiah.

스물셋
'seumulset'

Daldust's POV

Five years ago…

'I really don't want to go,' I say to my friend Mark, standing outside my building's front door.

'No, you need to come with us. You've been in London for a month and haven't met anyone. You are coming to the party,' he says.

I have met people, just not people interesting enough for me to talk to outside of parties.

'That girl you saw the other day will be there.' The other one tries to convince me.

'It doesn't matter, she has a boyfriend.' I look up at the dark night sky.

'So what? They're not married, and you need friends,' Mark says, giving me the bracelet to enter the party. So this is the type of friend he's expecting me to make.

I accept it, not for them, but for her, to see her at least one more time.

'Park will be there,' Justin tells Mark, playing with his car keys.

'Yeah, I know, he's the host.' Mark pushes his tongue inside his cheek. A habit I picked up that he has when that guy gets mentioned.

'Who is Park?' I ask.

I only know Justin and Mark here in London, and it happened by chance. My mum works for Mark's mum so I met him at a dinner. Justin came along; I believe they're best mates.

They aren't my preferred type of friends, but it will do for now.

'He's a dude who thinks he's the best, just because every girl wants to get in his pants,' Justin says as I see Mark's jaw tense.

I have a sense that there's history there, and it's most likely not a nice one.

'The party is at ten. We will meet you there,' Mark says, and they leave.

Like I mentioned, not my type of friends. My type would at least take me there, since I have no clue where the party will reside.

A few minutes after I walk inside my small flat, the door opens.

'*Omma* (mum)?' I lean towards the entry to check on whoever is coming inside.

'*Ne* (yes),' she says, stepping into the living room.

'I'm going out tonight. Don't wait up,' I say, knowing that my socialising will at least bring joy to one of us.

'I'm happy you are making friends,' she says in her cute little accent. I love how she practises English even at home; she's the hardest working person I know.

I help her prepare dinner and we sit down to enjoy each other's company.

She misses my dad. I see that every day, especially when we eat. Her eyes keep glancing at where he would sit. I miss him too.

It's been two years since he died and even though the pain has lessened as we get used to it, it's still hard.

The reason we came to England was because my mum was struggling to be in Korea. We plan on visiting as often as we can because we have our house there, but for the time being, we are here. She needed a change of scenery from the places they frequented daily.

My heart ached to hear her cry every night as she lay alone, but ever since coming here, it aches less.

The infusion of fresh faces, experiences, and places has brought a sense of healing to her soul.

'How was work today?' I ask.

She is working as a cleaning lady for Mark's family. Some people might think less about housekeepers, but she loves to clean and get everything organised. To me, it's the perfect job for her; she always returns home smiling after taking care of a house where a family is complete.

'It was good. I cooked today and Ms Harmony liked it a lot.' Her dimples are showing. Ever since I was a kid, I've found them adorable.

My mum had me when she was young, so she never got to live her own life. She says she didn't mind it, that she enjoyed raising a child like me, but it's been wonderful seeing her live now. She's forty, but still very young at heart.

'What's the door?' I ask Mark, arriving at the street address he sent me by text.

'28, just listen from which floor music is coming out,' he says before hanging up the call and I sigh.

I shouldn't have come. They'll just send me off and go make out with someone.

After verifying my entrance by displaying my bracelet to security, I continue walking past the door and am instantly engulfed in a dense cloud of smoke.

'Sorry, mate,' the guy who just puffed smoke into my face says. He chuckles at the person next to him—both with bloodshot eyes—and it's only quarter past ten.

I shrug it off and walk further in as he gets out.

Deafening music is playing in the background, and the mix between alcohol and weed floats in the air. The inability to move well because of the crowd causes tightening in my throat.

But for just tonight, I'll try to fit in. My thoughts travel to the girl I met a few times since I got to London; I wonder if she's here.

We have never spoken, but we've been in the same circle of people. Her boyfriend is friends with Mark and that means he can't be that good of a person either.

She's not very talkative, but when she talks no one can outspeak her. The undeniable passion for life, and for him, is always present in her eyes.

I walk towards the island in the kitchen and pour myself whatever drink they have on display. I don't know the name, but it burns like hell when you drink it; my throat is on fire.

I walk to the sink and pour myself a glass of water to soothe the pain.

As I wait to run into the people who invited me, I ponder sitting on the sofa, wondering how many white spots would show up under a blue light.

Time goes by, but I can't figure out how much. I haven't seen either Mark or Justin around. Are they even here yet?

I heard music in the background of our call, but I won't rule out them being at a pre-party. Apparently, those are a thing.

I'm tired of those guys. Our time together is coming to an end.

'Hey. I've never seen you around,' a guy says, sitting on the filthy sofa next to me. Tattoos cover his right arm and I can't stop staring at them. They are beautiful.

'Yeah, I've never been around here.' I trace my eyes back up to his. He's Korean, or at least has traces.

'Who did you come with?' he asks, scanning the room.

'Mark and Justin, but I haven't even seen them yet.'

He chuckles. 'Those kids are outside, trying to get laid. I'm Elijah, by the way. Elijah Park.'

So he's Park. *Wait,* he threw the party. Of course, he's asking who the strange kid that invaded his place is.

'Oh, you're the owner of the place,' I say, glancing back at his arm. 'Nice tattoos.'

'Thanks, you want some?' Elijah asks. His smile contrasts how the other ones described him, but then again, they don't seem the type to know who's decent or not.

'One day.' My eyes take in my bare arms.

'When you want them, just go to my parlour. It's called InkPark. It's two streets down.' The guy stands up, looking at someone who just called for him.

I take his lead to move around the place as well.

On a corner some people play darts and beer pong, while on the opposite side others make out. Each side has doors with a sock on the handle.

This seems like the fraternity houses I see in films. I've never been in one, and even though the films are fictional, they have to be based on something.

I leave through the open window in the back that leads to the fire escape stairs, up to the roof.

'Mate, you're here!' Mark says as soon as he sees me.

This must be the outside that guy Park was talking about.

As always, Justin comes along. 'Welcome, dude. Let's get you acquainted with some people.'

'Hey,' I say, energy levels down to minus one percent.

As we walk towards a circle of people, someone stands out to me. It's her. She is here.

They introduce me to everyone, as if I had never met them before. It's the same circle they always hangout with, but people never notice the introvert.

After a while, some of them disperse and I go sit on a sofa they have up here. The reason for a roof sofa in this house is still very much shady, but the view compensates for it.

The full moon bewitches me every time. Its luminous serenity is enough to remind me to breathe. As I inhale, the sofa bounces a bit and my attention moves to the side.

'Hey,' she says, sitting down.

My vocal cords forget how to work, and I can only look at her big chocolaty eyes.

'I'm Lilah, Lilah Scott.' Her hand reaches out and waits to meet mine.

This is a turn of events I never imagined. The girl I have been chasing ended up coming to me.

'Hi, I—' I shake her hand. Her soft skin brushes against mine as our hands depart, making me long for more.

'You are the guy who Mark and Justin keep introducing, even though we have met multiple times,' she says. Her teeth so white they could compete with the moon.

She remembers me.

'I'm flattered you remember me.' I say a full sentence at last.

'Yeah, you don't seem to fit in with those guys. Why do you hang around them?' Her wavy brown hair sways with the wind and she rubs her hands over her bare arms.

I take off my jacket and place it on her back. 'Take it.'

'Aren't you cold?' she asks.

I shake my head with a soft smile. Bringing a sweatshirt under it was a smart move on my part.

She accepts the jacket and pulls it closer around her. It's a few sizes too big—probably because I like the oversized look on me—and it makes her look cute.

'Thanks.' Lilah's eyes squint with joy.

'I'm not,' I say, and she frowns at me. 'The type to hang out with them. They're just the first people I met when I got here.'

'Oh. Where did you come from?'

'South Korea.'

'That's cool. I wish I could travel somewhere now,' she says, looking up at the sky.

The light cast on her face deepens the shadows. I wish I could take her picture right now, but I'll surely draw her later.

'Well, the sky is the same anywhere in the world,' I speak, and she chuckles.

'I guess so, yeah.' I can see that she has already had a bit to drink.

'Where is your boyfriend?' I ask, looking around the roof for him. He's nowhere to be found.

The sound is so loud downstairs that it arrives here with only a slight muffle. Lauv's *Lonely Eyes* plays as I watch her stare at the full moon.

'I wish I was a bird.' She ignores my question. 'They can fly anywhere at any time. Imagine how it is to be that free.'

'They're lucky. Our legs aren't as strong as their wings to travel the world.'

'He's somewhere around the house. He never leaves the place, but he always leaves me. I don't even know why I come to these things anymore.' She looks down at her hands, playing with her fingers. Maybe she was considering if she would answer or not before.

I knew it. He's a prick.

I glance at her face and see her watering eyes shining with the moonlight, so I grab her hand and she leans her head on my shoulder.

It's strange how quickly we've become comfortable with each other, considering we just met.

Lilah cleans her tears with her free hand and lets go of mine with the other, sitting up straight. 'I'm sorry, it's just been a rough month.'

'It's okay,' I say. 'You know, we can't be birds. We are human after all, but we can be free.'

'We can, but I couldn't just spread my wings and go now, like a bird. And I really want to go now.' Her voice gets lost in the wind as she looks at the buildings in front.

My chest tightens hearing the hurt in her tone. I really want to hug her right now.

But that would probably be weird.

Thankfully, the muffle in the music grows—they must have lowered the sound—so I catch her words.

'If you want to go, then go. You should feel free at least once in your life.'

'Here you are,' someone says. We turn around and the guy who should have been comforting her stares at me.

'Vance,' she says.

'Let's go, the guys are getting food and I'll drop you off at home,' he says, tightening his lips. I don't like his tone.

'Are you going home afterwards too?' she asks him.

'No, I'm coming back here. The party will go on until the morning, but I know you get tired early.' He tries to sound like a considerate boyfriend, but I can see through his act.

He doesn't care that she gets tired early. If he did, he would stay with her. He simply doesn't want to have her around for long, especially after he gets drunk and wants to do whatever.

'Oh, okay.' Lilah's sigh tells me I'm not the only one who sees through his words.

With her head down, she gets up, and they make their way to the stairs. While I keep my gaze fixed on them leaving, she unexpectedly turns around and rushes towards me.

'Here, I almost forgot,' she says, taking off my jacket and giving it to me. 'Thank you, not just for the jacket. I'll try to be free.'

I give her a small smile and she leaves to catch up with him, where he's already waiting by the stairs. I'm glad she's going home because I know he wouldn't give her his jacket and she would feel cold the whole night.

Before walking down the stairs, she looks at me once more and waves with a smile.

It was at that moment, as the wind swept her long, brown, and wavy hair back, revealing her beautiful face, with big doe eyes, that I was certain I would never come across anyone quite like her again.

Present time...

I walk towards the bakery near my workplace when I'm stopped by the writing in cursive pink letters above the door. I'd never noticed the name until now: *Sweet Delilah*.

I stand by the door, feeling the cool breeze brush against my face, while she waves from the inside, her smile visible through the window.

Just like that night, she smiles and waves at me, this time not saying goodbye, but welcoming me into her life.

It's you. It has always been you.

Dear Lilah Scott, you never asked my name that night, but I never forgot yours.

스물넷
'seumulnet'

'You got a letter,' my roommate says as I walk into the living room.

'A letter?' Daldust doesn't send me letters home. I wonder what she's talking about.

'It's on the kitchen table.' She presses play on the show she's watching and her undivided attention remains there.

The beige envelope with the gold foil letter brings back childhood memories. These were the invites my parents would send out for their Christmas gala. The funny part is they told me I couldn't take part until I became of age and by then I was out of their house.

But they never sent me an invitation. Why now?

Maybe it's a farewell party before they leave for Beverly Hills?

This whole thing gave me an idea, in fact. I walk back to the living room and stand in front of the TV, making sure Elisa listens to me.

'What do you think of us hosting a Christmas dinner?' I ask.

Her eyes swiftly rise to mine. 'A dinner? You want to host a dinner?'

'A small gathering, just you, me, the boys, Sofía, Rebecca and Jeremiah, and if any of you want to bring someone you can, but just let me know so I can make food for everyone.'

'I'm still stunned. I never thought I would hear you say you want to organise a party. You. Being around people.' The woman gets up and hugs me. 'I'm a proud mama.'

I laugh. 'I've been happier lately, and being around you guys doesn't scare me at all. I can't say much about everyone else, but you, I'm actually eager to hang out with.'

'It sounds perfect,' she says, stepping back from the hug, smiling. A moment later, her eyes deviate to the kitchen and she frowns. 'But where will we put everyone? We only have a small kitchen table, no dining room.'

'I have an idea, but first I need to talk to the boys. I'm getting my tattoo today, so I'll ask them there. Now I need to go to work. Bye!'

'Can't wait to see what the tattoo will look like!' she says as I walk towards the exit door in a rush.

Arriving at my street, I peek at the tattoo parlour to check if the guys are there already, but it's still closed.

As I'm organising to open the bakery, my phone rings. I glance at it and a name I haven't seen in a while pops on the screen.

First the invite and now my mum is calling? Who's dying?

'Hello?' I say, turning off the ringing.

'Lilah? It's mum.'

'I know. I saw the name on the screen.'

'That's good. I didn't know if you had it saved.' Her condescending tone is making me regret having picked up the call. 'Did you receive our invitation?'

'Yes. It was surprising. I'll admit that.'

'We figured it was time. This little tantrum of yours has been going for way too long, Lilah. Your father misses spending time with you.'

Misses me so much he's moving thousands of kilometres away.

I scoff. 'There's no tantrum going on, mum.'

'Well then, why don't you ever call?'

'Why don't you?'

'Because you always have a mocking tone whenever I do.'

'I wonder why...' I say, taking a deep breath before she ruins my mood for the day.

'It's impossible to speak to you. I thought being twenty-seven would mean you were a bit more grown up, but you're the same as you were when you were seventeen.'

'That's where you're mistaken. At seventeen, I had to answer to you. There was no escaping because you were my guardian, even if it was Nana who took care of me most of the time. At seventeen, you had me on a tightrope, unable to act outside of your rules. You wanted me to be the younger version of you, but being you was my worst nightmare.' I'm appalled at myself, but I can't stop. 'And it took me almost five years after leaving that place to become my person. Bloody hell, it's taken me ten to heal.'

My eyes burn as I continue to pour my heart out. 'When you trap a child into behaving only a certain way, caring too much about other people's opinions, to be in constant awareness of the world around them and to make sure they smile through all of it, for they would not want to cause their family any disgrace. When you cling so much plastic wrap around them, you make them unable to breathe. The moment they find a tiny little hole that won't make them feel as if they're drowning with every day that goes by, they fight their way out. It might take a while to be free of all the cling wrap, but bit by bit comes off, and when it all does, there's no going back.'

'I'm not going back, mother. And I don't have to answer to you any more, even if that makes you look bad in the eyes of the Elite.'

'Delilah Scott, that's no way to speak to your mother.'

'You're right, I shouldn't be speaking to you at all. Please, wish Dad a marvellous Christmas.'

I hang up the call and fall on the chair behind the counter. It's amazing how a year of healing that seems to only be doing minor improvements can show all at once.

A call that would have ruined my day before now makes me smile. I laugh like a crazy person, crying streams down my face, and for the first time in a long time, I actually feel proud of myself.

'Lilah, Lilah, my beautiful blank canvas, Lilah,' Elijah says as I enter *InkPark*.

'Someone is happy.' I smile.

'You have no idea how eager I am to corrupt that silky skin of yours.' He rubs his hands together as if he was planning something mischievous.

The owner of the parlour walks closer to me and lowers himself enough for his mouth to stop near my ear and whispers, 'In a way I haven't already corrupted it, I mean.'

'Your flirtiness will be the bane of your existence.'

'Unless you become it first.' His words sink into my heart. This phrase would have made me the happiest a few months ago, but now it only brings a gut-wrenching guilt.

'Elijah...' I say.

'I'm joking. Being flirty, like you said.' He gives me a small smile, but I know there's truth in what he said. He's not joking.

'Hey.' Moon Hee enters the shop, giving me a breach to lighten up.

'Hey,' I say, avoiding his gaze. It's been over two weeks, but I still can't believe I said those things to him...

You'd be constantly checking your messages if I did that. What was I thinking?

'Do you have the drawing?' Elijah asks his partner and he nods.

'You drew my flower?'

'I hope you like it. I had an image when you talked to me about it and wanted to try to draw it.' He hands me the paper.

I stare at the white page with black ink on it. He used a fountain pen.

It's stunning. The way the trace thickens and thins in all the right places; strokes of a professional.

'It's better than what I had imagined. It's beautiful.' My mouth can't close with such astonishment. 'I had no idea you drew this well.'

He looks down and in a low tone says, 'Thank you.'

'Let's get it started. Onto the chair, Ms Scott,' Elijah demands.

I enter his office and sit on the black leather chair.

'Oh, before I forget. I have something to ask you two,' I say. 'I was thinking of doing a Christmas dinner and wanted to know if you're available and if I could use your dining room, since the only table we have is too small.'

'My parents are probably going to your parents' dinner,' Elijah says. 'So I'm in.'

'Can I take my mum?' Moon Hee asks.

'Of course! I would love to meet the woman who raised such an amazing person as you.'

Not again, Delilah. I should just keep my mouth shut.

Elijah looks between us, lips tight.

Fuck.

'Let's get me corrupted or not?' I ask him, attempting to divert his attention.

'Let's do it,' he says, before turning to his colleague. 'Can you watch the front?'

Moon Hee nods and leaves the office. Elijah closes the door behind him and places himself in front of me, my legs between his.

'Elijah?'

His hand tucks my hair behind my ear, and he nips my earlobe. 'It's been a while, and I've pictured us so many times in this chair.'

'Elijah...'

'I told you I didn't want the benefits to end. Do you?'

Do I?

'It's a bit weird, no?' I ask.

'Not for me. Before feelings were involved, there was an attraction that hasn't changed.' He starts a trail of kisses on the side of my neck, knowing exactly how in the mood that puts me.

'But this is your workplace…'

'I get it disinfected constantly, don't worry.' He smirks, grabbing my waist and pulling me to the edge of the chair.

He brings his lips to mine and caresses my breast with one hand while the other unbuttons my jeans. The wet feel of his tongue in my mouth gets me drooling down there and at the spark of his fingers with my clit I lose all temper.

I take off his shirt and down his bottom wear as he trails kisses over my collarbone and chest line.

My hand fills with his cock and I stroke gently, getting him harder.

'You really know how to make a man beg for more,' Elijah whispers in my ear, taking off my shirt and underwear.

He places my legs above his arms and lifts me up. I hold on to his neck as he enters me while standing.

Every time my body lowers, he gets deep inside me and, as much as I'm trying to control myself, there's only so much I can take. His moves quicken and a loud moan comes out of me. From then on, his mouth doesn't leave mine, muffling all my audible pleasure.

Elijah sits me back in the chair and turns me around, pushing me down flat, only my ass up.

This time his hand is the buffer, pushing my head back, while his other holds my waist, making sure every thrust is as intense as the stare he's giving me.

I always love it when he's rough, but this time there's more to it. I've never felt him so possessive. And I don't think it's only because of how he feels about me. I think he's catching on to the vibes between me and Moon Hee.

He already told me he thought I liked his flatmate, but even I've noticed a change in us. Perhaps that's what's putting him off.

A few moments later, he comes on top of me, giving me a kiss on the shoulder before stepping back to get some tissue to clean my back.

'This was fun,' I say, faking a smile while putting my clothes back on.

'It sure was.' His eyes don't meet mine and I feel awful.

'I don't think we should keep doing this,' I admit.

His head swiftly lifts, staring at mine. A few weeks ago, I saw his eyes shining before he cried. This time, the look in his eyes doesn't come from tears. In fact, it's the lack of shine that shows me how hurt he is; not from me not wanting to have sex with him anymore, but that I don't want us to be more.

'You're right, we shouldn't.'

I walk closer to him and wrap my arms around his waist, resting my head on his chest. 'Can we still be friends?'

'I'm not going to lie and say it won't cost me at first, but I care too much about you,' he says. 'But I think you should ask Moon Hee to tattoo you. He drew the flower, so I'm sure he'll do a better job than I would.'

'The last thing I wanted was to hurt you. You know that, right?'

He grabs my chin, lifting my head to gaze at him and smiles. 'I know.'

I nod and leave his office.

Behind the entrance desk, Moon Hee sits writing something down.

'Hey,' I say.

'Lilah.' His eyes widen. I don't know how soundproof those offices are, but I'm praying he didn't hear me. 'How's the tattoo?'

'Oh, something came up for Elijah. Do you think you can do it?'

'It would be my pleasure.'

He leads me to his office. It's identical to Elijah's, the only difference being in the art hung on the wall.

'These are beautiful,' I say, checking the framed drawings

before sitting on the chair. The fountain pen strokes stand out to me. 'Did you make them?'

'Yeah.' He looks back at me before returning to gather the materials.

'You really are talented.'

'Thank you,' he says, scratching the back of his head.

Watching Moon Hee in his element is hypnotising. I close my eyes for a while, allowing him to work; both for me and him because seeing him this close to me gets my heart pumping faster than it should when you're dealing with needles.

But I can still feel his touch through the black rubber gloves, his breath on my skin as he gets closer, his grip on my arm to steady me. Even with my eyes closed I'm pulled to him, and when I open them his sole focus remains on the tattoo.

I never knew being focused could be such an attractive look on someone.

After a couple of hours seeing him in the zone, I could tell how much he enjoys what he does. He's a creative and a bloody good one.

'How is it?' he asks.

'Beautiful. I couldn't have asked for better.'

'Can I ask why the lilac?'

'It's a long story, but it has a deep meaning for me.' I smile at the flower now forever engraved on my skin.

'Well, now that you have your first tattoo, come back whenever you get the bug for more.' He winks.

'Trust me, I will! And we still have to figure out one to do all together.'

'We have time.' He tilts his head, eyes deepening into mine, and I nod, leaving the shop before I get even more in my head about how much I shouldn't be feeling what I am.

Before I walk back into my bakery, I stop by *Greener's*.

'Hello, my favourite twins,' I say to Jeremiah and Rebecca.

'I bet we're the only ones you know,' Becca jokes.

'You're not wrong.' I chuckle.

'How's the bakery been? The restaurant has been full,' Jeremiah says.

'These collaborations sure give us a bigger audience. It's better every time we do it.' I grab a seat to eat.

'Late lunch?' the woman with copper locks asks.

'Yes, I closed the shop for a three and half hour lunch time because I went to get my first tattoo, and now I'm starving because I haven't had lunch.'

'First tattoo? Wow, can I see?' Rebecca asks before turning to her brother. 'Table nine is calling.'

He nods and leaves with a smile.

My long-sleeved shirt is too tight to roll up. It was awkward enough to tie it around me while doing it, so Moon Hee wouldn't be staring at my black bra. But as the professional he is, he didn't even comment on it.

'It's in the back of my arm, a bit tricky to show with this shirt without flashing everyone in here, so I'll show you another time.'

'Understandable. Not that I don't think some customers wouldn't appreciate the show.' This woman is such a joker and I love her for it. If there's anyone able to lighten up the mood, it's her. In a way, she reminds me of Elijah for that.

'Oh! But I wanted to invite you and Jeremiah for a little Christmas dinner I'm having at home, if you'd like to come and don't have any plans for the holidays.'

'Our parents are back in Ireland this year, so we would love it! I can't believe I'm finally going to see your house after four years of being business neighbours.'

'I guess it was about time.' I smile, thanking Jeremiah for bringing my plate.

'I have to ask,' she says. 'Will the cuties you hang out with be there?'

'Cuties?' I laugh. 'If you are referring to Elijah and Moon Hee from *InkPark*, then yes, they'll be there.'

'Great! The one with the tattoo sleeves is always a sight for sore eyes.'

After that my friend leaves to help her brother and it gets me thinking.

Elijah and Rebecca…That would be an interesting pair. Both are playful people, with a bright smile and so much love to give. He's a lot more reserved than her, but I have no doubt she would break down his walls.

Arriving home, I remember I haven't responded to Daldust. With the collaboration, *Sweet Delilah* has been so hectic I always arrive home exhausted. I must write to him today so I can send the letter tomorrow, otherwise another weekend will get in the way and it will take longer to receive more letters.

"You couldn't have prevented it. If she was as in love with her boyfriend as you said she was, nothing you could have said would've prevented her broken heart. Some things in life just can't be helped and one has to accept them to move on. I've learned that the hard way. And I know you will find someone as special or more than her. You will share your happiness.

We will meet one day.
Delilah"

스물다섯
'seumuldasot'

Taking one last glance around the bakery, I close the door until Monday. Christmas Eve is tomorrow, and I reserved the day for cooking the dinner at night.

I walk past my neighbouring restaurant and spot the twins still working inside, so I enter.

'Hey hey,' I say.

'Hey,' Rebecca says before pointing to my purse. 'Finished for the day?'

'Yes. I closed earlier today because I need to go by the post office and buy some last-minute ingredients for tomorrow's dinner.'

'We'll be closing earlier as well.'

'I just passed by to say that you can show up anytime from 6 p.m. and dinner will most likely be around seven-thirty.'

'Great! We'll see you there!'

Saying goodbye to her and Jeremiah, who entered the kitchen after waving at me, I continue my journey to the postbox to see if I have any mail from Daldust.

To my delight, the box isn't empty when I open it, so I grab the letter and save it in my purse before going to the market for mushrooms, carrots, chickpeas, and more tofu to make sure I have enough for seconds and leftovers. I refuse to have people starving at a dinner I serve.

At home, I save all the ingredients in the fridge and grab some dates to snack on while I read my pen pal's letter.

"Dear Delilah,

I have another chance now. I found her again, and like I said, she doesn't remember me. She is different. I can see how life must have affected her, but I still see the girl I met that week. I can see her coming back bit by bit. And I'm happy to help her, even if she doesn't know who I am yet.

And before you tell me to tell her, I will. I just want to help her first. This time, I'm not letting her go. Although I'm not sure if she's falling for someone else, I know this time I will do my best for her to see me as she did that night on the roof.

And because it's the season to be jolly, I wish you happy holidays, in whatever you celebrate, or not.

Yours truly,
Daldust"

I'm unsure of how to feel. I know I'm happy that he found her again, but for some reason, I can't help but be protective of him. All these months of talking have made him someone I've come to care for. I'm not sure if he shares the same opinion, but to me, a friendship has blossomed.

I smile, thinking of how I opened up before the snow melted. A tear rolls down my cheek and my heart tightens. This feeling of being proud of myself is still so foreign.

"I hope you get her this time, but remember, you can't force anyone to fall in love with you. I know that better than anyone. So, if she likes someone else, the only thing you can do is show her how much you care for her; be there for her. Whatever happens, keep supporting her, but if she never ends up seeing your worth, move on or you will be suffering for someone who doesn't deserve you. Respect and care for yourself first.

Besides, I'm here for you. For whatever you need. I hope you know that.

Happy Holidays!
Delilah"

For the rest of the day I plan out the dinner's menu and help Elisa prepare the decorations, so tomorrow she can do everything quickly and by herself.

Before going to bed, I receive a text message from Moonie.

Don't forget to apply the cream ;P

He's been sending me those a few times a week to make sure I hydrate the tattoo and help it heal correctly. That day after doing it, he spent a solid ten minutes giving me a full on course on how to take care of a fresh tattoo, all the dos and don'ts.

I apply the bottle he recommended to me and lie down to sleep. Tomorrow is the first social event I've organised, and I'm all jittery about it.

'Lilah! We're out of tape!' Elisa says, panicking with fairy lights on her hands.

'See if the boys have some.' I glance up at the clock and it's half-past two. We still have time, but I know it will be gone in a jiff.

We're decorating our flat and the boys' dining area, since after dinner we'll come here to hang.

A moment after I hear Elisa leave the flat, the doorbell rings.

Did she forget the key?

I swiftly wash my hands in the kitchen sink and move to open our front door.

My eyes widen when instead of being greeted by my flatmate, I'm faced by Moon Hee and a small Korean woman standing next to him.

'Lilah,' the man says. 'This is my mother, Yun Yu Ra.'

'*Annyeonghaseyo* (Hello), It's so nice to have you here.' I smile with a bow, reaching my right hand forward while my left holds under my wrist. Something I've seen people doing to show respect.

'So happy to be here,' the woman says. Her cute accent and smile melt my heart.

'We also brought food.' Moon Hee lifts an enormous shopping bag.

'Oh, you didn't have to. I'm making enough food for everyone.'

'*Omma* (Mum) wouldn't take no for an answer.'

'All Korean food. Good for you,' she says, her round dark eyes shining. I see the mother-son resemblance.

'Well, come on in.' I stand to the side, allowing them to walk into the house.

I lead them to the kitchen and while I mix the cranberry sauce I'm making to accompany some homemade seitan, Moon Hee rests the bag on top of the kitchen table.

His mum tells the name of what each container contains as she takes them out of the bag. '*Kimchi*, *Kongnamul Muchim* (Seasoned Soybean Sprouts), *Sigeumchi Namul* (Seasoned Spinach), *Oi Muchim* (Spicy Cucumber Salad), *Mu Saengchae* (Spicy Radish Salad), *Gamja Jorim* (Braised Potatoes), *Hobak Bokkeum* (Stir-fried Zucchini), *Manduguk* (Korean Dumpling Soup) and *Jeon* (Korean Pancakes). All vegetables; my son tells me you eat only vegetables.'

'Thank you so much. They will be a wonderful addition to the main meals. Now please, sit and relax,' I say, pointing to our navy blue sofa. 'Do you want a beverage?'

'*Mul juseyo* (Water please).'

'I'll get it. You're cooking, Lilah,' her son says.

The lady walks over to the living room and sits on our sofa, observing the space around.

'There really was no need for all of this,' I whisper to the man beside me. He's reaching for a glass to fill with water.

'For my mum, it's not a meal without infinite side dishes.' He chuckles.

'I'm eager to try them! And thank you for telling her about my food preferences.' My gaze locks on his and we smile.

Since that day at the tattoo parlour, I have seen little of him and none of Elijah. I'm giving him space, and I'm sure he's doing the same because he hasn't even been hanging out with Elisa.

I'm nervous about seeing him today. I hope he doesn't hate me.

Moonie's eyes travel down, and he rests the water glass on top of the counter, disappearing from my peripheral vision. My back warms, and I know he's getting closer. His breath passes my ear and I turn my head to the side to see his face over my right shoulder. His hands grab the hem of my sleeve and he pulls it back.

'You and your sleeves always hanging when they shouldn't.' His tone is low as he rolls both my sleeves up.

The beating of my heart pounds as fast as the sauce bubbles right now. I turn off the heat in the stove, but mine keeps burning. Having him this close to me messes with my entire system.

'How is that tattoo of yours? Is it healing nicely?' He changes subjects, his chest still touching my back.

I nod, unable to formulate words through the pounding of my heart.

'Good girl,' he whispers in the shell of my ear.

I hold a gasp, pinching my lips together, and before I can say anything else, he's off to hand his mother her glass of water.

Oh my. I read too much romance for those two little words to not turn me into mush.

The sauce is ready, but I keep mindlessly stirring it, repeating what he said in my head.

When I peek to my side, his eyes are already on me. With his head tilted, he winks, prior to continuing his chat with his mum.

The wink gives me a strange flashback, a blurry vision similar to a dream from a long time ago. I don't know what the dream was about, but it dries my mouth to even think of it, and unlike the frightening tightness I get in my chest when I do, Moon Hee's face has the power to soothe me. A firefly in the midst of darkness.

Five…four…three…two…one…

I inhale deeply and slowly let go of the image in my head as the breath leaves my mouth.

'I finished the dining area,' Elisa says, distracting my mind.

'That's great. So, they had tape?' I ask.

'Unfortunately no, but I went to Sofía's, and she saved us.'

'Good, good.' My eyes travel down to the cranberry sauce and I let go of the spoon, transferring it to a container. 'Have you met Moon Hee's mum? She brought a lot of food.'

'I met them in the hallway. She seems sweet.'

'I think so too.' I mumble, remembering the one person who I haven't seen in a while. 'Have you spoken to Elijah? He's still coming, right?'

She gives me a soft smile and a tap on the shoulder. 'He wouldn't miss it.'

A spark of comfort involves my heart and gives me enough strength to pass on to the next dish.

Elisa enters back in the living room and continues her job as a decorator when Moon Hee's mum returns to the kitchen.

'Could I watch?' she asks, pointing at the pan on the stove.

'Of course!'

The lady picks a chair from the table and moves it closer to the counter.

The moment her shoulders relax and her full attention is on

me, we hear a loud thump of a door closing.

'*Yu Ra Ssi* (Ms Yu Ra)!' a coarse man's voice sounds.

I look in the sound's direction and a tall, dark-haired man stands in the kitchen's entrance.

'Elijah!' I say and mindlessly run to him.

'Did you miss me this much?' he whispers as I hold him tight between my arms.

I guess I did.

'It was strange not having you around.' I lift my head from his chest and meet his eyes, staring at me.

He will make another woman so happy one day.

I let go of him, and he directs himself to Moon Hee's mother.

'*Yu Ra Ssi, jal jinesseoyo* (Ms Yu Ra, how are you)?'

'*Gwaenchanayo* (I'm fine),' she says, grabbing Elijah's hands between hers.

'Are you watching this amazing cook do her magic?' With his chin, he points at me.

'I'm learning, yes.'

The blood rises to my cheeks. 'Learning? I should be learning from you, *Yu Ra Ssi*.'

'Nonsense! I'm a simple cook, you have a bakery.'

'Exactly, I bake mostly. This is different. I'm no chef.' I gesture with my hand for her to get closer to me and hand her the wooden spoon. 'This is the view of a chef.'

Moon Hee walks behind his mother and whispers something that makes her laugh.

I frown my eyebrows and his mum says, 'I'm a five-star Michelin.'

The whole room chuckles at her cuteness.

'Five stars indeed,' Elijah says, a radiant and warm smile on his face. His eyes truly light up gazing at her. They must be close.

'Now please, anyone who isn't cooking or involved with food, out of the kitchen.' I point at the exit and watch the guys sit on the sofa as Yu Ra Ssi sits back on the chair and watches me sauté vegetables before I move on to frosting some cupcakes with green icing and a yellow star on top.

※ ♥ ♥ ♥ ※

'Can you take this to the table, please?' I ask my best friend as I stand in the hallway with a food platter.

As I'm about to turn away and enter my flat for the thirtieth time in the last hour, someone calls my name.

I turn my head to the end of the corridor and watch two ginger heads waving at me.

'Rebecca, Jeremiah! I'm so glad you're here,' I say. 'Come here, let me introduce you to everyone.'

They follow me to my flat's living room where the guys and Moon Hee's mum are conversing.

'Everyone, this is Jeremiah and Rebecca, the amazing chefs at Greener's.' I reach my hand to each. 'And this is Elijah, Moon Hee, and Moon Hee's mum, Yun Yu Ra.'

'Pleased to meet you,' Elijah says, walking closer to them and shaking each twin's hand. Moon Hee follows him and the twins approach *Yu Ra Ssi*.

'This is for you.' Jeremiah hands me a tall shopping bag.

I peek inside and take out a bottle of wine. 'I know nothing about wine, but this looks expensive.'

'Just a complement to the wonderful dinner I'm sure you've prepared.' His sister smiles.

'Thank you.'

Elisa appears behind the twins. 'I was wondering why I was alone in the boys' flat.'

'Elisa, you've met Jeremiah and Rebecca, right?'

'Nice to see you again,' she says.

'You came just in time. We are finishing up taking all the food to Elijah's and Moon Hee's flat, because their dining table is bigger.'

'Oh, we'll help!' Jeremiah says.

'Where can I leave this?' Becca asks, looking at her purse and jacket in her hands.

'Here, come with me. Jer, do you also want to leave your jacket here?'

He nods and hands me his outerwear before joining the rest of the people carrying plates and platters.

I lead my friend towards my room and set everything on my bed.

'So, that's Elijah...' she says.

'Yes, he is...' I chuckle, knowing exactly what she's thinking.

'He's even better looking up close.'

'He certainly doesn't fall short on beauty,' I say.

'Do you think he'd give me his number?' She fiddles with her thumbs.

'For sure. Just let him pick up on your charm and he'll be the one asking for the number.' I wink and she sighs, smiling.

We leave the flat and meet up with the rest of the gang already seated at the table.

'Sofía, have you been introduced to Jeremiah and Rebecca?' I ask.

'To Jeremiah, yes. It's nice to meet you, Rebecca.' The woman with brown hair smiles.

I'm sitting between Elisa and Rebecca, with Moon Hee in front of me and Elijah to his right, in front of Becca.

'Let's eat!' Elijah says, rubbing his hands together.

I was worried the twins would have a hard time fitting in with the group, but I forgot how much of a social butterfly Rebecca is and how she refuses to leave her brother behind. Their loyalty to each other is impressive to me as an only child, but when your parents send you to another country to give you a better chance at life at the age of eighteen and you're faced with handling adulthood on your own, you grab on to the one closest to you, and that is experiencing the same.

Rebecca told me their story a few years ago and how poor

they grew up. Their parents did everything they could for them, saving up every penny they could to send them to London, so they could live out their dreams. She always tears up a bit when speaking of them because they rarely see each other.

They got to London with a lease for a one-bedroom flat and a job offer at a relative's restaurant, washing dishes and cleaning the place. They spent five years there learning everything they could and growing to be the chefs they are now. They saved up by staying in their tiny flat so they could open their own restaurant, the one they got six years ago, the one that is so sought after for the last three.

'Are you having a good time?' I ask Jeremiah, who nods. He's me when I met these people, enjoying their outgoing personalities and laughing at their silliness but too shy to speak.

'Becca, can you pass me the wine?' Elijah calls out.

But my friend doesn't pass the wine. She grabs his glass and pours it, looking straight into his eyes. She's been doing this for so long she knows when to stop pouring without glancing down.

The smirk he gives her when she hands him his glass back shows me Rebecca just got revamped in his mind.

I glance at Ms Yu Ra, who's smiling, watching us kids enjoy a proper meal.

When everyone finishes, we move to mine and Elisa's flat for dessert and games.

Everyone's enjoying the sweets stand I created with cupcakes, Christmas cookies, chocolate mousse, and key lime pie as I glance around the room and notice a person missing.

'Jer, have you seen Moon Hee?' I ask.

Jeremiah teams up with Yu Ra Ssi while Elisa and Sofía are chatting, and his sister and my neighbour flirt with each other.

'I think I saw him leaving the flat.'

'Thank you.' I smile and move to the hallway.

Music sounds from the door in front of mine, so I knock.

Moon Hee peeks in the small opening he created, wearing

pink gloves. 'My hands are all wet. Can you push?'

I chuckle and push the door to enter.

'What are you doing here? You should be enjoying the food.' I frown.

'You cooked. It was only fair for me to wash the dishes.' He turns his front to the sink and continues his task.

'I won't deny that, but you could do that later.'

'I don't know if you've noticed, Lilah, but I like to keep my space clean.'

I do a quick scan around the flat and notice how it sparkles beyond the fairy lights hanging on the walls.

'Yes you do, Moonie.'

'If it was up to Elijah, the flat would be a mess. I can't help it. It's the neat-freak Virgo in me.'

'I had no idea you were into astrology.'

'I'm not, I just…stuff shows up when I'm scrolling social media and some things do make sense.'

I walk to his side and pop my elbow on the counter, placing my chin on my hand and turning my head to his, batting my eyelashes. 'Tell me more.'

My glance meets his at the corner of his eye and I watch his lips contort, resisting a smile.

'That's all,' he says, paying his full attention to the last fork he has to wash.

I laugh and tap his shoulder, going back to the entrance of the kitchen.

'Shall we?' I ask, tilting my head to the door.

He takes off the pink gloves and nods.

As I'm walking, I hear his steps quickening until he stretches his arm around my shoulders.

'I love it when you call me Moonie,' he whispers to me.

26
스물여섯
'seumulyeosot'

I haven't had such a fun Christmas in a while, and I'm so glad I took the step to have my first dinner party.

Today I have an appointment with Ms Julie's colleague, and the fact that I've dropped almost everything I held in my hands until now isn't enough to express how nervous I am.

I watch the clock on the left wall of my bakery, counting the hours until 9 p.m. It's a late appointment, but it was the best she could do, and I'm grateful for it.

There's still eleven hours left.

I've cleaned the tables twice, even though most of them haven't been used. I'm grasping for anything that will take my mind out of thinking about tonight.

I know I want to know. I need to know what was so awful that my mind had to shut down, but I'm so scared because of that same reason. *My mind had to shut down to protect me.*

I told Elisa this morning where I was going in case I didn't catch her at home before I left for the appointment, but deep down I wish I wasn't going alone.

Thankfully for me, a flood of customers entertain me for the next two hours.

At lunch hour, I walk by the post office. If I had a letter, at least I would have something else to think about, even if just for a little. And as always, Daldust reads my mind.

I grab the letter and walk back to *Sweet Delilah* to read it as I eat leftovers from Christmas dinner. We spent the entire weekend eating leftovers and they're finally gone.

"Dear Delilah,
Wow, the student just became the master. I think you need to tell your therapist to be careful. You might take a run for her job, haha just kidding xD
But thank you, I will keep that in mind.
Why do you say that you know that better than anyone? What happened that made you learn you can't force someone to fall in love with you?
Yours truly,
Daldust"

My hand searches under the counter for the pen and paper I usually leave under here, in case I need to write something. I always write these letters in my room because they feel so private, so I like to have a secluded place to gather my thoughts and not get interrupted.

But this shop is my place as well, and it's still closed for another thirty minutes, so I think I can manage.

"Oh, so it's my turn to spill the tea on my dating life, I see.
**My parents are part of a very famous group of wealthy people here in London, so they've always had their eyes set on who I should date. I'd never had much opinion when it came to that. In high school I had a boyfriend because our families wanted us to be the "it" couple—so no one would even dare to get close to "royalty"—and even though we supported each other because no one wanted to be in that place, we didn't like one another and rumours spread that he was cheating

on me with someone else. I knew it to be true because he told me about it and how much he liked her. But once the rumours were out, everyone turned the girl's life into hell for even daring to be mentioned with The Elite's children. She had to move out of the city. He was devastated and we...we had to pretend everything was okay until high school ended.

In university, I moved out of my parents' house so I was able to get a bit more freedom, but I was too shy around guys, I had never been around anyone but my "ex" (I put quotes because it never felt like a real relationship, it was all for pretend), not even with his friends I spoke because technically we were in a set of schools, one for girls, one for boys that were side by side, so the students only interacted outside of the gates. Inside I had my girlfriends, and outside I would hang out with him. Anyway, long story short, my flatmate convinced me to go to some parties, and I met someone, someone I later found out was also a son of The Elite, so my parents were thrilled, but this time he was someone I liked. He showed me a different side of life and even though we were different, I liked how he challenged me; I lost my shyness, and eventually, I became social. We dated for three years until one night...one night that changed the course of my life. I don't remember much of what happened around that time. They say traumatic events can block our memory. But I remember how I felt. I remember not leaving my bed for a week and locking myself in for a month. The memories from that era might be blurry, but the hurt is crystal clear. I do know I broke up with him later. I'm not sure if it was because of what happened or because I found out he was involved with a close friend of mine at the time.

After five years, I'm finally open to date again, with baby steps, but I'm open to it.

Delilah"

I sigh. Every minute that goes by makes the events more real. I mean, who knows if I'm even going to remember? They say it helps, but it's not one hundred percent foolproof.

What if I'm making a storm out of nothing? What if I end up not remembering?

Would it be that bad?

I think I could handle that, because at least I know I have tried. I know that if I don't remember it's because I shouldn't.

I take a deep breath and put a smile on my face. That's right, whatever is meant to be, it will be.

I walk outside the counter and turn the sign on the door to *Open*.

Most of the afternoon, I get myself out of my overthinker state, being able to focus on the day and my customers. I catch myself watching the hours from time to time, but nothing too alarming, until two hours remain. The moment I close the shop, I walk to deliver my response to Daldust's letter and rush home.

My shower takes less time than the night my parents invited some of their friends to our house and their kids without my knowledge. The moment my mum placed her eyes on me, who'd just arrived from a volleyball practice, all sweaty and a messy hairdo, she rushed me upstairs to wash myself and come greet our guests. She excused my lateness, saying I lost track of time focused on my studies as the successful student I was.

I park my car in front of a tall, light building. The warm lights coming off the street lamps make it appear yellow in this dark sky.

I walk inside, where I'm greeted by a woman in her twenties reading a magazine behind the C-curved marble desk.

'Hello,' I say, clearing my throat.

Her eyes move up from the *British Vogue* and she straightens her back, placing the magazine by her side. 'Evening. How can I be of service?'

'I have an appointment to see Ms Lewis. It's under the name Scott, Delilah Scott.'

'Yes, I have it here. She's expecting you. Just walk up the stairs to your right.' The woman smiles, pointing to where I should go.

I leave the bright white entrance hall to a zone where my eyes don't burn from the light. The currant-coloured carpet leads to a dark wooden door, contrasting from the walls.

'Hello?' I say, knocking on the door before opening a breach and peeking inside. 'The girl at the front desk told me I could come in.'

'You must be Delilah. Julie spoke wonders of you,' the counsellor says with a smile. 'I'm Diana.'

'Nice to meet you.' I sit on her mocha sofa. I find it peculiar how soft the material is and the way it moulds to you.

'Julie also spoke about what you were coming here to do. She didn't disclose details, but you are interested in trying to recover a memory from five years ago, if I'm not mistaken.' The woman with long sleek black hair squints her eyes, trying to recall.

'Yes, exactly. Ms Julie says that sometimes the mind can block traumatic events.'

'And are you certain you want to unblock them?'

'I am.'

'Tell me what you remember about that day.'

'The day I don't actually remember, but I don't think it was in the sunlight that something happened. I remember going to a party that night with my ex-boyfriend and…and…we…we left the party early. He was…taking me home, but we stopped in a dark and empty street. After that, I don't remember anything else.'

Ms Diana nods and takes out a paper and pen. 'I'm going to need your signature, to have it on paper that you allowed me to hypnotise you.'

'Oh, okay.' I grab the pen and lay down the paper on the table in front of me.

'Tell me Delilah, are you familiar with hypnotherapy?'

'Not first hand, but I've heard of it.'

'In the document, you can also read the steps it takes and all you can expect from it. I'll give you time to read it through.' She grabs her notebook to divert her attention while I read.

Once I finish, I lay down the pen and reach the paper to her. Ms Lewis's eyes lift from the notebook at my movement and she asks, 'Are you ready to start?'

I nod, and she tells me to lie down and pay close attention to her finger.

I follow it as it moves around, creating a pattern, one my mind recognises after a few tries, making it easier to focus.

'When I snap my fingers, you'll be taken back to that night five years ago. Your boyfriend and you are driving through a dark street. You just want to get home, but he stops. Remember what happened as the engine died down.'

At the sound of her fingers snapping, my mind goes black.

'Lilah?' I hear as soon as Ms Diana snaps her fingers again. 'Are you okay?'

I glance down at my knees tight on my chest as I wrap my arms around my legs, sitting on her sofa. I have no idea when I moved positions.

My throat is heavy as the only sound coming out of it are sobs that have lasted longer than I can recall.

I leave her office, taking only enough steps to not block the entrance, before I fall down to the floor. My breathing is too heavy and audible.

A river floods my face and my vision is too blurry to see the faces that pull me up. With the back of my hand, I clean up my eyes enough to recognise them.

'What are you doing here?' I say in between breaths, my voice breaking.

'We're here for you, Lilah. Do you really think you'd have to go through this alone?' Elisa says.

'Never again,' Moon Hee adds.

'You're stuck with us,' Elijah joins.

The three of them wrap their arms around me, allowing my tears to flood over my water line once more.

I feel a mix between pain from the past and hope for the future. I've been through this before. I remember everything now. But last time I had no one, and the pain twenty-two-year-old Delilah must have felt makes my heart ache.

They somehow get me to Lisa's car and drive me home—I'm too much in my mind to notice the world around me moving. Elijah drives behind us in mine, so I don't have to pick it up tomorrow.

I'm in the backseat, my head resting on Moon Hee's lap while he gently strokes my hair. My head is still trying to make sense of all the information it hid for the past five years.

Memories flashing through my head. Too many to focus on each. So many, my mind takes a while to connect them all.

Moon Hee lowers himself enough to whisper in the shell of my ear, 'You're not alone anymore.'

A wave of tiredness weighs on my eyes, so I close them. Between the silence in the car, the tears still rolling down my face, diminishing as the faucet seems to run out, and Moonie's caressing, my mind relaxes enough to drift off.

스물일곱
'seumulilgob'

It's been a few days since my appointment. I closed the bakery for the week, saying I was ill. In a way, it wasn't a lie. It still makes me sick to think about that night, but I've been taking my time to heal. I even unscheduled my session with Ms Julie for yesterday because I'm still not ready to talk about it.

My friends check up on me constantly, and Moon Hee keeps bringing me warm food to eat—he says sandwiches and cereals are not enough to keep me healthy—but they don't ask about it; they know I'll go to them when I'm ready.

'Lilah?' My flatmate knocks on my door.

I get up from my bed, still in my pyjamas, and open it. They let me sleep to my heart's content this week.

'Yes?' I rub my eyes. I'd been awake for a few minutes, but hadn't found the strength to get up.

'It's New Year's Eve...so I was wondering what you think of having a small gathering here with the boys and Sofía.' She glances behind her to the living room as a sign that they are here.

'Wouldn't you rather go to a party or something? You always go to parties on this day.'

'I would rather spend the night with my best friend. You always went to bed early on this day, so I had no other choice than to go out. Will you stay awake this time?'

I'm not much in the mood to socialise, but her glimmering

eyes take the best of me. 'Sure, sounds good.' Besides, spending time with them has been preventing me from going down the depression hole again, even if it has been just one or two at a time and not all like tonight will be.

'Yay, I'm so excited! You just relax and I'll take care of everything.' Elisa goes back to the living room and tells them the news.

A few seconds later, my tall, tattooed neighbour walks my way, even before I close my door.

'My dearest Lilah, did you sleep well?' Elijah has been a sweetheart. Even after I broke his heart, he's stayed by my side.

'I did, thank you,' I say, looking down.

It's weird to think that even though I've remembered both the night and the following weeks, I still feel so down. It's not as if I'm going through it again, but it brought up all the old feelings. Like painting a room in the same colour, you know how it looks, yet with the paint still fresh, it seems renewed.

He wraps his arms around me, his warmth giving me all the comfort I need without words. Elijah knows words aren't his strong suit, but he's improved in comforting people, at least with me. Sometimes a hug is worth more than any word.

'Are you really up for tonight?' he asks, stroking my back.

'I will be,' I say into his shirt.

He pats the top of my head and lets go of me with a sympathetic smile. I know this is hard on him too, being around me like this.

'Have you talked more with Rebecca since the dinner?' I haven't, but I'm hoping they have.

'We text sometimes, but my focus isn't on her right now.'

'Ouch,' I say, lifting my right hand to my chest. 'You have a gift to make a girl feel guilty.'

'I have a gift to make a girl feel. Period.' The man smirks, and watching the left corner of his mouth lift is all I need to know he's getting over it, over me. 'I'm joking. I'm focusing more on myself. Moon Hee even got me reading one of his self-help books.'

'He got you reading? Now, he's the one with the true gift.' I chuckle, and he rolls his eyes.

'Join us when you're ready.'

'I will.' I nod.

I take my time in the shower, washing every inch in my body twice. I've been doing that since Monday. It's been five years, but I have again the need to scrub myself. It's not as bad as before. I remember one day when I scrubbed so hard my entire body was raw after my shower. I had to change the clothes I wore after an hour because they got all bloody red.

I'm limiting myself to a gentle scrub twice and a great amount of moisturiser after.

Entering the living room, they all sit on the sofa watching a film.

'What are you watching?' I ask.

'*Love Actually*,' Moon Hee says as we exchange glances for the first time in a few days.

I've been avoiding him the most.

My therapist would be proud of me, because I'm choosing to let myself feel instead of reaching for the one thing I know could make me forget everything—in this case, the one person. Him.

Allowing Moon Hee in would mean I would feel happier when I want to be sad. When I want to grieve.

But I also know I can't avoid him much longer before he starts asking questions. He's made it clear he's not afraid to be blunt with me, and I know he'll ask me why I'm avoiding him. And if he does…I'm not sure how I'll hide my feelings for him anymore.

'Great film…' I say, pursing my lips together and slowly taking my gaze from his, not to cause any suspicion.

I move to the kitchen to eat something. When I turn to our table, there's a pot lid covering a dish. On top there's a yellow sticky note with the words 'Just heat it up. PS: They might not be as good as yours'.

He didn't sign it, but I know who it's from. I uncover the lid and a plate of pancakes stares at me. With the sticky note on one hand and the pot lid on the other, I smile.

He made a smiley face with chocolate chips.

I grab the plate and warm it up for a few seconds in the microwave. As the plate warms, I peek into the living room and as if he had a Delilah radar, he looks in my direction. I smile and give him a finger heart. He smiles back.

I haven't had anything other than cereal for breakfast all week, so these pancakes taste like heaven.

As I lick the last remains off the fork, I'm startled when Moonie says near my ear, 'Were they tasty?'

The fork falls on the plate, making more sound than I expected. My hand presses into my chest. 'You bloody scared me!'

He chuckles. 'I missed your smile.'

I swallow, avoiding his gaze. 'Thank you for this and all the food you've been bringing me.'

'I wouldn't want you to lose those pretty curves of yours.'

My eyes widen, and shocked isn't enough of a word to express what I'm feeling. 'Wow. I would expect a line like that from Elijah, but you? Who are you and what have you done to my Moonie?'

He chuckles. 'You just haven't seen all sides of me.'

'Moon Hee,' Elijah says, entering the kitchen. 'We should go see your mum now, so we can get ready for tonight after it.'

'Yeah, we should.' Moon Hee straightens his back and turns his body to Elijah.

As they leave the room, my designated chef for this week stops and turns his head back to me, giving me a finger heart, before turning the corner of the wall where my eyes can no longer see him.

'What do you think?' Elisa asks, spinning in her new see-through turquoise dress covered in small turquoise rhinestones.

'You look good in everything.'

Her dark complexion makes bold colours suit her so much, unlike my fair skin, which only pastels and neutrals suit.

'Do I need to get all dressed up like this? We're at home...' I say.

'You were at a home as well for my birthday and got dressed up, so get your ass up and go to your closet.' My friend lifts me up off the bed and pushes me to the closet.

I open it with a growl and rummage through it to find something pretty but comfortable. I come upon my lilac dress, the fabric feeling like soft clouds on my skin. Perfect.

'This one.' I show her the dress. 'I only accept this one.'

'Fine, it's cute. But you're letting me do your makeup.'

I nod. I wouldn't want to do it either way.

The doorbell rings throughout the house and Elisa moves to answer it.

'Hi babe,' I hear, letting me know it's Sofía. Good, I'm not ready to face men yet.

'You look amazing!' Sofía says to Elisa.

They come to my room, and I greet Sofía with a wave and a smile.

'That's such a cute dress, Lilah. I love it,' Sofía says, wrapping her arm around Elisa's waist.

'Thank you.'

Every time I see them together, I feel so happy for my best friend. She really found someone that sees her and treats her like the queen she is.

'Let's let her get ready,' Elisa says, closing the door on their way out.

When I'm dressed in the comfiest dress I own, some black tights and my white fluffy slippers, because I refuse to hold my feet hostage at home, I meet with Elisa to do my make-up. I tell her to do something simple, so she gives me a lilac eyeshadow and a cat eyeliner. Some highlights here and there and finishing with a non-stick lip gloss with a slight hint of pink, appearing almost as my natural lip colour when blood pumps in them after a kiss.

'There's some liquor and snacks in the kitchen, and the boys are getting more. As soon as they arrive, we're ready to party!' Elisa claps her hands together.

A few moments later, we hear the doorbell and since I'm closest to it and the girls are cuddling, I go to open it.

'Hey,' I say as two Korean men stare in my direction. Whenever I forget they're my friends and look at them as more, I'm constantly astonished by their beauty. And it's not just one, it's both.

Elijah wears black suit pants and a white shirt, the three top buttons hanging free and sleeves rolled up, showing all his black tattoos. Moon Hee is in a similar outfit, but his shirt is black and there's only one tattoo peeking in his right arm—although the ink on his chest peeks to greet me.

'Hey,' Moon Hee greets, staring at my outfit before his eyes stop on mine.

'Hey, beautiful,' Elijah says, giving me a peck on the cheek before walking in. 'Let's get this party started!'

'Elijah, my dearest party friend,' Elisa says, walking in his direction as we get closer to the living room.

'Gorgeous as always,' he says, placing an arm around her shoulders. 'You look lovely as well, Sofía.'

'Moon Hee, Moon Hee…Wow, I see your flatmate's sense of fashion has rubbed off on you.' My best friend stares at him, nodding her head.

'He said I couldn't leave the house with my normal clothes.'

'You and Lilah,' she says, pointing between us. 'Two peas in the same pod.'

He glances at me with a raised eyebrow, so I explain, 'She also made me dress up,' and he nods.

'And you did amazing,' Moonie says low enough for only me to hear.

I sense the blood reach my cheeks so I try diverting the attention to him. 'So did you.'

'Where do we put this?' Elijah asks, raising two plastic shopping bags.

'Kitchen. I'm going to turn on the music,' Elisa says.

The boys arrange the extra drinks and snacks on top of the kitchen table and as I look at what they brought, I spot *tteokbokki*.

'I'm definitely having this.' I grab a pot of instant *tteokbokki*.

'Don't eat it all, that's our go to snack,' my tattoo-sleeved friend says.

'You should have brought more, then.' I smile.

'It's okay, we have extras at home. I can go get it if needed,' Moon Hee says.

'You really are a Virgo,' I joke and he sighs, most likely regretting telling me about his interest in the zodiac.

I never knew I enjoyed teasing him as much as I do.

'Let's grab our drinks for now. We can eat after.'

We are all mingling in our main room when B.I's song *BTBT* plays.

'OMG,' I say to Elisa. 'You have this song on your playlist?'

'Spotify suggested this song, and I liked it. I didn't even know it was Korean until I checked the artist.' She takes a sip of her cranberry vodka.

'I'm so proud, I converted you to K-Pop.' I purse my lips, pretending to be about to cry, and place my hand on her shoulder.

'You did not.'

'All it takes is one song. More will come, trust me.'

My flatmate rolls her eyes, turning to speak with her girlfriend again.

The music in the background merges with my thoughts as I sway with a drink in hand. My eyes closed, feeling the beat around me as the alcohol enters my veins.

The song *Tattoo* by Loreen rises on the speaker and I open

my eyes to Moon Hee's looking at mine. His intense glare as he leans on the wall drinking pulls me closer to him.

'You look like you're having a good time,' he says.

'And you look like you're having a good time watching me have a good time.'

'What can I say...You're stuck on me like a tattoo...' The corner of his lip lifts.

'I must be in invisible ink, then. I don't see it.' Grabbing his arms, I study them, searching around for another tattoo.

He steps away from the wall, straightening himself in front of me, close enough that I can smell a faint sweet soap scent coming from him.

'You smell nice,' I say, stepping even closer to him. My feet are touching his.

'And you're drunk.' Moon Hee places his hands on my shoulder to steady myself.

'Just a little bit.' I smile with closed eyes. 'Oh!' My eyebrows rise. 'You know what I could go for now?'

He shakes his head.

'*Tteokbokki*!'

As I'm about to turn around to go to the kitchen, my foot trips on the other. While I'm leaning forward, seeing the floor as my destiny, Moon Hee's grip on my shoulders tightens, pulling me back to him.

My back hits his chest as I hear him going against the wall.

'Are you okay?' I ask, turning my face to the side and looking back.

With his arms wrapped around me he says, 'Sit here, I'll get you *tteokbokki*.'

'Guys, ten seconds to midnight!' Elisa says, raising her glass to count backwards.

I turn around to face the man behind me, whose arms stay around me. My gaze looks up at his as he leans still on the wall.

'Three...two...one...' my other friends yell as Chase Atlantic's

Slow Down roars around us.

My eyes watch as his darken, looking down at me, his hands marking my skin. My chest feels his getting quicker, matching the pace of my breath.

His lips part, and his tongue peeks out to wet the bottom lip that's fuller than the top with the perfect cupid's bow. The intensity in his gaze runs down my body, electricity bursting through it. I don't know if it's the liquor, how good he looks, the faint smell of vanilla soap, or the fact that his face is closing in on mine but the need to join my lips with his grows on me.

My mouth can taste the alcohol on his breath as he pauses a third of an inch from me and turns his head to the side, whispering in my ear, 'Happy new year, Delilah.'

♥ ♥ ♥

I stand behind the counter of *Sweet Delilah*, replaying Saturday night's event in my head. As I imagined, being around him made me forget all the worries that burdened me all week and for the past five years, and having his face so close to mine, despite much of the night being a blur, is marked into my brain in bold.

We crossed paths Sunday when he left my house, but I was too shy to even look at him.

My eyes stare at the street outside through the window when the gold bell on top of the door rings, bringing my attention to it. I only came here to grab a notebook I left before Christmas and forgot. Since I'm only reopening the bakery on Wednesday, I didn't even bother to lock the door.

The one thing I wasn't expecting was Moon Hee's face to be overtaken from my mind by the one who should have stayed in the past but stands in front of me.

Vance.

28
스물여덟
'seumulyeoldolb'

Five years ago...

'I thought you were taking me home. Why are we stopping here?' I ask my boyfriend.

As we approach the dark warehouse, the silence of the empty street becomes even more pronounced. I've been here once but the daylight still shone. The eerie atmosphere that surrounds us now sends chills down my spine.

'I'm just grabbing something to take to the party after. You can stay in the car if you want.'

I glance back at his new white Mustang standing out from the old and beaten cars along the street, surrounded by a few people in a detrimental state. Going with him is scary, but staying behind sounds even more terrifying.

I walk behind him, holding the back hem of his shirt, hyper-aware of my surroundings.

He stops, making me almost bump into him, and knocks on the door.

Someone on the inside asks, 'Password.'

'Sugar crush,' Vance says, and the door opens.

We enter the warehouse, whose door is being guarded by a man in black.

A man with a teardrop tattoo under his eye, and others

peeking through his collarbone, approaches the man beside me.

'What do you want, Vance?' he says, tightening his lips.

I glance up at my boyfriend, who's looking down at the floor. I've never seen him this way; it's almost as if he's afraid. Vance Harris doesn't get scared. He's the one people fear.

'Can you just...lend me one more gram? I-I promise to give you everything by the end of the week.'

'That's what you said last week.' The man crosses his arms.

My gaze moves beyond him and his guard, who dresses identically to the man at the door, to the women sitting around some tables, packaging white blocks. They're all wearing denim mini skirts and a bra, even in this chilly weather.

'Who's this?' I hear the strange man ask, returning my gaze back to him. When his gold teeth make an appearance, my eyes move down to the floor.

'No one you need to worry about,' my boyfriend says.

The man closes in on me and his fingers brush my hair back, making me more uncomfortable than before.

A sudden pull on my hand gets me to walk one step behind Vance. I trace its source and locate my boy's hand holding mine.

The feet that once stood in front of me take a few steps back.

'Okay,' the man says.

'Okay?' The swift rise on Vance's head leads me to lift mine as well. 'Thank you man, I won't let you down this time.'

The man chuckles, looking back to his guard, who smiles on cue. 'But she stays.' He winks at me.

Those words get stuck in the air. I look up at Vance, who's wide eyed, staring at his dealer.

I wait for him to say something, but nothing comes out of his mouth.

'Vance?' I nudge at him, but his only reaction is to swallow, so I repeat, desperation brewing inside me. 'Vance?'

I glance at the man smiling at me as his eyes trace my body, and the thought of being alone with him blurs my vision.

'Fine, I'll bring you the money today,' Vance says at last.

The man deviates his gaze from him, allowing me to breathe again. 'She stays until you bring the money.'

I should have stayed in the car.

I should have stayed in the car.

I should have stayed in the car, I repeat to myself as running footsteps sound away from me. A door closing a second later.

'Let's go on a date,' the man pulling me to him by the waist says. My vision is too blurred to see the floor straight.

My whole body is trembling by the time we arrive in a closed room.

The floor is still the only image in front of me, but the image I think of as he slides his hand down my back gets me airless.

'Let's sit here,' he says, lowering himself to the sofa on the right of the room.

I attempt to sit away from him, but he pulls me closer and wraps his arm around my shoulders. I sit straight, pushing my legs as close as humanly possible, his exact opposite.

'What's your name?' His gaze weighs on me, but I'm too scared to look up.

'You don't say much, do you?' he asks, grabbing my chin so my eyes meet his.

The dim light in the room doesn't allow me to know his exact eye colour, but it's a light one leading more towards brown. From my peripheral vision I catch his bodyguard standing by the door, watching us.

I hope Vance doesn't take too long.

He licks his teeth, releasing my chin, and chuckles. 'A date is for people to get to know each other. If you don't talk, I can't get to know you...and I *really* want to know you.'

The last thing I want is to make him mad at me, so I say, 'Lilah.'

'Lilah...A pretty name for a pretty girl.' His hand moves from my shoulders to my bare thigh as he puts pressure on my skin.

My hands grab on the hem of my dress, pulling it as far down as the fabric stretches.

'I truly like pretty girls,' the man with gold teeth says.

I swallow hard. *Please, Vance, please.*

'If your boyfriend takes too long, I'll get bored...I'm sure you don't want me to get bored.'

The guard receives a call and hands it over to the man, saving me some time. While he's distracted, I grab my phone to check the time. It's been half an hour since we entered the warehouse, so I'm assuming twenty minutes since he left.

He should be returning at any minute, thank goodness. One question keeps lingering in my mind. How does he owe money? His family is richer than mine.

Finishing up his call, the boss sits in his previous place. 'I'm sorry, I had to take that. Where were we?'

'Right,' he says a couple of seconds later. 'I'll give him ten minutes to return before you and I move to the second stage of this date.'

Each minute that goes by seems slower than the one before. *Where the bloody fuck is Vance?*

'I'm being too benevolent, aren't I?' he asks his guard. 'I've even given him five minutes extra.'

His guard stays silent, nodding only, so the man turns back to me. 'He must not like you very much. Unfortunately for him, I like you too much.'

The moment his tongue wets his lips, my eye gives up, releasing a tear down my cheek. His smirk says everything I need to know about him.

'Turn on the camera and stay outside. Make sure no one interrupts us,' the man says to the one dressed in black.

Camera?

The hand on my thigh traces up as his other grabs mine to free the dress's fabric. I attempt to stray away, but that only makes him smile harder. The sick sadist.

My mind is racing too fast for me to come up with a decision.

He wants to see me suffer, so I shouldn't give him the glee. But if I fight back, maybe it will give Vance more time to arrive. But what if he doesn't arrive on time? *What if he doesn't come at all?*

This time both my eyes give up, sending a stream of tears down my face.

He grabs both my wrists and lowers me on the sofa, holding them above my head. His knee tries to part my legs, but I keep them closed while moving around.

One of his hands takes over in holding my wrist while the other goes to hold my legs still. In that transition, I release myself and end up hitting him on his face with my elbow.

His smile fades, and a frown appears instead. This is the moment I know I fucked up.

'P-Please don't,' I say, my hands shaking.

He slaps me across the face, and the hand on my legs lifts my dress. The other holds my neck, making it harder for me to breathe.

'Bitch,' I hear under his breath.

My eyes close, attempting to take me away from this moment. Tears cool down my burning face as my body stiffens under his touch.

'You don't need to fight; I'm not going to hurt you. Just have some fun.' His hands trace my breasts, and he cups them before sliding down to the rest of my stomach. 'Don't worry, you'll still be pure for your boyfriend. I just want to taste every inch of your skin.'

I should have stayed in the car.

The monotonous expanse of the grey floor has held my eyes fixated for the past few hours. His bodyguard placed a blanket on top of me, as if that would provide any protection. My chest warms my legs as my arms wrap around it; a position that provides some comfort despite its lack of protection as well.

I've felt afraid, but I've never felt so unprotected, so out of control, at least not until now.

'Lilah?' someone asks, but my strength isn't enough to lift my eye line.

'Look who decided to show up after all,' Gold-teeth says.

'What did you do to her?' the other person asks, running towards me.

He slowly crouches down, gradually coming into view. My bare legs feel a sudden jolt as his fingertips make contact, causing me to flinch.

Vance.

I thought I'd feel happier seeing him, knowing I'm finally getting out of this hellhole, but my face is unable to move. I leave the comfort of my position and stand up, the blanket dropping behind me in the process.

My boyfriend takes off his jacket and places it around me, covering the parts my dress no longer can.

'Here's your fucking money,' the man beside me says.

With each step he leads me towards the exit, the sight of my light blue undies resting on the cold, grey floor draws my gaze.

'Are you okay? What happened?' Vance asks inside the car, but still I'm unable to speak.

The bright moon shines on the starless dark sky, making its presence as strong as the heaviness in my body. Outside, the buildings take their time to pass by us, or so it seems. Time feels like nothing but a façade at this moment.

Freedom was what I wished for tonight—to be a bird—but this body is trapping me even more now.

As we arrive at my house, the sun is waking up. Vance lays me down on my bed and gives me a peck on the forehead, leaving shortly after.

The world around me is nothing but a blur, one I see change

colours. From dark to light and back to dark as I lay on my bed wearing nothing but a ripped dress in a trance where only heaviness exists.

I've felt happy, sad, angry and many more emotions, but this is the first time I feel nothing. Empty. A bare shell on a soulless body.

Present time...

'Vance?' I blink hard, hoping it's a hallucination.

Not here. Not in the one place I control. *Not here.*

'Hi Lilah.' The man who caused the worst night of my life approaches me.

'What are you doing here?' I ask, closing the cash register.

'I wanted to see you,' he says.

'You've seen me, now go.'

I know he wasn't the one to do that to me, but I can't forgive the way he treated me. Especially knowing what he saw.

'I wanted to apologise for that night.' He walks closer to the counter, looking me straight in the eyes. 'I'm clean now. I have been for two years and one of the steps is to apologise to those I've hurt. I don't expect you to forgive me, but I truly wanted to express my regret.'

'Good, because I will never forgive you. The way you treated me...not only before but when I needed you the most!'

I've been holding on to these thoughts for too long. At the time, I wasn't able to tell him how I felt, but I'm ready.

'I never understood how we were so good at first and then you started abandoning me at parties, cheating on me—yes, don't think I didn't know—ignoring me, and that night...' My waterline floods and the tears threaten to cascade down my face, so I exhale. 'That night, you took so long. Why did you take so long?' But I can no longer control them. Tears roll down my face as I yell my heart out. 'And you didn't even bother to check up on me later. I didn't hear from you for weeks! If I didn't contact you, I probably wouldn't have seen you again. What did I ever do to you to deserve that?'

'Lilah, I'm-I'm so sorry, I swear, I—'

'I'm not done yet. I needed you, I needed you to comfort me, to help me, especially with my parents when he posted that video. They scrutinised me, and I had no one. No one on my side! I needed you to tell my parents you were the reason we broke up. I needed you...'

My eyes are too blurry to see someone going around the counter and embracing me. Vance stands still in front of me and when that person's thumb rubs away the tears blocking my vision, his face gives me the comfort I so desperately needed all those years ago.

'Moonie,' I say under my breath.

'I'm here.'

스물아홉
'seumulahob'

Moon Hee's POV

'Can you close up? I want to see if Lilah will serve me a coffee,' I ask my boss. I know she's closed, but I saw her going inside the bakery a few minutes ago.

'Sure, I'll be at Lisa's after,' he says, opening the cash register.

'Oh, and Elijah? I'm going to tell her soon.'

My friend stares at me for a while before nodding and lowering his head to the money with a forced smile. 'It's about time.' I hate that this has grown into a tension between us, but I know we'll get through this.

'You know I couldn't have it done before.' I look outside, thinking of the time I had to wait to be as I am with her now.

'You could. I did.' His gaze lifts to me, but his jaw stays clenched.

'Exactly because of it. She needed to sort out her feelings for you first. You were her crush.' I stare back at him.

'And I had my chance to be more, right? Is that what you're thinking?'

'*Hyung*...if she'd chosen you, I would be happy for you both. Sad for me? For sure. But I would cheer for you. That's why I stayed away from her since our first hang out, no matter how much that cost me.'

His eyes lower as the skin wrinkles between his eyebrows. 'That night...You talked more with her than all the nights after...'

'If I hadn't seen how she looked at you back then, I would have shot my shot earlier. But she needed to know how she felt about you, not to mention that she needed a friend more than she needed a boyfriend at the time.'

He stays silent, his head lowering to the cash once more.

As I'm walking to *Sweet Delilah* across the street, I watch Lilah talking to a man. I've never seen him around, but she doesn't look thrilled to see him.

The closer I get to the door, the more her eyes gleam. I've never seen her like this. They must know each other. I can hear her voice all the way out here.

'I'm not done yet,' she says as I enter the bakery. She doesn't see me or hear the bell.

I don't like this.

'I needed you. I needed you to comfort me, to help me, especially with my parents when he posted that video. They scrutinised me, and I had no one. No one on my side! I needed you to tell my parents you were the reason we broke up. I needed you.'

Oh fuck. I drop my backpack on the floor and run to her. The guy watches me as I round the counter and pull her to me.

Every time I see her cry, she holds my heart hostage. It's fucking painful.

I stood by as I saw my dad hurt, because I didn't know what to do...and I stayed quiet as my mum grieved for him, mad at myself for not helping him out of the dark hole he dug. If my mum wasn't as strong as she is, she would have gone the same path.

I won't let Lilah have the same fate. *Not her*. I promised myself I would never stay put again, and as if the universe heard me, it's been getting me at the right place, at the right time. My arms are ready to strip the pain away from her.

'Moonie.' She looks up at me, her lips trembling.

'I'm here,' I say, squeezing her harder against me.

'What the fuck did you do to her?' I turn to the man standing in front of us. If my stare could kill, he'd be lying on the ground by now.

'Lilah, I'm truly sorry. I was so messed up back then. If I could take your pain away, I would.' He ignores me.

'You can't, but you can take yourself out.' The woman in my arms stands upright but doesn't let me go.

The way her hands wrap around my waist is enough to tempt my mind to go places inappropriate for the moment. But it feels so fucking good.

No wonder Elijah caught feelings. I've only had brief encounters with her touch—with clothes on—and they're enough to send me over the edge. I can't even grasp what it's like to have her wrapped in my arms, nothing keeping our skin apart. And since this weekend, the thought of it has been coming more often than not.

His footsteps become less prominent as my eyes fixate on her. Delilah's face seems sad as she watches him leave, exhaling when the bell above the door rings and it closes.

Her eyes move to mine and for a few seconds, as the leaves flying outside stop moving and the street becomes empty, it's just me and her. Our eyes lock, reaching for the deepest parts of each other, searching for the secrets we buried under the moonlight to tell us we're not alone.

I'm the first one to break the silence. 'I have another song for you.'

I watch the black dot on her stunning brown eyes widen and as the corner of her lips lift, 'You and your songs. Which is it?'

'*I Hope You Know* by Sofia Carson.' How I wish you could read my mind, Delilah Scott.

Her eyes squint harder as her smile grows bigger. This face of pure joy, that's the one I strive for every time we're together. 'You're a box full of surprises, Kim Moon Hee. Who knew Sofia Carson was in your playlist as well?'

'I don't listen to songs for the artist but for their artistry.'

'Well, I would love to know what else is on your playlist.' The bell on top of the door rings, bringing us back from our utopia.

'I'm sorry, are you still open?' a woman with long and curly ginger hair asks.

Delilah's hands drop from my waist and she composes herself, turning her body towards the customer. 'Yes, of course, come in.'

'I just wanted a coffee to go,' the client says.

Delilah smiles and nods, turning around to the coffee machine. As her hand grabs the cup, I notice it shaking.

I reach for it, my hand on top of hers, both to calm her down and to take over. 'Go relax, I'll take care of this.'

'Do you know how?' Her hand heats mine as I try my best to keep it still.

'I've worked at a café before.' I smile, and she releases the cup, leaving me longing for her touch.

Lilah sits on the stool near the counter, and I prepare the other woman's order, taking a coffee for myself after she leaves.

'Thank you,' she says. 'Once more.'

'Stop thanking me as if I'm doing you a favour. We're friends, Lilah, and I really care about you. Besides, I just wanted a coffee for myself, anyway.' I wink to lighten the mood.

She chuckles with my comment and stands up to close the shop. I help the one my heart screams for and walk her to her house.

When we enter the girls' living room, Lisa and Elijah are sitting on the sofa talking. His eyes turn to me and Lilah, but stay fixed on mine. I shake my head, letting him know I haven't told her, and he nods.

'Hey,' I say, and they greet me back. 'Sofía isn't joining us today?'

'No,' Lisa says, standing up and walking into the kitchen. Her face turned too serious to be okay.

I turn to Lilah and whisper, 'Is everything okay with Lisa?' She gives me a shoulder shrug as a response.

I don't know Lisa as well as Lilah or Elijah, but I do care for her well-being. I walk to meet her and even though I have no clue on how to approach her, I pretend to go for a glass of water and I say, 'If you need to talk I'm here.'

She's sitting on the back counter, looking at her feet bouncing in the air.

'I've just been feeling weird. Sofía and I are great, and things are going amazing. But that's the problem. She's ready for more and I'm just not sure.'

'Why do you feel like you're not sure when you know how good things are?' I ask, walking to the counter by her left and leaning on it.

'I don't know. That's why I say I feel weird.'

'Look, Lisa, I don't know you that well, and I don't want to make any assumptions, but from all I've seen and heard in the past year we've known each other, Sofía is the first person I've seen you spend more than two weeks with and I see how you look at her. She makes you happy.'

Her eyes now lay on me, her feet still. 'How do you know you've found love?'

'Love doesn't find you—passion and desire yes—but love...love you create by choosing that person and fighting for them every day. So don't be afraid of falling in love with her, because that's not something you can control, but you can control if you want to love her. And if you don't want to lose her, choose her.'

The woman with chocolate and blueberry locs nods with a small smile and gets down from the counter. 'Thank you.'

'Anytime.' I smile and stand straight, extending my arm for her to lead the way back to the living room.

On the sofa, Elijah and Lilah sit next to each other, his arm around her. This dynamic is so unfamiliar to me. I know they are good friends and I know nothing else will come out from there, but it's still so strange to know that they slept together from time to time. Especially knowing that if it was up to Elijah, they'd be more than friends.

'Lilah, when is our turn?' I play, getting everyone's undivided attention. 'I mean, I'm the only one who hasn't slept with anyone from this group. I could've asked Lisa, but she's dating, so…when is our turn, *Delilah*?'

Elijah's gaze is somewhat in shock and sad at the same time, and Lisa is just amusingly watching us. But it's Lilah's choke on the air that gets me to clear things up.

'I'm joking, relax. It's funny how Elijah has been with both of you.' I chuckle.

'Woah, in my defence, that was a stupid drunk night when we met. We soon realised we were better off as friends,' Lisa says, gesturing with her hands, as she does when trying to make a point.

'True that.' Elijah points at her while nodding.

While everyone else is laughing, Lilah remains silent, fixing her gaze on me. Part of me hopes she can see past the joke and understand my sincere longing for us to have our own special moment. Her expression gives me a glimmer of hope, but I'm uncertain if she feels the same way.

I wonder if this magnetic pull I have towards her is mutual. Does she feel the same need to be close when we are in the same space? That any stolen touch is a percentage of battery recharged?

Does her world stop when our eyes interconnect? Is the impulse to grab her close to me and kiss those luscious lips getting harder each day for her, too? Does her mind fill with the thought of us making love, making it more difficult to concentrate on the simplest tasks?

She's my favourite song on repeat.

The want to pull her aside and tell her everything, tell her how destined we are, is stronger today, but after the encounter she had, I don't think it would be the best idea.

As *omma* says, 'Patience is a virtue,' and I'm nothing if not patient.

'Well, what film are we watching today?' Lisa asks, deviating Lilah's gaze from mine.

'I'm feeling horror,' Elijah suggests. 'I want to see who you ladies grab when a scare comes.' He winks, teasing his tongue out.

'We all know you're the one who needs to grab someone,' Lisa says, and we laugh.

'As long as we're grabbing, I'm fine with it,' he plays.

'You choose, I need to go to the loo first. I'll make the popcorn when I come back,' Lilah says, getting up from the sofa and walking to the room's entry.

'Take your time. I'll make the popcorn,' I say.

She nods and leaves the space without another word. I hope I didn't make her too uncomfortable before. She's been so dispirited.

A few minutes later, as I turn around from the microwave after placing the bag of corn inside, Delilah shows up in front of me.

There's something different from before. Her head stands tall as her foot takes a step closer to me, making me take one back and hit the counter behind.

She takes another step and I hold my breath.

Where is this confidence coming from?

Her head tilts to the right, peeking in the microwave. My heart beats faster with each corn exploding inside the paper bag. Her gaze finds me once more and she leans in to me, standing on her tiptoes.

Her breath meets my ear, sending infinity chills all over my body. 'I know you don't want me to thank you, but let me at least tell you how much I appreciate you.'

A flame rises inside me and my hands grab her waist, stopping her from stepping back as her feet lay flat back on the ground. The sight of her tongue slightly wet her bottom lip before she pulls it between her teeth makes it impossible to turn my eyes back up to hers.

Our bodies touch as I lean on the counter, her head looking up as I look down, with my hands on her waist, tempting my patience.

I'm not sure I can hold it in anymore.

I look up from her lips to see her gaze down on mine. *She wants me too.*

In the split second I'm about to risk it all, as I lower my head to meet hers, the microwave beeps, startling us both.

Fucking popcorn.

서른
'seoreun'

My bedroom's ceiling has been through multiple luminosity stages as I lay in my bed, gazing at it. Tonight's events marked on my mind.

Not only tonight's event, but him. He's marked on my mind. The way his round, beautiful dark eyes weren't so rounded as his desire shone through. The way he couldn't stop staring at my lips, enticing my own desire to kiss him, for the second time.

It's weird how this came out of nowhere. I've tried to pinpoint the moment I stopped seeing him simply as a friend, but I come out blank every time.

He came to me as a small splash in the ocean that as it went over it collected more water and grew, and when I finally saw it, it had grown so much that it drowned me.

During the film, I couldn't concentrate on the plot. All I saw was him, and he saw me. Whenever I took a glimpse of him, he was already looking at me. I'm not even sure if he ended up watching the TV screen. We kept our distance, though. I sat next to Elisa on one end of the sofa and he sat on the opposite. We decided it was better because we were afraid of anyone seeing what we saw. The invisible fire that surrounded us, that tempted to burn us with its beautiful, yet extremely dangerous, flames.

The funny thing is that because of him, a day that I would have spent reminiscing about the past otherwise became a day to remember for all its good. Vance's visit was shocking to say the least, and all the memories that it brought to the surface were overwhelming at best, but that one brief moment with Moon Hee overshadowed everything once again.

The more I think of him, the more my heart wants to burst, palpitating so hard as if it's trying to leave my chest. My mind floods with every memory of him.

All the times he held me as I broke down, in a way no one else had ever done. I used to be alone in those moments, but suddenly someone that started as a stranger appeared in the background, ripping my bubble to hold my hand and tell me everything would be okay. And it was, because he was there.

A stranger that for some reason feels like someone I've known for years; someone that was dormant in the deeper parts of my heart and erupted like a volcano, covering it with lava.

The day has risen through my window and without checking the time, I give up on sleep, getting up to move to the kitchen. I went to bed earlier than the rest because I needed to calm my mind, which ended up backfiring on me, so it comes as a surprise when I walk to the living room to find two men sleeping.

I quickly return to the hall and peek in my flatmate's room. The bed is made, and she's nowhere to be seen.

What the hell happened after I left?

I walk to my room and grab my phone to check the time and see if she texted.

Ten past seven. And a message from three hours ago.

Sleeping at Sofia's. The guys fell asleep watching another film

I place my phone back on the nightstand and when I go to turn on my door's nob, a slight tap on the door comes through.

'Lilah?'

His voice stops me midway. My heartbeat speeds up again, overriding all of my previous doubts and thoughts.

I open the door, grab his hand to pull him inside, and close it again.

He's facing the window, the sunrise glimmering over his features. His eyes stare at me, pupils widening. I wonder if it's from the light or because of me.

'I heard you walking around,' Moonie says.

'It surprised me to see you sleeping there.'

'Yeah, we fell asleep.' He rubs his hand on the back of his head, tousling his silky black hair.

'I couldn't sleep.' My eyes meet the floor, and I turn around to watch the sunlight. 'So, I was going to bake something.'

'Let's do it.' His hands brush my shoulders, landing as a feather on my skin.

My face turns to my right to find him gazing outside.

I walk back until my back meets his chest and his arms wrap around me, hugging me from behind. The warmth in his body transfers to mine, reaching places the sun can't. We stand like this for a while, watching the bright light rise through the window until I say, 'Let's go.'

He unwraps me from his arms. 'Thank god, I'm starving.'

I laugh, and he gives me a wink back, waking up the butterflies.

We enter the kitchen in silence. I place my index finger vertically on top of my lips, signalling to sound-asleep Elijah, and I grab the ingredients to make pancakes.

'You can sit there while I make breakfast. This is fast,' I say to Moon Hee.

He walks close behind me. 'I would love to stay back and appreciate you wearing only that shirt, but I don't know how much I would enjoy seeing Elijah's eyes on you when he wakes up.'

I glance down at my white baggy shirt. *I'm not used to having men around in the morning.*

'Don't worry, I'll grab you some pants,' he says, leaving me to prepare our food.

While I'm mixing the pancake batter in a bowl, by hand as to not wake our guest up, the man that has been stirring all the emotions in me returns with black trackies.

'I apologise in advance if I took anything out of place in your room, but I had to rummage through it a bit to find these.'

I chuckle. 'It's okay, thank you.'

I put on the pants and heat the pan.

'The only vegan pancakes I've tasted were from when I made them for you,' he says, looking at the batter. 'I also never had any other dessert vegan before entering your shop, and I would have never guessed if you hadn't told me. But I'm sure yours are way better than mine.'

'Elisa loves it when I make them.' I smile.

'Oh, I believe it. You have magical hands in the kitchen.'

'Not just in the kitchen.' I lick the spoon of batter, my eyes fixated on his.

Moon Hee licks his bottom lip before one corner of his mouth lifts and when his breath brushes my ear, he whispers, 'I'll be the judge of that.'

Fuck.

Fuck. Fuck. Fuck.

That's all I can think to do with him now.

The sizzling from the pan startles me, liberating my mind of those thoughts, at least for the time being.

He sits back on the table, and I finish the pancakes. As I'm plating them, a silhouette shows up on my left.

'Yummy...What smells so good?' Elijah says.

'You're up.' Moonie states the obvious, eyes wide.

'Yeah, the smell woke me up. I'm starving.'

'Go sit then,' I say, grabbing an extra plate for him.

'*Kamsamnida* (Thank you). This looks so delicious,' Elijah says.

'They're delicious,' Moonie says.

I smile at them and satisfy half my cravings. The other half are sitting next to me, and I'm not sure if we're ready to tackle them.

'Are you feeling better?' Elijah asks me, pouring syrup over his pancakes.

'Yes, thank you for asking.'

Moon Hee's possessiveness surprises me. I didn't take him for that type of person, but the glare he's giving Elijah makes it crystal clear. I never noticed his reactions before, so I don't know if this is something new or not.

I reach my hand under the table to his and squeeze it gently. His gaze turns to me and I give him a soft smile.

'Elisa and I are going to the arcade today. Do you want to join us?' he asks.

'Hmm…I'm not in the mood to go out today,' I say.

'So, both introverts stay.' He chuckles, lifting another bite to his mouth.

'Why aren't you going?' I ask Moon Hee.

'I'm also in the mood to stay home.'

We're both staying behind. Alone.

Is this a sign?

Don't be stupid, Delilah, you stay behind all the time. Why would this time be any different?

I'll stay in my house, and he'll stay in his. That's it. Nothing more.

I sense his gaze on me while I murder my pancakes by poking on them with my fork.

'Should I come over later?' he whispers to me.

My fork drops and my eyes look back and forth between him and his flatmate, who's distracted by scrolling through his phone. I lift my eyebrows and point with my eyes to him, as if telling him, 'Are you crazy? What if he heard you?' but he only smirks at me.

I'd never seen him smirk before, and it's happened twice today already. There's a whole new side of him I'm unfamiliar with, and deep down I'm eager to discover it.

Once the boys leave, I embark on a frenzy of cleaning, scrubbing every surface in sight. From the ceiling to the floor, this house gleams with cleanliness. Baking is my go-to remedy for stress, but I wouldn't say I'm feeling stressed at the moment. Faced with a cluttered mind, I tackle the task of cleaning the house, hoping it will bring some mental order as well.

Not long ago, I ended things with Elijah, and even though he took it well, I still know how he feels about me. Moon Hee is his best friend, and I'm afraid us together would hurt him.

Elisa left to meet Elijah a few hours ago, and there has been no sign of Moon Hee. Maybe he was joking before about coming here.

I sit on the sofa, nodding to myself. I guess it's for the best.

I reach for the remote and zap through the channels. Nothing sparks my interest, so I stand up once more. I walk to my room and glance around at something to do, but there's nothing out of place.

Daldust.

That's right, I picked up a letter yesterday before I went to the bakery. With everything, it completely slipped my mind.

I go through my bag in search of the letter and when I find it, I sit at my desk to read.

"Dear Delilah,

It seems like you've been through a lot relationships-wise. I'm glad you know your worth now and that you have people you trust, people who love you.

After that girl I tried dating, but nothing ever lasted because she was always on my mind.

Are you interested in someone now? If it's okay to ask, of course.

You got me curious and you already know I'm interested in someone ;)

Yours truly,
Daldust"

I do have people who I trust and love. That's so foreign to me. It has been only me since my Nana died. She was the one and only form of love I knew in my childhood. I've had fleeting love, but nothing compared until now. I found people I know I can count on, where we'll be there for each other, to support and cheer.

This might sound weird, but I know I've known Elisa for the longest time and she's been the closest form of love I had, but somehow these past months we've gotten even closer. Perhaps it was me who learned how to let people in, perhaps we both grew in ways we hadn't before. Either way, I can't wait to see where the future takes us because this friendship still has a long course to go.

"Honestly, I am.
But I'm scared to fuck up our friendship.
I'm just so grateful to have him in my life. To be able to talk with him without any insecurities. He's one of the few people that can relax me and increase my happiness.
You said you lost her because you realised your feelings too late and didn't tell her about them.
I'm learning from your mistakes. I don't want to regret my life and not be able to have a relationship because he's always on my mind. So I'm going to tell him soon. I'm just gathering the courage to expose myself in that way.
And isn't it about time I get to know your real name? Delilah"

We seem to have an unspoken connection, clear from everything that has transpired, but until we voice our feelings, it remains a mirage within my thoughts. Uttering those words will bring them to life, and I'm not sure if I desire that reality.

Not that I don't fantasise about it, but I dread all the consequences that might come with it. As I wrote to Daldust, I'm scared to fuck up our friendship, not just mine and Moon Hee's, but the group's. I don't want to unbalance our energy.

I fold the letter and place it in an envelope, saving it in my purse, so when Monday arrives, I can send it.

When I step out of my bedroom, a loud thump sounds on the flat's exit door. I turn my attention to it and go check what's on the other side. My hand lifts the little black peephole cover, but all I see is the top of a head.

'Who's there?' I ask.

'Moon Hee.' The voice outside sounds strenuous.

I open the door to find my front-door neighbour picking the lid of a pot off the floor.

He looks at me and chuckles. '*Eottoke...* (What do I do...) I hit the pot on the door when I went to knock and the lid fell down.'

I smile and grab the pot away from him. 'Come in. What is this?'

'Just some seaweed soup I made,' he says, closing the door behind him.

'But it's not my birthday.' I've always seen them make that soup on someone's birthday.

'I know. I just had the ingredients and wanted to do something home-cooked for you, especially after the wonderful pancakes you fed us for breakfast.' He's the only man who can make me question every previous thought I had when I was alone.

'Thank you.' I walk to the cabinet and take out two soup bowls. 'Let's eat while it's still warm.'

He nods and sits across from me at our little dining table.

'I was beginning to think you were joking about coming here,' I say.

'If there's one thing you need to learn about me, it's that I never joke when it comes to you, Delilah.'

A thousand sun rays involve my heart as those words leave his mouth. 'What else do I need to learn about you?'

'Whatever you want. For you, I'm an open book.'

'Why did you recently start calling me Delilah?' He's the only one who does it, everyone else always calls me Lilah. My Nana was the only one who used my full name.

'It's funny, but I didn't know you were Delilah until recently because everyone calls you Lilah all the time. Why is that?'

'Oh...' I reminisce about kindergarten times. 'When I was young, there was another Delilah in my class and my parents refused to have me be *common*, so they began calling me Lilah, saying to everyone it was a variation coming from lilac, a colour that is sweet, endearing, and welcoming. That's why my grandmother called me Sweet Delilah and why I named it my bakery. In her honour and because that's how I want people to feel as they walk into it.'

'My lovely lilac,' he says, reaching his hand to my face, wiping a tear I didn't notice.

'Sorry, I tend to tear up every time I think about her.'

'She must have been a wonderful person to have raised such an incredible woman as you.' There is no one besides him and Daldust who understands me so well. Him even more, as he can see through my eyes, deep into my soul.

'I'm sorry, I can't do this,' I say, standing up from the table and walking into the living room.

'Lilah, wait!' He rushes after me. 'What's wrong?'

'I can't do this.' I point between us.

He holds my hands near his chest. 'Why not?'

I stare down at the ground, avoiding his gaze. If he saw my eyes, he could tell right away.

'Talk to me,' he says, leading me to the sofa.

We sit down next to each other, hands warming one another. I watch the pot on the counter from across the room and sigh.

'I don't want to make it awkward between us and Elijah. He's your best friend and I know he has feelings for me.'

'I understand.' One of his hands lets go of mine, moving to my chin and pulling it towards him. 'I also know how he feels about you, but he knows how I feel, too.'

My eyes, which had been avoiding him, lock with his in a heartbeat. 'He does?'

'Yes, before the two of us got any closer, he and I spoke. He knew I would be speaking to you soon. It was sooner than expected, but I guess it was when it needed to be.'

'For today, can we just talk?' I ask.

'I would love nothing else,' he says. 'Now let's go eat the soup before it goes cold.'

I nod and we move to the table once more.

Time with Moon Hee slips through my fingers like grains of sand, impossible to hold on to. Ever since our first encounter, I've realised that everything else pales in comparison, as he becomes the sole focus of my attention.

The room grew darker as our conversations flowed, K-Drama episodes played, and we indulged in snacks. The peculiar thing is that the same peacefulness I feel when I'm alone, engrossed in my passions, is mirrored in his presence, only heightened by the knowledge that I'll never feel alone again.

서른하나
'seoreunhana'

Elisa's POV

'Did you have fun at the arcade on Tuesday?' Lilah asks me, cleaning plates to store them back on the shelves.

'Yes, but I'm sure it would have been better with you there,' I say as I sit at the table, a blank page on the computer staring back at me.

I don't normally work here, but I needed a change of scenery.

'What did you do?' I ask. I know she spent time with Moon Hee because when I was walking in the hallway to the flat, I saw him leaving our place.

'Not much...I cleaned the house, wrote a letter to Daldust, and then Moon Hee showed up here.' Even though she has her back turned to me, I can hear it in her voice, how normal she wants to make it pass by.

'Seems like a productive day.' Maybe by pretending to play along, she'll tell me something more. 'How are things between you and...Daldust.'

The way she stopped before I said the last name makes me want to laugh. Something is definitely going on between her and Moon Hee.

'Everything is going well. I've been really enjoying getting to know him. I feel like we connect, you know? He's been a good teacher too.'

'Moon Hee, hi!' I say. My flatmate almost breaks a plate at

the sound of my voice, turning to the entrance of the kitchen in a flick of lightning.

'Elisa, what in the bloody hell?' Her eyes widened at me, one hand on her chest and the other holding her to the counter.

'Did you hear a doorbell?'

'No...'

'They don't have a key, do they?'

'No...'

'Then how would it be him?' I chuckle. 'What's been going on between you two?' I'm not that patient of a person.

'It's weird. We both know we have feelings, but we can't seem to cross the line.'

'That's so funny, thinking you and Elijah didn't exactly have feelings but crossed the line so easily.' I close my laptop's lid. This conversation is pulling me more than the report I need to write for the efficiency analysis of a website I created a few weeks ago.

'Yeah, life is funny like that.' Lilah pulls out a chair from the table to sit nearer to me.

'Have I told you how proud I am of you?' The eyes that once sat on the table rise to mine.

'Proud?'

'Fucking proud. One year ago you never went out unless it was for work, and then therapy. The simple mention of me bringing someone home would lock you in your room. Six months ago, you actually started walking around the house with others here, like a tiny mouse running around trying not to be seen, but it was progress already. And now? When was your last panic attack?'

'A month ago...I've been able to stop myself before I got there.'

'A fucking month ago! You just had a dinner party. Never did I think Delilah fucking Scott would organise a dinner party. You went on holiday with me and three other people. You even hang more with your other friends. And being around guys? Even if you're still cautious about all the others, you've become friends with two! Not just one, two! One that got you active in bed again.' I wink. 'And another that's stealing your heart. So yeah. Proud.'

'Looking back, it's like the snowball effect,' she says. 'For a long time it didn't seem to be working, but little by little I think I progressed and since I started writing to Daldust, it's like he opened my life to all kinds of possibilities.'

'He might have helped you, but *you* opened your life to possibilities. You took the first steps, you went out of your comfort zone, and you kept growing.'

'Do you remember five years ago?' she asks, now playing with her thumbs.

'After Vance?' I ask, and she nods. 'I remember coming home and not seeing you or hearing you for a week, seeing a shadow walking around the flat, simply existing. Your skin was so pale all the time.'

'Yeah...I think the biggest difference from then and now is how alone I was. And when you are used to going through everything alone for so long, it's weird to know that you have someone you can count on.'

'The thing is, Lilah, you were never alone. You felt alone, but I was there for you every time you needed it, just like you are for me and as I'll continue to be. I gave you space back then because no matter what I did, you were existing inside your mind. I remember being the one to clean your room and change your bedsheets. Making sure you always had something to eat in the fridge.'

'You did all that? I honestly don't remember. For an entire month, my life was a blur and after that many hours of the day were too. Thank you for doing those things.'

'Can I ask what happened?'

My friend leans back in the chair and takes a deep breath before telling me how one normal evening became the turning point in her life. How Vance left her with someone that violated her private space, and even though he never penetrated her, he touched her every crease, kissed it, licked it. Got off of seeing her tremble—afraid he would go back on his word at any time—rubbed himself on her, came on her skin, and recorded the whole thing.

'What a sick psycho...Wait, was that the video I heard people talking about?' I ask, remembering some chats.

'People saw?'

'From what I remember, no, they saw the thumbnail of the video, but if they went to click it, it wouldn't work. Your parents must have taken it down right away.'

'Having that around would ruin their reputation.'

'I don't believe it was just that. I remember your mum coming here when you wouldn't leave your room. She came a few times after too, but the same way you didn't see me, you never saw her.'

Lilah's eyes stare at me with raised eyebrows, her mouth slightly parted as she interiorises my words.

Faint as the wind on a clear sunny day, I catch her saying, 'She did?'

'I know you two don't have a good relationship, but she texts me sometimes, asking how you are.'

I stand up from the chair and walk to my room to grab my phone that had reached eighty-eight percent in charging. I hand her my blue-cased phone with the chat from her mother opened on the screen, backing five years of texts.

'She texts at least once a month...' Her finger keeps scrolling up. 'Why didn't she just ask me? I rarely hear from her.'

'I don't know. I think that's a conversation you should have with her.'

'Thank you for showing me this,' she says, handing me the phone back. I smile, taking my computer from the table and returning to the office space I created in my room.

I place it on the left side of my corner table, turn on the desk computer, and click the little button under my two lower screens and the top one—to give me a more ample view of the workspace. I grab my workout ball today and sit on it while putting on my black and blue headphones that match the aesthetic of my cloud blue room.

The purple, grey, and blue clouds projected on the ceiling and the blue LED lights on the walls are enough light to focus on getting this report done. When my one-hour Ghibli piano soundtrack ends, I write the last dot on the Word document, finishing up the work I had for this Saturday afternoon.

I grab my phone and send a text to Sofía.

Are you free today?

One more hour and I'll go to you <3

It's funny to think this little Spanish woman brightens up my days. I haven't had someone like that for a while.

I've always seen myself as a self-sufficient person, happy, single and surrounded by others. But the truth is, even though my nights were roaring loud, my days felt lonely, especially when the one friend I have was going through so much she couldn't spend all the time I wanted with me.

We always had our film nights and meals together, but as an extrovert, every time she held herself in her room, my day became gloomy. That's why meeting our front-door neighbours and having another extroverted friend was a game changer for me. I would still do my work, workout, and play a game for a while, but whenever I was done with my entertainment, I could just call Elijah and they would come over.

I've been living on my own since I was seventeen and from all the people I've met throughout the years, I can say I've found my crew at twenty-seven. It took me twenty years, but my dream has come true.

The lights in front of me blur together as I reminisce on seven-year-old Elisa sleeping in a room with five other girls, all wishing for someone to come take them to their new home—one where they could finally say they have a family.

Mine might not be the standard formation, but it's the one I've built and will accompany me as I extend it in the future.

I know Lilah has always seen me with a cool aunt vibe, but deep down I long for a big family, to be the mother of boys, girls, and all they choose to be.

And as strange as it might seem, because I've met her so recently, I see that future with Sofía and I know she sees it with me.

I grab my copy of The Last Of US Part I and insert it into the PS5. I can almost play this game with my eyes closed by now.

When Sofía texts me saying she's finished work, I stop the game and walk up to open the front door.

'Hey babe,' my gorgeous girlfriend says.

Her delicate chestnut lips tease me as they touch with each word she speaks. I place my hand behind her head and pull her to me.

I can't imagine getting tired of kissing her in this timeline. Our lips were made for each other.

The soft touch of her hand on my back sliding down to my behind makes me grab her hand and lead her to my bedroom. When she closes my door, her soft touch turns ferocious, pushing me to the bed and standing on top of me, lifting my chin so our mouths connect again.

My hands grab the hem of her shirt and lift it above her head. *I love a braless woman.*

Sofía follows my lead, leaving us exposed.

The sweet gaze she has when she looks at me is one of many things that made me fall in love with her. Her kindness is boundless.

'Can I tell you something?' I say, popping myself on my elbows as she stands in front of me at the edge of the bed.

'Always.'

'I've never...done it...with a girl, I mean.' I bite the inside of my lip.

'I know.' She smiles.

'You know?'

'When your friends talked about all the relationships you had, on your birthday weekend, I thought to myself how odd it was for a woman so open with her sexuality and seemingly so active with it too, to be dating me and every time I try to go a little further, for the last two months to avoid it. I just figured you were taking your time.'

'But, they talked about women too…didn't that make you think about it?'

'At first, yes, I thought it could be just a me thing. Maybe you wanted to take it slow, but I could feel it in your touch, your nervousness when I touched you in certain places.'

'I guess you do know me.' I chuckle. 'Every girl I was with, we only made out dead drunk. In the morning, they wouldn't remember half the night, so they never questioned if we ended up doing something.'

'The one thing I haven't quite figured out is…why didn't you do it with any of those?'

'I wanted to be sober for my first time.'

She gets herself on her knees in front of me and asks, 'Are you sober now?'

I nod and kiss her drug-like lips before sitting nearer the edge of the bed.

Both her hands pull down my yoga pants and undies in one go. I instinctively close my legs, but she puts her hands on my knees and opens them again.

Her face gets closer to me, disappearing between my legs. When something wet, hard, and with a rough texture touches my clit, I gasp, energy buzzing through my spine.

I close my eyes, allowing myself to enjoy every slide, touch, and movement. When her lips join the mix, followed by her fingers, every fragment of negativity or bad vibration leaves my body, making me feel closer to a higher dimension than any drug I've tried has.

I've always let my sexuality flow where it wanted. I'm not attracted by outer organs, but by the inside nature of a person. And at this moment, Sofía is all I'm attracted to.

Attracted to the small mole under her eye as she stares into my soul, attracted to all the parts of her body that she uses to pleasure me, and the ones that make her love me. Attracted to the soft hair touching my legs, the warm hands holding my thighs and the devious smile she has on now that she has tasted me.

Everything she's doing is enough to make my heart beat faster than a Formula 1 race. My legs tremble more than an earthquake and the air slips out of my lungs as if I'm being drowned by the only sensation I feel: euphoria.

'So, was it worth the wait?' my girl asks.

'Every bit of it.' I open my eyes to watch her lie down next to me on the bed. 'My turn,' I say.

She chuckles as the back of her fingers caresses my cheek. 'I'm okay. Seeing you was all the pleasure I needed for now.'

'Are you sure?' I ask.

'I am. But don't think you're off the hook...I have so much I want to do with you.' She winks.

'Can you pass me the water bottle?' I ask, and she lifts herself to grab the bottle on the nightstand near her. 'Thank you.'

'You and your big ass water bottle. You don't go anywhere without it.'

I laugh and look at my three litre bottle. 'I need to keep my water intake in check.'

'Health freak,' Sofía jokes.

'Have you been drinking enough water? Are you using the reminder I installed on your phone?' I take a sip of water and place it on the floor beside me.

'Yes, mum.'

'Good.' I smile and wrap my arm around her, pulling her closer to me.

Her head lies on my chest as I look up at the projected clouds on the ceiling and play with her hair.

Serenity fills me as I picture my future. Seven-year-old Elisa couldn't fathom dreaming of something as beautiful as my reality.

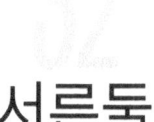

서른둘
'seoreundul'

I'm still appalled by what Elisa told me about my mother. Never in my life had she given me a reason to believe she cared. Not when I had school presentations or events and Nana was the only one to show up. Not even at my high school or university graduations.

Not on all the birthdays she'd sent me a gift through one of our maids because she'd gone on a business trip with The Elite. Not even when my grandmother died…

So, why? Why does she ask my flatmate if I'm okay? And not once dare to come up to me and question it to my face?

I don't understand.

London's weather matches my mood today. Cloudy with a high expectation of rain.

The small drizzle I caught on the way to the bakery warned me to not put out my outside tables. And as I prepare the ones inside, placing a few alive flowers in the centre, I ponder if I should call her.

'Lilah?' I hear in between my thoughts. I sigh, not connecting the dots that someone had called me until I look up to a warm smile.

'Moonie, hi. I'm sorry I didn't notice you coming in.'

'Is everything okay?' he asks, eyebrows closing in on each other.

'Lost in my thoughts, that's all.' I give him a small smile and grab the cleaning spray and cloth, walking behind the counter.

'It's been a while...'

My eyes rise to his, momentarily forgetting all that troubles me. He has a power over me I haven't been able to understand.

'I'm sorry, I have been all over the place lately,' I say.

'Has the issue with your ex made you get panic attacks again?' My eyes glance down at his hands laying on the counter, so inviting.

My hands lie on top of his and I meet his eyes once more. 'As strange as it might sound, no. I haven't had them in a long time. It's almost as if my body has finally managed to relax after all this time. No matter how stressed or worried I might be, it all seems to vanish with a thought.'

'A thought?'

I smile but say nothing. I have not yet gathered the courage to say: you.

'I actually came here to ask you something...' he says. 'I wanted to invite you. On a date.'

'A date?' My eyes widen at the words, and butterflies run through me. My body lightens so much I feel like I'm levitating.

'I want to spend time with you. Just us. We don't have enough of that.'

'That's true.' I look down, biting my lower lip. We're almost always surrounded by our friends. The only day we had alone was a week ago and after he left, I already wanted to have another. 'So, what do you have in mind?'

'Not to sound too cliché, but I was thinking of a film and then a walk under the moonlight?'

'Sounds perfect,' I say, trying to play cool. 'What will we watch?'

'I want you to choose the film. I'm fine with whatever you want.' Both his hands turn palms up and hold mine.

'Oh, I don't know...' I mumble, my heart racing. Every date I've been on, I never had a choice in the planning. I've grown to enjoy a multitude of genres and things because of it. 'I think it would be easier to choose something you like, because I'm sure I'll enjoy it too, than to choose something I want and risk you not liking it.'

'Delilah, my dear lilac, I don't mind what you choose, because the whole point is not for me to watch the film, but for me to watch you enjoy it.'

No one has ever cared if I enjoyed it or not. It was always about them enjoying it. And I was happy seeing them happy.

Someone saying they are the ones who want to see me happy is so foreign.

He releases one of his hands from mine and lifts it to my chin, bringing my gaze up to his. 'See what's in the lineup and then tell me the time.'

I nod and he retreats outside.

I seem like a teenager again with a stupid grin I cannot subside. I grab my phone to check what's playing tonight in the theatre, but when my face sees the screen, I get the impulse to text my mum.

Can we meet this week?

I proceed with my search, keeping his words in mind to find something I'd want to watch instead of looking for something I think he would enjoy.

Until closing time, my mind crosses multiple subjects, including the difference between when Elijah asked me on a date versus Moon Hee. I was a wreck back then, but it's so weird that not an ounce of anxiety travelled through my body now. No matter the progress I've made, I'm sure if it were someone else, I would have reacted differently.

Before entering my flat, I glance at the door behind me and smile.

'You look happy,' my flatmate says when I walk by the living room towards my room.

'I am happy.'

'Any reason in particular?' She grabs a handful of popcorn, switching her eyes between me and the TV.

'Moon Hee invited me on a date.'

Her head turns to me in a flash, eyes wide and mouth full. She reaches for the remote and pauses her show, coughing a bit from the speed chewing. 'He what?'

'Yeah...' The blood rises in my cheeks and the more I think about it, the more emotions flow over me.

Tears flood my waterline, but I don't want to cry. 'I don't know why I'm so emotional,' I say, wiping my eyes.

'He fucking finally did it...' Her tone is low as she looks down before meeting my eyes with a grin. 'He fucking finally did it!'

My friend gets up from the sofa and reaches her arms around me.

'Is it weird that I'm so happy I want to cry?' I ask.

'No, it's not. I've noticed your energy and girl, I fucking want to scream that this is finally happening. After I saw you so close on New Year's Eve, I really thought that something would happen then...but you guys are fucking slow!'

I laugh. 'We haven't even said how we feel about each other.'

'You don't need to. Your eyes are shouting it every time you look at each other.'

A sudden thought of another friend of ours drops my smile. 'But I still feel bad about Elijah.'

'Lilah, today is not the day to think about Elijah. I know you are a sweetheart who wants everyone to be happy, but trust me, Elijah will be fine. And he'll be happy seeing you happy.' Her words soften my heart. 'I saw you smiling when you were having the best time with him, but I've never seen you glow like when you are with Moon Hee.'

'He does bring out the best in me...' I tight my lips, smiling.

'And you bring out the best in him.'

'Okay, but now...What am I going to wear?'

'I know exactly what,' Elisa says, leaving towards her room.

I follow her but stop by the door, peeking at what she's looking for. A few minutes later and with a few undone drawers, she takes out the perfect dress for me.

'It's stunning,' I say, feeling the soft silk fabric in my hands.

'I've had it for years, but never wore it. The colour doesn't suit me at all. But you're my opposite on the colour wheel, and I think you'll look great in it.'

'Elisa...It's absolutely perfect.' I place it in front of me and check her full-body mirror.

The long, thin, and flowy sleeves give the dress a romantic feeling I only get from fairytales. Its baby blue shade reminds me of a colour only found in aesthetic boards on Pinterest. The lower hem stops above the halfway mark on my thighs, giving me an illusion of longer legs.

'Go try it on!'

I speed to my room and change clothes. It fits like a glove, which is strange because of how different my body and Elisa's are.

Walking out of the room, I watch my best friend's eyes lit up. 'Lilah! Please don't ever take that off again.'

I chuckle, but don't resist asking, 'The dress wasn't just sitting in your room because it didn't match your tones, wasn't it?'

She sighs, looking down. 'You caught me...I bought it for you a few years ago, but never found the right time to give it to you until now.'

'Thank you,' I say.

I take a quick shower and get ready, texting Moonie when I'm finished.

Moments later, the doorbell sounds through the house and my flatmate gives me two thumbs up, whispering, 'You got this.'

The grin that hasn't left my face the whole day grows when I open the door and find a bouquet of white lilies and purple lilacs being held by two hands.

From behind the bouquet, a head peeks to the side with a gentle smile. 'Hi.'

'Moonie...You shouldn't have...'

'If I want to make this night unforgettable, I had to,' he says, handing me the giant amount of flowers. 'And wow,' he says, his eyes travelling down on me. 'You're pretty unforgettable too.'

I think there was no point in putting on blush because I have a feeling my cheeks will flush all night long.

'You look pretty good too.' He's dressed in a similar outfit from New Year's, but this time instead of suit pants he has black jeans, giving it a more casual look.

I enter the kitchen to put the flowers in water and Elisa gives me a look with raised eyebrows. I know she'll want me to spill the entire night when I arrive home.

'Let's go,' I tell the man whose eyes don't stray from me.

'I have a little confession to make...' he says when we arrive in front of the theatre.

I glance up at him and he wets the lips I couldn't stop thinking about a few nights ago, before speaking again. 'I rented the whole film session for us. Just to make sure no one else would be there.'

My jaw drops. 'You weren't kidding when you said you wanted it to be just the two of us.'

'I've been waiting for this night for way too long to not have it be perfect.'

'Oh yeah? How long?'

'More than you think,' he whispers in my ear, warming my whole body with his breath.

His face finds itself a third of an inch from mine again, his breath brushing on my lips.

'Moonie...' I mumble.

'Yes, Delilah?' I can almost taste the scent of mint coming from his mouth.

I swallow hard, getting ready for this to be the moment our mouths finally touch, when the corner of his mouth lifts.

'Don't get any ideas just yet. The night is still young.'

I gasp, unsure if the coarse tone of his voice was the reason for the breath caught in my throat or the fact that he insinuated that something will happen tonight.

He stands up straight and walks into the theatre, and I follow.

We sit in the dark, empty room. The perfect mood light surrounds us as ads play on the big screen.

'I'm not sure how you feel about rom-coms, but I've wanted to see this one since it came out.'

'I love rom-coms,' he says, a soft smile on his face.

My hand brushes the side of his hand when I place it on the armrest and as I'm about to take it, afraid to make him uncomfortable, he grabs it.

Without words, or a slight glance in my direction, Moon Hee holds my hand tightly as he watches the trailer for an upcoming film and I feel the butterflies levitating me again.

There we stay, getting closer as the film plays. With each laugh, either I move towards him or he moves to me. By the end, my head rests on his shoulder as we watch the two protagonists kissing and declaring their love for each other.

'That was funny,' he says when the lights turn back on.

Neither of us move, his hand still holding mine and my head resting under his.

'Moonie?' I say, lighter than a feather.

'I'll never get tired of hearing you call me that,' he says. 'What is it, Delilah?'

'I...' My mind is having trouble coming up with the words my heart feels.

'I know.'

'But how do you know?' My head leaves his shoulder and stares at him.

'I just do.'

'You're still such a mystery to me,' I say.

'Which is funny because I'm the one who's been wearing his

heart on his sleeve the most.'

I never noticed it, but from what I've been told and if I objectively look back, what he says makes sense. He's been quiet, letting me live my life and make my own decisions. Waiting for the day I noticed him, the day he'd become the one in my eyes. He's never hid his feelings towards me, he's just didn't shout them, allowing only the ones who would truly look at him to see.

'Let's go for the walk?' I get up from the seat.

'Yes, let me just go to the loo quickly.'

I nod and he leaves the room.

I grab my things and take my phone out of silent mode, noticing a text on the screen. My mum replied.

I'm free Wednesday.

That's in two days...Will I still have the courage to face her then?

I'm waiting for my date by the door, outside of the theatre, when I make up my mind to go through with it.

Meet me at the bakery at 7 p.m.

'We can go now,' Moon Hee says, behind me.

I try to shake the thoughts of Wednesday for now and focus on the moment.

'So, do you have anything else special prepared?' I ask.

'You know I do.'

I smile, excited to see where the night leads us.

We're walking along the street between the film theatre and the park near our shops when I spot fairy lights drawing a path.

I glance at Moon Hee, and he smiles, so I keep walking. In front, the fairy lights move up to two trees, a blanket and basket between them.

'A picnic?' I ask.

'I thought you might be hungry after the film.'

I run to the trees and sit on the fuzzy cream blanket. I'm glad it's not a windy night.

I watch as he approaches me and sits by my side, opening the basket. Inside there's a bottle of *soju* and two shot glasses, as well as two sandwiches wrapped in foil and some plastic containers.

He takes everything out and I check the containers. Chocolate-covered strawberries fill one, homemade *tteokbokki* fills the other.

'You never got to eat your *tteokbokki* that night, and homemade is always better than store bought. Besides, it goes so well with *soju*.'

'Strawberries for dessert, I'm assuming?'

'Something sweet for a sweet someone.'

My eyes close as my mouth opens wide, laughing. 'You're really going at it tonight.'

He laughs with me. 'I'm going to pamper you so much you'll be feeling the void of it for the rest of the week.'

With the biggest grin, I grab the sandwich and take a bite.

'Hmm...delicious,' I say.

We stare at the sky as we eat, and each take a shot to warm us on this cold night.

'I haven't been completely honest with you,' Moon Hee says to the sky. I frown, looking at him, but his eyes stay on the moon. 'Don't worry, it's not something bad, but the reason you think I'm so mysterious is because I have a secret. One I want to tell you, but not now.'

'A secret?'

'Can you trust me and wait a little longer? I promise I'll tell you soon.'

I'm unsure of what to think. He's never given me a reason not to trust him, but I wonder what the secret is.

'Can we just enjoy tonight?' he asks.

'Why did you tell me this now when you could have hidden it for longer?' I ask.

'Because there's something I want to do, and I want you to know where I stand.' His eyes meet mine, dark as all the times I've seen a spark of desire in him before. 'Do you trust me?'

'Yes, I trust you.'

'Good,' Moon Hee says before turning to the side. His hand slides to the side of my face and he comes closer, eyes fixed on my lips. This time, he doesn't stop. His lips meet mine; an infusion of alcohol, spice and sweet slides in my mouth, completing me.

My eyes close, intensifying my sense of touch. The way his soft lips push against mine, the way his tongue teases me. How one of his hands travels down my back while the other holds the back of my head. His body leans in on mine, leading me to lie on the blanket.

He holds himself on top of me, never breaking our kiss. If I didn't know it was a winter night, I would say we were in summer from how hot my body feels right now. My heart beats faster as our kiss gets more passionate, my hands on his back as one of his traces my silhouette.

Loud thumps sound in the distance, and he releases my lips, looking toward the sound. I glance with him and watch as multi-coloured fireworks fill the sky next to us.

My eyes quickly travel to his as if asking, *'Did you do that?'*

He lowers his head back down, nearing mine, and whispers in the shell of my ear, 'I told you I wanted to make this night unforgettable.'

Bloody goosebumps rise all over my body. Nobody has ever seemed as hot to me as he does right now.

He joins his lips to mine again, both of us kissing as if the other was our source of air. Reaching for every breath we never knew we were missing.

⸻

I can still feel his lips on mine as I walk into my bedroom. My finger traces the skin he kissed only a few moments ago as we stood in the hallway, not wanting to let go of each other. And the way he said, 'Goodnight, Delilah,' with the most perfect expression of *this is not over and I can't wait to get my hands on you again*, will make me have dreams I don't think I'll be able to repeat out loud.

I jump on my bed, kicking my feet in the air as I cover my face with the pillow to avoid making loud giggling sounds that would wake up Elisa.

Once I calm down, I remember I still have a letter from Daldust I didn't get to read from when I picked it up today at lunch hour. I grab the envelope with a full heart.

"Dear Delilah,
I think it's time for us to meet.
I know where your bakery is. I pass there almost daily. Please don't think I'm a creep. It's on my way to work. I didn't tell you because I wasn't ready for you to know who I am, but now I'm ready.
I'll pass by again on Friday. I'll show you who I am and what my name is. Wait for a guy in a red shirt.
For now, here's a hint: Dal means Moon in Korean, so my nickname is in reality Moondust.
I love the moon.
Yours truly,
Daldust"

This Friday?

I lay my back on the mattress, eyes wide open. *I'm meeting Daldust this Friday?*

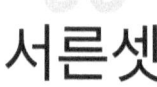

33
서른셋
'seoreunset'

My brain slowly wakes up when I pick up a notification sound in between dreams. Moon Hee sent me another song, but this time he wrote something under it.

Thinking of you displays on my screen under UMI's song *wish that i could*.

I glance up at the time on the right upper corner. A quarter to seven—my alarm would ring in fifteen minutes—so I decide to turn it off and lower the volume on my phone, placing it near my head on the pillow before I click play on the song.

I can't hide the fact that I love the way he communicates through songs with me. I love that he's thinking of me when he hears them or they remind him of me. Something that only he and I know. Our little secret.

I replay the song three times before getting up. Another one to add to my Moonie playlist.

The morning is calm; the sun hasn't risen in full and the streets haven't swarmed with people. I love the quiet of being awake when no one else is, whether that be at night or dawn.

I remind myself to take a few deep breaths, a trick Ms Julie taught me for when I want to make sure I'm present in the moment; something to slow down when I'm overwhelmed, to connect me back with my body. I take my time in the bathroom, pampering myself before I face the day.

When the days all blurred together I forgot myself, forgot to take care of me, but I've learned that I need to take care of myself before I can take care of anything else. Because if I'm not at my best, I can't give my best.

I leave my flat earlier today and walk up to the roof. I want to eat my breakfast in the open and with a view.

Taking my first step outside, I spot someone else up here. Their back faces me, but that's a physique I've been becoming more familiar with, one I'm becoming quick to recognise, no matter what he wears.

With my feet light so he can't hear me, I step closer to him from behind.

'Hey,' I whisper in his ear.

His face meets mine after a small jump of his torso, and my eyes stare into his big dark ones.

'Hey.' Moon Hee's smile turns devilish at the sight of my lips.

He reaches his hand to the side of my face and brushes my bottom lip with his thumb. I place my plastic container on the edge of the table beside us and wrap my arms around his neck, getting on the tips of my toes. His head leans down until our mouths connect and we breathe again.

'How I wish I could be your lover...' he says, taking a step back.

I bite my lower lip, gaining the courage to ask what's been on my mind since I heard the song for the first time. 'Do you want to be my lover?'

'More than anything.' His stare deepens, reaching every inch of my soul and making me feel more seen than ever—more desired than I've ever felt.

My eyes smile, but I don't know what else to do. He stripped all my layers down. I'm bare in front of him, even with my clothes on.

His gaze travels behind me and back. 'You brought breakfast?'

'Oh, right,' I say, looking back at the table. 'I came here to have breakfast with a view.'

'I couldn't imagine a more beautiful view than you.'

All the heat in my body rises to my face, and I grab my container to hide it. I sit on the chair next to the table and open it.

'Do you want something?' I ask, reaching my hand out with the food so he can take a better look at what it is.

'Mini pancakes…I might just take you up on the offer,' he says.

Moon Hee grabs another chair and pulls it closer to mine, sitting by my side and placing his hand on my thigh.

His warm presence soothes my body, and his fingers slightly grazing my leg send me a sensation of comfort I've never found outside my room. We eat as the sun rises, taking our time to enjoy the moment.

'Well, I need to go to work now,' I say, closing my plastic container and lifting myself off the chair.

Moon Hee gets up after me and turns to face me. 'Can I see you afterwards?'

'I'm meeting my mum after, but we can see each other later.'

'What about a drink here, under the moonlight?' His hand moves to the small of my back and he pulls me to him. My chest hits his.

'Sounds perfect.' I smile.

He gives me a kiss on the forehead before turning to the door.

'Wait!' I say. 'I've been meaning to ask you what your name meant in Korean…' I've always found Korean names interesting; they always have an intricate meaning and ever since we met, I've had this question floating in my mind.

His head spins back at me, and he sighs before speaking. 'Moon is usually connected to literature, writing, or letters, and Hee means joy or happiness. My mum likes to say that speaking with me is like reading a letter that gives her joy.'

My mouth opens halfway but no words come out. He turns back to the rooftop's exit and leaves.

He's a happy letter. A letter I eagerly wait to receive because it gives me joy. Like Daldust...

Moon Hee is a letter of joy, and Daldust is actually Moondust...

Could it be? But how?

I keep thinking about it all morning, trying to find answers until that night from five years ago pops back in my mind. The last moment of the night I felt safe, the only peaceful moment I had in a long time. I remember the guy next to me looking at the moon, his eyes big and shiny from the light. The blurry face comes into focus when I recall him looking at me as I waved goodbye.

It was him...all those years ago. *It's always been him.*

The day goes in a flash when you have something occupying your thoughts...and today outpaced many. But that also means the moment I've been dreading is arriving.

High heels sound on the floor when the door opens—a specific sound that always reminds me of someone. I turn around from the coffee machine I'm cleaning and huff at how sharp my hearing still is.

'Lilah,' my mum says, nearing the counter.

'Thank you for coming,' I say.

I walk to the door and put up the *closed* sign. Signalling for her to sit at the table next to me, I pull out the chair and sit.

'I can't say I'm not surprised by your invite, especially after our last talk,' my mum says.

'You and me both.' I look down at the table, gathering my thoughts. 'Why do you ask Elisa how I'm doing, but not me?'

She gasps. 'I have no idea what you are talking about.'

'Don't play dumb with me. I saw the texts.'

'How could you expect me to ask you when every time we speak, you treat me so poorly?' She crosses her arms. I've learned from a young age that's her move when she's defensive; an armour to protect her.

'I know I don't treat you the best now, but that's because I got fed up with everything you put me through.'

'What did I do that was so bad? I never understood.' The look in her gaze shows me she really sees herself as a victim. How could she not know what she was doing, gaslighting me all those years?

'For starters, you've never been a mother. You've been a financial provider, but not a mother. Tell me the last time you held me in your arms? The last time you were happy for me, genuinely happy? The last time you told me you loved me?'

Her head turns to the side, but she stays silent. After a few moments, she exhales and turns back to me, and the most fragile tone I've ever heard comes from her. 'I know I've never been a mother…I didn't know how. My whole life my goal was to be part of The London Elite, be someone people respected. That's how I was raised.'

The light in the bakery reflects on her eyes, making the sparkle coming from the tears she's trying to hold back visible, but she keeps her posture and continues. 'My mother grew up poor and everyday she would come home from a job she hated, beaten up, and would stare at me and say, "Veronica, never allow people to think less of you. Don't be like me; be strong. Be someone people respect, someone people fear, someone unstoppable," and so I did. I worked my whole life to be like that.

She wasn't a bad mum. We had great moments when I was little, but as I grew, she became distant and tougher, only smiling when I achieved something. I strived for a smile. My entire foundation to become better came from wanting to see my mother smile. When I was younger, I never aspired to be a mother. I never wanted to pass on that burden. Society is too cruel, especially to young women, but then I met your father and that man turned my entire world upside down. He was everything I wasn't: serene, happy, compassionate…but I stole that from him. My harsh personality rubbed off on him. And I think that happened shortly after we had you, when our busy life wasn't allowing him to be the father he wanted and because I've never had the mother instinct, I couldn't understand him.'

Before I went to my grandmother, I remember seeing my father smile every time he got home, always asking for his precious Delilah, but it all changed soon. He grew distant, and stopped holding me, or even looking for me after his trips. He would get home and lock himself in his office. I became invisible.

'If I'm being honest, I think he shut down and longed to be away from home because it pained him to not be there for you and instead of enjoying those fleeting moments he sent you to his mother, the one person he knew could care for you the way you deserved. Delilah, I did what I thought was best for you. I also didn't want you to be stepped on, and when I saw what happened to you, I knew I'd failed. I failed as a mother, as a caregiver, as a person. I couldn't face you after that, but you're still my child and despite what you might think, I care about you.'

'Thank you for being honest,' I say, unable to hold my posture like her, allowing the tears flooding my waterline to spill. And for the first time in my life, I see my mother cry.

'I'm so sorry, Lilah.' She holds my hand. 'I haven't been a mother for the past twenty-seven years, and I can't promise to know how to be one. But we're both adults now, and maybe, if you'd like, we can try again.'

Her face is too blurry for me to see, but I know she means it. We never had a good relationship, but maybe we can try.

'I'd like that,' I say and take a few papers from my napkin dispenser on the table to wipe my tears.

We get up and stand by the door, her back straightened as if she didn't just cry and pour her heart out, but this time she's smiling.

'I'm very proud of the person you've become, Delilah. And I'm so glad you didn't take my advice.' She comes closer to me and wraps her arms around my body. I hug her back, enjoying our first hug since I was four.

The moment she leaves the bakery, I sit back down, my energy stripped from this emotional turmoil. I could really use that drink now.

'Hi Elisa,' I say, entering our flat.

'Hey.' She walks into the living room, and I follow her.

'I barely saw you these past two days.' When I left work, she wasn't awake and when I came back, she wasn't home.

'I know, I stayed at Sofía's yesterday.'

'Oh, okay.' I want to tell her about what happened, but I'm not sure if she wants to know. I sigh and sit on the sofa next to her.

My flatmate stares at me. 'So? What are you waiting for? Tell me about your date!'

I chuckle, happy that she does want to know. 'It was amazing.' I haven't been able to think about that day without blushing. 'He rented the film room for us, and then we had a picnic prepared, filled with fairy lights and to top it all off...fireworks! He had fireworks playing in the background as we had our first kiss. I honestly thought these types of things only happened in books.'

'Ah! I'm so happy for you!' She beams. 'It does seem straight out of a fairytale. And the kiss?'

'Perfect.' I bite my lip at the thought of him.

We look like two teenage girls, all giddy with excitement.

'I'm meeting him tonight on the roof for a drink, which after today I need,' I say, propping my head on the back of the sofa.

'What happened today?' she asks.

'I had a talk with my mum...and I'm still processing everything.'

'Was it bad?'

'No, quite the contrary. She gave me answers. I cried, *she* cried and hugged me...It was a mess. But in the end we decided to try again, to try to have a good relationship.'

'She cried?' Her eyebrows rise.

'I know.' If I had never seen my mother cry, Elisa hadn't even seen her smile...

'Wow...Now that I did not expect!'

'I honestly had no expectations when I asked her to meet. I stopped expecting anything from her a long time ago, but this surpassed any that I could ever have.'

'I'm glad you worked things out.' My friend smiles.

'Me too.' I sigh. 'I'm going to eat something and then meet Moon Hee. Are you doing anything today?'

'I'm having an early night, because I barely slept last night. If you know what I mean.' She winks, and I laugh.

When my belly is full, I knock on my neighbour's door.

'Hey,' the man that hasn't stopped making me smile, says.

'Hey.' I look beyond his shoulder, seeing if someone else is there.

'He's out. On a date, actually.'

My eyes meet Moonie's. 'On a date?'

'Yeah. I have a feeling about who he's with, but he doesn't want to tell me, yet.'

'Who do you think it is?' I pry.

'Your friend, Rebecca.'

'Oh my god, yes! I was rooting for them!' I'm so happy that Elijah is dating again.

'Now, shall we?' He extends his hand for me to hold and, interlocking our fingers, he leads me upstairs.

'I swear the view at night from here is so beautiful,' I say, standing near the roof's half wall.

'I always come here when it's not raining.' He takes a deep breath, closing his eyes to enjoy the gentle wind.

'Wait!' I startle him. 'We didn't bring anything to drink.'

'Jesus, Lilah, you scared the shit out of me.' His hand touches his chest, calming him down. 'Follow me.'

He takes me to a corner of the rooftop where a brown waterproof cover protects a pile of things and takes the cover off, showing a mini fridge.

'This is where Elijah and I keep our stash,' he says, taking out two bottles of *soju*.

'You have a secret spot here and didn't tell us?' I place my hand on my waist.

'If we did, it wouldn't be a secret, would it?' He winks.

'Well...it only has to be a secret for everyone else. Elisa and I aren't everyone else.'

'No, you're not.' His hand reaches behind my back as he closes in on me, our chests connecting.

'What?' I ask as he stares quietly at me.

'I've never met anyone like you, as beautiful as you. I could stare at your features forever and never be able to transfer your essence into paper.'

'I'm no Mona Lisa.'

'You're art, Delilah, and I can't wait to be the artist to decode you,' Moon Hee says.

A fire ignites inside of me, heating my body, my face burning up like wildfire.

His head lowers to meet mine, and I close my eyes. After a few seconds of not having the action I was expecting, my eyes open again and find his eyes glued to mine.

He smirks and joins my lips to his. I didn't know he could be such a tease.

The softness of his lips does everything but calm my fire. As his hands hold my waist—after he grabbed both the bottles we were holding and threw them to the lounging chair with a fluffy mattress—I grow wet between my legs, throbbing for him.

Moon Hee pulls me as close as possible to him and I can feel a hardness growing on him. I swallow, my breathing getting heavier, more desperate for him as his mouth travels down my neck and up to my ear.

'I want you so fucking bad,' he whispers, and I join my lips to his again, my passion telling him exactly how much I want him too.

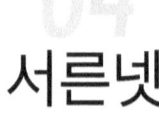

34
서른넷
'seoreunnet'

His fingers dig in my skin as he leads me backwards towards the lounging chair he threw our *soju* bottles on.

When my legs hit the edge of the chair, I stop and he helps me lower myself without breaking our kiss. With my back to the mattress, the alcohol bottles now on the floor, and his legs parted, each knee by my side, his kisses trail down to my collarbone as his hand moves up to the hem of my shirt.

Sparks flow through my body while the warmth of his hand travels under my shirt to the top of my bra, his lips caressing my skin as his tongue teases it.

Moon Hee breaks his trail of kisses and looks up at me, asking, 'Are you sure?'

'Yes.' I smile and close my eyes as his breath touches my skin again.

He unhooks my bra and lifts my shirt, exposing my chest.

'A fucking work of art.' His voice is raspy, with a hint of desire.

My back arches the moment his tongue finds my nipple, sending shivers all over my body. I never knew how sensitive to the touch someone could make me until him.

I grab the hem of his shirt and pull it above his head, getting my hands on his defined torso and feeling all the creases as my fingers slide down to his pants.

I stop at the edge of his bottoms and look up at the eyes already on me.

His tongue peaks out to wet his bottom lip, and he smirks. 'Don't get shy now. I'm all yours, my lilac.'

His words make me shyer than before, making my hands retreat from his pants to cover my face. I hear him chuckle and then he grabs my wrists, holding them by the sides of my head, to see me.

'No hiding. I need to see your beautiful face,' Moon Hee says, letting go of my wrists to take off his pants.

My hands stay where he left them, waiting for him to return to them.

He unbuttons my pants and slides them down, leaving me with my black lace undies.

The moon behind him casts a shadow over his front, making him more alluring when he cocks his head to the side and lowers himself on the end of the chair. His hands grab the sides of my undies and he pulls them to him. Moon Hee's face approaches me and my bent legs close as an instinct.

He places his hands on my knees and tears my legs apart. 'I said, no hiding.'

His nose rubs on my clit before his tongue meets me. I hold the top of the lounging chair while he fills me with pleasure, making my wetness overflow as he sucks on me, the tip of his tongue teasing me in the exact spot he picked up so fast that gets my eyes rolling back. One of his hands cups my breast, massaging it, and the other slides two fingers into me.

I moan, my body unsettled and oversensitive, and the hand that once laid on my breast now covers my mouth.

'As much as I would love to hear you scream for me, it would wake up the whole neighbourhood,' Moonie says.

His fingers slide off me and rest under my belly button, holding me steady, as my legs tremble to the rhythm of his tongue.

Moans try to escape his hold, my breath hitting his palm. My beating heart runs faster and my fingers dig deeper in the chair. I hold my breath; the tension building up to euphoria, until I release, panting as my legs fall tired.

'That's a good girl.' He hovers over me and replaces his hand on my mouth with his lips.

With his hand, he takes one of mine from where they have been waiting for him and leads it to the bulge in his briefs. Feeling him gets me pulsating again in the place he just left.

I slide my hand over the fabric through his length a few times before grabbing his briefs and pulling them down. My eyes catch his cock, and I bite my lip. I want to taste him.

'Stand up,' I say and he follows, staying where he once sucked me, only this time I'll be the one with my mouth on him.

Sitting up, the breeze of the night hits me. My body has been so hot I almost forgot we were outside in the middle of winter. He must notice my shivering because he grabs his jacket and places it on my back.

'Sorry I didn't bring a blanket. I wasn't expecting this to happen,' he says, chuckling.

'I don't think either of us was expecting it.' I laugh.

I wrap his length with my hand and stroke it while my tongue teases the tip. Then I move my tongue down, licking him as if he was the dessert I didn't have for dinner, until my lips wrap around his girth. His smooth texture slides perfectly between my tongue and the roof of my mouth.

My eyes look up to his head slightly tipped back so I watch his torso, seeing the tattoos on his chest that have always piqued my interest; tattoos I only got to glance at sometimes. I'm so lost tracing the ink of the *kitsune* fox on his chest, I don't notice when his head turns down. Our eyes meet and something inside me erupts; a feeling, a need.

I get up on my feet and meet his luscious lips. My arms surround his neck and his hands slide down to my ass to squeeze it. In synchrony, I jump to wrap my legs around his waist and he holds me to give me a lift. Moon Hee leans us down until my back hits the mattress, hovering over me.

I let go for a second to wet his dick by first sliding my fingers through my tongue and then around him. He holds himself, wetting my entrance before slowly opening me up.

I gasp when he fastens his pace and his mouth meets mine, engulfing all the moans. My nails dig to the skin of his back as he moves back and forth, our bodies dancing together. One of his hands cups my breast as the other holds him up. His kisses trail away to my ear, licking the lobe, and then down my neck. I could have him doing that all day.

I hold my lips close, trying to make as little sound as possible, but when he hits the spot, I can't contain myself.

'Fuck it,' he says, reaching the hand on my breast to my neck and choking me enough to not cut my breath but to make my desire grow. He pounds harder, hitting all the right spots with each thrust.

My voice fills the air as we enjoy the moment. A few minutes pass and he fastens his pace, pulling back right before coming all over my belly.

Moon Hee gives me one more passionate but short kiss and stands up. He grabs his briefs and cleans me with them.

'I guess I'm going home commando,' he jokes, and I laugh.

My head is still trying to process what just happened. What he just did. Me and Moon Hee. Us.

'This was...' I say. 'Wow.'

He smiles and sits on the edge of the lounging chair, caressing my leg. 'Better than I pictured.'

I blush. He pictured it. My smile is uncontainable and I sit up, closing in on him, my chest on his back.

My mouth opens, wanting to say something I don't remember the last time I said it. Those three words that mean so much. But no sound comes out.

I know in my heart that I mean it, but there's something holding me back, so I choose to ignore it and focus on what is right in front of me—an amazing man with whom I just had an amazing time.

'You should get dressed before you catch a cold,' he says. I love how thoughtful he is. I've noticed from the beginning how much he cares for others.

'Yes, *we* should.' I give him a peck on the shoulder and get up to find my clothes. When I pass in front of him, he slaps my butt, making me shriek in surprise and him chuckle.

In the end, neither of us needed a drink. We got high on each other.

Today is the day I'm meeting Daldust.

I try to keep calm as my heart attempts to leave my body. All this time he has only been on paper, like a fantasy in my head, but today he'll become real. Will he be who I think he is?

Millions of questions rush through my head, but all I want to do is hug him.

I shake my head, focusing on the present moment. There's no need to worry about something that has nothing to do with the now, as Ms Julie says.

Leaving my bed behind, I make my way to my wardrobe. Although I don't want it to seem like I'm dressing up for him, I still want to make sure I look my absolute best.

But I decide to stay true to myself by grabbing a pair of black jeans and a purple sweatshirt.

'Morning.' Elisa smiles, and I leave the lavatory as she enters. That reminds me, I haven't told her what will happen today.

'Good morning,' I say before she closes the door. 'I'm meeting my pen pal today.'

My flatmate swiftly turns around, eyes wide open. 'Oh my god! How are you feeling? Are you excited? Nervous? Where are you meeting? I want to hear all about it afterwards.'

'You sound more eager than me.' I laugh. 'I'm a bit nervous, but I'm looking forward to it. We are meeting at the bakery.'

'Go get him, girl. I'm really proud of you, you know? Something like this would have made you anxious even to leave the bed in the past. Look at you now, saying you are looking forward to it.' My best friend beams.

'Thank you, I'm proud of myself too.' I head over to hug her.

We move on with our paths after it and I go to work.

I love watching the shop before opening. There is something about the morning's silence that gives me peace.

As soon as I open the bakery, a couple walks in for their breakfast meal.

'Good morning,' I say. 'What can I help you with?'

'Good morning!' the lady says. 'We'll have two coffees and three chocolate croissants.' The man who walked with her is already sitting at a table.

'I'll get right on it. You can go sit and I'll take your order to the table.'

She thanks me and leaves to meet her mate.

It takes a while until more customers come in, but every time a guy would arrive the first thing I looked at was his shirt. No red shirt, yet.

The movement is slow for a Friday. Maybe today people are more eager to get home from work, or try not to eat so many sweets because they know they'll mostly relax at home, since it will be raining all weekend.

I don't mind it though since it gives me more time for baking. I walk to the back of the shop towards the kitchen so I can bake some cupcakes for tomorrow.

Only a few customers have come, so I'm still entertained baking when the bell above the door rings. I walk to the front of the shop to see who it is. The bright red shirt on the man I've never seen wearing colour makes my heart pump as fast as it did last night, and when I meet those dark, round eyes, it stops. An overwhelming wave of emotions comes crashing down on me. I run to him and hug him like I never have.

'It's really you,' I say as he stands in front of me.

'When did you figure it out?' Moonie asks with a soft smile.

'I had a feeling after you told me your name's meaning.'

'Yeah...I knew you would. I wasn't sure if knowing Dal meant Moon would lead you to me, but you had to ask the meaning of my name in Korean. In a way, I hoped you'd think it was a coincidence.' He chuckles, rubbing the nape of his neck.

'Did you know all along? Was it why you accepted me?' I have so many questions. 'And I have to ask, you have colour in your wardrobe?' The last one might be the biggest one at the moment.

'I don't. I had to ask Elijah for it.' He chuckles. 'And I didn't know from the beginning, only after I found your bakery's name.'

He steps in closer, reaching for my hand and I give it. His touch is warm, leaving a sensation of comfort swirling up inside of me.

He feels like home.

'I'm sorry for not remembering you...I tried to shut down that night because it was when my life turned upside down. I knew I had talked to someone. I never forgot our conversation. It was the best moment of the night, but because I'd drank a lot, I didn't remember your face and I never got your name.' Memories of the starry night flash before my eyes.

'It's okay, it wasn't our time. But I also said that I wouldn't let another chance pass by me. I would say what's in my heart, even if that meant I could get hurt. So, I have something I need to say, something I should have said a long time ago. Something I already knew in my heart, and the time we have been spending together and writing to each other just made it clearer.'

I stare into his eyes and wait for him to say what I couldn't last night.

'Saranghae.'

'*Saranghae.*' My eyes smile.

For years I've feared *I love you's*. I dreaded them, since I felt like no one ever meant them like I did and it only meant they had the power to break my heart.

Moon Hee helped me understand that being in love is a blessing, not a curse. Being able to open up, be vulnerable, to someone is beautiful and the real and raw human connection. That connection is rare and if we ever find it, we should embrace it, not run away. Being scared is normal. It only means what you feel is true. And even if we fear being heartbroken, being able to love while we can will always be worth the risk of being alone in the end.

This family I found by chance showed me there's more than romantic love. The spectrum is too wide to be put in a box. And those who never love will always be alone, because being able to give and receive love is how we know we are alive.

'I live so I love' — Kim Namjoon, Trivia 承: *Love by BTS*

Epilogue
에필로그

9 months later

'Hello Delilah,' Ms Julie says as I enter her office. 'How was this month?'

A few months after Moon Hee and I started dating, Ms Julie said I had been doing so well, she thought it was time to reduce our sessions to every other week. Six months later, here we are: my first session in a month.

'It was great, actually. The bakery has been doing so good that I'm thinking of expanding it. I saw a for-sale sign on the shop next to mine and I can imagine tearing down a wall and making the space bigger, which now that the cold months are coming will be very handy.'

'That's fantastic! I rarely mix business and pleasure, but I'm very tempted to go try some of your famous baked goods.'

'You can visit on Tuesdays. I'm not working on that day. That way, no mixing is done.' I laugh.

Because of the latest success, four months ago I had to hire help. Nora, my twenty-three-year-old employee, is working solo on Tuesdays since they continue to be the slowest days. That way I can have two rest days and she has the weekends off, so I'd say she got a good deal.

Moon Hee also took Tuesdays off so we can spend more time together, even though we see each other every day.

'I sure will!' My therapist smiles. 'But now returning to you, how are your nightmares?'

'They've been subsiding significantly. I only had one this month—at the beginning—and since then it's been quiet.'

When my mind calmed down from everything going on with my love life, I began dreaming about that night. It was awful at first. I spent a week afraid of falling asleep and waking up crying. There were days I had to take sleeping pills to see if I could rest, but I didn't want to abuse them, so Moon Hee came to sleep with me every night. I felt bad for waking him up so many times, but after a month of reliving that nightmare, we finally got a good night's sleep. Having him there for sure helped relax me.

'Trauma takes a long time to overcome, but seeing you heal for the past two years has been a blessing. You've done a terrific job.'

'There was a time when it really seemed impossible.' I feel the moisture build in my waterline, but no tear is shed. After crying for so long, my body has become relaxed just at the thought of it.

'When it comes to personal growth, everything is possible.'

I give Ms Julie a summary of my month and, on my way home, stop by *InkPark*.

'Lilah, Lilah, my dear Delilah,' Elijah says, smiling, as soon as his eyes land on me walking through the door.

I still remember seeing his forced smile around me and his flatmate in the first months, but time does heal the heart and his has moved on to someone who deserves him.

'Elijah, Elijah, my dear…Sorry, I don't know what to call you.' I laugh and he joins me.

'Your man is with a client, but you're free to wait.'

'Actually, I wanted to schedule a tattoo.' I place my forearms on the counter and lean forward with a sheepish smile.

'Another? You're addicted,' he jokes. 'I might as well open a tab for you since you've become a regular.'

'Says the man with two complete tattoo sleeves, and I spot a brand new tattoo around your neck.'

'You're looking at your future.' He copies my posture and stares into my eyes.

'My measly five tattoos still have a long way to go.' I wink. 'But I want you to do my next one.'

He forces a gasp, eyes wide with an overdramatic open mouth and a hand above it. 'You would betray your boyfriend like that?'

I swap my hand on his arm and roll my eyes. 'I'm still waiting for the tattoo made by you that you promised me almost a year ago.'

Elijah straightens his back, and picking up a pen, says, 'For when?'

'End of the month?' I peek at the agenda to see if he has a spot.

'Done.'

'Thank you.' I make a heart with my hands and walk towards the door.

'Lilah!' he says, and I turn my head around. 'Becca and I will pass by your flat later.'

'Okay.' I smile and close the door behind me.

Never in my life did I think I would have such a close relationship with a guy I wasn't dating the way I have with Elijah. I love the way we're so comfortable around each other and how he always brings out my loud side.

I walk inside my home, the house I've lived in for the last ten years, and sigh. So much has happened in a decade, yet the place remains the same. The walls haven't been painted, the sofa is the same, the small dinner table remains in its corner. Memories fill this place, but I'm getting ready to make new ones.

Elisa must be at Sofia's. Sofia said she's moving, so they're most likely packing. It's a shame she's leaving though because they won't be as close as now, but I'm sure they'll figure it out. They've been dating for almost a year, so they'll probably be taking the next step soon.

The moment I place down my purse, my phone vibrates on

the table. I glance over at the screen and the word MUM floats in bold.

'Hi mum,' I say, pressing the green button.

'Lilah, hi. I wanted to confirm your presence and Moon Hee's for dinner next Monday.'

After our conversation about trying to start over, my parents cancelled their move to Beverly Hills. They said they had a reason to stay after all.

'It's confirmed. We'll be there at seven.'

'Also, I think it's time to meet Ms Yu Ra. Do you think she'll want to come also? Your father has been pushing on it for a while and I agree.'

'I'll check,' I chuckle. 'Send kisses to Dad. As soon as she gives me an answer, I'll tell you.'

'I will. See you Monday.'

Parents meeting each other means something big, but I know we're ready for it. It's funny to think back to how my mother judged Moonie when she saw him the first time here, and now she can't get tired of him—he's the son she never got. And even though I still notice how my dad tenses from time to time when I'm there, I also don't remember the last time I've seen him smile so much.

I saw how much of a burden our relationship was for all of us and it's been a blessing to see us heal from it.

Daldust's letters sit on my desk in a transparent box. I like to reread them from time to time. They helped me as much as Moon Hee did in real life and even though I know I can simply talk with him now, sometimes I miss the pen and paper.

The sound of the doorbell rings and I walk out of my room to check who it is. I look in the peephole, but all I see is my neighbour's door, so I open mine.

I glance around, but the hallway remains empty. *Did I imagine the sound?*

As I'm about to close the front door, my eyes stop at the floor. A grey envelope lies near my feet.

I pick it up, but the only word written is Delilah. There's no reference to the sender.

I walk inside and open the letter in my room.

"Dear Delilah,

I know it's been a while, but I missed this. I missed you.

I know your life has been through a lot of changes in the past year and I can't tell you how proud I am of you.

Proud of how strong you are while still being vulnerable. Proud of everything you accomplish and simply proud because you exist.

You bring light into my days, and I just want to repay you by making you the happiest. Seeing you smile is the same as breathing for me. And I want every day to be a breath of fresh air.

I hope to make you smile today.

Yours truly,

(Your boyfriend) Daldust"

He just did. Receiving this letter was as heartwarming as it was strange.

My smile turns suspicious. *Why would he send me this?* I've told him I missed his letters, but my gut is telling me there's more to it.

I shake the thought and focus on tonight's hang out. We're now three couples and Jeremiah. I'm thinking of setting him up with Nora. She seems like his type. I just need to figure out her type.

For tonight I'm baking a few croissants, pigs in a blanket, and pizza, with a key-lime pie and a banana bread for sweets. Everyone always eats as if they've been starving all day just for our Friday nights.

My headphones fill my ears with music while my hands mix up batter and my ass shakes to the rhythm of the tunes. This is my time, when I get to forget the world outside and focus on me.

An hour later and a few batches of food done, I'm bopping my head to the sound of OOHYO's *Pizza*, which I found to be fitting for tonight's menu, when a hand wraps around my waist.

I do a tiny jump, surprised I'm not the only one in the room, and turn my head around to find his dark eyes smiling at me.

My lips meet his and he sneaks a finger in the banana bread's remaining batter before licking it and passing the flavour on to me.

'Delicious,' Moon Hee says. 'Just like the baker who made it.'

He never fails to heat my cheeks.

'I didn't hear you come in.' I gave him a key when he came to spend nights here and since then, he never bothers to ring the bell again.

'Of course not. I'm trained like a ninja.' He chuckles.

'Oh, that must be it, not the noise-cancelling headphones.'

'I knew you'd see the truth.' He wraps his other arm around me and pulls me closer to his chest. 'How was your day?'

'Perfect now that you're here.'

His head tilts to the side. 'That should have been my line...'

'I've learned from the best.' I wink.

My man lifts me to sit on the counter and places his lips on my neck's skin for a few seconds before whispering into my ear, 'Do you think we have time?'

I open my eyes. 'Elisa has been gone for a while, so I'm not really sure. She could be coming back any second or stay until after dinner.'

'Works for me.' Moon Hee picks me up over his shoulder and walks us to my room, slapping my ass on the way.

'Wait! I only have twenty minutes before the bread is done.'

He puts me down with my back on the bed. 'No time to waste then.'

I laugh, and he takes off his shirt. I'm not the only one growing my tattoo collection.

'Your sleeve is almost done,' I say, watching his arm.

'Yeah, next week I'll be finishing it up.'

I'm about to make more conversation when his mouth finds mine, making me forget all the words I was thinking. His hands trace my figure in a slow, caring pace, and when they touch my nipples, a shiver runs down my spine.

My hand finds the bulge in his pants, and I know he's as ready as I am. Maybe twenty minutes will be more than enough.

He lifts my shirt and meets my breast with his lips. I'm glad I'd already taken my bra off, one less layer to remove.

A moan escapes my mouth when he sucks my nipple and unlike the times we needed to be quiet for having flatmates, this time nobody's home.

His kisses trail down my belly, and his hands continue to please my breasts before they remove the sweatpants I'd changed to when I got home. Moon Hee traces his middle finger through my undies and I inhale at his touch.

'You're already so wet...' he says with a smirk.

He kisses my undies between my legs before removing them and meeting his tongue on my clit. My eyes close and I grab the sheets as his hands hold me at my waist while he works down there with his mouth.

His pace fastens and my hand moves to his head, my fingers mixing with his hair. 'Oh, Moon Hee...'

Two fingers enter me and I know I won't last long this way, but I stop him by taking his hand out and pulling down his cargo pants.

'I want to come with you inside me,' I say.

'Your wish is my command.' My boyfriend wets his lips before meeting mine concurrently as his length finds my entrance.

I moan into his mouth as pleasure fills us. Skin to skin, in the rawest form of connection, the entire world vanishes, and it's just us. Our time.

Our fingers interlock and we make love to each other, moving our bodies as one. With every groan and moan, we are getting closer to utopia.

Not long after, I sense my body stiffen under his, my legs trembling around him, and I squeeze his hands while coming undone, panting. The moment he sees me relax, he unlocks our fingers, wrapping his hands around my wrists, and fastens his pace, kissing me harder as he comes.

I've noticed how incredible he is at holding himself back, making sure to pleasure me first, so we both end up satisfied.

He lays next to me and as his eyes stare into mine, his hand places my hair behind my ear.

'I love you, lilac,' he says.

'I love you too.' My head is on his chest, my hand tracing his skin, when a thought pops into my head.

'Oh my god!' I say, getting up in a flash, grabbing my robe and running to the kitchen.

My banana bread.

I turn off the oven and open it; thankfully we were fast, so it hasn't been that long, but the top was already getting burnt.

I take the bread out of the oven and place it on the counter to cool.

I'll just remove the top. It's fine.

A messy-haired Moon Hee wearing only his black cargo pants appears in the kitchen. 'Did it burn?'

'It's fine,' I say, observing how long his hair has grown. His fringe now reaches his eyes, even though he likes to part it more to the sides so his forehead peeks out, but his mullet has fully grown.

'It completely slipped my mind,' he says, leaning on the kitchen's entrance frame, making me desire a second round.

'The food is done. We should get ready for the others.'

He nods and walks to my room so we can get dressed. Glancing over to my desk, I spot the letter and remember to ask, 'Why did you send me a letter?'

He looks back at where I'm staring. 'I just wanted to have in writing how much you mean to me. Did it make you smile?'

'It did.'

'Then mission accomplished.' He sits next to me on the mattress, and I place my head on his shoulder.

'It was really just that? No hidden agenda?'

His silence makes me think there is, in fact, a hidden agenda. Moon Hee can't lie, he knows that, I know it too, so he prefers to stay silent when he doesn't want to tell the truth.

'I guess I'll find out later,' I say, and he gives me a peck on the forehead.

Half an hour later, Elisa and Sofía enter our flat. Moon Hee and I ended up going to the sofa and watching an anime episode, since they're a lot smaller than a K-Drama one would be.

'We brought drinks!' My flatmate lifts two white plastic bags.

'For the month?' I ask.

'Trust me, more than half of it will disappear tonight,' she says.

'Are we playing a drinking game?' Moon Hee asks.

'Aren't you a smart one?' Elisa winks at him.

Not long after they arrive, the doorbell rings. I get up and walk to answer it.

'Hey hey,' the woman with long copper locks says, arm intertwined with Elijah's.

'Hey Becca. Hello again, Elijah.' I look behind them, but the place her brother usually occupies is empty. 'Where's Jeremiah?'

'He's not coming tonight, already had plans with his new friends.'

'New friends?' I ask.

'He met a group of people when he went to the arcade and apparently got along with them very well. Also, I think there's a girl in the group he's interested in, so...' Rebecca chuckles.

'Can we come in?' the man beside her asks with a sigh. 'I'm hungry!'

'Let the baby go ahead,' I say to his girlfriend.

'Thank you.' Elijah kisses my head as he walks by me, but I notice how Becca's eyes turn to the side.

'Are you uncomfortable with how Elijah and I interact?' I ask her as she walks inside the flat.

'I'm just not used to it,' she says, avoiding my gaze. 'I know there's nothing going on with you.'

'We're really just great friends. Besides, he's totally infatuated with you.'

She chuckles, her eyes meeting mine. 'It took a while for him to accept to go out with me. After you, he isolated himself; to heal, he said.'

'I'm just glad you didn't give up. Look at you now.' I smile.

Becca glances back at her man and the corners of her lips lift. 'Yeah...'

'Let's go. Apparently, there's a drinking game tonight.'

'Uh...Fun!'

We walk into the living room and all four people present glance at us in silence. Did we walk in on something?

'*Kaja* (Let's go), let's get this party started!' Elijah claps his hands together.

I go over to take a croissant and a glass to drink. I pick the first one in front of me. It has a blue stripe across it—each glass has a different colour so we can better identify our cup—but it disappears from my hand in a second.

'I already got a glass for you.' I glance to my side and watch Moon Hee put the blue-striped glass back on the table.

'Oh, okay, thank you.'

We start with a normal card game to warm up and enjoy the food and conversation, but after half an hour Elisa goes to one of the white bags and gets out *Do or Drink Naughty Edition*.

I stare at her, my mouth half opened. 'We're playing that?'

'I thought it would be fun since it's just couples, so Sofía and I went to buy it. I'm so eager to try the game!'

'You knew it was just couples tonight?' I ask.

'Yeah, I talked with Elijah earlier and he mentioned Jeremiah wasn't coming.'

'That's why you said you and Becca were coming tonight when I was at the parlour?' I turn to Elijah.

'Yeah.' He nods.

Moonie wraps his arm around my waist and pulls me closer. 'Are you okay?' he whispers in my ear.

'Yes...Just...I don't know. I think I'm reading too much into everything,' I say in a low tone, for only him to hear.

He turns my head to his and joins our mouths. The softness of his lips always eases my mind.

'Lovebirds, leave that for the game,' Elisa says.

'Who starts?' Rebecca asks.

'Oldest and youngest do rock-paper-scissors to see who wins. The winner goes first,' Elisa says.

'*Joayo* (I like it),' the men say in sync. They look at each other, surprised, and laugh.

'Okay, so...I'm twenty-eight,' I say. 'Elisa is still twenty-seven and Elijah is twenty-eight. Moonie just turned twenty-six a few days ago. How old are you, Sofía and Becca?'

'I'm twenty-six too,' Sofía says.

'Ah, I'm the oldest...I turned thirty last month.' Rebecca hides her face behind her hands.

Elijah turns to his side and pulls hands away so he can look her in the eyes. 'Still sexy as always.' Her smile grows and her head leans on his shoulder.

'So by default, Rebecca is against Moon Hee because he just turned twenty-six while Sofía's birthday was back in March,' Elisa says.

'*Gawibawibo*,' Moon Hee says.

'Paper wins rock.' Rebecca smiles.

'Okay, draw the first white card,' Elisa says, handing her the deck.

'Vote: on the count of three, every player has to point at the person they think is better in bed,' she reads.

'Juicy. We're starting well!' Elisa beams. 'Everyone got their answers?'

Fuck. Fuck, no.

'Okay, one…two…three,' Rebecca says and everyone points at their significant other except me and Elijah.

Is he having the same problem as me? Sex with him was fun, but the intensity with Moon Hee is out of this world. The way he can be sweet but be choking and spanking me the next second is enough to send chills all over my spine. But I don't want to hurt Elijah's feelings, because he is very good too.

'Lilah?' Elisa asks, frowning. 'Elijah? Don't you know your answers?'

Elijah glances at me and I can see the despair in them. He's not having the same problem as me. My eyes widen and I slightly shake my head no to him, hoping no one saw it, but knowing everyone is looking between us. Everyone except Moon Hee…I sigh, a weight on my heart.

Now he thinks he's not my first choice.

I look once more at Elijah, who gives me a small nod and we each point at our partner. In the end, sex should be better with Rebecca because their intimacy transcends the physical.

I grab Moon Hee's hand and whisper to him, 'Sorry for hesitating, but I didn't want to hurt Elijah's feelings. It's definitely you.'

'Even if you don't mean it, now I know I need to step up my game, so next time there won't be any hesitation,' he whispers back.

'But I do mean it.'

'I still want to make sure.' His smirk tells me I have a lot waiting for me tonight.

We face back at the group, and Elijah takes a card.

'Draw a black card,' he says.

'Yes!' Elisa claps.

'Take off a piece of clothing every time someone drinks until you're down to your underwear. Stay like this for the rest of the game or drink two shots.'

'You're lucky. Besides my girl, everyone has seen you naked. Not fair, you got an easy one,' my flatmate says.

'I've seen him in swimwear, so it will be the same. Yeah, an easy one.' Sofía nods.

'Jesus, do you want me to take another card?' he asks. 'I'll take another card.'

'Draw a black card, again,' Elijah reads. 'Spin the bottle and make out with the person it points to, both of you must do this or take two shots.'

'That's better, thank you,' Elisa chuckles and gets up to grab an empty bottle.

The bottle spins and stops right in front of him.

'Sorry mate, but no,' he laughs. Both he and Moon Hee take two shots.

Then it's Moonie's turn to take a card. 'Guessing Game: guess the most sensitive spot on the body of the person on your right.'

'That's easy,' he says and closes in on me, licking with the tip of his tongue on the space between my ear and neck. I inhale, and he sucks on it.

'He definitely knows,' Rebecca says with a chuckle.

'He's doing the one that's appropriate for the viewers,' Elijah says to her.

Our heads move to him, and his flatmate's lips tighten. 'They didn't need to know that.'

'It's okay, it's not like it's a secret,' I say. I don't know what's going on with Elijah today. 'My turn.'

I draw a black card and read it out loud. 'Sit on the lap of the person to your right for the next round or drink twice.' I look at Sofía and smile when she pats her legs for me to sit.

'How you doing?' she says, and we laugh.

Then Sofía needs to demonstrate her first kiss to a player, so I get off and let her dramatically French kiss her girlfriend, which makes us all laugh, then I'm back on my new spot until it's my turn again.

'Text a random number "want to get freaky?" or drink twice.' Elisa chuckles and grabs her phone. 'I'll just tell them later it was for a game.'

We go for a couple more rounds until Elijah gets up to go get more food from the kitchen and I follow him.

'Hey,' I say, and he glances at me. 'Is everything okay with you today? You're making it seem like you're not over me after all.'

'It's not that,' he chuckles. 'I'm perfectly happy with Becca, I just…I found some photos of us on my phone and it brought back memories and for some reason, I got jealous. You're still the one who understands me the best.'

'I get that, but think about how uncomfortable you're making your girlfriend.' I pat his shoulder. 'You just need to let yourself open up to her. I know it's funny that I'm saying this, but it's true. Only then you can live up to your full potential.

Before I walk over to the living room he speaks again. 'Hey, Lilah…I really am happy for you.'

'I'm happy for you too.' I give him a soft smile.

Joining us, Elijah whispers something in Rebecca's ear and kisses her. Maybe he apologised.

When I grab my glass to fill it out, something sparkles on the bottom. I frown and turn it around to find something taped to the bottom. Because of it being concave, I hadn't noticed something in the middle every time I placed it down on the table.

It's a key.

I look up and see everyone watching me. Moon Hee takes the key and turns to me.

'Delilah Scott, after having a wonderful nine months by your side, sleeping almost every night together, either in your flat or mine, I thought it was time for us to have our own place. Will you move in with me?' he says.

'Oh my god, Moonie. Yes, of course I will!' I hug him and everyone cheers. 'This is why you wanted me to have this cup!'

'Yeah, I was hoping you'd finish the drink to notice.' He chuckles.

'You all knew?' I ask.

'You're staying in Sofía's flat, and she's moving here. This way, we're all still close to each other and we don't need to run around between houses. And you, Elijah, will have one all for yourself. Rebecca and you will have fun, I'm sure,' my soon to be ex-flatmate says.

He smiles and places his arm around his girlfriend's shoulders, kissing her temple.

'What if I said no? What would happen to that plan, since Sofía is all packed to go?' I ask.

'Well, we didn't think you would, but if that was the case, she would still move in with us.'

'And I would still move to hers. That way we could have more privacy,' Moon Hee says.

I turn to him and kiss the bloody hell out of his lips. I can't wait to move in with him. Like I said, I'm so ready to create fresh memories, and as long as the people in this group are present in them, I know they'll be happy ones.

'Shall we continue to play? We still have a long night ahead of us,' I ask, and they agree.

My smile never fades throughout the night as we laugh and have fun the way only people who've found others that match their energy can. *The way only we can.*

The End.

Do you want more?

Read Bonus Chapters

Ream

www.reamstories.com/evachauauthor

Get Character Art

Website

www.evachauauthor.com

Acknowledgments

Modern Pen Pals started as an idea in my head in 2021, where I began to write it —those who have been with me since then might know it started on Wattpad. But something in me didn't feel prepared to write this story the way it was supposed to be told, so two years later I picked it up again after simmering it in my head. So many things changed since I thought about it in the first place (fun fact: it wasn't supposed to be a love triangle! The characters had a mind of their own and I only became aware of it halfway through it), but the meaning remained.

This book and these characters became very special to me as the story bled to the paper, not only because of the message this story carries but because of how much more meaningful you made it.

My amazing Beta Readers - Lia, Chelsea, Julianna, Drusilla, Emily, you girls got me so excited to share this story and it wouldn't be the same without you! Your love for the characters made me want to scream mine. Thank you, thank you, thank you, for all of your comments and support ♡

Sarah Ward - I'm so glad I ran into you on Threads, you took Modern Pen Pals to the next level, thank you for answering all my questions and for being an awesome editor ♡

My Street Team - You've helped me spread the word about this book, and for that I'm forever grateful! I loved meeting all of you and some I'll for sure continue to rely on. Thank you for supporting me ♡

Swipethebook PR Connect and Authors PR - Publishing is all fun and games until marketing comes into place, and if I'm completely honest it's not my favourite, that's why working with you helped so much spreading the word about Modern Pen Pals. Kriti and Sanjana (swipethebook), Débora and Marina (Authors PR) I thank you for all your hard work ♡

Bangtan Sonyeondan aka BTS - I know you'll never read this, but you made this book happen. If it weren't for you I wouldn't have fallen in love with the Korean culture or maybe I'd just find it later in life. You guys helped me in ways you can't possibly imagine and I can't begin to word it, but I know I don't need to because the bond ARMY and BTS have transcends the written language; transcends any language. 아포방포 ♡

You - If it weren't for you reading this book I wouldn't be able to publish it, you make all the blood, sweat and tears worth it. I love to write, and I do write mostly for myself, but it wouldn't be the same if I couldn't share it with people who resonate with what I have to say. Thank you for reading ♡

About the Author

Eva Chau is a Portuguese romance author who loves to swoon readers with her character-driven stories, seasoned with a hint of open-door spice. She loves to learn new languages and often includes that in her books by giving them a multicultural dimension.

Her books often have a lighthearted romance but touch some heavy topics while she strives to make characters relatable, both with their struggles as with their personalities, so readers can connect with them and feel less lonely in the world.

Connect with the author

Website
www.evachauauthor.com

Instagram/Threads/TikTok/Pinterest
@evachauauthor

Subscribe to her Newsletter for giveaways, exclusive access to previews of her new books, life updates and more.

www.evachauauthor.com/mailing-list

Other books by the Author

Hope by Eva Chau

In darkness, the only way for love to shine is through...*hope*.

Sweet, kind and strong-headed Ema Mendes moved to London with a goal in mind: to get her degree to become a successful interior designer. That's what she worked her whole life for.

Until those mysterious caramel-eyes caught her attention. She knows he's an infuriating distraction, one she swore off.

He's her roommate's brother. Her partner in class. The only one who can bring out emotions she's never felt.

He continuously shakes her hope in humanity until...he becomes her first love.

***

Read a sample

Ruthless, cold and successful Nathaniel Blackburn has all the university's girls at his feet, but after what happened last year he has only one rule: he won't sleep with the same girl more than once.

What he wasn't expecting was the lost girl he met on campus to be his sister's roommate. The one who should be off limits.

She drives him insane in every way, but is also the reason he's able to sleep well at night.

Her hope in the world is something he mocks until...she teaches him the meaning of love.

She saw the darkness. He saw the light. They found each other.

Hope is a New Adult Contemporary Romance with grumpy/sunshine, roommate's brother, forced proximity, inexperienced/experienced and college tropes.

www.ingramcontent.com/pod-product-compliance
Lightning Source LLC
LaVergne TN
LVHW091709070526
838199LV00050B/2332